Death Upon the Wicked Stage

Death Upon the Wicked Stage

Judith Johnson

Kismet Mysteries

Library of Congress Control Number: 2023923426

ISBN 979-8-9896511-0-8 (paperback)

ISBN 979-8-9896511-1-5 (ebook)

To Max and Margo, who fired up the dream.
To Jack and Anne, who made it come true.

Chapter 1

Please Say Yes

T HE WALL PHONE IN the kitchen rang once ... twice ... and Ruth Carson muttered to herself.

"Damn! It always rings when I'm up to my elbows in something!" She stopped kneading the rye bread on which she was working and quickly wiped her hands on a small towel. On the fourth ring she picked up the invading phone gingerly, trying not to get it dirty.

"Carson's," she said somewhat curtly, getting rye flour all over the phone. Although her husband, Tom, had been dead five years, Ruth still answered the phone as if he were living there. *In this day and age, I feel much safer if people don't know I live alone,* she had decided.

"Ruthie!" The woman's voice on the other end was chirping excitedly. "Guess what, Ruthie? Fritz is having auditions tomorrow night. I just saw it in the St. Paul paper. They're doing *Show Boat*. I *love* that musical! We've got to audition! You know almost everyone who auditions gets in. Whaddaya say?"

Ruth felt immediately guilty for sounding snappish when she answered the phone. It was her long-time friend, Angie Corbello. Ruth switched gears and chuckled, "Hi, Angie, how are you?" She wiped off the phone with a towel and sat down on a kitchen stool. *This might take a while,* she thought.

Angie Corbello's enthusiasm for the Como Park summer theatre outshone her enthusiasm for almost anything else in her life, except perhaps for her little aging terrier, Charlie. She lived for the musicals that played there each summer. Auditions were held sometime around the second week of April and closing night was usually the second Saturday in August. Those were the months when Angie truly lived. September through March were seven months 'to be endured,' until the next summer theatre season rolled around.

"Oh, Angie, I don't know," Ruth sighed. She straightened the pale blue and yellow patchwork table runner she had made to accent her white kitchen table. "Don't you think we're getting kind of old for this? We should probably let the young ones take over."

She glanced over at her graying blonde hair in the small mirror near the telephone and lifted a few strands near her temple. The face that looked back at her was pleasant, with rounded pink cheeks and a small, upturned nose on which perched a pair of trifocals with mauve-colored frames. It wasn't a face that announced to the world, "I'm 62 years old." When Ruth looked closely, she still couldn't see many lines except the ones at the corners of her blue eyes. "Smile lines," her late husband called them.

"Old?" Angie snorted. "Whaddaya mean, old? They need us! We've still got strong voices. You know we do."

Angie will never be old, thought Ruth—*at least not in spirit.* Angie loved to laugh. She dyed her long ponytail bright red, and even though her aging body grew a bit plumper each year, her attire of choice was usually a pair of black leotards and a gaudy flowered top. On special nights those tops sported sequins.

This would be their eighteenth year together in community theatre. Their troupe, the Como Park Pavilion Players, performed musicals every summer on the big stage of St. Paul's Como Lakeside Pavilion.

The pavilion, which reminded Ruth of something she's seen in a Maxfield Parrish painting, was located in Como Park on the edge of serene Lake Como (named after the lake in Italy). Built in the early 1900s, it was a graceful, white, stucco structure supported on all sides by Corinthian columns. It had a roof but was otherwise open to the elements. One side held a stage that faced the lake, allowing performers to look out upon the audience while also viewing the lake in the background. On good nights, the pavilion's dark-green benches accommodated about 600 eager theatre-goers.

Attached to the pavilion, directly behind the backstage area, was a large, white, two-story Romanesque-style building that housed a restaurant. There you could buy hot dogs, hamburgers, fries, malts, cones, popcorn, and other picnic fare to be eaten in the restaurant or taken out into the pavilion.

Ruth first found out about the community theatre when her daughter, Hannah, and Angie's daughter, Tracey, had been chosen from their schools to play two of the Von Trapp family children in *The Sound of Music*. Fritz, the director, needed more nuns and noticed Ruth and Angie sitting on the benches in front of the stage while watching a rehearsal. He asked them point blank, "Do you girls sing?"

"Uh ... yes ... um ... in choir at church," Ruth had said, hesitantly, putting down her knitting and looking at Angie for help.

Angie was going to be no help at all. Setting her can of Diet Coke down with a "clack" on the bench, she bounced quickly over to the gray cement steps leading up to the stage. "We sure do!" she said with more enthusiasm than Ruth felt.

"Well, then, get up here," Fritz barked. "I need you. I gotta have more nuns in this show!" He continued to look at the small audience of assorted parents and grandparents who sat waiting for their children and grandchildren to finish the rehearsal. Most looked down intently at something in their laps, avoiding his gaze. "I can't do this show without more goddamn nuns," Fritz muttered under his breath as he turned his attention back to the performers on stage.

And so it began: an eighteen-year-long love affair with the Como Park Pavilion Players, a deepening friendship with bubbly Angie Corbello, and an ongoing association with the sometimes brilliant and funny and often exasperating, Frederich Gerhardt, known to the theatre crowd as Fritz. Ruth probably would have retired from the stage after *The Sound of Music*, but stage-struck Angie would have none of it.

"Pick me up at a quarter to seven, okay Ruthie?" Then Angie bellowed, "Charlie! Get down! Bad boy! Then she crooned, "You're such a bad boy. You're mama's bad little boy."

Ruth winced as she held the phone away from her ear.

"Anyway, Ruthie," Angie continued, "can you run me by that Red Owl on Grand Avenue on the way to auditions? They have a sale on Charlie's special doggie vitamins—not that he really needs them. Charlie! I said get off mama's chair! Bad boy! Come here, mama's little bad boy, you little mooshie-face, you ... give mama a kiss. Here's a treat, you bad, bad boy! So, you up for it? Huh? Ruthie?"

"Alright, Angie, I give up. Tomorrow night, at quarter to seven in front of your building. I'll see you then." Ruth shook her head and laughed to herself as she said good-bye to her friend and hung up the phone. She looked at her two cats, Morrie and Grizelda, who had come into the kitchen hoping for a treat, and said to no one in particular, "That Charlie has to be the most spoiled, rotten dog in the Land of 10,000 Lakes." Then she returned to the task of kneading her bread.

I'll bring Angie a loaf of this tomorrow, she thought. While greasing the bread tins she began to absentmindedly hum one of *Show Boat*'s most famous songs: "Life Upon the Wicked Stage."

It was pouring rain the following night when Ruth dashed out the back door of her cottage-style home. It faced Lake Elmo (the lake) in the historic town of Lake Elmo (same name), about twenty miles east of St. Paul. She ran out to her garage, her long jeans skirt flapping in the wind, as she fumbled with the wrapped bread, her purse, and her umbrella, trying not to get her navy-blue silk blouse wet. Once in the garage, she got into a little beige Toyota Corolla, put everything on the passenger seat, turned the key, and flicked the garage-door opener.

While backing out, she saw her cats watching intently from the back porch window. She looked at her neat little house with its spacious lawn and numerous oak trees. She glanced appreciatively at the lake at the end of her front yard. Even in the rain her property was beautiful.

I am so lucky, she thought. *Tom left me well-cared for. I own my home. No mortgage. My kids are near, at least Hannah. I live on a lake. I have a car that runs. I'm retired. I'm healthy. I can do whatever I want.*

As she pulled out of her driveway, her eyes welled up a little, thinking of Tom. He had had been gone five years. The year he died, 1985, was a hard year, one she would never forget. How he used to laugh when he came to our performances. He never expected the actors to be professionals, but always made opening night special, bringing flowers for the curtain call, always taking everyone out after the play, always paying for Angie's dinner.

Oh Tom ... Ruth fingered the little comedy/tragedy key-chain ornament that he had given her after one of those opening nights. *I miss you so much!*

Once on the road, she turned off her car radio and inserted a CD of *Show Boat*. "Why Do I Love You?" was playing when Ruth reached West Wind Terrace, the high-rise apartment building that Angie and her little dog, Charlie, called home in St. Paul's West Side neighborhood.

The building had seen better days, as had most of its inhabitants. Angie had been watching for Ruth out of the streaked lobby window when she saw Ruth pull up. She dashed out the door and through the rain to Ruth's car, holding an old newspaper over her head.

Ruth noticed that Angie had dressed up for her audition. Her red ponytail was wrapped into a tight bun and fixed to the top of her head with some glittery barrettes. She wore one of her more subdued outfits: black velour pants and a matching tunic. For dramatic flair she added a huge rhinestone necklace and matching earrings that dangled to her shoulders. Her shoes were silver toeless pumps, so high she tottered when she ran in them. And she carried a silver purse.

Ruth, who usually wore blue-jean skirts with blouses in subdued colors or muted plaids, smiled when she saw her friend. "Hi, sweetie!

Well, they'll pick you out of the crowd, for sure! Ruth quickly grabbed the rye bread off the front seat before it was squashed.

"You don't think it's too much, do you? I can go in and change to different shoes. Maybe I should have taken my black velvet purse?" Angie plopped down on the front seat and pulled down the visor that covered the mirror on her side. She looked at her reflection doubtfully.

"No, no, you're fine. You look like a diva!" Ruth leaned toward the woman and gave her a one-armed hug. "Hello, my dear, how's 'his highness'?"

"He was sitting in my chair watching TV and eyeing the Kleenex box when I left. He'll probably have Kleenex all over the apartment when I get back." Angie looked up at her ninth-floor picture window. Even though there was no face there, she waved and cooed, "Bye-bye sweetie, mama's going to give you some good vitamins when she gets back. Oh! What's this? For me?" Angie eagerly grabbed the package Ruth gave her. "It smells like home-made rye bread. Wow! Thanks, Ruthie!"

Angie's husband had run out on her, she had once told Ruth, "after he knocked me up!" Angie had laughed ruefully. "Just as well. He wasn't much of a husband and he probably wouldn't have been much of a father." That was more than twenty years ago.

Angie's life hadn't been easy. Ruth knew that. But the spunky woman had raised her daughter, Tracey, by working hard and steady in a series of low-paying jobs. Tracey had graduated high school with honors and got a scholarship at the University of Minnesota, where she'd majored in business administration. Angie was justly proud of her. Ruth knew that her friend only worked part-time now—usually temp jobs—but her spirit never flagged. She always seemed happy.

In many ways, she's one of the richest people I know, thought Ruth.

Ruth and Angie drove over the Robert Street Bridge, which spanned the Mississippi, and on through downtown St. Paul. Getting on I-94 was tricky, especially in the rain, but Ruth finally turned onto Dale Street, taking them into the upscale Grand Avenue district.

Ruth watched for the traffic and Angie nibbled pieces off the loaf and exclaiming "Umm, mmm, good!"

If they hurried and made all the lights, Angie could get her dog-vitamins and Ruth could get cat food and fruit at Kowalski's Red Owl and still get to Fritz's auditions on time. They were in luck. The rain stopped and there were few people in the check-out lines. Kowalski's, the only supermarket on that part of Grand Avenue, was a popular and well-stocked store.

"Can you believe the price of these oranges?" Angie whispered, putting down a net-like bag full of the succulent fruit.

Ruth picked it up. "I'll just buy one big one and we'll split it," she told her friend. "I can't possibly eat a dozen oranges before they go bad." Ruth knew Angie was on a tight budget.

"Let me pay for half," Angie said as she dug into the silver purse.

"Don't be silly," Ruth said as she laid her Visa card on the counter. "Anyway, I don't pay for them, I just use this little magic plastic card!" They both laughed at Ruth's lame joke.

Back in the car, the women rode the five blocks to the Gerhardt Music Studio singing "Fish gotta swim and birds gotta fly!" The rain had started up again, accompanying them with a staccato on the car roof.

Ruth turned the little Toyota onto Portland Avenue. Once a street of large single-family homes, it now included apartments and duplexes.

Many of the oldest houses had been converted into rental units. Yards that used to show off elaborate flower gardens were now strewn with tricycles and children's toys. Ruth carefully edged past the rows of parked cars on both sides of the street. They arrived at one of the last-remaining single-family homes on the block: a sedate, three-story Queen Anne that housed Vivian and Fritz Gerhardt and their famed Gerhardt Music Studio.

As Ruth and Angie drove up, they immediately noticed the flashing lights of a waiting ambulance. Two white-uniformed attendants were easing a gurney down the Gerhardt's inclined driveway, maneuvering it between two police cars parked next to the house. Belted to the gurney was a large form completely encased in a blue body-bag.

Chapter 2

An Ominous Way to Start

"WHAT IN GOD'S NAME?!" Ruth exclaimed as she pulled up to the first available parking spot. She had barely shut off the ignition before Angie opened the door and bounded out.

"Hey! I just finished a CPR class," she called to the men. "Can I help?"

Ruth heard the answer as she exited her car. "Lady, this guy is way beyond CPR. Please back up. Give us some room."

They finished loading the body and were shutting the doors of the ambulance as Ruth came up and put her arm around Angie's shoulders. Angie just stood there, a forlorn crease in her forehead. "Geez, who is it?"

"Excuse me," said one of the attendants as he elbowed past Angie and Ruth, carrying a clipboard over to the police car.

"Come on, Angie." Ruth gently took her friend's arm and guided her up the driveway and out of the way. "We'll find out inside." They headed toward the side door, which stood next to an elegantly lettered sign that read "Gerhardt Music Studio."

Fritz Gerhardt, wearing a black t-shirt emblazoned with "Just Call Me Maestro," stood in the doorway. He beckoned frantically for Ruth and Angie to come in. His countenance was deathly white.

"Oh my God!" he rasped. "Lionel's been murdered! It stopped raining for a few minutes and he said he was just going out for a smoke. Someone stabbed him out in the alley!" Fritz was breathing much too rapidly for a man his age. "Oh my god oh my god oh my god ... Lionel!" He held his heaving chest with both hands.

Fritz's wife, Vivian, stepped up beside him and handed him a juice glass full of water and a small white pill, which Ruth assumed must be for his anxiety attacks or his heart. Most of the older cast members knew about Fritz's hysterical outbursts and had seen Vivian administer medications before. No one took it too seriously; they just assumed that Vivian would handle it, whatever "it" was.

"Come on in, girls, hurry," Vivian whispered to Ruth and Angie. "Get in here before the police decide there's too many people inside."

Vivian ushered them in and quietly closed the door behind them. Fritz, still pale, swallowed the pill and leaned against her, clutching her arm and breathing heavily. She took the glass and helped him down the stairs to the basement studio.

Vivian Gerhardt carefully eased her beloved Fritz into an old brown leather chair that sat next to a table full of ball-point pens and audition sheets. As he moaned, "Oh God! What are we going to do? What are we going to do?" Vivian took a thin notebook and fanned Fritz with it, "shushing" him as if trying to quiet a cranky toddler. Her very presence seemed to calm the man.

She said quietly, but firmly, "Fritz … Fritz. Settle down now. Look at me. There's nothing we can do about it now. Do you want me to send everybody home or are we going on with auditions?"

Vivian had been Fritz's wife for a little over twelve years. She married him when they were both in their early fifties. The rumor among the theatre crowd was that they had been sweethearts long before finally marrying. Vivian Gerhardt was Fritz's exact opposite. Where Fritz was wiry and slender, Vivian was pleasingly plump in a European style that bespoke the "good life." Where Fritz was excitable to the point of apoplexy, Vivian exuded calm. Where he was argumentative, she was reasonable. Tonight, when Fritz's heart pounded so hard you could see his chest move, Vivian Gerhardt was a life-saver.

"Everyone, take five," she said with composure, looking around at the stunned folks assembled in the basement studio. "He'll be all right in a moment or two. Then we'll decide what to do."

Fritz Gerhardt and Vivian Zoltoff had lived across Portland Avenue from each other for almost three decades. They had known each other since their late twenties, when Fritz played in the all-city orchestra and Vivian sang solos in a community chorus. The volatile Fritz had been immediately smitten with the quiet, lovely soprano. He was also devoted to his "mama," a well-known local diva who kept her only child busy managing her lengthy and productive operatic career.

Ruth had never known Madeline Bouree-Gerhardt, but photos of her adorned the Gerhardt's basement studio. Each picture was framed and had a small label, printed carefully in ink, apparently by Fritz. "Mama at Carnegie Hall 1952," "Mama with Senator Humphrey," "Mama with Governor Anderson," "Mama at the Vienna Opera House," etc.

Madeline, as nearly everyone in the Twin Cities music world knew, had been almost solely responsible for bringing opera and, eventually, musical theatre to St. Paul. Old-timers in that city recalled how single-handedly she took on the Minnesota Legislature and demanded that they fund a program encouraging youthful musicians and singers. She agreed to match their funds with an inheritance left to her by her late husband.

People who had known Madeline would always smile at the mention of her name and shake their heads in awe: "That woman sure had a set of pipes. And she wasn't afraid of anybody or anything. She knew what she wanted and she nearly always got it. God help anyone who was in her way!" To the St. Paul musical community, she was a legend. And Fritz adored her. It was only after Mama Gerhardt died, having lived well into her eighties, that her son married the other love of his life: the ever-patient Vivian. Now the two were inseparable. Fritz lived for music and Vivian lived for Fritz.

The west wall of the studio was covered floor to ceiling with laminated show-bills, each from a past opera or a musical performed in St. Paul over the last half-a-century. The wall was a testament to the Gerhardt's energy and commitment to the arts. It also gave cast members who rehearsed there a sense of being part of something with a long tradition—a tradition that tonight seemed in jeopardy.

Vivian Gerhardt, however, was not going to let anything happen to that tradition if she could help it. She said quietly to her husband, who remained collapsed in his old leather chair, "Come on, Fritz, the show must go on."

As if by magic, that old cliche—so common in the theatre that it was almost a parody—brought Fritz to life. He stood up, squared his thin shoulders, smiled at his wife, smiled at a group of children in the front row, and then smiled at the adults who milled around behind them.

"People! Ladies and gentlemen," Fritz said as he edged toward a black metal music stand that served as a podium. He cleared his throat and looked out at the small crowd of would-be cast members. Out of habit, everyone quieted down when he spoke. "We've had a tragic happening here tonight. Yes, take your seats. Thank you. You all knew Lionel, our wonderful Lionel. He ..." and here his voice broke, "... he was one of us and we all loved him. We don't know what happened out there on the street tonight, but Mama would want us to continue the audition. The show must go on!"

Fritz continued, his voice becoming stronger and more dramatic. "Do you feel up to auditioning tonight, people? Should we do this show for Mama? For Lionel?" Fritz stared at his people with his piercing brown eyes and waited, his slender fingers folded on top of the music stand, as if in prayer.

The group of twenty or so adults and children, who by now were all seated in four rows of folding chairs, mostly stared back. A few glued their eyes to the dark-green painted cement floor, not knowing what to answer. The uncomfortable silence was broken only by the hum of a small fan on a table in the corner, laboring to provide air.

He is amazing, thought Ruth as she watched him. *He plays a crowd like a violin.* It was so still you could hear people breathing. Finally, one of the older men in the back raised his hand.

"Maestro, if we could maybe have a few minutes to catch our breath, and maybe get a drink of water."

That was Vivian's cue. "There's a big pot of coffee and some punch in the kitchen and there are some bars in the dining room. I was saving it for after the auditions, but why don't we have it now?" She looked at Fritz for his approval.

"Alright," he said with a gesture of his hand toward the narrow stairs that led up to the kitchen. "Let's take a small break. Fifteen minutes. Be back in your seats at ..." he looked at his watch, "eight thirty-five." He glanced at Vivian and sighed as he sat down again.

The older cast members, who knew the Gerhardt house by heart, trooped up the creaky wooden basement stairs toward the bright cheerful kitchen. Vivian always served refreshments in the formal dining room, which was just beyond a cozy breakfast nook.

As they went, you could hear the whispers. *"What happened? Did you see anything?" "What if they're still out there?" "Will you walk me to my car when this is over?"*

Vivian, who held onto Fritz's wrist as if taking his pulse, looked up and called to Ruth. "Ruth, would you please just take the coffee and punch into the dining room for me? Everything else is already on the dining room table." Ruth nodded to her as Vivian continued her instructions. "The coffee is plugged in on the kitchen counter and the punch is in the fridge ... and Ruth, could you please pour punch for the children? Maybe the youngest ones can sit down at the breakfast nook. My dining room carpet was just cleaned."

"I'll take care of it. You stay with Fritz," Ruth reassured her before hurrying up the stairs. *She's so organized,* thought Ruth. *And he's so lucky to have her!*

For people who had just witnessed death, the cast member's appetites were amazingly healthy. Vivian, renowned for her pastries, had made apple strudel bars and frosted almond bars. Both were quickly consumed. Ruth saved one of each to take down to Vivian and Fritz. She assumed that Vivian would want coffee and that Fritz would probably want his usual Pepsi. She assumed correctly because he smiled and gave her a "thumbs up" when she came down the stairs with their tray. "I found this in the refrigerator," she told him. "I thought you'd probably want it."

"You are an angel from heaven!" Fritz popped the top and, ignoring the glass of ice Ruth had brought, gulped it straight from the can.

"Fritz," Vivian cautioned him, "drink it slowly. Come on, now. You know how you get." Smiling indulgently at her husband, Vivian rolled her eyes and shook her head at Ruth.

"He looks a lot better," Ruth told her.

"I *am* a lot better!" Fritz answered back, stuffing both bars quickly in his mouth and washing them down with another swig of Pepsi. Then he burped. "Oops! Sorry Mama," he said with a grin. He wiped his mouth with the back of his hand. "In China, that's a sign that the food was good."

Vivian scowled. "Well, we're not in China," she countered, and gave him a look.

Ruth thought that right about now was a good time to retreat. "I'm just going to go up and make sure everything's cleaned up"

Vivian nodded and motioned with her hand for Ruth to go. "Thank you, my dear," she said quietly.

Knowing the maestro's penchant for punctuality and how risky it was to disregard it, the older members of the would-be cast soon urged everyone down the flight of stairs from Vivian's kitchen and into their seats.

By precisely eight thirty-five the theatre folk sat quietly, waiting for Fritz's directions. They filled the four rows of chairs, adults in the back on risers, children in the front, floor level.

Some of the newcomers turned their heads to the right, gawking at the colorful mural that covered the north wall of the studio. It was a mountain scene, painted in a somewhat primitive style. Looking like an illustration for the story "Heidi," it consisted of a half-timber Alpine cottage surrounded by pine trees and a meadow full of edelweiss. The focal point was a young girl wearing traditional German dress who stood next to two grazing goats. She appeared to be calling or perhaps singing to the goats.

Because cast members had been conscientious about putting all of their used paper plates, cups and napkins into the large waste-basket in the kitchen, Ruth didn't have much to clean up. She had only to straighten the table cloth and bring the coffee pot and punch pitchers back into the kitchen. While descending the stairs to join the others, she noticed Angie beckon and pat the vacant chair next to her. *Well, this is an ominous way to start*, she thought as she slid in beside her friend.

Chapter 3

The Opera Star

RUTH SQUIRMED UNEASILY ON the uncomfortable folding chair, trying to relax and breathe deeply. Deep breathing, she had once learned in yoga class, was supposed to calm the nerves. She looked at the familiar pastoral scene on the wall nearby and thought, as she had done every time she sat in the Gerhardt's basement studio. *Why didn't the artist paint those pine trees more realistically?* Then her thoughts shifted to the immediate challenge at hand. *In a few minutes I will have to sing in front of this group. I don't like singing alone in front of people. That's why I always audition for the chorus. Lord, do I even remember the words to my song?*

Without answering the questions in her mind, her thoughts wandered back to the mural. The inept rendering of the pine trees had always bothered her. *They look like little Alfalfa's hair, parted in the middle,* she thought to herself, remembering the old "Our Gang" movies. Ruth had been an art teacher for twenty years before Tom got sick and she retired to take care of him. She continued to paint landscapes as a hobby and was actually quite accomplished.

I wish they would let me in here for an afternoon with my paints and brushes, she thought, laughing to herself. *I could fix those stupid trees!*

Suddenly Ruth's eyes met those of a tall, distinguished-looking Black man who must have just arrived. He stood in the front of the room, talking with Fritz. She quickly looked down in her lap, looked up again, trying not to stare, and noticed his slender frame and graying temples.

He's really handsome. I wonder who he is?

Angie saw him too. "Wow! Look at Mr. Gorgeous, will ya?" she whispered to Ruth. "I wouldn't kick *him* out of my bedroom!"

"Shh," whispered Ruth, poking her friend gently in the side.

Just then Fritz made another one of his announcements. "Ladies and gentlemen," he said as he put a hand on the man's arm, "I have the great pleasure of presenting Mr. Delancy Mays, currently just finishing his role as Rigoletto at the Lyric Opera in Chicago. He has graciously agreed to give us some of his time this summer to play the role of 'Joe'."

There were appreciative murmurs and applause. Al Rosenberg, one of the actors and obviously an opera buff, rose from his seat, nodding affirmatively while he clapped.

To Fritz, getting someone of Mr. Mays stature was an obvious coup.

"Mama always thought you could sing better than me!" he kidded the embarrassed-looking, home town opera star, who smiled and shook his head and again tried to sit down.

Fritz would have none of it. He was on a roll and he held tightly to the man's arm. "Del always got the good roles, even though I was older and much better-looking," he told the group, who laughed as if on cue. Fritz, who couldn't sing a note and who looked somewhat like an aging troll, was always making jokes at his own expense. That was part of what endeared him to the theatre crowd.

"Of course, he had been a top student at Julliard," he winked at Mr. Mays, "and I was only a lowly bassoon-player. Mama would pay me ... not to sing!" At this the crowd laughed again, although it was a joke that Fritz often repeated. Fritz's total lack of singing talent was legendary.

At this, Delancy Mays finally extricated himself from Fritz's clutch, patted him on the shoulder, smiled, and sat down in a chair next to Vivian.

Oh Lord, he's helping with the auditions! Now I have to sing in front of an opera star! Ruth closed her eyes and tightened her grip on the Kleenex she held in her hand. Even though Ruth routinely made it into Fritz's choruses—musicals always needed singing villagers—the mandatory auditions made her nervous. Earlier that afternoon she had practiced singing to her own piano accompaniment of "Somewhere Out There," from *An American Tale*—a song she thought of as "her song" for Tom.

It's silly, she thought, *but I always think he hears me when I sing this.*

Ruth's reverie was cut short when Vivian gently led the first child up to the front. He was a chubby little fellow, about ten years old she guessed, with thick coke-bottle glasses and red hair. His face was pale and his freckles stood out like dots made with a magic marker. Ruth nodded her head and smiled at him in encouragement, a reflex left over from her days as a teacher. She thought there was something familiar about his face, but couldn't place it and thought no more about it.

The boy handed his music to Vivian, who sat down at the well-worn baby-grand Steinway that the Gerhardts kept in perfect tune.

"Isn't Susie here?" Fritz asked Vivian. "Where's Susie? I'm paying her for rehearsals. She oughta be here."

"She called me earlier," Vivian gently reassured him. "She's having car trouble. She'll be here and I'll fill in until she comes." She flexed her fingers and started the introduction to "Make Believe," from *Show Boat*.

Oh, Fritz is letting him audition with a song from the show—kind of a strange selection for a kid to sing, though, thought Ruth, who remembered it as Kathryn Grayson's signature romantic song. Fritz always told them not to audition with songs from the show they were doing. It was one of his cardinal rules. Ruth supposed it was because they wanted to know what kind of music people chose to use, and perhaps because he would be unduly influenced by hearing someone sing a song for the part they wanted. She craned her neck to get a better look at the child. She was glad that Fritz had relaxed his rule a bit.

Little Rodney Olson stood for a moment looking out at the assembled would-be cast, his red hair plastered in sweat on his forehead, his glasses slightly fogged. His short, plump arms hung at his sides. His little barrel chest could be seen expanding the blue and gray polo shirt he wore. And then he opened his mouth. And sang.

A clear, brilliant, heart-breaking sound filled the room.

"We could make believe, I love you ... only make believe, that you love me ..."

The crowd fell quiet. Even the children in the front row stopped fidgeting as their eyes and mouths opened in surprise at such incredible beauty coming from the throat of one of their own kind.

Rodney continued to the end of his song. Fritz didn't cut him off mid-way through as he usually did for most of the singers. Ruth noticed that Fritz's eyes were closed and that he was smiling as though he didn't want the song to end. Ruth had never heard anything so lovely—and heart-rending. As he sang, you forgot his appearance, his age, his glasses. All you heard was a clear, wonderful voice, floating through the air, filling the room. Ruth dabbed at her eyes with a Kleenex. She looked at Angie and saw a tear roll down her rouged cheek.

As Rodney finished singing, Fritz stepped away from the podium and put his arm around the boy's shoulders. "That was just wonderful, son," Fritz said beaming, and then quietly whispered "When you are older, I'm going to cast you as a leading man. We'll do a show just for you and you'll be the star." He looked at Vivian and Delancy and gave a nod that meant Rodney was definitely in.

As the red-faced, but grinning future star took his seat directly in front of his mother, Ruth saw the woman reach her arms around Rodney's chair and hug him from behind. She leaned over, kissed him lightly on his moist cheek, and whispered something in his ear. When the boy leaned back into the hug, Ruth felt the love between them.

Rodney's mother, Rhonda, who auditioned later, looked young, possibly in her late twenties. She was pretty, but thin to the point of looking frail. She had large glasses and her brown hair hung straight, touching her shoulders. Ruth thought the sturdy little boy looked very well-fed and well-dressed, compared to his mother. Ruth noticed Mimi Rosenberg, one of the older members of the group, reach over and pat the young woman's arm, giving her a smile and thumbs up sign.

The rest of the audition went with a familiar routine. The children auditioned first so they could leave early. Most were fairly good singers, although none as superb as Rodney Olson. One little girl danced as she sang, looking for all the world like a little Mexican-American Shirley Temple.

All the children will probably get in, thought Ruth, *because Fritz is savvy enough to know that each child on stage adds at least ten or twenty ticket-paying family members to the audience.*

When it was her turn, Ruth sang a passably good "Somewhere Out There" to her beloved late husband, Tom. She tried not to look at Delancy Mays, or at anybody for that matter, riveting her eyes instead upon the back wall, just above the heads in the last row of seats. It was something she learned from her high school choir director.

Angie sang a lively rendition of "We've Got Elegance," complete with a little dance, from *Hello Dolly.*

The usual coterie of slightly paunchy balding tenors, baritones, and bases in their forties and fifties sang "Stouthearted Men," "They Call the Wind Maria," and "I Did It My Way." One darkly handsome man—younger, hairier, and more muscular than the others—sang "Maria," from *West Side Story,* sending shivers up the spines of most of the women in the audience.

A real lady-killer, Ruth thought to herself.

Two old hands in the troupe, Al and Mimi Rosenberg, sang a duet from *Annie Get Your Gun.* Ruth thought their interpretation of "Anything You Can Do, I Can Do Better," was good enough to be on a professional stage. She roundly applauded them, cheering, "Brava!" and "Bravo!" along with the rest of those present.

The Rosenbergs bowed like real theatre folk do, holding each other's hands high and then sweeping them down as they bent low before the crowd. Fritz nodded "yes," at Vivian and then joined the others with applause as the tall, thin Mimi and the shorter, portly Al took their seats.

The audition was at times amusing. A mezzo-soprano, auditioning for the comedic part of "Ellie," sang "Itsy Bitsy Spider" in torch-song style. It was roundly funny and by then most of the group seemed to have forgotten about the body that had lain on a gurney, scarcely an hour ago, in Fritz's driveway.

When the singing was over, Fritz wiped his brow and thanked Susie, who had finally arrived half-way through the audition, for her playing. He told the cast that they should thank her too, and everyone dutifully broke into applause. Susie, who always seemed embarrassed when Fritz called attention to her, ducked her short dark curly head behind her music but waved her hand at them.

Fritz spoke briefly with Delancy Mays, who then excused himself and left. After that, Fritz chatted with some of the older auditioners, including Ruth and Angie, thanking them for coming. "It's going to be a great show!" he exclaimed.

Vivian, always the organizer, double-checked everyone's phone number, reminding them that there was one more audition the next night, in case they had any friends who wanted to try out. She promised to call with the cast-postings within the week.

As Ruth and Angie walked to Ruth's car, it finally hit them. "Lionel was probably going to be cast as Ravenal," Angie said quietly. "I wonder who'll take his place?"

"Unless someone really good auditions tomorrow night, my guess would be the *West Side Story* guy," Ruth softly answered as she opened the passenger door for Angie. She was careful to look into the darkened back seat before her friend got in.

"Why are we being so quiet? God! What a way to start a production," Angie pronounced as she eased her ample frame into the car. She trembled. "Ooh! Someone just walked on my grave."

"Don't say that!" chided Ruth as she clicked the four-door lock and turned the ignition key.

"And that cool Black guy ... whoa!" Angie grinned. "He was checking ya out. I saw him."

"Angie!" Ruth shot back. "He was not." She turned the car carefully into the street. "Anyway, he's probably married, with six kids."

"Well, I wouldn't mind having *his* kids!" Angie's earthy humor showed.

"Honestly, Angie!"

"Once ya have Black, ya never go back,"

"For God's sake, put a sock in it!"

By the time they exited Portland Avenue on to Dale Street, the rain had stopped. Ruth opened her window a crack to let fresh air in. Angie followed suit and breathed deeply, leaning back luxuriously in the seat. "I don't know why, but I just love being in these shows," she laughed ruefully, "although I don't know why anyone would want to look at this old wreck up on a stage."

"Well, Angie ..." Ruth looked sideways at her friend's ample frame. "Just remember Mae West. Everyone loved her, especially the men!"

"Oh yeah, they're beatin' my door down, beggin' me for a date."

"This group is darn lucky to have you," Ruth said, and started singing *"Life upon the wicked stage ain't ever what a girl sup-po-ses!"*

Angie joined in, *"Stage-door johnnies aren't bending over you with gems and ro-ses!"*

The two women laughed and sang and engaged in the kind of banter one finds only among trusted old friends. They were oblivious to the car following them.

Chapter 4

Attacked

Because the audition had lasted longer than usual, due to Lionel's murder and the ensuing shock and commotion, Ruth and Angie didn't stop for a cup of tea and piece of pie on Robert Street, as they typically did.

"Don't feel you have to take me to Baker's Square tonight," Angie told her. "It's late. I'm bushed and Charlie is way past due getting outside to take care of his business."

"Okay," Ruth agreed. "I'm tired too—but at least my cats have a box."

After a few minutes had gone by, Angie started in again, "Really, though, tell me honestly. What do you think of that Mays guy?"

"Angie!" Ruth laughed. "You have a one-track mind!"

"Maybe so ... " Angie shot back, "but he looked classy."

"Like I said before, Angie," Ruth quipped back. "Married. Six kids."

"Maybe not. Maybe he's a widower ... lonely ... needs a little TLC ... a little home-made rye bread," Angie grinned as she waved what was left of Ruth's bread under her nose.

"From your mouth to God's ear," Ruth told her, shaking her head and laughing.

The dark-colored sedan was still following Ruth's Corolla as she pulled into Angie's high-rise parking lot. It slowed down when she did, parking down the block from Angie's building, carefully avoiding the street lights.

That night, back at her lake home, Ruth had trouble getting to sleep, tossing and turning in her upstairs bedroom. She finally got up and sat in her big blue and white chintz-covered easy chair, putting her bare feet up on the matching ottoman. She looked out at the full moon over the lake, which shimmered in its light. On one hand, she was deeply troubled by Lionel's murder.

He was such a nice man ... so courteous to everyone ... so gentle, she thought. *Who would ever hurt such a man?*

On the other hand, she felt the stirrings of something she didn't really want to deal with. "Mr. Delancy Mays as Joe," she whispered to herself, smiling at the moon.

Within a week, Vivian Gerhardt had called all of the principals, those with actual speaking parts, and all of the chorus members. She knew how to gently let down those who had hoped for bigger parts but did not measure up to her husband's musical standards. To these, she usually offered a place in the chorus, which most gladly accepted. Just being in one of Fritz Gerhardt's productions was enough of a plum.

On Wednesday, Ruth got her call for the chorus, which she both expected and wanted. "Oh, thank you so much, Vivian!" she exclaimed breathlessly. She had been working in her back yard flower garden and had to run to get to the phone in time, pulling her gardening gloves off as she went. "Have you heard any more about Lionel?"

"No," Vivian answered. "The police don't seem to be investigating anyone in the company. But other than that, they really haven't told us much. Fritz calls them just about every other day, but they just keep telling him, 'No new developments.'"

"Good grief, I should hope they don't suspect anyone in the company," Ruth said. "Did Lionel have a family?"

"Not really. He had a long-time friend, an older gentleman, a Mr. Hurd, who shared a house with him. I met him once, a very nice man. Seemed kind of quiet. We've heard absolutely nothing from him. Fritz tried to call him to find out when the funeral was and the line had been disconnected."

"Oh dear." Ruth felt sorry for a man with no family to mourn him. "Poor Lionel. I wonder who could have done such a thing?!"

"We think it was a gang-member," Vivian told her. "This neighborhood has changed in the past thirty years." She went on to tell Ruth about how she and Fritz used to go for long walks after dark, sometimes to a soda-shop up on Selby Avenue. "Not any more. We have to be watchful when we go out to get our mail."

"I'm sure it has changed," Ruth told her. "But when we have rehearsals at your house there are so many people coming and going, I always felt safe. Poor Lionel."

"Ruth," Vivian interrupted, "would you do me a favor and call Angie for me and tell her she's in the chorus? And also tell her she should be ready to take on a small character role. I know she's a good friend of yours and her line is always busy when I call."

"I'd be glad to ... and yes, I know ... she does get long-winded on the phone," Ruth laughed. "If I can't reach her today, I'll tell her tomorrow. We're going together to buy fabric for our costumes." Even though she didn't have to, Ruth enjoyed making her own costume and she usually helped Angie, who wasn't as proficient a seamstress.

"Thank you," Vivian said, adding, "I wish you could call Gloria-June Kimmel for me too. I know she'll turn me down flat for the chorus." Vivian spoke freely to Ruth, who was one of the old-timers in the company. Vivian knew Ruth could be trusted not to repeat theatre gossip. Fritz knew this as well, and so the Gerhardts frequently confided in Ruth, asking her advice or to perform favors during the run of the show.

Oh no, thought Ruth, grimacing. *There's no way I'm going to deal with Gloria-June!*

Most people were happy to be in the chorus, thinking it was an honor just to sing under Fritz. The one exception, however, was Gloria-June Kimmel. Gloria-June, being a transplanted southern belle, used both her first and middle names. She always refused a place in the chorus if she didn't also get a speaking part, however small. She was a star-wannabee and her husband, Howard, blessed with a wonderful resonant voice, almost always got a principal role. Gloria-June, on the other hand, had a voice that wandered slightly off key. At best, she could be described as an "average" singer.

Ruth remembered one summer when Gloria-June was given a small but important role. She had been so hard to work with that Fritz almost kicked her out of the production. "I'm sorry Vivian, but I think I'll pass on calling Gloria-June," Ruth laughed. "Especially if it's with unwanted news!"

"Well, thanks anyway," Vivian replied. "See you Monday night for chorus rehearsal, seven o'clock sharp, at the studio."

"We'll be there," Ruth assured her. "I love the music in *Show Boat*. I'm really looking forward to this show."

"By the way," Vivian remarked, chortling a bit as she did so, "Our wonderful Mr. Mays noticed you."

"What?" Ruth was embarrassed, but her heart did a little flip. "What do you mean, 'noticed' me?"

Vivian continued. "After you sang, he scribbled in the margin on your cast sign-up sheet, "lovely," and then, after Susie arrived and I sat down next to him again, he pointed to your name and whispered, "This one is in, I hope.""

Ruth laughed. "That doesn't mean anything. He just wants some old-lady singers in the chorus."

"Maybe," Vivian told her. "It was how his eyes lit up when he said it. I would watch out, though, if I were you."

Ruth was flustered. "I have no intention of ev ... watch out for *what*?"

Vivian's voice had an edge to it, "Well, rumor has it that Del has been seeing Blanche Voorhees."

"Not *the* Blanche Voorhees!" Ruth had seen her perform once at the Orpheum in *Carmen*. She was a diva in the true sense of the word, and then some. "Didn't I read somewhere that she tried to poison ..."

"... tried to poison a rival in order to get a part?" Vivian interrupted. "Yeah, that's the story. They never proved it, of course, but I wouldn't put it past her. She started out, years ago, with Fritz, you know ... singing leads in his shows. She grew up in South St. Paul, even though she would have people believe she's descended from de-throned European royal-ty. She was a real pain in the patootie then and she's even worse now."

Ruth was surprised that the usually composed Vivian sounded so virulent. But she listened.

"Once there was this sweet little girl from White Bear Lake," Vivian recounted. "She had an absolutely lovely voice, so Fritz had this little gal and Blanche share the role of Julie in his production of *Carousel*, singing on alternate nights. Blanche hated the fact that she had to share the spotlight and she really hated that this other girl was not only prettier but a better singer."

"Better than Blanche Voorhees?" Ruth was incredulous.

"Anyway," Vivian continued, "Blanche got wind of the fact that this little gal was going to audition for the Chanhassen Dinner The-atre. And wouldn't you know it, when this sweet young thing showed up to audition, they said, "Why are you here? You called and cancelled your audition last night. You said you had found a better part," Vivian sniffed. "The girl told me this, later—even though she tried to explain to them that it hadn't been her, they didn't let her audition."

Ruth gasped. "And you think that Blanche Voorhees made that call?"

"I know for a fact that she did. I overheard her. I remembered hearing her call someone from the phone in the restaurant during one of our breaks." Vivian sounded really angry now. "At the time I thought she was just calling for something she wanted to cancel, but now I know she was out to ruin this little gal's chance to audition."

"God in heaven!" Ruth whispered. "I sure wouldn't want to get in her way."

"I don't know what he sees in her," Vivian snorted. "A nice man like that."

"Well, that's something I don't have to worry about," Ruth assured her. "I have no designs on anybody." Inwardly she felt a little disappointed.

"And she hates Fritz," Vivian went on. "She doesn't ever want her 'humble' roots to be exposed, and once when he was being interviewed by the *Pioneer Press*, he mentioned that she was a former star in his shows at Como." Vivian laughed. "She read the article and had a hissy fit! She called us and ranted on and on because she thought Fritz was referring to her as a has-been." Vivian rolled her eyes. "You can imagine what Fritz told her."

"Yes, I can imagine ..."

"Well," Vivian continued, "at least she won't dare to show up at rehearsals. Fritz would tell her in no uncertain terms to leave. That's for sure!"

Ruth and Vivian said their good-byes, after which Ruth slumped in one of her big blue winged-back chairs. *Well,* she thought, *that's that. It was silly of me to even think about Mr. Delancy Mays.*

Her cats, Morrie and Griselda, came up to her, perhaps sensing that she needed comfort. Griselda hopped in her lap and Morrie jumped to the back of the chair, rubbing his head on hers. "Oh you guys," she cooed. "You always know when mama needs you." She petted them and listened to them purr.

By late afternoon Ruth was at her kitchen table, about to bite into a tuna fish sandwich on whole wheat toast with some Sun Chips, which she'd prepared for an early supper. She also had a cup of Earl Grey tea with a small slice of lemon. Knowing her friend's talkative nature, Ruth thought she might as well sit down and enjoy her meal while they chatted, something they frequently did. She called Angie, but the phone rang and rang.

Finally, a man's voice answered. "Hello, who's calling please."

Surprised to hear a stranger's voice answer Angie's phone, Ruth responded somewhat formally. "This is Ruth Carson. May I speak with Angie Cobello, please? I'm a friend of hers." *Who the heck is that?* Ruth wondered. *And why would he be answering Angie's phone for her?*

She could hear Charlie's whining cries in the background and she instantly got a sinking feeling in the pit of her stomach. She pushed her sandwich aside.

"Mrs. Corbello has been taken to Regions Hospital. Did you say you are a friend of hers? Could I have your name and phone number?"

"What? Who *is* this?!" Ruth gasped. "And why is Angie in the hospital?"

"This is Sergeant Michael Sullivan, St. Paul Police, ma'am," he replied crisply, "and I would like your full name and phone number, please."

Startled, Ruth answered more meekly and gave the sergeant her number. Then she asked, "What's going on? Is Angie okay?"

"Ma'am, if you could come down to the main precinct station and give us some information, we'll be able to tell you more."

"But ... but ... is she alright? Ruth could feel her fear mounting. *Oh Angie! No, not Angie!* Her breath was coming in short gasps.

"It looks as though someone broke into her apartment last night and attacked her. That's about as much as I can tell you right now. She was alive when they transported her to St. Paul-Ramsey Hospital," the sergeant said, more kindly.

"Thank God!" Ruth said, beginning catch her breath. "I live in Lake Elmo, but I'll come as soon as I can. Is your police station the one on Tenth Street?"

"You said you were a good friend?"

"Yes, I ... good friends. For many, many years." Ruth tried to stay composed and keep from sobbing. *Oh Angie,* she thought. *Please, Angie. Please be alright!*

"Well, Mrs., uh, we do need someone to take care of her dog."

"Charlie?" Ruth asked. "You want me to take Charlie? Uh, that's her dog's name."

"When we called her daughter, she said she could not take the dog. If you can't, we'll have to bring it to the pound. You are certainly under no obligation."

Ruth really didn't want to deal with the little guy, but her loyalty to Angie prompted her to action. "Okay. I guess. Do you want me to come over there and pick him up?"

"No, ma'am," the man replied. "We're having someone take him over to the station now." Ruth could hear frantic yipping in the background.

"Okay," Ruth sighed. "I'll be there as soon as I can." She hung up the phone and started to cry, her shoulders heaving, her hands covering her face.

Chapter 5

The Hospital

R UTH SLAMMED HER BACK door shut and ran into her garage, almost tripping over some boxes she had left on the floor. "Dammit!" she cried, regaining her balance, only to hit her hip on the side of her car.

Rubbing her sore hip, Ruth eased into her Toyota and turned the key. As she backed out of her garage, she narrowly missed hitting the frame of her garage door. "Angie!" she cried. "Hang on, Angie. I'm on my way!"

She hardly remembered the drive to St. Paul's downtown police station. A generally cautious, polite driver, she honked her horn and blinked her headlights at people whose driving deterred her from reaching Angie quickly.

As she pulled up to the police station, Ruth looked briefly at her reflection in the rear-view mirror.

My God, I look a fright! she thought to herself, as she tried to smooth down her hair. "I didn't even put on any makeup!" She pulled into a visitor's spot in front of the station. *At least I'm dressed okay to go and visit at the hospital.*

She was wearing a dark blue, wrinkle-proof blouse with black pants and a thin black jacket she had thrown over her shoulders at the last minute.

Ruth jumped out of the car and ran into the building, breathless as she hurried into an uninviting tan-colored room. A young Asian woman in a police uniform sat at a reception desk, protected behind a heavy mesh security screen.

"I'm looking for Sergeant ... oh, ah ... Sullivan, I think his name was."

"You must mean Michael Sullivan," the officer replied. "Is he expecting you?"

"I was on the phone with him about 45 minutes ago. He asked me to come down here and answer some questions. It's about Angie Corbello. She was attacked last night in her apartment. I think I'm supposed to take care of her dog."

"What's your name?"

"Ruth Carson."

"Hold on, please." The officer picked up her phone and pressed a number.

"Don? There's a Ruth Carson here to see Mickey. Says it's about someone who was attacked last night ... and something about a dog."

She nodded as she listened and then turned to Ruth.

"You can go right up." Ruth heard the loud click of latch being released on a heavy metal door to her left. "Go through there," the officer said matter-of-factly, nodding at the door, "and go up the stairs. Turn left in the middle of the hall. It's the third door on the right-hand side and it says "Homicide" on it. Just go on in. They won't hear you if you knock."

Ruth thanked her and started for the stairs. ... *up the stairs ... turn left ... third door on the right-hand side ... If they have Charlie and expect me to take him right away, I don't know what I'll do. I certainly can't take a dog to the hospital with me*, she thought. *I hope they can keep him while I run over to Regions to check on Angie.*

When Ruth found the door marked "Homicide" she walked in. The first thing she saw was a small white terrier held tightly by an older-looking officer. The animal was squirming wildly, trying to get away.

"Ah, excuse me. I'm Ruth Carson," Ruth said. "I'm looking for Sergeant, uh ... Sergeant ... "Sullivan?" the officer answered. "Come on boy, I won't bite," he said as he held tightly to the dog's collar. "Mickey brought this little fellow in. I mean Sergeant Sullivan," he added with a smile.

"Well, it looks as if Charlie's being a handful," Ruth reached out to scratch the little dog's ears. The animal shut its eyes and cringed. "Charlie," Ruth cooed, "don't be afraid. You remember me."

"He's pretty upset. So, your name is Charlie, is it?" he said to the dog. He put it on the floor, tied a rope to its collar and secured it to his chair. "Are you the woman who's supposed to pick him up?"

"Yes, I guess so. I'm Ruth Carson," Ruth explained once more, "Angie Corbello's friend." She went on to explain that in order for her to go over to the hospital and check on Angie, he would need to keep Charlie about an hour longer.

The officer shrugged. "Well, I suppose so. I guess I don't mind his company for a while longer. He rose and offered Ruth his hand, "I'm Don Olson ... Sergeant Olson," he told her. "I'll just wait here until you get back."

"I thought Sergeant Sullivan was going to ask me some questions," she said.

"He had to respond to another case that just came up. He wants to talk to you, though. He'll call you."

Ruth thanked him and started out the door. As she did so, she saw Sergeant Olson break a bagel in half and offer half to the dog, who backed away from it.

Ruth paused, "Do you know? Was Angie conscious? Did she say anything?"

"I think she said something about not being able to be in some show."

"Oh!" Ruth cried. "Yes. We are both in community theatre. We were going to be singing in *Show Boat* this summer."

"So you're in that theatre group Ms. Corbello was in?"

"Yes," Ruth told him, "Angie and I are both in that group, the Como Park Pavilion Players."

"Well," he sighed, "okay then. See you later. But if you're not back in a couple of hours I can't keep him and we'll have to bring him to the pound."

Ruth thanked him again for watching Angie's dog. "Don't worry, I'm sure I'll be back soon." She drove to the hospital as quickly as the downtown traffic allowed. Parking was at a premium but she eventually found a spot in the hospital ramp.

"Finally!" she muttered to herself as she carefully edged into the tight space.

Hurrying as fast as she could to the intensive care unit, Ruth told the nurse on the floor that, other than Angie's daughter, she was as close to immediate family as Angie had. The nurse led her down a darkened hall, past a young uniformed officer keeping watch, to another nurse inside a darkened room. It was a small room, lit dimly. Lights from an assortment of monitors blinked yellow and green.

"Has she been conscious at all?" Ruth whispered.

"In and out," whispered the nurse in return. "Please don't stay too long. We limit our ICU visits to ten minutes, maximum, and her daughter will be here in about an hour. We don't want to overdo it."

The nurse stayed in the room while Ruth looked down at her friend. Tears welled up in Ruth's eyes and she began to sob quietly. Seeing her genuine sorrow, the nurse quietly turned away, ostensibly to check on some tubes that were running from Angie to another machine.

"Oh Angie ..." whispered Ruth, "what have they done to you? Who would ever hurt you? Angie, sweetie, it's Ruth. I'm here." She choked back tears. "Don't worry about Charlie. I'll take good care of him. He can stay with me. You know I love that little guy. And I love you too." Ruth turned away, overcome by the sight of her bruised and broken friend.

"Is she, will she, be alright?" Ruth questioned the nurse. The once vibrant Angie lay still and pale except for terrible bruises around her face and neck. Dark circles ringed her eyes. Her red hair was matted to the sides of her head. A tube fed oxygen into her nostrils.

"I've seen a lot worse recover," the nurse said gently. "We'll take good care of her." She adjusted the covers slightly at Angie's feet. "We really need to let her rest, you know."

"Of course," Ruth said and turned to go, "It's just ... just ... she's so dear to me. I can't believe anyone would hurt her. She's such a loving, giving person." Ruth shook her head in disbelief.

"It's a crazy world with some pretty sick people," the nurse said as she set her jaw in the resigned manner of someone who had seen it all. "Don't worry, we'll do everything we can to help her."

"Thank you," Ruth murmured. "Please ask her daughter to call me. I'm keeping Angie's dog at my house and she might want to come and get him. Here's my number." She hurriedly scribbled her name and number on a piece of paper she found in her purse.

The nurse nodded, taking the paper and putting it in her pocket.

"I hope they catch whoever did this to her," Ruth whispered. "He must be some kind of animal."

"No, not an animal," the nurse responded as she looked squarely at Ruth. "Animals only kill for food or to protect their territory."

Ruth quietly let herself out, nodding to the officer as she left Angie's room. Then she stopped and turned to him. He looked familiar. *Where had she seen him?* She looked at him again, more carefully, and then it dawned on her. "Were you ... didn't you audition for *Show Boat* at the Gerhardt Studio last week? Singing 'Maria?'"

The muscular, good-looking young man immediately stood up and extended his hand. "Yes, I did. I'm Danny Ancino. How 'ya doin' ?"

"I'm Ruth Carson." She held out her hand, wincing when Officer Ancino gripped and shook it vigorously. "I auditioned for the chorus," she said, and added more quietly, "I'm a close friend of Mrs. Corbello, the lady you're guarding. She's also in the theatre, in the chorus with me. We've been in Fritz's shows for years."

The young officer frowned. "You're kiddin! That lady? The attempted homicide? Whew!"

This young man exudes raw power! Ruth thought.

"Please, please take good care of Angie," she told him. "She's so dear, so good-hearted. Will there be a guard here all the time, around the clock?"

"Probably not. We usually hang around for the first few days to see if they wake up and say anything we can use as evidence." Changing the subject back to himself, he said, "Ya know, I just got a call from Ms. Gerhardt yesterday. I'll be doing Gaylord Ravenal. He's the lead, ya know." He all but strutted as he said this and then added sourly, "But geez! I don't like that stupid name—Gaylord."

"Congratulations!" Ruth said. "I'm sure you'll do a wonderful job." She thought to herself that he looked a bit too beefy and coarse for the part of Ravenal, which in the film version had been played by the virile, yet debonaire, Howard Keel.

"Yeah, I guess they were going to give the lead to some other guy, but he got killed right before auditions. So I got the part."

Danny Ancino bounced up and down on the balls his feet in nervous energy and smiled in a way that made Ruth feel uncomfortable. She instinctively backed away from him. "I, uh, suppose I'll see you at rehearsals."

"Sure thing. Can't wait." Danny Ancino expanded his chest and flexed his biceps. "See ya!"

Oh Lord, Ruth prayed silently as she walked tearfully down the stark hospital corridor. At that moment she forgot about Delancy Mays and any other distractions or worries in her life. Ruth's thoughts were only to plead for her friend. *Please, please take care of Angie, Lord, and Lord, please bless Lionel, too. He was a good soul, a wonderful man. Let him be with you, oh Lord. Please. Amen.*

Chapter 6

Cats and Dogs

R UTH'S JOURNEY BACK HOME with Charlie Corbello on the front passenger's side was harrowing, to say the least. The little dog, anxious at being in a strange car, peed on and then began chewing the immaculate front seat of Ruth's Toyota.

"No, no! Charlie! Bad boy!" Ruth tried to sound stern, but loving, as she did with her two cats. The dog eventually settled down and appeared to fall asleep. Ruth drove the rest of the way in silence, hoping he would stay that way until she reached Lake Elmo.

When Ruth pulled into her garage, the dog awoke, looked at her and whined. Ruth scratched his ears and lifted him out of the car.

"Here you go, boy. You're going to be all right. You'll be going back home soon." She carried him out into her back yard and put him on the lawn, where he immediately relieved himself again, this time under her lilac bushes. "That's a good boy," she cooed. "Come Charlie, here boy, here boy."

He ran from tree to tree, bush to bush, and around the house. Ruth followed him, trying to herd him indoors.

He's just like an excited kid.

When he reached Ruth's dock he stopped, not certain if he wanted to go closer to the lake. It was there that Ruth caught up with him. Using a small piece of rope from the garage, she gently led him up the back door steps and into her house.

While investigating her kitchen and helping himself to the cats' water and food, Ruth went into the living room to shake out the old red and black plaid blanket that Morrie and Griselda sometimes used when they lounged in front of the fireplace. She plumped it up, folded it, and put it back in front of the hearth. The little dog came trotting in, sniffed it, walked around it a few times, and then laid down and started chewing on one corner.

"Well, guys," Ruth said to her two cats, who were on top of the beige sofa and her dark blue wing-back chair, eyeing the newcomer warily. "Be nice now, we've got company." The cats didn't move. Griselda growled in a low, menacing manner while Morrie just arched his back and stared at the newcomer. Charlie stopped chewing for a moment, wagged his tail, and looked up at Ruth as if to say, *are they friendly? If not, get me out of here!*

"Come on, now, "Ruth chided the cats, "Charlie's had a rough day, so be a little hospitable, will you?"

She reached up to pat Griselda on her soft gray and white head but the angry feline jumped up and bounded up the stairs. Morrie followed.

"Okay, sweetie," she stated as she reached down and scratched the little terrier behind his ears. "I guess it's just you and me. Let's get you your own water dish and some food." As if he understood, the terrier followed Ruth into the kitchen.

It was twilight by the time Charlie finished exploring Ruth's first floor and finally ate some of the dry dog-food that Ruth always kept handy for the times her daughter Hanna's dog—a large, sociable black lab—came to visit. She took Charlie outside to do his "business" again and he once more chose the lilac bushes that lined Ruth's back yard. "Well okay, Charlie. Maybe that will make them grow," she said as he finished the task.

After Charlie had looked around her yard again, sniffing the bushes, the trees, the garage, house, and porch steps, he trotted over to a stone angel in her garden and looked up at it, head cocked. Ruth sat on her wrought-iron bench, watching.

"Don't worry, little guy. She'll be all right. You'll be home soon." As if he understood, he came over and nosed Ruth's hand.

They sat like this for a time under the huge oak tree, while Ruth scratched his ears and talked quietly to him about Angie. "She'll be home soon. It's okay. I'll take care of you until she comes to get you." She was really reassuring herself. After a time, she led the little dog back into the house. The terrier went right into the living room and settled in upon his blanket.

Ruth looked around for Morrie and Griselda, but they were nowhere in sight. Then she remembered the mess in her car and decided to clean it. She had just finished up when the kitchen phone rang.

It was Fritz Gerhardt.

"Ruth," he said in a raspy voice, "I need to talk to you; I want your advice." Fritz often called Ruth during the run of the show. He knew he could trust her, not only to give him sound counsel, but to not repeat to others what he told her.

"Anything I can do to help, maestro." Ruth addressed him with the title "maestro" in deference to his age and experience. "You know you can count on me." She stretched the extra- long phone cord into the living room and settled down on the sofa; Fritz's calls were usually drawn-out.

"Do you remember the person who did costumes for us last summer?" Fritz asked.

"Marie, something? Young? Blonde?" Ruth tried hard to remember. After a while, all the summer shows seemed to run together.

"Well," Fritz said with a worried tone, "she rented or bought a lot of the costumes and went way over budget. I don't know what we're going to do this year," he sighed with a cough, "and I wondered ... could you ... would you handle it this year?"

Oh God! thought Ruth. To Fritz she said, "My sewing skills are pretty limited. And I'm a slow sewer. You need someone who can work fast and ... and ... set-in sleeves are a real problem for me. It takes me forever to do sleeves. Have you asked Gloria-June?" Ruth knew that Gloria-June Kimmel designed and made most of her own outfits.

"That ... well, I won't say it 'cause you're a lady, but she'll want a leading role if I ask her to do anything as big as costumes. She always comes with a price." Fritz coughed again. "Are you sure you can't manage it?" he said in a pleading tone.

Ruth could hear his rapid breathing over the phone. "Fritz, I wish I could say 'yes' to you. I really wish I could." She took a deep breath. "I'm just not a good enough seamstress." She could hear Vivian talking to him in the background.

"Vivian wants to know ... can you make your *own* costume?"

"Of course, and Angie's, too," Ruth replied. "I can manage two costumes. But that's about all I can do. And I usually don't finish those until just before dress rehearsal."

"Well, okay. I just thought I'd ask you first. You're easier to work with and I know you'd try and save us money. Gloria-June will spend like a drunken sailor!"

Ruth smiled at his description. "Maybe I can help find props?" she offered. "I love to go to thrift stores. Why don't you have Vivian give me a list and I'll start collecting some of them. That will be my gift to the company." Ruth knew they always worked with a frugal budget.

"Well, that would be wonderful!" She heard Vivian again say something in the background. "Vivian wants to know if you reached Angie?"

Ruth wasn't sure how to even begin. She stammered and said, "Well, ah, today I received a phone call from the ..."

"Sorry!" Fritz interrupted. "I've got to go. Vivian! Will you get that? Somebody's at the front door. Ruth, I'll talk with you later." And he hung up.

Saved by the bell, Ruth thought. *I would hate to be the one to tell him about Angie. He's so excitable, I'm afraid he'd have a stroke.* She decided to wait a few days and perhaps she'd be able to tell the Gerhardts something more specific and positive.

For the next few days Ruth called the hospital every day to check on Angie, hoping to hear some good news to share with Fritz and Vivian. The nurses who ran the Intensive Care Unit got to know her voice and were always cordial, but told her gently that there had been no change. Ruth had been hoping against hope that Angie would be well enough to go to the first rehearsal. She told the comatose Angie so when she visited her.

Twice that week, Ruth stood by Angie's bedside, holding her friend's limp hand and stroking her long red hair. Ruth talked about Charlie, about the show, about how Angie's daughter needed her, about the weather, anything she could think of, hoping Angie might hear and regain consciousness.

One day when Ruth came to visit, Angie's daughter, Tracey, arrived at the same time. Ruth waited in the hall while Tracey checked up on her mom. The girl came out and hugged her.

"The nurses tell me you've been here a lot, and calling every day. Thanks!" she said, wiping her eyes. "And the police told me you took mom's dog to your house. That's so nice of you! I've been meaning to call you. I just wish I could take him off your hands," the petite brunette said ruefully. "My work schedule ... it's so crazy right now it just doesn't give me any time to care for him. I hope you won't have to keep him too long," she said, fighting back tears.

"That's okay, honey," Ruth said. "I can keep Charlie as long as you need me to."

Tracey slumped into a chair. "My mom is so lucky to have a friend like you."

They sat there for a while, talking quietly, although Tracey did most of the talking, usually about her mom. She told Ruth about the hours she and her mom had spent doing crafts together. She talked about little trips they had taken, about how her mom, while not a great cook, thought everything Tracey made was delicious. Tracey laughed and cried. Ruth let the girl ramble on, knowing it was good therapy for her.

Meanwhile, they waited.

Morrie and the dog were actually beginning to get along. When Ruth came home from the hospital, she found them sleeping together, almost nose to nose, on the rug in front of the fireplace. Griselda kept her distance, however, and now slept in the big blue wing-backed chair.

"So, you've decided to call a truce. Good!" she told them.

Griselda looked up as if to say "Fat chance."

After two more visits to Angie's bedside, Ruth decided she had better call the Gerhardts and tell them about Angie's break-in.

"Oh my god!" exclaimed Fritz. "Rehearsal starts next week. Will she be all right?!"

"I don't know," Ruth told him, "but I don't think we can count on her for this show."

"I'll set aside comp tickets for her in case she's well enough to at least come and see us," Fritz said.

Chapter 7

First Rehearsal

THE FIRST NIGHT OF rehearsal was always Ruth's favorite night. Everyone was relieved not to be auditioning, happy to be in the show, and glad to see old friends. Former cast members came early so they could visit a while before rehearsal, well aware of the Maestro's "German punctuality," as he called it. They also knew that during the rehearsal, when Fritz gave directions, they needed to listen attentively and not converse.

New cast members who came late or wanted to use rehearsal time for chit chat soon learned that Fritz Gerhardt ran a tight ship; if they transgressed, they got "the look."

You only get "the look" once, Ruth remembered, *and then you either shape up or ship out.* She recalled the time when a young man yawned loudly while Fritz was explaining something to the cast. She never saw that fellow after that night, nor did she see him in another show.

Fritz began by telling everyone that there was no new information about Lionel's murder. He also told them that Angie, an alto in the chorus, had been attacked and was in the hospital. The stunned cast members murmured among themselves about whether this a jinxed show or coincidental bad luck.

Good grief, thought Ruth, *I've never seen more superstitious people than theatre folks.* She shook her head. *Some bad things just happen. That doesn't mean a show is jinxed,* she reassured herself. *Lionel and Angie? Just a coincidence.*

While Vivian was distributing scored scripts, Fritz assigned seats to the various sections of the chorus: soprano, alto, tenor, bass. The principals were in another small room, loudly practicing their lines. Ruth could hear them clearly through the door. Everyone who played the Como Pavilion knew that once they were in the place, they had to practically holler their lines in order to be heard and so it became a habit to rehearse that way. Fritz had the principal characters meet two nights a week, once by themselves and once with the chorus so they could learn their parts, and then fit them into the whole fabric of the show. The principals had met two nights ago so this was their first night with the whole chorus.

As the "stars" came in from their practice room, Ruth noticed Danny Ancino flexing his muscles in front of slender, pretty, dark-haired Sandy Westerling, who was to play the part of Magnolia, the leading lady.

He looks more like he belongs in "A Streetcar Named Desire" than "Show Boat," Ruth thought to herself.

Ruth looked over at Delancy Mays, who was showing Rhonda Olson something in his script. Rhonda was playing the part of Julie, the woman with "mixed blood" who must leave the show boat because she was found to be married to a white man.

It's good that things are better now in the South, Ruth thought to herself. *But don't even think about Mr. Mays. Remember Blanche Voorhees.*

Fritz called the group to order and the principals quickly took the folding chairs in the front row. First, he told them the history of the troupe. Although Ruth had heard it many times, she never tired of hearing how his mama, Madeline, had started the company. Besides, the new people hadn't heard it.

"The Como Park Pavilion Players are going to be fifty-five years old this summer," Fritz announced with a broad smile. "Mama would be so proud! The final cast party will be at our house and it will be a gala fifty-fifth birthday party ... and our new governor will be invited." The entire cast applauded.

Fritz then gave a thumbnail synopsis of *Show Boat*. The musical centered around the cast and crew of a late nineteenth century Mississippi River show boat called the *Cotton Blossom*, owned by Cap'n Andy Hawks. In Act I, Andy's daughter, an aspiring actress named Magnolia (Nola), falls in love with Gaylord Ravenal, a raffish riverboat gambler. She is warned, however, by Joe, a Black deckhand married to the boat's cook, to be wary of men like Ravenal. Julie La Verne, the troupe's leading lady, also warns Nola about Ravenal, as does Nola's mother, Parthy Hawks, but the pair falls in love. In the meantime, Julie, who is married to the troupe's leading man, Steve Baker, is discovered to be biracial passing as white. This forces her and Steve to leave the show boat because this is the Jim Crow-segregated deep south, where interracial marriage is illegal. Ravenal becomes the troupe's new leading man and Nola its new leading lady. Act I ends as they marry, in spite of Parthy's objections. Things spiral downward in Act II, but conclude with a bittersweet yet optimistic ending.

As they went through each song, Fritz paused and told them what was happening in the story line. As a teacher, Ruth always appreciated Fritz's explanations. It made the music mean something, especially for the younger people who may not have been familiar with the show. He pointed out that *Show Boat* was not only a love story, but also about racial prejudice and squandered opportunities.

Fritz told them he had changed some of the lines so as not to offend present-day audiences. "We're going to sing, *'Here the folks work on the Mississippi, here the folks work while the others play,'* instead of saying 'colored folks and white folks.' Please mark that in pencil in your books if they are not already marked."

Ruth looked around and the only Black person there was Delancy Mays.

He's a bit elegant for the part of Joe, she thought, looking at his handsome profile. Just then, as if Mr. Mays had read her mind, he turned in his chair and looked directly at Ruth and smiled, nodding at her as if to say "Hello."

Embarrassed, Ruth looked quickly down at her book, only to glance up again and see that he was still smiling at her.

Honestly! I'm acting like I'm in junior high school, Ruth chided to herself. *He's cordial to everyone. Get a grip, girl!*

She pursed her lips and forced herself to look at all of the other principals also, just so she wouldn't stare at the man.

Parthy and Captain Andy were played by two old hands in the theatre, Mimi and Al Rosenberg.

They don't even have to act, Ruth laughed to herself, *because Mimi bosses Al around just like Parthy bosses the captain.* Mimi was tall and angular, with a long gray braid wound around her head. Al was short, bald, and rotund. They looked like the proverbial "odd couple," but old-timers knew them to be devoted to each other.

Ellie and Frank, the "comedians" of the musical, were played by two young people. Ruth did not remember the man, but Ellie, a smallish woman with noticeably prominent front teeth, had sung "Itsy Bitsy Spider" during auditions. She was introduced as Shirley Hammond. The man playing Frank was obviously a friend of hers. She hung on his arm and introduced him as Ed Daily. Ed was dark-haired with dark eyes, a throwback to the fifties, complete with a duck tail haircut and a pack of cigarettes rolled into the sleeve of his white tee shirt.

Both of the Kimmels were there. Howard, wearing a casual short-sleeved navy polo shirt with grey trousers, was cast as both a deck-hand and a gambler. Gloria-June had dressed to the nines in a hot pink satin suit with a very short skirt and matching toe-less pumps. She was chosen to play Queenie, an important part.

Hmm ... I wonder how that happened? thought Ruth. *I'll bet she's doing the costumes.* She smiled to herself and breathed a sigh of relief, glad that chore wasn't hers.

Rodney Olson, the young red-head with an angelic voice, was also present. He stayed by his mother's side. The little "Mexican Shirley Temple," introduced to the group as Elena Cordova, was there with a stout woman who looked like her grandmother. Elena had been given the part of Kim, the daughter of Gaylord Ravenal and Magnolia.

Rehearsal went well. Fritz joked that they might open sooner than July. "Maybe next week!" It was an old joke, one he used every summer, but each year when he repeated it the cast would laugh nervously.

"We'll be rehearsing in the pavilion basement in three weeks," Fritz proclaimed. "We'll be blocking by then. And I want all parts and music memorized by then. No books out at Como!" There was a collective groan from the cast and chorus. Fritz grinned. He loved getting reactions from "his" players.

When rehearsal ended, Ruth gathered up her things and had started up the stairs when Vivian stopped her.

"Have you heard any more about how Angie is?" Vivian's forehead was creased with concern.

"I've been there several times and no change, I'm sorry to say. I'm also taking care of her little dog until she gets better," Ruth told her. "He's getting used to my cats and they're gradually getting used to him."

Susie, the accompanist, overheard. "Oh, I remember Charlie. Such a cute little dog!" She smiled, shaking her dark, pixie haircut. "I remember at Rhonda's baby shower, how he tore up some of Angie's decorations," she laughed. "Quite a little scamp!"

Ruth did not remember Rhonda's shower, but then there had been a few years when Tom was ill and she had taken a break from the company. "Charlie is cute," she told Susie, "and he's been awfully good, but I know he must miss Angie. I can't wait until she can hold him again."

Just then, Delancy Mays, script in hand, started up the stairs. Vivian was blocking Ruth's way out, so she had to back up against the wall to let Del move past her. As he got closer, Ruth could smell his after-shave, a clean, citrus-like smell. Her heart started to beat a bit faster and she looked pleadingly up the stairs at Vivian, who looked back at her like a Cheshire cat. "You've met Mr. Mays, haven't you, Ruth?" Vivian said with a grin.

"Ah … not … formally," Ruth stammered. Her face felt hot. She started to reach out to shake hands with him and dropped her music book on his feet. "Oh I'm sorry," she spluttered, "I'm such a klutz!"

"No harm done," Delancy laughed as he retrieved the book and pressed it into Ruth's hands. "Someday I'll have to tell you about the time someone dropped a whole side of a house on me, during the rehearsal of *Rigoletto*." He met Ruth's eyes. "I'm Delancy Mays," he said, still holding onto Ruth's book himself.

Ruth took a deep breath, trying not to sneak another peek at his well-fitting jeans, looking instead at his crisp white shirt and his rolled-up sleeves. "And I'm Ruth Carson, one of the altos," she told him. "I hope you didn't get hurt—from that house, I mean," she laughed nervously.

Vivian was grinning at both Ruth and Del, holding fast to her place at the top of the stairs, keeping Ruth from moving away from Del.

Why, she's enjoying this, the old matchmaker! Ruth thought.

"I think I must be like a cat," Del said as he smiled down at Ruth. "I may have nine lives."

Suddenly, a thunderous blast rocked the house!

Chapter 8

This Kind of Thing Can Snowball

EVERYBODY SCREAMED, RUTH TOO. She stumbled but was caught by Del. They both sat down hard on the stairs, their arms around each other.

"What was that!?" Ruth cried, clutching Del for dear life.

"Something must have blown up," Del said, extending an arm to encompass Vivian, who had plopped down beside them.

"Fritz!" Vivian cried, "Fritz! Are you okay?"

Fritz was already pushing past them up the steps. "Is it the house? Please God! Not my house! Not my house!"

There was pandemonium upstairs. Danny Ancino ran to the studio door and yelled, "Where's your phone? Somebody call 911!"

"What happened?!" cried Vivian.

"Somebody's car just blew up!" Danny yelled. "It's an inferno out there! We gotta call 911. Hurry!"

Del regained his composure first. He gently removed Ruth's hands from his shoulders, got up, found the black wall phone, dialed 911 and told them that a car had just blown up in the street. He carefully articulated the address, repeating it twice.

Del, Ruth and Vivian then joined Fritz and a growing crowd of cast members and neighbors gathered on the driveway and lawn in front of Fritz's house. A parked car, or rather what was left of it, was engulfed in flames.

"Oh Lord! Was anybody in it?!" Vivian cried.

"There almost was," Al Rosenberg said hesitantly as he clutched his sobbing wife's arm. "It was our car."

Within minutes three police cars showed up, followed quickly by a fire truck and paramedics with an ambulance. The fire-fighters made quick work of the flames, but the little sedan was a total loss. No one appeared to be hurt and the ambulance returned to the station.

One of the policemen took charge. Sergeant "Mickey" Sullivan herded everyone back into the Gerhardt Studio and proceeded to question the adults. He started with the Rosenbergs but Mimi couldn't stop crying and Al seemed to be in shock, so the sergeant moved on to the adults who had children in the troupe. The children were cranky and tired, and after one mom complained that it was a school night, he let them all go.

Rhonda Olson offered to drive the Rosenburgs home. Ruth thought Rhonda looked shaky, leaning on Rodney as she walked up the stairs. She could see him trying to brace himself in order to hold up his mom. Ruth's heart went out to them both.

After that, Sergeant Sullivan, who looked frazzled, questioned Del and Ruth and the rest of the cast. By now it was almost ten p.m. Ruth had the beginning of a splitting headache. "Do you know anyone who might have wanted some harm to come to the Rosenbergs?" He asked everyone the same question.

"Certainly not," Ruth replied, shaking her throbbing head when it was her turn. "They're wonderful people. I can't imagine anyone who would do such a thing."

"Is anyone mad at this theatre company for any reason?" he asked, looking over the group.

"What?" Fritz responded angrily. "Who would be mad at us?" He shook his head in disbelief. "All we do is good for this community! Why would anybody ... of all the goddamn idiotic ..."

"Sir, sir." The sergeant gently took Fritz's arm to stem the tirade that was beginning to pour out. "All I mean is, by our records, well, you have one actor dead, one in the hospital, and now two who would have died if they'd been in their car a minute or two earlier. Doesn't that look like a pattern to you?" He peered intently at Fritz, who was still shaking his head.

Fritz was ashen-faced. "I don't know. I don't know." Vivian, always watchful for her husband's well-being, came up and put her arm around him.

Mickey Sullivan went on. "I don't want to frighten anyone, folks, but this kind of thing can snowball. I saw it once in San Francisco when I worked out there. It was about fifteen years ago. Some nut decided to get rid of this little community theatre group out in Sausalito, near San Francisco. Half-a-dozen people died before, whoever it was, just stopped."

There was dead silence in the room. Ruth couldn't even hear people breathing.

Fritz gained back some of his composure. "What can we do? Are you saying we should disband and close the show?"

Someone in the cast immediately said "No!" and others began to echo the sentiment. "Never! ... Absolutely not! ... This isn't San Francisco ..."

After a few more minutes of discussion, the sergeant relented, "Okay, okay, I can see it won't do any good to try to shut you people down. But I'm telling you, all of you, be careful. There's something going on here that's dangerous. Watch each other's backs. Be on the lookout for strange faces that appear to be lurking around. Call us immediately if you see anything out of the ordinary ... and Mr. Gerhardt, I need to talk with you some more. Maybe tomorrow morning? At the station downtown? Say, around ten?"

Fritz nodded.

Before Ruth left for home, Del asked her, "Are you sure you're alright?" He looked at her and smiled. "You could leave your car here and I could drive you home. We could pick it up tomorrow."

"Oh, no ... thank you," Ruth said. "That's very kind of you. But I live quite a way from here. Out in the country." She put her hand on his arm and squeezed, "Thanks, though."

"I'll see you at the next rehearsal then." He squeezed Ruth's arm back.

What a kind man! Ruth thought. She looked up at him and smiled. "Yes, next rehearsal."

As Ruth drove home, trying to keep her head still so it wouldn't hurt, she thought about what Sergeant Sullivan had said: "Some nut decided to get rid of a little community theatre group. Half-a-dozen people died before whoever it was, just stopped."

It sounds as if they never caught the person responsible, she concluded.

The aspirin Vivian had given Ruth was beginning to work and she kept mulling the recent events around in her head. *These must be mere coincidences. Things like this just don't happen, not here. Maybe in California, but not in St. Paul. People are pretty decent here. Nobody would be that crazy. Lionel was probably stabbed by a gang member looking for drug money. Angie was beat up by a mugger. The Rosenberg's car was ... maybe faulty wiring?*

But the fact was, Lionel was dead, Angie was in the hospital, and Mimi and Al had almost been blown to smithereens. *Could it be,* she thought, *that someone has it in for us?*

By the time Ruth pulled into her driveway her headache had subsided.

Thank goodness! she thought. *Maybe I'll be able to get a good night's sleep after all.* As she entered her kitchen, she was met by all three of the animals, especially Charlie, who was anxious to go out. She noticed that her telephone message machine was blinking.

"You will just have to wait," she told the flashing red eye. "Come on, Charlie, Good boy!" She led the little terrier out the back door, flicking on all the lights as she went.

After Charlie had finished his business, Ruth took a deep breath and pushed the "play" button. The crisp voice of Angie's night nurse came on. "This is St. Paul-Ramsey Hospital, ICU Unit calling. Mrs. Carson, would you please call us?" The nurse left a number.

Ruth wrote the number down as the next message started:

"Fritz here, Ruth. Sorry to call so late, but would you do me a favor? That policeman wants to meet with me tomorrow morning at ten and I need a ride. I also need someone I trust to go in with me. Could you go, Ruth? Please, call me back tonight. I'm not going to be asleep. Not after all this. You know my number." Neither of the Gerhards drove, relying instead on taxis or the bus, or (as was often the case) on the kindness of willing friends and neighbors.

Then came the final message. It was a faint, indistinguishable voice and Ruth wasn't sure if it was male or female.

It said "Angie Corbello is the ..." The next words were garbled, but at the end of the message she heard, "... and it's not over yet."

Chapter 9

The Injured Comes To

Ruth dialed the ICU unit. Her hand began to shake as she waited for the hospital to pick up. Finally they answered, "Regions Hospital, ICU. Can you hold, please?

Ruth waited patiently for about a minute.

"Hello? Who's calling?"

"This is Ruth Carson. I'm returning the ICU nurse's call."

There was silence on the line and then the ICU charge nurse's voice came on.

"Mrs. Carson?" she said crisply, "thank you for calling us back. You were on Angela Corbello's immediate family call list and we wanted to let you know that she is doing well. She wanted to talk to you, but it's too late now tonight. She's asleep. Can you call back tomorrow after nine in the morning?"

Ruth was overjoyed with this news. "Oh, thank you so much for telling me. That is wonderful to hear. I was so worried! Yes, I'll call back tomorrow. First thing after 9:00. It will be so good to talk to her. Thank you, thank you again!"

That night, Ruth forgot everything except that Angie was alive and doing well. She sat in her blue wing-backed chair and held Charlie. "Your mama's going to be okay. You know that, boy? She's okay! She's okay! I'm going to call her tomorrow. Maybe even see her." Ruth was so happy she went into pantry cupboard and took out a bottle of champagne that her daughter, Hannah, had given her last Mother's Day. She managed to pop the cork and poured a juice glass full to the brim. "To Angie," she told the dog and two cats before taking a big swig. Charlie, sensing her celebratory mood, danced excitedly around while the cats watched with benign expressions. Ruth had another glass and, feeling tipsy by this time, fell asleep on the big sofa in the living room, covered by her blue comforter, surrounded by Charlie, Morrie, and even Griselda, who had finally decided to be sociable.

She woke up slowly the next morning. "Sorry guys," she said as she pushed the animals off her. "I guess I was in a pretty good mood last night." Groggy, with a bit of a headache, she shuffled out to her kitchen and made herself a strong cup of tea, took two aspirin, and ate some raspberry yogurt. She let Charlie out, let him back in again, put fresh water and food out for all the animals, and then, at precisely nine o'clock, called the hospital once more. When she reached the ICU unit, the nurse told her that someone wanted to talk to her. Ruth held her breath.

"Ruthie? Ruthie, it's me, Angie. Are you there?"

Ruth's heart leaped with joy. "Angie! Oh my God! Angie!"

"Hey, Ruthie." Angie's voice was hoarse, but unmistakable. "I don't remember anything. Is Charlie okay?"

"He's okay, Angie." Ruth was crying now. "He's here with me. My cats love him! Well, at least Morrie does." Ruth wiped her eyes on her sleeve. "How are you?"

"I've been better." A long silence. "I don't look so good right now."

"Oh Angie!" Ruth sobbed, "you're the most beautiful person I know!"

"Sez you!" Angie quipped.

Ruth talked with her friend for about five more minutes before the charge nurse took back the phone, interrupting their conversation. She informed Ruth that her patient needed rest but, if Ruth wanted to visit, she could come over in the afternoon. "I told her daughter she could come too," the nurse told her.

"I'll be there in the early afternoon," Ruth told the nurse.

Ruth showered, dressed, and busied herself with deferred household chores for the rest of the morning. She heard Lake Elmo's noontime siren as she locked the house and walked to the garage. Soon she was on the highway, almost to St. Paul to see Angie, when she suddenly remembered: "Oh no! I forgot to call Fritz back!" She glanced at her dashboard clock. Twelve-thirty.

Aghast at her forgetfulness, Ruth pulled up to a convenience store, hurried in and dug through her purse for the quarter needed to use the pay phone. "Don't bother. It doesn't work," declared a tattooed, teen-aged boy behind the counter. He looked up from his car magazine.

"I've got to make a call. It's really important," Ruth said pleadingly.

"I guess you can use the store phone," he said, "if it's local and you keep it short."

"Thank you so much!" Ruth took the phone he handed her. She had Fritz's number written in a little notebook she kept in her purse. She dialed but only heard a busy signal. "Busy," she sighed, looking at the young man.

"You can try again in a few minutes if you want to."

She debated for a moment and then told him, "No, thanks. I think I'll just go over there."

"Suit yourself," he shrugged, returning to his magazine.

As she drove to the Gerhardt Music Studio, Ruth went over in her mind what she'd tell Fritz.

I'll just tell him the truth. I was so excited to talk with Angie, everything else just fell by the wayside.

It was nearly one o'clock when Ruth got to the Gerhardt residence and studio, arriving just as an immaculate white Lexus, driven by none other than Delancy Mays, was pulling slowly into Fritz's driveway. She honked her horn and the Lexus stopped. Ruth jumped out of her car and ran up to the driver's window. Delancy rolled it down. "Well, well, it's good to see you again, Mrs. Carson." He extended his hand to Ruth with a grasp that was firm and warm.

Fritz was sitting in the front seat next to Delancy with Vivian sitting behind.

"Fritz! I'm so sorry I didn't call you back," Ruth said apologetically, "but Angie is awake! I talked with her this morning. I learned late last night that she was okay and I was so happy I broke out a bottle of champagne that I had been saving and I celebrated—just me and my pets—and I probably had a little more of it than I should have. Anyway, then this morning I was able to talk with Angie on the phone. In all the excitement I completely forgot to call you."

"Hee hee!" Fritz laughed. "That's alright, Ruthie." His grin widened. "I would have had a snort myself if I'd heard that Angie was all right."

"Did she say who hurt her?" Vivian asked from the back seat.

"She doesn't remember anything. But I think she's going to be okay and that's all that matters to me." She realized that Mr. Mays was still holding onto her hand. Embarrassed, Ruth pulled away from him and patted her hair self-consciously, tucking a few loose strands into the French roll she wore. "I was just on my way to see her and then I remembered your call. I'm so sorry."

"That's okay. I was going to ask if you could take me to the police station this morning, but my chauffeur here offered to take me to take me there instead. We're just getting back." Fritz patted Delancy on the shoulder.

"And his 'chauffeur' would be delighted if you would join us all at the Lexington for a late lunch," said Delancy with a smile. "We just stopped by the house first to pick up Fritz's jacket before heading over. It'll be my treat."

"Oh, oh, I can't. I would love to ... but Angie's expecting me at the hospital. Her daughter will be there too. Thank you though." Flustered, Ruth could feel her face heat up.

"Another time, then?" Delancy's smile was genuine but he looked disappointed.

"I'd better get over to the hospital. Again, I'm really sorry I didn't get back to you this morning," Ruth said as she looked at Fritz and then at Vivian.

"That's all right, dear," Vivian answered. "We know you're dependable. We're so glad to hear this about Angie. Please greet her for us."

They said their good-byes and Delancy took Ruth's hand again and squeezed it gently, which she felt right down to her toes. When she got back into her car she took a long, deep breath.

Whoa, girl. You're way too old for this kind of thing.

Angie was no longer in ICU and had been transferred to a regular double room. No one else shared it, so it was more like a private room. Tracey was already there when Ruth arrived. Ruth knocked lightly on the open door.

"Come on in, the party's here!" Angie sounded stronger, but still not like her usual self. She was still connected to some tubes and monitors.

"I can see that," Ruth smiled, as she handed Angie a bouquet she had purchased in the hospital gift shop. "Here. I know you like pink carnations."

"I should get beat up more often," Angie quipped.

"Mom!" Tracey clucked her tongue and shook her head. "Honestly!"

"Angie," Ruth echoed in a quieter voice, "do you remember *anything*?"

"Well, I still don't know who it was. The creep! I remember taking Charlie outside to do his business, and then we went up the elevator back to my apartment. I opened the door and Charlie ran in. I was a little surprised because all the lights were out and I usually leave them on when I just go to let the dog out. I thought maybe the electricity had gone out.

It does that sometimes. I walked in and, *bam!* Someone hit me hard a couple of times on the head. I don't remember anything else until I woke up here." Angie let out a long breath. She looked as if just remembering it had been exhausting. She fell back on the crisp, white hospital pillow, her matted red hair framing her pale face.

Tracey turned to Ruth. "Mom will be here another week, they said, and then I'm going to take time off from work and take her to my apartment ..."

"No you're not!" interrupted Angie. "You just got promoted in that job. She's head of the computer division," she told Ruth proudly. "You are not taking time off now to take care of me! I'll be okay. I just need to get these tubes out of me and get back home and ..."

Now it was Ruth's turn to interrupt. "And then you're going to come and stay at my place. Really, Angie, wouldn't it be fun? Charlie's already there. You can have Hannah's old room. You told me you liked that room."

"Oh geez!" Angie shook her head. "I can't do that."

"Why not? You'd do it for me."

"Well, let me think about it." Angie closed her eyes for a moment. "Okay, but only if I can cook."

At this, Tracey burst out laughing. "Oh yeah, mom. That's a real incentive!" She looked at Ruth. "Are you sure about this?" Ruth assured her that it was. "I'll want to come over to visit and spend a little time with her," Tracey said.

"Monday nights would be good," Ruth told her. "We have our rehearsals then ... and by the way, Angie, you'd better get well soon. You're in the chorus of *Show Boat.*"

"I might have to sit this one out." Angie closed her eyes again and let out a breath.

"You'd better rest now," Ruth told her. "Come on, Tracey, let me buy you some lunch or a cup of coffee or something in the hospital cafeteria. I think we should let your mom sleep."

Just then a petite Hispanic nurse walked in with a tray full of meds and something that looked like a malt. "She needs her medication and some nourishment," the nurse said quietly, "and rest."

"Sure," Tracey whispered. "We're just going down to the cafeteria. We'll be back in about a half-an-hour."

"If she's asleep, don't wake her up," the nurse instructed. "Sleep will heal her."

From your mouth to God's ear, Ruth thought.

While Ruth and Tracey had the hospital cafeteria's sweet and sour chicken, which wasn't too bad, they worked out the logistics of getting Angie's things temporarily moved to Ruth's house. Tracey insisted that she would bring her mom's stuff there and Ruth agreed. Ruth didn't really want to go to the apartment where her friend had been attacked, and Tracey would know what to pack to make Angie comfortable.

When Ruth got home, she listened again to the strange, garbled message on her answering machine.

Who is it, and what does it mean? she thought. *Angie Corbello is ... what? And what exactly isn't over yet?* Ruth listened to the cryptic message three more times and then decided to call Sergeant Sullivan about it.

She dialed the St. Paul police station and was put through to Mickey Sullivan.

"Hello. Sullivan here."

"Hi, Sergeant Sullivan?" Ruth took a deep breath. "I'm Ruth Carson, one of the people in the Gerhardt theatre group? You said we should call you if anything came up and, well when I came home the other evening ... well, I had a very strange message on my phone answering machine. I think perhaps you should hear it."

Sergeant Sullivan sounded interested. "Can you repeat it?"

"It was hard to understand. It said "Angie Corbello is ... and then it was garbled. I couldn't make it out. And then the voice said, "it isn't over yet." Ruth held her breath.

"One minute."

Ruth could hear him speaking to someone else in the room.

"Mrs. Carson?" he said, returning to the phone. "We definitely want to listen to your answering machine tape. Could you remove the tape from your machine and bring it down to the station? We'd be very appreciative. Can you do that?" His voice sounded concerned.

"Of course," Ruth answered. "Anything to help." Then she asked, "Can you tell me anything about who might have assaulted Angie?"

The sergeant sounded more official now. "I'm sorry, Mrs. Carson, I can't discuss the case. But please know that we're doing all we can. And please do bring in your tape."

"Of course." Ruth reached down to scratch Charlie's ears. "I'll come in tomorrow."

Ruth made herself a strong cup of tea. Then sank back into the big chair by her fireplace and sipped it. Charlie put his chin on one of her knees.

"Your mama's going to come here soon, little guy." Her eyes became moist as she looked at his little face. "Won't that be wonderful? As long as you and Angie need me, you'll always have a home here."

Morrie jumped on the back of the chair and nuzzled Ruth's head. Griselda even came up and joined the group.

Ruth surveyed her menagerie. "Good for you, Griselda, you're finally being hospitable. Too bad people can't be as good to each other as you animals."

That night, she lay on her bed and gazed up at the white ceiling. She thought about Angie, her infectious laugh, her outrageous outfits, the excitement she always exhibited on opening nights, and Ruth gave silent thanks for her friend's life. She also thought about Delancy Mays, his kind eyes, his warm hand shake, his arms around her that time on the stairs. And she finally fell asleep.

But sleep that night was troubled. Ruth had dreams—nightmares really—about cars and houses burning up and pets at the windows howling to get out. She wanted to rescue the animals but couldn't move. There was a long stairway and a little white dog trapped in a cage. She tried to help him, but she was encased in some sort of period costume that held her arms and hands in a straightjacket-like coat that changed and became pulleys for a theatre curtain.

She awoke early, not refreshed, but glad to no longer be dreaming.

Ruth went straight to the police station that morning.

"Thank you for coming in," Sergeant Sullivan said. "Can I get you a cup of coffee?"

She declined and took her answering machine out of a canvas carrying bag, pushing it across the desk to the sergeant. "I couldn't figure out how to take the tape out," she said apologetically, "so I brought the whole machine."

"That's fine, we can do it," he told her as he examined it. "When did you say this message came in?"

"The night before last," Ruth told him. "I found out that same night that Angie was going to be okay, and I visited her the next day, and to be honest I was so excited about that I just completely forgot about this strange message."

"Can we keep this for a while?" he asked her.

"Of course," Ruth told him. "Keep it as long as you want. I don't think any of us has a clue about this whole thing. Why? Who's doing these things? Lionel, Angie, the Rosenburg's car. We all find it just unbelievable! I've been in this troupe for eighteen years and I've never met a more wonderful group of people." She dabbed her eyes with a Kleenex.

"Please, Mrs. Carson," the sergeant said gently, "we only think there *may* be someone targeting your group. We don't know for sure." His eyes were kind. "Just be careful. Be on the look-out. And stay together."

"What I don't understand," Ruth said as she looked intently at the sergeant, "is why this person left a message on *my* phone?"

"I don't know. Are you a long-time member of that group?"

"Yes, but…" Ruth looked aghast. "Are you saying that, whoever it was, knows who I am? And where I live?"

"I understand your worry," the police sergeant answered. "You live on the outskirts of the Twin Cities, don't you?"

"Yes, in Lake Elmo, and I live alone. My husband died a little over five years ago."

"Could you call a neighbor you trust and have them keep an eye on your place? I'm afraid there's not too much we can do unless someone tries to break in. Do you have a dog?"

"Well, yes, I guess I do have Angie's dog for the time being. Yes."

"A dog might help. But I'd recommend that you also have dead-bolt locks. Put the outside lights on at night. Secure the windows. Maybe don't have a lot of shrubs around the foundation of your house. Maybe it would help if you had someone stay with you for a while."

"Angie's going to be staying with me when they let her out of the hospital," Ruth answered hesitantly, "so I won't be alone."

The sergeant kept her another half an hour, getting names of cast members, past and present, anyone connected in any way with the theatre group that Ruth could think of. She told him she couldn't imagine anyone in the troupe who would have wanted to kill someone. It was simply too nice a bunch of people.

Except for Blanche Voorhees, she thought to herself, but she didn't mention it to the sergeant.

Chapter 10

No Scripts Tonight, People!

ANGIE FELT WELL ENOUGH to come home to Ruth's house within the week. Her daughter Tracey brought her, along with a suitcase full of clothing. Ruth was delighted to see her friend. Charlie, however, acted nervous.

"I must still smell like 'hospital,' to him," the hurt Angie told them. "He'll warm up to me in a day or two."

Tracey immediately changed the subject and handed Ruth a bag of Chinese takeout.   "Mom insisted on cooking tonight. We thought this would be great heated up." Tracey hugged her mom. "And there's more than enough for three, if you don't mind me horning in. I can't seem to get enough of her." She hugged Angie again.

"Of course not! I'd love to have you stay," Ruth assured the girl. "Smells good. What is it?" She peeked into the white bag.

"Orange chicken with white rice and egg rolls with sweet and sour sauce. It's my absolute favorite," Angie chirped, sounding like her usual self again. "Here, Charlie," she said as she took a piece of egg-roll and tried to tempt the little terrier out from under the chair. But the dog backed away. "Oh, I guess he'll come around." Angie said uncertainly.

"That sounds perfect," Ruth told her. "I even have some leftover champagne to go with it. I opened a bottle the night you woke up." She smiled at her friend. "It'll go flat if we don't drink it."

Angie felt well enough the following Monday to go to the second rehearsal for *Show Boat.* There was applause when she slowly made her way down the basement steps into the Gerhardt Studio. As usual for Angie, she basked in the attention and made a low, sweeping bow to the group.

"Every day above ground is a great day," Angie joked as she took her chair.

At Ruth's house, however, Charlie still avoided Angie. He most often stayed in Ruth's bedroom, sleeping at the foot of the bed. Angie, trying to make sense of it.

"After all," she said to Ruth, "the poor little guy saw me get beat up. He's probably still afraid."

After three more choral rehearsals in Fritz's basement, which were—thankfully for the cast—uneventful, the next rehearsal for *Show Boat* was at the Como Pavilion. During the first complete run-through the actors still weren't one hundred percent certain of their music or their lines.

"No scripts tonight, people!" Fritz bellowed out as the actors filled the benches nearest the stage. The afternoon sun was still glinting off the lake. There was a slight wind, pleasantly cooling off the pavilion space, which was open on three sides. On the stage side, the set was almost finished, making the stage look as if it was the deck of a large show boat on the Mississippi. Fritz was busy going over changes in the score with Susie, the accompanist, whose electric piano was immediately under the stage area and close to the audience. But like an omniscient god, Fritz also kept an eagle eye on his cast. Susie patiently listened as Fritz made some minor adjustments to the accompaniment.

"I've already changed the orchestral scores," he told her. "They'll all be here for the dress rehearsal. It'll sound good, you'll see." Susie didn't look too happy, but she penciled in the changes.

Ruth laughed to herself. She and Angie had gone over their music at her home and knew it pretty well, but she could see little scraps of paper coming out of many of the actors' pockets and sleeves. Al and Mimi Rosenberg, who came in a new red Mazda, had xeroxed their scores, cut them up, and made them into ingenious little booklets—anything to aid one's memory.

If Fritz noticed these lame attempts by cast members to have "crutches," he understood enough to look the other way—as long as they weren't too blatant about it and had everything memorized by the dress rehearsal. Ruth looked at the little calendar she always carried in her knitting bag; the show opened in three and a half weeks.

Ruth loved rehearsals when they did run-throughs with the entire cast. This was when the show started to feel real to her, like a genuine Broadway show! The rehearsals were long and sometimes tiresome, but she loved them nonetheless. Ruth always brought her knitting along; it was something to do when others were running through their parts. Tonight was no exception. The chorus in *Show Boat* had a lot of down time when they didn't need to be on stage, and Ruth was not one to waste this time. Besides, she finished many of her Christmas presents this way.

She was working on a blue vest with a light gray pattern for her granddaughter. Ruth looked up from her knitting in time to see Fritz whisper something in Susie's ear and see her sharply shake her head, "No."

Looking across to where the principal actors were sitting, she could see Delancy Mays smiling and laughing with Al Rosenberg. It looked as if Al had told him something amusing.

Stop staring at the man! He's not interested in some old widow from the sticks. She wondered about him, though. From the gray in his hair, she guessed he was close to her age.

"He is *so* hot," Angie whispered in Ruth's ear.

"Shh!" Ruth answered. "He'll hear you."

"Not out here with all this noise." Angie told her. "Say, Ruthie, can you get home by yourself tonight? Tracey's picking me up early and taking me to her apartment. She has some windows she wants me to make curtains for. It's just straight sewing and I can handle that. I'm going to stay overnight there. Tracey's taking a day off tomorrow and we're going shopping for the fabric. Tracey says she misses me, and I don't think Charlie will miss me much." Her voice trailed off.

"Oh Angie, Charlie'll get friendlier. Just give him time. He's in a strange house and everything. You have my key, don't you? You can get in if I happen to be out. Tomorrow?"

"Sure, I can. And I wish Mr. 'Hottie' would ask you out."

"For God's sake, Angie. Behave yourself!" Ruth chided.

"Well, that's no fun!" the red-head retorted.

Once the cast had done the initial choral and musical rehearsing with Fritz, it was time for William "Billy" Hammer, the company's dramatic director and Fritz's fellow Mason, to do the blocking and directing.

"Billy" was a good-looking, outgoing, middle-aged St. Paul businessman who loved the theatre. He owned a restaurant on the east side of St. Paul, rental property on the west side, and another restaurant in the midway. Billy, it was rumored among the cast, also had his fingers in a number of Twin Cities real-estate deals.

Ruth remembered in the old days, at least fifteen years ago, when Billy had been a leading man, handsome and divorced. Once Mimi Rosenberg had whispered to Ruth that, according the ladies who played opposite Billy, he "loved 'em and left 'em." Ruth didn't put too much credence in rumors. Besides, she reminded herself, that all happened while Billy was divorced. Billy's second wife, a willowy blond named Lorene, was one of the loveliest women Ruth had ever seen. She doubted very much he would stray from her.

Ruth had always enjoyed Billy. She saw him as a high-energy, type-A sort of guy, the kind who sometimes kindled the jealousy of others. Personally, Ruth found him easy to work with and he certainly seemed to know what he was doing.

Well, he should know his way around the stage, Ruth thought to herself, remembering Billy's rousing characterizations of Curley in *Oklahoma,* Billy Bigelow in *Carousel,* and the king in *The King and I.* She and Angie had been in the chorus for all of those productions.

Ruth had heard it said by more than one cast member, "if Billy Hammer's not at a cast party, then it's not much of a party." He had the kind of personality that announced, upon walking into a room, "I'm here so now the fun can start!"

Billy's once red hair was turning gray and his once trim abdomen had grown a little paunchy, but his voice was still strong and his brilliant blue eyes and ruddy cheeks gave his face a youthful quality. His robust, out-going personality enabled him take charge and make people do exactly what he wanted—and convince them to love it.

What Billy wanted, right now, was for the chorus to "Get your butts up on stage!"

Chapter 11

The Dark Costume Room

As RUTH HURRIED TO get in line with the other chorus members, Angie nudged her and moved quietly behind the curtain. Ruth could see Tracey waiting for her mom by the steps that went up to the stage. Ruth gave them both a conspiratorial little wave as she moved on stage and began to sing with the rest of the chorus:

> *"Cotton Blossom, Cotton blossom,*
> *Captain Andy's marv'lous show!*
> *Thrills and laughter, concert after,*
> *Everybody's sure to go!"*

Before they knew it, Billy had reorganized them into small groups, all singing to Al Rosenberg, who was extra-manic as Captain Andy.

> *"Captain Andy, Captain Andy,*
> *Here's your lemon cake and chocolate candy,*

Quince preserves and ain't that dandy?
Mama always sends her best to you!"

Ruth was blocked next to little Rodney Olson, whose astounding voice continued to belie his age and appearance. Again, she marveled that such a sound could come out of a child! He needed no "crutches" either, she observed. *Well, the young have less in their minds, and so have an easier time memorizing things than the rest of us,* she thought as she slipped the small index card with the lyrics to the songs into her sweater pocket, just in case she had a "senior moment." She looked at Rodney and then over at Billy.

I'll bet Billy looked a lot like that as a kid, she surmised.

Al Rosenberg seemed to have recovered completely from the incident with the car. Mimi was uncharacteristically quiet, however, and looked pale. Ruth attributed it to the stage lights that made everyone look rather ghostly when not wearing stage makeup. Mimi's "Parthy" was a bit more bitter than Ruth remembered Parthy being played.

Maybe she's mad at Al for something?

She thought Danny Ancino was unexpectedly good as a kind of "macho" Ravenal, swaggering across the stage, flashing his dark eyes. His smoldering rendition of "Make Believe" probably made more than one young woman in the troupe shiver.

Sandy Westerling was passable as the blushing young *ingénue*, Magnolia, also called Nola.

A little too restrained, thought Ruth. Why, she even looks frightened. Maybe she just needs to get used to Danny Ancino's arm around her waist. Well, at least the chemistry between them makes the show interesting.

Shirley and Ed, the young couple playing Ellie and Frank, were absolutely delightful. Ruth had not enjoyed the actors playing "Frank and Ellie" in the movie production of *Show Boat* as much as these two. Their voices were no great shakes, but they were funny. Their dances together were rollicking, and their comedic timing brilliant. When Shirley finished singing "Life Upon the Wicked Stage," the entire cast spontaneously applauded. Fritz beamed. So did Billy.

Rhonda Olson. Little Rodney's mother, played the tragic leading actress, Julie. With her lank brown hair pulled back in a ponytail, and her hazel eyes hidden behind the same thick glasses her son wore, she surprised everyone. For such a slender woman, she was truly a torch singer in the rich, gutsy "old style" of torch songs. Her rendition of "Can't Help Lovin' That Man" choked up the more mature women, Ruth among them.

No wonder little Rodney sings as well as he does, she thought.

The man playing Julie's husband, Steve, seemed a little old and portly for the part. His name was Alex Johnson and Ruth remembered him singing "Stout-hearted Men" at auditions. Another man, playing the part of Pete, the villainous ship engineer who would try to woo Julie, was better cast. At least he *looked* like a villain. Introduced as Alex's brother, Ray, he had the countenance of a prize-fighter, complete with a nose that appeared to have once been broken and badly set.

The Kimmels were in their usual form. Howard was sterling in whatever part he played and Gloria-June, well, Gloria-June was marginal. Tonight Gloria-June was dressed in a tight, low-cut, bright green, satin dress with black satin piping.

They must be going out, afterwards, thought Ruth. She also wondered how they were going to make the fair-skinned Gloria-June into the elderly Black cook Queenie.

I'm sure glad I'm not in charge of make-up.

Delancy Mays was wonderful as the aging dock worker (and Queenie's husband), Joe. His voice was no surprise to Ruth, who had heard from Al Rosenberg that he had sung on the stages of both the Lyric Opera in Chicago and in Carnegie Hall in New York. Mr. Mays had the grace and stage presence of one who spent his whole life in front of the lights. His "Old Man River" was, well, Ruth shivered at its beauty.

He is gorgeous. He moves as if he was born for the stage, she mused. *What beautiful hands ... and that profile!*

After finishing his song, Delancy looked over at Ruth, as if for approval. She smiled and gave him a thumbs up. He smiled back and made a telephone with one hand, pointing to Ruth with the other. "Can I call you?" he mouthed.

Ruth became flustered. Extremely happy that Angie had already left with Tracey, she looked back at Delancy and shrugged her shoulders, nodding her head yes. "Okay," she mouthed back at him. *What could he want?* she wondered. *Probably help with his costume.*

The rehearsal of the first act went as well as could be expected for an initial run-through. Billy kept his notes to a minimum and gave directions that were up-beat and funny. Ruth noticed that Susie the accompanist left before it was over because Danny had to sing "You Are Love" with Vivian sight-reading on the piano. This upset Fritz, who slammed his fist down on the podium and muttered quietly to Vivian, "I pay her scale! Where the hell did she go?"

It was after nine-thirty when the chorus and principals were finally allowed to leave. As he dismissed them, Billy passed out flyers with the performance dates and reminded everyone to tell their friends about coming to the show. The cast took the flyers and dispersed quickly; it was late and they had worked hard.

Delancy approached Ruth.

"I need to get right home tonight. I'm waiting for a call from the Lyric. But can I call you tomorrow?"

"Uh ... sure ... um ... do you have my number?" Ruth asked.

"Of course," he grinned. "Vivian gave it to me. I'm sorry not to be a gentleman and walk you to your car, but I'm running late and this call is important. I'll see you later." He turned and was off at a run.

Huh! she thought. *At least he knows he* should *be a gentleman. Lyric my foot! The call is probably from Blanche Voorhees ... or from his wife and six kids.* Ruth mentally scolded herself. *My God, I'm getting jealous!*

By the time Ruth finished using the bathroom in the pavilion basement, everyone in the cast had gone. She'd convinced herself that even if Delancy Mays did actually call her, which she doubted, she would not give him the time of day.

The lights were still on as Ruth walked up the long-familiar basement stairs, feeling around in her knitting bag for her car keys. She knew that she had wrapped her keys in a hanky and stuffed them in the bottom of her knitting bag, under the yarn. Feeling exhausted, she thought she would drive through McDonald's on Snelling and get a Diet Coke to keep her awake for the drive home. She continued searching her knitting bag for the keys, thinking, *all I want to do is get home without falling asleep and going off the road. Then I'm going right to bed!*

"Where the heck are my keys?" she muttered to herself. Her stomach tightened. Not only were her keys missing, but the hanky in which she wrapped them was gone!

What do I do now? How will I get home?

She went back down the stairs and into the ladies' room but didn't see her keys. Then walked back upstairs and looked under the bench where she had been sitting. Nothing. Perhaps someone had found them and turned them in. She walked around to the restaurant to ask the people who ran the concessions. It was closed.

Ruth walked back down the stairs and took another tour of the ladies' room. Still nothing.

Clutching her knitting bag, Ruth was grateful that at least she had an extra car key in her purse, but it was locked in her car. "Okay ..." She took a deep breath and quietly said to herself, "Find a hanger, slip it around the window, pop up the lock post and open the door. There's an extra key in my purse." Her nervousness grew more palpable as she neared the costume room. "Calm down," she murmured to herself. But she knew she was becoming scared out of her wits.

The lights in the basement of the pavilion threw an eerie cast on the cluttered hall leading to the costume room. Ruth picked her way through partially-built sets that lined the passageway, careful not to rub up against the fresh paint she smelled. She hoped that the door to the costume room hadn't been locked. She tried the knob and, hurray! it opened.

The room was pitch black, but she could see the row of costumes from assorted past productions hanging there, like ghosts, illuminated from the dim hallway light. She groped for the wall switch just inside the door and then felt a dusty costume being suddenly pulled over her head and wrapped tightly around her neck and shoulders.

"Auugh!" she screamed as she fell back against the wall, her panic-stricken cry muffled in layers of nylon-net.

Chapter 12

Yet Another Attack

GAGGING AND COUGHING, RUTH struggled against the rough fabric scratching her face and neck. Layers of musty cloth filled her mouth as she tried to get enough breath to scream. Frantically ripping at the cloth, Ruth's first instinct was to get air. She twisted her head and shoulders, lashing out at her assailant with her feet. As her foot hit solid flesh, she didn't hear a sound, but felt the person break apart from her.

"Ouuff!" Ruth cried out, feeling a sharp pain in her right side as something heavy hit her and she fell backwards. Something was on top of her! She reached up and felt a cardboard box, full of ... more costumes!

Then, as suddenly as she had been attacked, Ruth knew she was alone. She pushed her way free of the box and its contents and finally managed to rip the musty costume off her head. All she could see was a heap of clothing in the dim light. All she could hear were her own sobbing gasps and someone's footsteps running up the basement stairs.

Ruth felt her side. It hurt but she could move. Leaning against the wall she breathed heavily, and just for a moment she put her hand over her heart, which was pounding.

"Help!" she cried weakly, "Please! Someone! Help me!" No one came.

Ruth knew she must get help, fast. Terrified, forgetting her knitting bag, she stumbled up the steps and headed for the outside door next to the restrooms, fearing that her attacker was still in the building. When she finally made it out into the night air her voice intensified.

"Help! Please! Someone, help me!"

But the place looked deserted. No one answered. She turned and ran through the parking lot toward Lexington Avenue, where a few cars were winding their way through the park. She began waving at the passing cars.

The first one, full of young men, sped by and honked for her to get out of the way. The second swerved and just continued on. But—thanks be! —the third car was a police car: Danny Ancino's! He slammed on his brakes and pulled over to the curb. In an instant, he was at Ruth's side.

"Oh, thank God you came along! I've been attacked!" Ruth was sobbing and struggling for breath, holding her chest again.

Danny put his hands on Ruth's shoulders. "Hey! It's me, Danny, from the show. What happened? You all right?"

Now that she knew she was safe, Ruth's heart stopped pounding. She straightened up, trying to compose herself. "I guess I am, but I was down in the ... I was mugged! I was attacked ... down in the costume room."

Danny looked toward the pavilion. "Where we just practiced? Geez! Are you sure?"

"I went down there to find a hanger to open my car. My keys were … I, I put them in my bag and someone must have taken them. My knitting bag … I must have left it downstairs. I fell when they pulled an old costume over my head." She knew she wasn't making much sense.

"Okay. That's okay. Go ahead," Danny said softly.

Ruth took a deep breath and began again. "I went to look in my knitting bag for my car keys. I keep them in there while I'm up on stage, but they were gone. I have an extra set in my purse, which is on the floor of my car." She took another deep breath. "I thought I could find a hanger down in the costume room so I could maybe use it to open my car and at least be able to drive home. That's when someone attacked me! Whoever it was, pulled a costume over my head so I couldn't see him. At least I think it was a 'him.' He also dumped a big box of costumes on top of me!"

"Did he hurt you?" Danny looked toward the pavilion.

"I'll probably have a bruise on my side where the box hit me." Ruth felt the tender place on her right side. "But I'm okay. I just think I should report this to the police."

Danny squared his shoulders. "Hey, I *am* the police, remember?"

Ruth, wide eyed, suddenly recognized him. "Weren't you just at rehearsal?" She didn't remember him being in a uniform.

"I still have to make a living." He flashed his brilliant smile at her. "I change into my uniform when we're finished rehearsing. I have a night shift that starts at nine-thirty. The timing is pretty tight on rehearsal days but I manage. My patrol includes this neighborhood. After my shift I get to sleep all day. It's the only way I can do the show."

"Well, what do we do now?" Ruth swayed a little on her feet.

"Get in the squad car and settle your nerves. And relax." He opened the back door for her. "You sit in here for a while." He swung his squad car into the lot and parked next to the darkened pavilion. "Stay here. I'll go downstairs to check that room out."

Ruth felt relieved, safe, and glad to just sit. She rested her head against the seat back.

Danny reached for a coffee thermos. "Here, drink this. I don't want you passin' out on me." Danny poured the steaming liquid into a Styrofoam cup.

Ruth took it, thinking, *I don't have the nerve to tell him I don't like coffee.*

"Just stay here. Keep the doors locked. I'll be right back." He patted Ruth's shoulder. "Don't open it for anybody."

As she heard the doors click, Ruth let out an enormous sigh. The coffee actually tasted pretty good. After Danny was out of sight, she lifted up her blouse and checked her right side. Even in the dim light she could see a nasty bruise beginning to darken. She touched it tenderly. *Too low to be a rib. That's good. This will probably be gone in a couple of weeks.*

About ten minutes later, Danny strode back to the car and opened the door on Ruth's side. "Here's your knitting bag—and I found these on the floor under all the clothes. Are they yours?" He dangled a bunch of keys in front of her.

"Those are my keys!" Ruth reached for them and felt comforted just by fingering the comedy and tragedy key-chain that Tom had given her. "Thank you, though I really don't know what they were doing in the costume room." She looked inside the knitting bag; both her hanky and her knitting were intact.

"Don't know," Danny said, shaking his head. "Maybe the mugger dropped 'em, or maybe you dropped 'em. Anyway, we got 'em." He shut Ruth's door, climbed in on the driver's side, and checked his dark, curly hair in the mirror, smiling at his own reflection. "Let's go up to Keys and get you another cup of coffee and a doughnut." He started the car with a roar and pulled out on the road, narrowly missing another car, cursing under his breath as he did so. Ruth started, covering her eyes with her hands.

"Really, no, I should get home," Ruth said, recovered enough to look back at the pavilion parking-lot. "My dog ... he needs to be let out. I have a long way to drive. Really, I can't go."

"Hey, 'you arguin' with a cop?" Danny laughed. "Not a good idea."

Ruth felt all eyes on the two of them as they walked into Keys, which was a local, family-owned and operated restaurant. Danny chose a booth toward the front. Ruth couldn't help noticing the patriotic theme with which the owners had decorated the place. Small American flags and white silk flowers, arranged in milk-glass vases were everywhere, on the tables and on small shelves that lined the walls. There was also a large sign on the wall that made Ruth smile: "In God We Trust, All Others Pay Cash!"

Ruth allowed herself a cup of tea and a doughnut with Danny, whose animal charm was certainly evident to the petite blonde waitress who served them. She never took her eyes off the young man.

She's actually batting her eyelashes! Ruth thought to herself.

"Hey, you must be feelin' better." Danny raised his coffee cup in salute to Ruth. "I see a smile."

"Yes, thank you," Ruth told him. "This hit the spot. It's just what I needed."

On the drive back to retrieve Ruth's car, they talked a little about the show, which was Danny's first.

"My Uncle Tony," he laughed, "he said, 'Danny boy, you're a good singer and I know you're goin' to get a lead in that show.' "So here I am."

"Is your Uncle Tony an actor?" Ruth asked him.

"Yeah," Danny laughed. "He's quite an actor—he acts up!" His laughter had a bitter edge to it.

"I don't understand." Ruth looked at him. "Why did your Uncle Tony want you to …"

"Hey! No more questions. Here's your car." Danny pulled alongside of Ruth's car and jumped out to open the door for her. "Don't worry. I'll report in your assault. Someone will call you tomorrow. You think you can drive home okay?"

Ruth assured him that she could, and thanked him profusely for his help. As she eased carefully behind the wheel, she instinctively pushed down the door-lock and glanced into the back seat. It was empty except for her purse, which lay on the floor where she left it. The caffeine and sugar she had consumed was beginning to take effect. She felt wired.

I probably won't get much sleep tonight, she thought as she drove out of the park and turned right on Larpenteur Avenue. She went over and over things in her mind, trying to sort out what had happened. *Did I just "think" my keys were lost?* She felt unsure now, wondering if she had merely missed them when looking through her bag.

No, I really searched through it. They weren't in there. I would have found them, she told herself emphatically. *Who attacked me? And why?*

Driving home, she promised herself that she would never again go down into the basement of the pavilion, or anywhere dark and deserted, alone. Never! She also made a mental note to herself to keep her keys safety-pinned inside her pocket after this.

As she pulled into her driveway, Ruth's anxiety began melting away. These were her trees, her flowers, her driveway, her house. "Thank God only Angie has my keys," she said to herself with a sigh of relief as she turned the key in her back door lock. "Babies, I'm home! Sorry I'm late," she called out.

No one came to meet her.

"Charlie! Griselda, Morrie, kitty kitty!" She tried again, hurrying to put her things on the kitchen table and get to her living room, where she assumed her animals were sleeping. But not a sign of them.

Running to her bedroom, Ruth called out, louder this time.

"Charlie! Here, boy! Here kitty, kitty, kitty!"

A little paw stuck tentatively out from under her bed, followed by Griselda's furry face. "What are you doing here, hiding from mama?" Relieved, Ruth chuckled and knelt down, gently pulling the cat from under her bed. She knelt further down and under the off-white dust-ruffle was Morrie, cowering in the farthest corner. "What is going on?" she asked the cats. "Where's Charlie?"

Griselda's answer was to cling tightly to her, Morrie's was to stay where he was.

Ruth searched for Charlie all over the house, including the basement, which she brightly illuminated before descending the stairs, but found no trace of the little white terrier. She called and called. She went into the yard, even into her neighbor's yard, but still no trace of Charlie.

As she looked through the house, she noticed one of the French doors out to her patio in front of the living room was open a bit.

I must have forgotten to shut and lock it when I left. He probably got out that way. Ruth was panicking now. "Where *is* he?" she panted as she ran around to all the out-buildings, and even down by the lake. But not a sign of him.

"Charlie! Charlie! Here, boy! Where are you?!"

After forty-five-minutes, she was bone-weary. She sat down in one of her big blue chairs and sobbed.

What am I going to tell Angie? Exhausted, she finally fell asleep in the chair.

During the night, both cats curled up in her lap.

Chapter 13

A Well-Loved Pet

AT EXACTLY NINE O'CLOCK in the morning the phone woke Ruth, who groggily stumbled out to the kitchen to answer it.

"Hello?" her voice a throaty rasp, not yet quite awake.

"Mrs. Carson? This is Sergeant Sullivan with the police. Officer Ancino reported that you were assaulted last evening and I'm calling to see how you are."

Ruth snapped awake as soon as she heard the authoritative voice. "Ah, yes. I have a slight bruise," she replied as she touched the sore spot, "but other than that, I think I'm fine, thank you." She stretched as she said this, trying to work the kinks out of her back.

The sergeant went on. "Can you remember anything about your assailant?"

Ruth sat down in one of the white kitchen chairs and then got up again to stretch. "I can't really tell you much, other than after rehearsal last night, I noticed my car keys were missing. I looked all over, and by the time I finished looking, everyone had gone home. So I went into the costume room in the basement to see if I could find a hanger to open my car door. I had another set of keys in my purse on the floor of the car."

"You were alone in the pavilion at that time?" Sergeant Sullivan sounded puzzled.

"Well, Angie had to leave early with her daughter and my car keys were missing. I had to get home," Ruth said defensively.

"Go on. Then what happened?"

"Well, when I went to turn on the light, someone pulled a costume over my head. I fought him, or whoever it was, and then I fell over, and then a big costume box fell on me or it was pushed on top of me. I don't know. It happened so fast, and then the person just ran away. I could hear footsteps running up the stairs."

"What did that sound like? Did it sound like a man running? Or a woman?" The sergeant sounded as if he was writing it all down.

"I don't know, it's hard to tell. But I think whoever it was wore sneakers. Yes," she thought, "definitely sneakers. Kind of quiet, not like regular shoes. I have to tell you, though," she said, "I have a much more pressing problem. Charlie, Angie's little dog, is missing. When I finally got home last night he was gone." She sounded tearful. "I've looked and looked. He's just not here and I'm just heartsick. How can I tell Angie he's missing?"

"Well, Mrs. Carson, I'm sorry about that, but a missing dog is hardly as important as an assault. You could have been badly hurt. Or killed."

"But, Angie's dog." Ruth was getting more and more upset. "Angie and her daughter are coming here this afternoon. What will I tell them?"

"Mrs. Carson," said Mickey Sullivan, sounding a bit irritated, "call your neighbors. Call the local animal shelters. But do it right away. Did the dog have a collar? Any identification?"

"No, no, he didn't. He didn't wear a collar."

"Well, after you check with your neighbors, call all the local animal shelters. Sometimes when a pet gets out and wanders away, some good Samaritan brings them to a shelter." Sergeant Sullivan cleared his throat. "But do it right away. The shelters usually don't keep animals for very long."

"Oh ...!"

And then he added, his voice sounding stern, "Mrs. Carson, I have to warn you. You've got to be careful. Don't go places alone, especially after dark. Whoever attacked you might try again." Ruth promised to be more careful.

Ruth hung up and looked down at her two cats. "Where's Charlie? Did you two see where he went? Okay, okay. I know you're hungry."

She filled the cat's food and water bowls, then went upstairs to take a shower. As she let the jets of hot water rinse the shampoo out of her hair and massage her aching shoulders and back, she kept rolling the events of the previous night around in her head.

I'm sure I didn't lose my car keys. But how did they get out of my bag? And how am I going to find Charlie? What am I going to tell Angie?

Then she thought she heard the back doorbell ring. Turning off the water, she listened for it and it rang again. Ruth stepped out of the shower and grabbed her long, blue terry-cloth caftan, looking one more time at the darkening bruise on her side as she carefully let the garment fall over her body. Quickly wrapping a towel around her wet hair, she ran downstairs. "I'm coming! I'm coming!" she called out. *I guess I'm covered up enough.* Ruth sometimes wore the blue caftan out to get the mail.

Angie and Tracey were already in the kitchen.

"Angie! Tracey!" Ruth cried as she hurried to meet them, "I'm so glad you're here. I can't find Charlie anywhere! When I came home last night, he was gone. He must have somehow gotten out, although I don't know how." She wrapped her arms around herself to get warm. "I'm so glad to see you! We have to start calling the animal shelters."

Angie stopped in her tracks. "What do you mean, "Charlie's not here? Where is he?"

Ruth told her about the previous evening—her assault at the pavilion and then arriving home to find Charlie missing.

"My god! Are you okay?" Tracey asked first.

"Maybe we should take you to a doctor before we look for the dog." Angie gave Ruth a hug and Ruth winced.

"Other than being a bit tender, I feel fine," Ruth assured her. "Besides, I want to ... I need to look for Charlie."

"Where should we start?" Tracey asked.

After giving Tracey the phone numbers of some neighbors, Ruth ran upstairs to dry her hair and dress. Angie ran out to the yard and began calling for her dog.

When Ruth came back into the kitchen, Tracey was still on the phone. Ruth made some tea and cut three slices of banana bread.

"Nothing," Tracey said as she hung up the phone. "No one's seen him."

They had the tea and banana bread to revive themselves and Ruth decided to first call the St. Paul animal shelter near the pavilion. It was the largest one in the area and the first one most people thought of. She doubted Charlie was there but felt she should call, just in case.

The woman at the shelter sounded like a teen-ager. "I'm not sure when he came in, but we do have a little white terrier in the third room. I think he's a fairly old dog."

After questioning her, Ruth found out that the "third room" was where older, sometimes sicker, animals were briefly kept before being euthanized.

"Please, our missing dog is old, and he might be the terrier you describe. Could we please come in this afternoon?"

"You better come right away, ma'am. We're closing in a couple of hours."

"Please!" Ruth pleaded. "Don't do anything to him. He may belong to us and he's very well-loved pet. We'll be there in a half-hour or so."

"Okay, we'll hold him for you," said the girl.

Ruth told Tracey and Angie that they should leave right away. Cups and saucers were left on the kitchen table and they hurriedly piled into Tracey's little blue SUV.

Tracey was a good driver and went just a bit over the speed-limit. She navigated expertly through Maplewood, then through Roseville, and finally into St. Paul. Tracey looked resolute as she drove. Angie was uncustomarily quiet. Ruth silently prayed the little dog would be Charlie.

Tracey parked with only two deft moves in front of St. Paul Animal Control.

"Let's hurry." Tracey, usually very thoughtful of others, jumped from the car and left Ruth and Angie behind to follow.

Once inside, Ruth went up to a large reception desk and explained that she had just called and that a woman said she would hold the dog for her.

"Right this way. I hope it's yours," said the young man who led them to the third room.

They walked straight to the cage of the little terrier. Angie started crying and cooing at the dog, pushing her fingers through the cage to pet him. Tracey asked the young man to please let the animal out. The dog was going crazy, jumping up and down and yipping.

This is Charlie? Ruth wondered, surprised. *He doesn't look exactly like the dog that was at my house.*

But seeing how overjoyed Angie was, and how the dog was acting, she said nothing.

"I'm afraid you'll have to pay for him," the attendant explained apologetically. "Since he had no identification, we can't let anyone just walk in here, say it's theirs, and take it home for free."

Angie and Tracey argued with him, but to no avail. They finally gave in, but told Ruth to put her checkbook away. Tracey insisted on paying for Charlie.

"You were buying his food," she told Ruth. "At least let me buy him back."

The dog was now in Angie's arms, licking her face and making joyful dog-noises.

"He loves me again!" Angie had tears of joy in her eyes.

The young man turned to Ruth. "Lady, if you like that breed, we have another dog who is almost the exact replica of this one. Wanna see him?"

"We have our dog. We don't need another, thank you," Tracey told him briskly, before noticing Ruth, who looked a little crestfallen.

"You're going to look at that other dog, aren't you?" Tracey said to her. "My god! You're as bad as my mom!"

"It can't hurt just to look," Ruth said expectantly. Angie nodded.

While Tracey took Charlie out to the front office to pay for him and sign the papers, the attendant walked Ruth and Angie through a couple of rooms full of cages holding animals of every description. There were dogs, cats, kittens, puppies, rabbits, even some gerbils, until they came to another room with only a few cages. In one was an elderly terrier, the exact twin of Charlie.

"His name's Toby. Someone brought him in who said he didn't want him anymore." The little terrier barked wildly when he saw Ruth.

"Oh, my sweet baby," Ruth crooned. The animal came to her instantly and licked her hands through the bars of the cage.

This is the dog I had at my house! she instantly realized with a shock. *But how could that be?* "He would be a good play-mate for Charlie, and Sergeant Sullivan told me to get a dog," Ruth said, more to herself than to anyone else. "Okay ... Toby, it looks like you're coming home with me." The dog barked excitedly as he was lifted from his cage and placed into Ruth's arms. Sold!

The ride home was exuberant. Charlie and Toby were in the back seat with Angie, jumping up and down, wagging their tales, and yelping with joy. They not only licked the back windows of Tracey's car, but licked each other, acting like long-lost buddies.

"Look how well they get along." Tracey smiled at the dogs through the rear-view mirror. "And they look just like twins, don't they?"

Ruth looked back at the almost identical dogs. "I know this sounds strange," Ruth finally told Angie, "but I'm sure that Toby is the same dog that the police gave me when I picked him up at the police station ... the dog they said had been in your house. I think I've had Toby at my house, not your Charlie."

"How could that be?" Angie countered. "Anyway, I don't care. I've got my sweet little mooshie-face back."

"Don't forget, Ruth, you've been under a lot of stress lately," Tracey interjected.

"Well, maybe," said Ruth, "but Toby seems to already know me."

Chapter 14

On the Mississippi

Ruth's two cats were not happy when Ruth, Tracey, and Angie brought Charlie and Toby into the house. Both felines jumped upon the back of the sofa and arched their backs. Griselda made low growling sounds. Neither would go near either dog.

Charlie ran here and there throughout the house, sniffing everything. Toby looked up at the cats as if to say, "Hey, you know me. I'm your old friend!"

Morrie finally jumped down, sniffing and rubbing up against Toby in a way that said "Okay, you can stay." Griselda held her ground on the sofa.

Later, as the three women sat at Ruth's kitchen table enjoying a bowl of tomato soup and a grilled cheese sandwich, they laughed at the antics of the two dogs cavorting on the kitchen floor. Charlie had one end of a throw rug in his mouth and Toby held the other—a tug-of-war!

"We'd better get these two some real toys to play with," Ruth laughed, "or they'll tear my house apart. You know, I wonder if they are from the same litter," she added. "They not only look alike; they seem to be about the same age."

"Maybe," said Tracey, reaching down to tickle Toby's ears. He let go of the rug and sat up, begging for a piece of sandwich. "Mom got Charlie from some friend of hers in St. Paul, didn't you, mom?"

"Yeah, she lived on Front Street." Angie gave both dogs pieces from her sandwich. As she returned to her lunch the phone rang.

It was Fritz. "Ruth, can you help me out this coming Saturday?" Fritz was in his usual no-nonsense, get right-to-the-point mode.

"Uh, I think so." She took a quick look at her monthly calendar. "Yes, okay, I don't have anything scheduled on that day. What's happening?"

"We've been invited to sing on the *Saint Paul Jubilee*," Fritz proudly announced. "It's a sternwheel paddleboat. The governor, the mayor, and uh, other dignitaries are having a 'day on the river,' and *we* are the entertainment. It will get us some great publicity for the show. What do you think of that?"

"I think our maestro has been hobnobbing with important people again," Ruth responded with a laugh. From experience she knew that Fritz was on familiar terms with "everyone who was anyone" in the Twin Cities area.

"Hee, hee, hee!" chortled Fritz. He loved it when someone realized the extent of his influence in certain political circles. "They're even going to feed us. After we sing, of course. We're singing during their lunch, and then we'll have an hour or so to sit and have a box-lunch and enjoy the boat ride. Doesn't that sound like fun?"

"It sure does. Count me in!" Ruth paused a moment—she hated to put a damper on Fritz's enthusiasm— "but what about costumes?"

"No problem. Vivian and Gloria-June have that all taken care of. They will have everyone's costumes waiting for them when we gather on the boat. Gloria- June has been working on costumes for weeks and she's volunteering her time. I don't have to pay her anything. All I had to do is buy the material."

Ah ha! thought Ruth. *I was right. That's how Gloria-June got a meaty role.* "Well, you know I always like to sew my own costume, and Angie's. I hope that's okay," Ruth stated.

"Of course. I told Gloria-June not to worry about your dress or Angie's. Say, would you call Angie for me?"

"I'll do better than that. I'll ask her now. She's staying with me for a while—but what was it you wanted me to do for you?"

"Oh." Fritz cleared his throat. "That was it. We are calling everyone in the cast to tell them about singing on the riverboat. This all happened at the last minute. So you can join us to sing some of our numbers on the boat on Saturday?"

"Well, yes, sure. What time?"

"Ten a.m., at the Harriet Island Landing. Okay?"

"We'll be there with bells on," Ruth assured him.

"You'd better wear a costume too! Hee, hee, hee!" Fritz laughed at his own joke. "This is a family show!"

"Okay, we will. Bye, maestro."

Ruth rolled her eyes as she hung up the phone and looked at Angie, "Oh boy! We're going to be singing several numbers on a Mississippi paddleboat and need to have our costumes made in exactly four days. I have some major sewing to do!"

"I'll take care of the animals, I'll make the meals, you sew," Angie said as she started to clear the table. "Don't worry about anything. Charlie is back home and now he has a best friend. All's well with the world."

Ruth glanced at the two cats sitting with doleful looks in the doorway to the kitchen. "Not everybody's world," she laughed.

Tracey excused herself, thanked Ruth, and hugged and kissed her mom. She wanted to get back to her apartment and routines. "I have so much laundry to do," she said, "and I haven't vacuumed in over a week."

"Poor baby." Angie made a face at her.

Ruth's sewing room on the main floor had once been Tom's den. She stored her fabric in large Rubbermaid storage boxes, which were crammed full of fabric pieces and scraps, organized by color. She searched in the box marked "blue" and again in the box marked "white," but couldn't find what she wanted.

I thought I'd saved some blue and white satin, she thought.

"Shoot!" she told Angie. "I probably used it for something else." She realized she'd have to run out and buy new fabric, quickly, if she was going to finish their costumes by Saturday.

She asked Angie if she wanted to go to the fabric store with her, but Angie declined.

"I'm gonna take the two *naughty boys* outside and throw sticks for them to fetch. They need exercise and I need fresh air. I spent too much time in that hospital."

"Okay then, have fun," Ruth said. I'll see you later." She hurried out to her car.

Driving down White Bear Avenue to a discount fabric store, Ruth decided to not spend any more than she had to. Once at the store, it took about thirty minutes of browsing before she found what she needed.

As she left the store, she decided to run into the Dollar Tree in the next block. She wanted to see if they had any small umbrellas—the kind you'd maybe find at wedding and baby showers. She was in luck.

I live right! she thought, as she picked up the last two such umbrellas they had. *I can cover these with fabric and Angie and I will look like authentic Southern belles!* Then she mused, *well, maybe not for the boat trip, but certainly by opening night.*

On the way home, Ruth started thinking about the design of their costumes.

We'll each need a bustle ... connected to the dress so we can get in and out of it easily. She went on to herself: *The bodice will have to be fitted. I have a pattern for that. And the front of the skirt will be straight to the floor, with the back of the skirt full and sweeping. We'll have to have long sleeves, yes, long, with puffs at the shoulders and very fitted at the wrists.*

By the time Ruth reached her driveway, she had a picture in her mind of how the costumes should look.

"Hi, Angie, I'm home!" she called as she let herself in the back door to her house. There was no answer, but a note had been left on the kitchen table. Ruth's stomach lurched as she picked it up.

Ruthie, Sergeant Sullivan called. He's got a lead. Your neighbor George is taking me in to St. Paul so I can talk to him. I'll bring back Subways for supper. Have fun sewing. Love, Angie.

Ruth's heartbeat returned to normal.

God! It's about time the police got a lead, she thought, and then, *how did Angie get my neighbor to take her to the police station?* Ruth pondered that as she went to the laundry room to pre-shrink all the fabric before cutting it out.

While the fabric was in the dryer, Ruth sat down at her kitchen table to wait for Angie.

I wonder who it was, Angie? Who would ever hurt you? What about Lionel? And why try to kill Mimi and Al? And why attack me? She was just starting to make herself a cup of tea when she saw her neighbor's car pull slowly into the driveway.

"They think they have the man who did it!" Angie yelled to Ruth as she jumped from seventy-year-old George Sandstrom's car. Ruth heard her say, "Thanks, George! I owe ya! How 'bout some Subways? We got plenty!" Ruth saw George laugh and shake his head "no" as he slowly backed his car out of her driveway. Angie swooped into the kitchen with two large white bags. "At least they *think* he's the one. Oh, and I'm sorry I just took off like that. I was talking to George out by the lilac bushes when the phone rang. George said he had to go to a hardware store anyway, so he drove me in to the station. What a nice guy."

"Yes, George is a real gentleman," Ruth told her friend. "His wife is in the Alzheimer unit in Good Samaritan ... and he's a wonderful gardener. He and his wife were both raised in this area. They didn't have any kids. I suppose he's lonely."

"Yeah, he told me about his wife. Sure is a shame. She doesn't know him anymore. Hasn't for over three years. Isn't that the saddest thing?" Angie looked out of the window where the car had disappeared. "I think he kind of likes me."

"Of course, George likes you. Who wouldn't like you? So, tell me who it is," Ruth said. "What did they tell you at the police station?"

Angie looked downcast as she took two turkey sandwiches with all the trimmings, including chips and cookies, out of the bags and set them out on the kitchen table. Ruth noticed Angie's hands were shaking.

"Sit down, sweetie." Ruth softened her gaze.

"They wouldn't give me a name. They just showed me a picture and asked if I recognized him. I thought it looked like someone who works in our building. I remember him saying 'good morning' to me once when I was out walking Charlie. Why would he do such a thing? Why would he want to hurt me? I never did anything to him!" Angie began dabbing her eyes. Ruth stood behind her friend and put her arms around her.

"I don't know," Ruth comforted. "It's okay … it's okay … just let it out. I don't know, sweetie. Some people are nuts. We don't know what's in their minds. At least they've got a suspect." *But,* Ruth thought to herself, *I wonder if he's really the right one? What about the others in the cast? Could this man be the guilty one?*

Ruth tried to sound positive for Angie's sake. "Come on, Angie, let's eat this wonderful feast you brought. Turkey and all these veggies. Look's good!"

While Ruth thought she'd save half her sandwich for another meal, Angie recovered quickly and tucked into hers with gusto.

"How did you know that this was my favorite?" Ruth said, trying to sound cheerful. She didn't want Angie to think that the killer might still at large, even though she believed he probably was.

"This is Tracey's favorite too," Angie continued as she chewed. "We always used to get this when we had a longing for sandwiches, along with the chips and chocolate chip cookies. Her favorite. Tears continued welling up in Angie's eyes, but she kept eating and talking.

Go ahead and cry, Ruth thought as they ate. *It's good to cry. Gets all the hurt out.* "Look, we've got company." Morrie, Griselda, Charlie, and Toby—all four—had smelled food and were lined up in front of the table with hopeful expressions.

"You little beggars!" Angie laughed, smiling through her tears. She started cutting up small pieces of turkey and putting it on napkins. "No, you can't have any more." She pushed gently at the greedy Griselda, who was nosing the others away from the food.

Ruth worked the rest of the afternoon and well into the evening on their costumes. She pinned the pattern pieces and Angie helped cut. Angie was a little more difficult to fit because of the extra weight she carried, but Ruth finally got her friend's bodice looking "respectable." Ruth had the basic bodices and skirts pretty much cut out when they finally went to bed.

"Tomorrow I'll sew them together, and the next day I'll do the hemming and put snaps on the bodices and sleeves," she told Angie before they turned in for the night. Ruth exceeded her expectations, because by late afternoon the next day, the costumes were finished, leaving time in the evening to transform the umbrellas into something resembling frilly parasols.

Saturday dawned bright and sunny.

What a perfect day to be on the river, thought Ruth as she got up and fed the animals. She briefly let the dogs run outside while she prepared her usual morning tea.

Angie was still asleep in the second upstairs bedroom when Ruth shouted up the stairs to her friend. "Come on, Angie! Rise and shine."

"Mmpf, is it morning already?" mumbled Angie, pulling the pillow over her head.

"Come on, lazy-bones!" Louder this time. "Get up! We need to get going soon."

Ruth stepped into her sewing room and looked over her handiwork. She wished the bustles were fuller, but they looked okay. *We've got big enough 'bustles' of our own,* she laughed to herself, *and, for the short time I worked on them, they look pretty darn good.* She thought the umbrellas needed more lace. *Or maybe not,* she said to herself. *I don't want to look too frilly.*

Ruth heard Angie humming and rummaging around in the kitchen.

Good, she thought, *she's up and probably feeling better. I wonder if we'll see Sergeant Sullivan on the boat today. Maybe we'll have a minute to talk.*

Just then, Angie came into the sewing room with a glass of orange juice for each of them.

"Have you had your vitamin C this morning?" Angie asked.

"No, I haven't, thanks."

They sat down and sipped their juice in silence.

Finally Angie spoke. "You know, I just don't believe it was the man from my apartment building. He never seemed angry or anything. Besides, I hardly knew him. It doesn't make sense."

"Well, let the police figure it out."

"Yeah, I guess so." Angie took the empty glasses back into the kitchen.

Ruth looked at her watch. "Whoa! We'd better be going. We need to be at that boat landing at ten, so we'll have to leave here by nine. And we have to get into our costumes first. No time for breakfast."

Angie returned to the sewing room, gathered up her costume, and ran up her bedroom.

Ruth hurriedly got into her own costume and quickly fixed her make-up, not knowing if there would be any time or place for it on the boat. She found a gray bonnet in her old costume closet, and as she surveyed her image in the long mirror in her bedroom, she sang, *"Put on your old gray bonnet, with the blue ribbon on it, and I'll hitch old Dobbin to the sleigh ..."*

She dug around her closet some more and found a straw hat for Angie. The ribbon on it almost matched the green of Angie's dress. *Close enough,* she thought.

At nine-fifteen, both women headed out the door.

"I'd better drive like the wind," Ruth told Angie. "We're late!"

"Do you think I look okay?" Angie asked as she pinned the hat over her red hair.

"I think I'll put more trim on your bodice later," Ruth mused, noticing Angie's ample cleavage. Then, seeing her friend's frown, she smiled, "In that green dress, you look like Scarlett O'Hara!"

Ruth was dressed from head to toe in the black and gray striped satin, complete with a black bustle and black trim on the neck and sleeves of the bodice. Her bonnet was gray, with a black tie under the chin, and little pink roses on the side.

"I'm still not sure about the parasols," she said to Angie, "maybe I can find some more lace for them?"

"They'd look even better with sequins." Angie quipped.

Ruth rolled her eyes. "We'll have some for opening night."

After Ruth found a spot in the landing's parking lot, she and Angie left their purses in the trunk, each putting some cash into the pockets Ruth had made on the side of their skirts.

Ruth looked around. *This could be a hundred years ago,* she mused. *Take away all the cars and we're right there. The paddleboat looks old … and so does the river.*

Delancy Mays, dressed as "Joe" was the first person they saw as they neared the boat. He stood on the dock, watching as they approached.

"Hello, Mr. Mays," Ruth said. *And how's your girlfriend, Blanche?* she added mentally.

"Please, call me Del."

"'Hey there, Del," Angie said with a wink. "Lookin' fine!"

"Thank you. You both look just lovely."

Ruth had to admit that even in tattered deck-hand attire, the man looked elegant. As he offered his hand to help her on the boat, she felt a little quiver, but dismissed it at once.

"Thank you … Del," she said with a brisk nod.

I haven't even looked at a man since Tom's death. Anyway, he has a girlfriend and I'm not about to tangle with her. She dismissed her "quiver" with a rueful shake of her head as Delancy Mays put his other hand gently under her elbow and lifted her to the deck.

She primly said "Thank you. It's quite a nice day, isn't it," and tried to dispel the subtle shift in her breathing. She'd loved Tom passionately, and hadn't felt like this since before Tom became ill.

"It is a nice day, isn't it?" He looked first at her, and then turned to assist Angie.

Ruth noticed the finely chiseled bones of his face. *He really is good looking,* she acknowledged to herself.

"Fritz wants everyone on the lower deck, by the bar," he said, pointing. "They have two small rest rooms to use for men's and women's changing rooms, but I see you ladies came prepared. Very nice. And very period."

Angie simpered and spun her body around for his approval.

"Ah, thank you," Ruth told him. "Well, we'll see you down below." She grabbed Angie's arm and moved her toward the stairs.

"Whoo-boy! He is one hot guy," Angie whispered.

"Shh!" Ruth shook her head.

But Ruth couldn't help stealing another glance at Del.

He really is handsome. And that voice! But—she reminded herself as they reached the bottom of the stairs—*he belongs to Blanche Voorhees.*

The *Saint Paul Jubilee* was an old paddle wheeler that had been rebuilt and updated to modern codes as an excursion boat. Convenient hand-rails were abundant and life preservers hung strategically on all the exterior walls. Nineteenth century touches, however, were everywhere evident in the design, with brass fittings, faux gas lanterns, and gingerbread Victorian trim painted white. Chairs and sofas were cushioned with a plush mauve velvet. It certainly looked like an old southern river boat.

"Ruth! Angie! You both look wonderful, just wonderful!" Fritz ran up to Ruth, hugging her and then holding her at arm's length, beaming. "Don't they look wonderful, Vivian?" He was dressed for a "rich man's" day on the river: navy-blue linen sports coat and gray slacks, complete with white shirt and ascot. Vivian smiled warmly at Ruth and Angie, nodding her head.

Fritz loved the promotional events that typically surrounded the opening of his musicals. When politicians and wealthy patrons of the arts appreciated his efforts and came out in force to his functions, he simply glowed! It was his life's work to bring music to the masses in Minnesota's capitol city, but it was Fritz's life's blood to be noticed and approved of—especially by the rich and famous.

Vivian was in costume herself. To help Fritz out, she sometimes sang with the chorus when he needed another soprano, and today was apparently one of those days. While he played "grand host," his ever-patient help mate struggled under a huge bundle of costumes. Ruth could see perspiration beginning to stain the tight bodice of her pale blue dress. Vivian looked at them again, rolling her eyes, as if to say, "men!"

Ruth and Angie hurried over to relieve Vivian of some of her burden.

"Here, let us take a few of those. What can we do to help?" Ruth asked.

"Oh, thanks." Vivian let out a deep breath. "You are life-savers." She shook her head and said, "I don't know where Gloria-June went and she has all my labels. I guess you'll just have to lay each costume over the back of a chair. There's one for each cast member, except for you two. I'll, I'll just get ..." Vivian looked harassed and nervous, not her usual calm demeanor.

"Geez, Vivian, chill out." Angie laid her hand on Vivian's arm. "You'll give yourself a heat-stroke goin' so fast."

Ruth thought, *Good grief! Everyone always worries about Fritz's health. Vivian takes on way too much to make sure he doesn't have any stress in his life ... and she's probably in worse shape. I should help her more.*

Ruth laid out the costumes, then asked Vivian, "Why don't I get you something cold to drink. You sit down for a minute while I find Gloria-June and then I'll bring something cool."

"Oh, that would be nice." Vivian plopped down in the nearest empty chair. "Either Seven-up or Sprite would be great. Thank you, Ruth!"

"I'll have a Diet Coke," Angie told her, as she sat her ample frame on one of the chairs and fanned herself with her hand.

Ruth didn't have to hunt for the effervescent Gloria-June because, just then, she made her grand entrance.

"Hellooo, everyone!" she sang out.

Ruth stifled a laugh. As "Queenie" the woman looked just like a madam—not that she knew any madams—but Gloria-June, resplendent in plum-colored satin with cream-colored lace trim, certainly looked like what Ruth would imagine one might look like.

"Ruthie," she cooed, "and Angie ... I simply do *love* your sweet little costumes ... Howie! Del!" she shrieked at the two men entering the room. "Bring those costumes in here. And hurry up! Cast members are starting to come and I still have to do my makeup and warm up my voice."

Angie shook her head and rolled her eyes, but kept her mouth shut.

Del was carrying a huge bundle of costumes down the narrow stairway. "Yassuh, Miz' Gloria-June. Ah shore don' think yo' need to warm up that voice none," he muttered *sotto voce* while making a face and winking at Ruth.

"Shh!" Ruth giggled, slipping by him on the narrow stairway. His after shave, or perhaps his close presence, made her feel a little giddy.

Howard Kimmel stumbled down after him, forehead beaded with sweat, carrying half of what Del had carried but barely able to handle it. Ruth's heart went out to him. "I'm coming," he managed to croak.

Ruth found a pop machine at the top of the stairs. Thankfully, it took dollar bills, and she had put some in her dress pocket. She purchased six cans of Seven-Up, and Angie's Diet Coke, thinking she'd treat the costume crew. As she was about to descend the stairs, she heard Fritz call out a greeting over the railing. The dignitaries were arriving, including Minnesota's quirky, colorful governor.

Ruth couldn't help it. She walked over to take a look at the governor's party, set the pop down on the deck, and leaned over the railing so she could see better.

The governor looked up, spotted her, and waved. Ruth waved back.

I'm sure he can see I'm part of the show. She gave a wide smile and waved again as the governor threw her a kiss. She threw one back. Then her breath caught as she recognized the woman right behind the governor and his wife. It was Blanche Voorhees.

Oh my god, she's here!

Blanche Voorhees wore a lime-green suit with a short, extremely tight jacket and long, slim skirt, which showed off her voluptuous frame to great advantage. The low-cut jacket revealed ample cleavage.

Lord! She looks absolutely predatory.

The diva's coal-black hair was pulled back and gathered in a bun at the nape of her neck. Long, snake-like tendrils of hair dangled around her face.

She's like Medusa.

Blanche walked like a woman with a mission, her high heels clacking on the deck as she made her entrance.

Fritz greeted the governor and his wife amid much banter and exchanges of hugs. Vivian stood by at the periphery, waiting to be acknowledged. Finally, Fritz remembered his wife and brought her forward. Ruth noticed that Vivian curtsied when she met the governor.

Then Ruth saw Blanche come up to Fritz. Saw him stiffen when the woman grabbed his shoulders and "air-kissed" him on both cheeks. Fritz muttered something—Ruth couldn't tell what—and saw Blanche's dark brown eyes grow wide and then narrow again, in anger. Vivian stepped forward and led Fritz away.

I'd better stop gawking at Delancy May's girlfriend and get the drinks to the costume crew, Ruth chided to herself as she turned from the railing and bent down to pick up the cans of pop.

"Here, let me help you." It was Delancy Mays, who had come up the stairs quietly and now stood behind her.

"Oh!" Ruth gulped. "You startled me." Her face turned crimson as she stood up quickly, dropping two of the pop cans. They immediately rolled down the deck.

"Sorry, I didn't mean to ... that is ... I ..." The words escaped him. With long strides, he retrieved the errant cans. Putting them in his vest pockets, he picked up two others while Ruth picked up two more. His hands brushed against hers as they did so. "Oops, sorry again," he told her. "Actually, I came up here to hide. I ... well, I guess I ... oh never mind," he told her, shrugging his shoulders. He held up one of the cold cans of pop. "Is one of these for me? I hope?" he asked her, diffidently.

"Yes, yes, it is. I thought I'd treat the costume crew." Ruth regained her composure and found Delancy's embarrassment endearing.

"You are a fine lady. A true lady, in the best sense of the word," he said. He stood close to her, looking into her eyes. "It's a rare quality these days."

"It's just Seven-Up," Ruth said, surprised and pleased. Her heart beat rapidly.

"Well," Del said, "let's go down and get thrown to the proverbial wolves."

Chapter 15

A Brave Rescue

As usual when in front of an appreciative audience, Fritz was in top form. Before the performance, he stepped onto the stage and briefly explained the plot of *Show Boat* to his audience. He had a way of mesmerizing a crowd.

Everyone seemed to take in the ambience: the large white paddle boat with colorful trim moving slowly down the Mississippi; the steep muddy banks held together, it seemed, by interlacing tree roots; the lush forest and meadows rising up beyond those banks; the warm, summer sky with its lazy clouds moving almost as slowly as the river. It was magical.

After Fritz's story-telling, he conducted the music. He even let the governor step up and conduct "Make Believe," stopping him several times to correct him (to the uproarious delight of everyone).

The governor, in retaliation, shared some funny anecdotes about Fritz's early days in the orchestra pit. The governor's uncle had apparently known Fritz "way back when" and he regaled the jovial audience with stories of "the only man in Minnesota ornerier than myself!"

The chorus sounded better than in any of the rehearsals, and the soloists were in fine form. Delancy Mays brought down the house with his moving rendition of "Ol' Man River." He even sang an encore reprise because the audience applauded and cheered until he agreed to do so. Ruth glanced over at Blanche Voorhees when Del sang.

She looks as though she's crazy about him, Ruth thought with a sinking heart. *Maybe he feels the same way about her—not that I blame him. I have to admit, she is stunning!* Then her thoughts shifted: *I wonder what just went on between her and Fritz?*

Ruth noticed that Billy Hammer and his wife Lorene were among the guests. Billy looked dapper in a summer-weight gray suit and Lorene was lovely in a sheer, pink chiffon dress that seemed to float as she moved.

There was a large police body guard that Ruth thought must be for the governor and his wife. She looked for Sergeant Sullivan in the crowd, but didn't see him.

I still want to talk to him about ... things.

Danny Ancino was dressed in his Ravenal costume. Ruth saw him being patted on the back and congratulated by an expensively dressed older gentleman whose thick fingers glittered with diamonds. Ruth guessed he was the notorious Uncle Tony.

Each of the children in the group who didn't have parents in the chorus was assigned to an adult who would watch over them. Those who did have parents in the show stuck close to them. Ruth could see Rhonda Olson and Rodney, looking out over the water.

She looks so young to be his mother.

After the performance, all members of the cast were given box lunches. Angie ran up to Ruth and whispered loudly, "Mr. Gorgeous wants you on the second deck toward the back of the boat, with your lunch. Go on. I'll eat lunch with Vivian," she winked.

"Who? What's going on?" Ruth asked.

"Just trust me. Go!" Angie grinned as she pushed Ruth toward the stairs.

I must be crazy to do this! Ruth thought, as she went up to the second deck and found a secluded bench in a shaded alcove near the stern. The drone of the engine in the bowels of the boat and the churning, sloshing paddle wheel were the only sounds that could be heard. She sat down, arranged her skirts, and tried to calm herself by looking through her box lunch. It had a turkey croissant sandwich, some potato salad, a pickle, and a bottle of iced tea. She took out her napkin and looked around nervously. *Did Angie make this up?* she wondered.

Del came up the stairs, smiling as he walked toward her. "Do you mind if I join you?"

Ruth's mouth went dry as she moved over on the bench to make room. Without saying a word, she opened up her bottle of iced tea and took a sip. *I feel like a school-girl!* she thought, heart pounding.

Ruth felt as though she shouldn't encourage him, but something in her also wanted to see how far this could go. She took a deep breath, and sipped her iced tea slowly, desperately trying to think of small talk. She avoided looking at Mr. Mays, gazing instead at the river.

"You know," Del said with a grin, sensing her discomfort, "I've already held you in my arms. Remember Fritz's basement stairs? It's not as though we're complete strangers." He put his hand on her arm and let it linger there.

Ruth's anxiety began to dissolve. "Yes, you have," she laughed as she looked at his hand. "That was quite a night, wasn't it," she said, recalling the explosion of the Rosenberg's car.

"It certainly was." Del frowned with the memory of it. "I was worried about being on a boat with this bunch. After all, anything could happen here and we couldn't get away … and I'm a lousy swimmer!" he chuckled.

"I'm a pretty good swimmer. But with this dress I'd probably sink like a stone." She self-consciously smoothed her dress over her thighs.

"It's a lovely dress … and I never got the chance to tell you how much I enjoyed your singing during the auditions. Have you ever heard Diana Krall? She sings jazz."

Ruth shook her head. "No, I'm not up on jazz singers."

"You sound a lot like her. I have some of her CDs. I'd be glad to lend them to you."

"That would be nice." *Hmm, maybe he has etchings, too,* she thought.

"My late wife loved this river," Del said quietly.

His late wife? So he's not divorced. Good, because if he was divorced, I would wonder why?

Del continued. "We used to have a farm about ten miles beyond those bluffs." He pointed southward. "I didn't farm it. I was too busy with my musical career, but Elaine did. Grew just about all our vegetables. Our daughter Elizabeth ate very few store-bought vegetables before she left for college." He sat silent for a moment.

"Do you still live there?" Ruth asked.

"Oh no. The suburbs were encroaching on it and a developer offered a very good price. So, after Elaine died, I sold it and moved to a condo in the Ramsey-Hill neighborhood. The farm was too much to keep up and, well, I felt alone out there."

He looked in Ruth's lunch box. "Why, they forgot to give you a brownie. Here, have half of mine." He broke his in half and gave the larger portion to Ruth.

"No, no, you keep it." She waved it away.

"I insist," he said, putting the dessert bar in her box.

"Well, okay, thank you," she said. "It does look good."

"How about you?" Del asked. "Vivian tells me your husband died ... what ... four years ago?"

"Yes. Almost five. I keep busy though." Ruth didn't want to sound as if she was lonely.

"My daughter Hannah and her husband, and their nine-year-old daughter Annika, live in Plymouth, but right now they're in Sweden working with a consortium to combat some kind of a global temperature change. My son, Robbie, is an elementary principal in Evanston, north of Chicago, so I sometimes travel to see him. And I volunteer at church. And I paint." She took a deep breath. "And I have a dog and two cats. Actually two dogs because one of them belongs to Angie and she's staying with me right now. Boy, do I sound boring!" she laughed.

"Not at all!" Del smiled down at her. "It sounds quite wonderful. So what do you paint?"

"Oh, landscapes, mostly. Acrylics. Nothing very ... you know ... just quiet little landscapes."

"Are you represented by a gallery? I'd love to ..."

Suddenly Ruth heard the clacking of heels heading in their direction. It was Blanche Voorhees, swooping down.

"Why, Delancey Mays," she purred, "I've been looking all over this boat for you, you naughty boy! The governor wants to meet you, and I said I would produce you, so come along!" Ignoring Ruth, she put her hands around Del's arm.

Del rose slowly. "Ruth, I'd like to present Miss Blanche Voorhees. Blanche, this is Mrs. Ruth Carson."

Ruth nodded and lied, "I'm pleased to meet—"

"Yes, yes," Blanche interrupted. "Come along now. The governor—"

"The governor can wait," said Del firmly, sitting back down. "Ruth and I are having our lunch."

"But Del. The governor wants to meet you—*now*."

"Ruth and I are eating our lunch," he said quietly but resolutely.

Blanche glared at Ruth, gave her a frosty smile, turned, and left with much clacking of heels.

Del looked at Ruth and smiled conspiratorially. "That went well, don't you think?"

"I don't know what to think," Ruth answered, perplexed. "What about the governor?"

"She probably made it up." Del sounded resigned. "Divas! Sort of like two-year-olds in adult bodies."

"Well, I certainly don't want to get on the wrong side of her."

"That awful woman? Don't worry, she's always upset with somebody." Del let out an exasperated sigh. "I took her to a cast party once. She called me and said her car was in the shop and she needed a ride." He shook his head. "When we got there, the place was crawling with reporters. She hung on my arm as if she was drowning. Our picture was taken and the rest, as they say, is tabloid history." He looked at Ruth. "Don't believe everything you see in the papers."

Ruth, relieved, smiled and leaned back. "Okay, I won't."

Del turned toward her, "Let's change the subject. My place could use some paintings. The walls are almost bare. What gallery shows your work?"

"Good heavens!" Ruth laughed. "I'm not important enough to be represented by a gallery." She shrugged. "I used to be an art teacher. Now I'm retired and I finally have the time to paint a little. That's all. And I will *give* you a painting if you'd like, for your poor bare walls."

"No, no," he insisted. "I would expect to pay for your artwork. Really, Ruth, I would like see them—and buy one."

"Absolutely not!" she said in mock anger. "You shared your brownie with me. The least I can do is share my paintings with you!"

By now, Ruth's uneasiness had dissipated. "So tell me," she said, "why you are involved in this production, singing with a bunch of amateurs like us? To be honest, this seems like a step down for you—someone who normally sings in big-time opera houses all over the country."

Del hesitated as he stared out toward the lush riverbank passing by. "I needed a break from all that. My schedule had been going full steam for too long and I decided to give myself a respite, something longer than the usual week or so before heading off to the next production. Somehow Fritz caught wind of it and called, asking if I would please, please take on this role since I was going to be staying in town this summer. The fact is, I owed him a favor—and he knew it—because of some big favors he had done for me when I was just getting started with my career. He had also been very supportive of my daughter, Elizabeth. She sung in a few of his shows when she was young."

"So here you are ..."

Del turned and looked into Ruth's eyes. "Yep. Here I am. I just couldn't say no to Fritz."

Ruth and Del spent the next half hour talking quietly and laughing often. If any other cast members saw anything unseemly in the couple's behavior, they said nothing. Both looked a trifle let down when the boat finally pulled up to the landing and the river cruise ended.

Del spoke first. "This has been one of the most pleasant afternoons I've had in a long time." He took Ruth's hand in his. "I would like it, well, perhaps we could go out to dinner? Or a concert? If you ... or ... your children, ah ... well, you know ... don't mind the *race* thing?"

"Del ... Del." She quieted him by holding up her other hand. "It's fine, and I would love to."

Just after the boat was secured to the dock, they heard frantic screams on the deck below. It was Rhonda Olson. "Rodney fell in the river! Help him, please! He can't swim! Help! Save my boy!"

Del was down the stairs in a flash, tore off his jacket, and unhesitatingly dove into the water where Rhonda was pointing.

I thought he said he was a lousy swimmer, thought Ruth as she hastily followed him down the stairs.

Del was under a few seconds and then rose up out of the murky water like a huge fish, the whites of his eyes wide and frightened-looking. He took a deep breath of air and dove under once more.

Ruth could hear Rhonda sobbing, "Oh, please! Please! Save him!" A few other passengers had come to the railing to watch.

Oh God! Please ... Del ... Rodney ... please be all right, Ruth prayed.

It seemed like an eternity, but it was probably only seconds when Del rose out of the river again. This time he held a choking boy.

Rodney was coughing up water but alive. Rhonda leaned over to take him from his rescuer, but the deckhands edged her out of the way and tossed a life buoy attached to a rope that Del could hang on to while they lowered a small life raft for the man and the boy. From the raft they pulled them both onto the deck.

"Come on, son. That's right. That a boy. Cough it up!" They leaned him forward and pounded on his back to get more river water out of him. Rodney's ashen face began to redden as he coughed and coughed. "You're one lucky kid, that's for sure!"

Rhonda knelt on the deck and hugged and kissed her son, then jumped up and hugged and kissed and thanked her son's very wet rescuer, who looked embarrassed by all the fuss. Angie, Ruth, the rest of the cast, and many of the passengers praised Del for his bravery. Clearly uncomfortable, Del just shook his head.

Someone had already called 911 and an ambulance pulled up to the dock minutes later. Rodney kept insisting he was all right, but Rhonda wanted him to see a doctor just in case. Ruth watched Rhonda Olson, her arm around her only child, walk down the gangplank and onto dry land. She saw the ambulance drive about a block away, and then make a quick U-turn and come back. A white-faced Rhonda came running up the plank once more, and Ruth was the first person she saw.

"Ruth!" the frightened woman whispered. "Warn the others! Rodney said he didn't fall. Someone pushed him!" Then, without another word, she turned and ran back to the ambulance and her waiting son.

"My God!" Ruth gasped. Just then, Del, who had been a few feet away, came up to her.

"Did she just say what I think she said?" He was wrapped in one of the boat's wool emergency blankets.

"Who would push a little boy off a boat?"

It was too much for Ruth. Tears spilled over her cheeks, her shoulders shook, and her hands made a helpless gesture as she tried to wipe her tears away. "Who ... who on earth would intentionally do that to a little boy?" she sobbed.

Delancy Mays took Ruth in his arms for the second time.

"Hush now, shh. He's safe now. He's safe."

Ruth let him hold her and rock her like a baby while she cried, feeling very safe herself in his arms.

Chapter 16

Any Press is Good Press

DEL HURRIED AND GOT a Coke from the boat's bartender to take to Ruth, who sat shivering on a bench near the gangplank. He also grabbed another of the boat's blankets and wrapped her in it.

Ruth didn't want the Coke because it wasn't "diet," but he insisted.

"You need the sugar," he told her. "I don't want you going into shock on me." Then, pulling the blanket closer around her, he excused himself. "Please wait for me," he told her. "I have to see the police and then change out of this wet costume. I'll be right back."

Ruth sat there as she was told, wrapped in the blanket, sipping on the Coke.

Del, still dripping wet, went to talk with the police. The governor and Fritz were there, too. They began congratulating him on his bravery. "Please," Del said, holding up his hand, "I need to tell you something. This is important." When they heard what Rhonda had told him, Sergeant Don Olson, who had been in charge of the police detail that day, wondered out loud why anyone would target a child.

"Don't worry, sir," he told the governor. "We'll find whoever did this. We have the passenger list and we'll go through it with a fine-toothed comb." The governor nodded.

"I think the target was anybody in the theatre group," Del said quietly.

"Why?" the sergeant asked. "Why would anybody target a bunch of actors?"

Del shrugged and left to change his clothes. Fritz just put his head in his hands.

Back on the bench, Ruth began to feel better. *At least Rodney is safe, for now,* she thought, looking up as she heard Angie's excited voice.

"Ruthie! Are you alright?" Angie looked bewildered. "I heard that Rodney fell into the river and then I saw you crying, but I was helpin' Vivian with the costumes and I couldn't get close to you. I had to put the dresses down first because Vivian didn't want 'em mussed up. Then Gloria-June started orderin' me around. God, that woman is irritating! Then I saw that Del was holdin' ya ..." Both women instantly turned their heads at the clacking of high heels. Ruth's heart sank.

"What is going on?" an angry Blanche Voorhees demanded to know. Ruth thought she looked disheveled.

"What do you mean, what's going on?" Ruth asked her.

"I mean, why was he all wet? Ignoring Angie, she all but stamped her foot in front of Ruth.

"You didn't see him rescue that little boy?" Angie asked her.

"What little boy?" Blanche turned to her, exasperated. "All I saw of Del was his back as he went into the men's room. And he was soaking wet and wrapped in a blanket! What happened? What did you do to him?" She looked menacingly at Ruth.

"Where were you," she asked the diva, "about fifteen minutes ago when Del dove into the river and rescued a drowning boy?"

"Yeah, where were ya?" repeated Angie.

Blanche pursed her lips. "I was up in the pilot house with the captain. He's an old friend and he was showing me how to steer the boat."

"Oh!" laughed Angie. "Is *that* what they call it now?" She rolled her eyes.

Ruth, noticing Blanche's mussed hair-do and rumpled appearance, remembered reading about Blanche Voorhees' sexual exploits, as well as her temper. "Yes, while you were busy in the pilot house, *steering*, Del was busy rescuing a little boy," she told her pointedly.

"I don't like your tone," Blanche said defiantly, "and I *really* don't like your messing around with my man!"

Angie let out a snort of laughter and stepped between the two women.

"What?!" Ruth squared her shoulders and peered around Angie. "First of all, I don't 'mess around,' as you so colorfully put it. And he is not 'my man.' And in any case, don't you think Del has something to say about who his friends are?"

"I know what Del needs, and it isn't some little arsty-fartsy theatre-wannabee from the middle of nowhere!" Blanche spit the words out at Ruth.

"Now you just wait a minute!" Ruth gently pushed Angie aside and stood up to her full five-foot four-inch height. She let the blanket fall from her shoulders. "If you think for one minute that I'm going to take this kind of abuse from a ... from a ..."

Ruth's words fell on deaf ears because Blanche Voorhees had already turned on her high heels and was clacking her way down the gang-plank toward dry land.

"Bitch!" Angie said loudly after her.

Just then, Del came up to the two women. He had seen Blanche leave. "I hope Blanche wasn't giving you ladies any grief." He picked up the blanket and put it on a deck chair.

"Hah! Ruthie and I can take care of ourselves," Angie assured him, hands on her hips.

"Oof!" Ruth looked up at him, exasperated. "What a terrible woman. How can you stand her?"

"I can't. I don't know why she has this 'thing' for me. It isn't reciprocated, I can assure you."

Ruth was incredulous. "She actually told me she didn't want me messing with *her* man!"

"Oh lord. I'm so sorry." Del shook his head.

"Well, *I'm* not sorry," Angie countered. "We got to see the real her." Then she patted Ruth on the back and said, "I'll be in the car if you need me."

After saying "goodbye" to Angie, Del turned to Ruth. "I talked with the police. They have a list of all the passengers. They had to with the governor's party. Extra precautions." Del looked in Ruth's eyes. "They'll find him, Ruth. I'm sure they'll figure out who did this. Don't you worry."

"I just can't believe it. Why hurt that sweet little boy?" Ruth stared out at the river.

"He's safe now." Del looked down at her with a smile. "Hmm, let's see. I wonder where could I buy us some supper? Or maybe just a drink and appetizer?"

"I'm so sorry. I can't. I want to go home," Ruth told him. "It's been too big a day and I'm absolutely exhausted. Perhaps another time." Ruth glanced down at her dress, still wet where Del had held her. "Besides, Angie and I came together, already dressed in our costumes. Maybe another day. Really, I mean it. I would like to go to dinner with you, but Angie and I need to get back ..." Her voice trailed off.

"I would love to take her, too," he assured her. "I think she approves of me." He smiled in the direction of Ruth's car.

"Please, Del. I can't go anywhere dressed like this."

"Alright. Okay. I'll take a rain-check. Are you sure you can drive?"

"Oh yes. I'll be all right. Thank you so much for the invitation, though. Maybe ... later this week?"

"How about tomorrow?" Del was persistent. "I hear the Sunday brunches at Lake Elmo Inn are especially good."

"I've got a better idea," Ruth answered. "Why don't you just come to my house for brunch—say about eleven? You can pick out a painting."

"It's a deal! But I will bring some wine. And the dessert."

Ruth let out a breath. "Ok, some kind of rosé I think, that will go with anything I make. As for dessert ..." She paused, trying to think of something.

"Something chocolate? I hope," he added.

"Chocolate's my favorite," Ruth assured him.

Del looked at his coffee-colored hands a moment and then looked up, his brown eyes twinkling. "Glad to hear it!"

Blushing, and trying not to smile, Ruth gave him instructions to her home and promised to be careful on the drive home.

Del walked her to her car and told her, "All kidding aside, I'm really looking forward to tomorrow!"

"Me too," she whispered as she slid behind the wheel. Angie was sound asleep.

Ruth drove home slowly. Angie murmured, smiled at Ruth, and closed her eyes again. Ruth had a lot to think about. When she was in that kind of mood, she drove slower than usual.

Who would have pushed Rodney in the river? And how did Blanche Voorhees find out so much about me? Artsy-fartsy? Theatre-wannabee? Honestly! she muttered to herself. She also thought about Del. *He's really something. And that smile! And those eyes ...* In spite of herself, Ruth was feeling things she hadn't felt for some time.

The ride to Ruth's home became more scenic as they neared Ruth's Lake Elmo home. The passing landscape—still mostly agricultural—calmed her as it always had. The trees were particularly beautiful along the lake as she drove down Lake Elmo Avenue. She loved this little town with its quaint main street and store fronts looking much as they might have, long ago. She turned down her street, past a few small houses with large yards, past a wooded area with birch trees bordering a small pond, and finally into her own driveway. Large oaks dotted her yard and the lake glistened in the distance.

When she stopped at her garage, Ruth said quietly to Angie, "Wake up, sleepy-head, we're home."

Angie muttered, "Hmpf! That didn't take long."

Ruth let the dogs out first thing, but kept an eye on them. Once they had finished their business, she called them back in, saw that all the animals were fed, and joined Angie in the kitchen after changing out of her costume. They had both decided that "comfy" was the right thing to wear for the rest of the day. Angie put on a large flowered caftan and Ruth slipped into navy-blue sweats.

Ruth fixed a large plate with some grapes, crackers, and cheese. She poured a glass of orange juice for each of them, brought everything into the living room, and turned on the television. She wanted to see if there was anything about Rodney on the 5:00 news.

"You suppose we're on TV?" Angie asked, helping herself to the crackers and cheese. "I'd like to see myself on TV, although I know it would make me look ten pounds heavier," she sighed.

"We're not important enough," Ruth replied, breaking off a cluster of grapes, "but the governor is. I suppose he'll be on. And maybe something about Del rescuing Rodney."

"Or that horrible Blanche Voorhees! She probably tried to get in front of the camera," Angie spit out.

Ruth laughed.

They watched the evening news on Channel 11, Ruth's favorite station, and saw full coverage of the river cruise and even the rescue.

"It's too bad they spent so much time talking about the rescue instead of the show coming up at Como Park," Ruth commented, "but Fritz always says that 'any press is good press,' so I suppose it's better than nothing." The segment showed Del, still in his wet clothes, talking to the police and the governor. There was no glimpse of the haughty Blanche Voorhees.

"Oh boy!" Angie chortled, slugging down her juice. "That'll get her undies in a bunch."

"I guess she was too busy 'steering' the boat," Ruth said, and they both laughed.

As they cleared the dishes away, Ruth realized that she had better get up to Gustafson's Grocery if she was going to have Del over for brunch tomorrow.

Angie settled down in her room to read a "trashy novel," as she put it, while Ruth checked her refrigerator. *Eggs, milk, butter, cheese … good, I can make omelets. I wonder if he likes ham? Better get some of that,* she thought.

Ruth let the dogs out once more, and as she stood at her back door waiting for Charlie and Toby to come in, she remembered, *Danny Ancino's uncle was on that boat … I think. If that's who he was, is he capable of such a terrible thing? My god, I hope not! And why would he want to kill Rodney?*

Outside, the two dogs sniffed each other and sniffed the small piles each had made under the lilac bushes at the edge of the yard. *Fertilizer,* Ruth thought, as she stood in the door and they headed back toward her. *Even if Uncle Tony wanted to hurt Fritz in some way, Rodney wasn't crucial to the show. It would still go on. Well maybe not if Rhonda couldn't be replaced.* Ruth finally gave up thinking about it. *I've got to stop this!* she chided herself. *I have a brunch to plan.*

She let the dogs in and looked at her two cats. "Okay, Morrie, Griselda," she said to the felines sitting expectantly on two kitchen chairs. "I'm not forgetting you. What do you think, babies?" She talked to all four animals: "Tomorrow mama and Angie are going to have a very handsome gentleman visitor."

After informing Angie she was going for groceries, Ruth grabbed her purse and ran a brush through her hair. She drove straight to Gustafson's, where she bought some thin slices of ham, some flaky croissants, and a can of tomato juice and a lemon. *He might rather have tomato juice than orange juice,* she thought. Then she added a box of strawberries and a box of blueberries. *I'll make muffins. Mine are delicious, if I do say so myself!* Then, feeling as if she had gone overboard, she started to put the croissants back, but hesitated. *No,* she thought. *If we don't eat them tomorrow, Angie and I can have them for lunch on Monday.*

Ruth paid for the groceries and briefly discussed the weather with the chatty girl at the check-out. Then she put the groceries on the front seat of her car and headed home.

I'd better get out some of my paintings and set them up in the living room. I hope he likes them, really, and won't just be polite. And I hope he likes my cooking... Okay, Ruth. Stop fretting. It's just a brunch... a couple of friends... nothing to get worked up about.

That night, Tracey called Angie.

"She was acting weird," Angie told Ruth after hanging up the phone. "I think she's got a new boyfriend. And she said not to call her unless it's an emergency—as if I would!"

Chapter 17

Lake Elmo

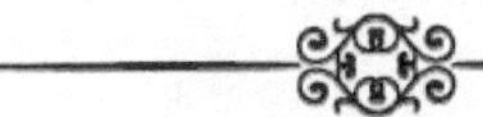

SUNDAY DAWNED OVERCAST AND chilly. Ruth was glad because she had a lot of cooking to do. Not wanting to miss church, however, she went to the early service at Christ Lutheran, which was only a five minutes' drive from her house. Angie slept in. Ruth sat toward the back and after the final hymn and benediction, she hurried out the door and headed straight home.

When Ruth pulled into her driveway, Angie was sitting under a tree, sipping a cup of coffee and watching the dogs frolic in the yard.

"I'm going in to start the egg dish, and muffins," she called to Angie, who gave her a thumbs-up sign.

While Ruth was getting things ready in the kitchen, Angie sauntered in. "I just talked with that cutie-pie, George, and, whaddaya think? He wondered if I wanted to go to Perkins in Stillwater." She looked at Ruth. "Just as friends, he said." Angie looked uncertain. "Do you think it's okay? He seems lonely."

"Well, you know I'm having Del over for brunch." Ruth looked uncertain.

"That's why I thought it might be a good idea for me to go with George." Angie told her.

"I think it's fine for you to go to brunch with George—as a friend." Ruth looked at her. "But to be honest, I thought I'd rather have you here today. Del will think I got rid of you on purpose."

Angie smiled. "I hope he does. Anyway, George told me I made him feel less lonely."

Not much later Ruth watched as a very solicitous George helped Angie into his car.

I guess they both deserve some happiness in their lives, Ruth thought. *And so do I.*

Del arrived early, just as Ruth was taking the muffins out of the oven.

"Oh god!" she muttered, running over to the kitchen mirror to fix her hair. Quickly, she grabbed her compact from her purse, powdered her nose and took off her apron, hanging it on its hook on the wall. Del was striding up to her back door when she opened it. "Welcome!" she beamed.

Both dogs ran to greet him, tales wagging furiously. "Well, well, who are you?" he said as he bent to pet them. "I see you have guard dogs. Good!"

Ruth laughed. "You can see how fierce they are." She held the door open for him, stepping aside as he moved past her and into her kitchen.

"It's beautiful out here," Del commented. "And this house ... I would say ... built in the 1930s. Am I right?"

"Very good," Ruth responded, glad to instantly have something to talk about. "Built in 1935 to be exact. My husband looked it up. He always wanted to know the years our houses were built."

Del looked at his watch. "I apologize for being early. I've never driven out here before. I thought it would take longer."

"That's all right, please sit down," She motioned to one of the white kitchen chairs before realizing that Morrie was on it. "I have a menagerie I'm afraid."

Del lifted Morrie gently and sat down, cradling the cat in his arms. To Ruth's surprise, the animal just yawned and found a comfortable position in Del's lap.

"That's a first," she told him. "He doesn't take to strangers."

"Animals usually like me." Del stroked Morrie's back with his long fingers. "We always had a cat or two at home, and dogs." He looked down at Toby and Charlie, who were sitting at his feet. "Something smells awfully good."

"We're having blueberry muffins, cheese omelets and ham, croissants, strawberries …"

"Oh no!" Del interrupted, looking dismayed. Morrie jumped off his lap and headed for the living room to join Griselda, who was watching from the doorway.

"What, are you allergic?"

"No, it's the chocolate. The dessert." Del groaned. "I bought some Bavarian chocolates at this very posh store in New York the last time I was there. I've been saving them for a special occasion, which this is." He hit his head with his hand. "I'm such an idiot! I forgot to bring them."

"That's okay," Ruth told him. "You've had a lot on your mind." She put her hand on his shoulder. "I have plenty of food. We'll enjoy them some other time."

Del put his hand over Ruth's. "Promise?"

"I promise. Now," sounding businesslike, "tea or coffee?"

"Tea, please. With a little milk if you have some. And I'm really sorry about forgetting the chocolates. I promised dessert."

Ruth poured his tea. "I will enjoy them all the more if I can anticipate them for a while."

"Are you teasing me, Miss Ruth?" he said with a wink as he took a sip of the tea.

"No ... yes ... I mean no ... I don't know why I said that." Ruth patted her hair nervously, fumbling for words. She turned to the stove. "Time for me to make the omelets now."

Del just sat there, silently drinking his tea. "So, where's Angie?" He'd finally noticed she wasn't there.

"Angie has found a friend in my neighbor, George Sandstrom. They took off for Perkins just before you came. I'm sorry," Ruth stammered.

"I'm not." Del grinned, setting down his cup and standing up. He went over to Ruth and put his hands on her shoulders.

"I don't really know what's happening here," Ruth said softly, not looking at him. "I'm not used to this."

Del leaned his chin on her head as his arms enfolded her. "I'm not either. I was married a long time, and there hasn't been anyone else since my wife—whatever the tabloids say about me and the awful Ms. Voorhees ..." He kissed the top of her head, gathering Ruth closer.

Ruth could hardly breathe. Del just stood there, holding her in his arms, before swinging her around to face him. He looked into her eyes.

"Let's take it slow," he said, "and get to be good friends. Let's see what happens. I just have a good feeling about you." He pulled her gently into an embrace again and then, just as quickly, let her go. "I did say 'slow,' didn't I?" he added smiling as he sat back down.

Flustered, Ruth said nothing before returning to her omelet preparation, pausing every once in a while to look reassuringly at Del. Finally, struggling for words, she settled on a cliché: "I believe if something's meant to be, it will be."

"Que sera, sera," Del sang. Glad to change the subject, he asked, "Did you see that movie? The one where Doris Day sang that song?"

"Yes, I love Hitchcock movies." Ruth also was glad to change the subject. "But I usually get nervous when they show them on TV, so I don't watch them if I'm here alone. I'm a little isolated out here ... and they're scary."

"Maybe we can rent one sometime and watch it together," Del offered.

"I would love that. I'll make popcorn." She flipped an omelet from the frying pan to a serving dish.

The omelets were good. The muffins turned out perfectly. And while they ate, they talked. Del was appreciative of Ruth's cooking. He ate heartily and praised the food so often that she finally blurted out, "Enough already! I'm not all that great a cook. My repertoire is limited, actually. Let's see ... I make good spaghetti, and good chicken in cranberry sauce, and ... well, okay, I can make reservations. I'm especially good at those."

"I like a woman with some reservations," Del shot back.

"Oh no you don't. Not that again," Ruth laughed.

"Okay, I'll behave." Finished eating, he wiped his mouth with his napkin and leaned back in his chair, "Now, how 'bout those paintings of yours?"

"They're in the living room," she said. "Go on in and look at them while I clean up here. That way I won't have to see your disappointed face when you first see them." Ruth started to clear the table.

"As if I'd have a disappointed face," Del snorted as he walked through the door into the living room.

A few seconds went by and Ruth held her breath. Then she heard Del exclaim, "Ruth, these are really good! Are they all for sale?"

"They are all 'for you,' if you like." Ruth stood at the door separating the two rooms, watching Del as he paced from one painting to another.

Ruth had set up four paintings—two large and two small ones. The large ones were winter landscapes, showing different views of the frozen lake and the trees around her property. The two smaller ones were also landscapes: a summer scene of the pond behind her property and a brilliantly colorful fall scene of a road winding through a grove of birch.

"I know just where I'll put this one," Del said as he picked up one of the larger winter scenes. "On the wall across from my bed, so I can see it first thing in the morning when I wake up." He hesitated. "Ruth, these are wonderful. You have to let me pay for these."

"Don't be silly," she told him.

"You can't mean that."

"I don't sell my work. I give it to people who appreciate it."

"Well, I can tell you that *I* appreciate it. You are very good." He picked up the small one with the birches. "We had birches on our farm," he added quietly.

"I'm glad you like them. Really, I want to have someone who truly *likes* them to *have* them." She put her hands up to her mouth for a moment. "I'm sorry you'll have to get them framed. Tom used to make all my frames in his workshop in the basement …" She got a lump in her throat and her eyes began welling up.

"Well then, I know what I can do to repay you," Del said heartily. "I can make some frames for you whenever you need them. I have the tools I need in my basement."

"Yes, I would love that." Ruth smiled at him, dabbing her eyes with a Kleenex. "Sorry."

"Don't be," Del assured her. "We're getting into unknown territory here. We are bound to be a little emotional."

They settled into Ruth's cushy living room couch for a while and Del told her where, in his house, he wanted to put the rest of her paintings. She explained some of the reasons she painted landscapes as she did, and he asked intelligent questions about her work, impressing her with his knowledge of art. The morning became afternoon and the time went quickly. When Del finally said it was time to leave, Ruth was sorry to see him go.

"Are you ready for a real date with me now?" he asked Ruth. She said she was, and agreed to go to lunch with him at the Muffuletta in St. Anthony Park the following Friday evening. "We aren't going to have many more Fridays left, but after the show is over, I'll take you someplace even fancier to eat, and maybe a concert somewhere," he promised as he started for the kitchen door. "I have a good feeling about us." He kissed the top of her head and exited the way he came in.

Angie returned home later that afternoon.

"You missed a good meal this morning," Ruth told her, looking up from the mystery novel she was reading. "There are some leftovers in the fridge if you're hungry. There's some ham and the blueberry muffins turned out especially good."

"We went to Perkins, and then we drove to White Bear Lake to look at condos," Angie told her. "I told him he'd be crazy to move out of Lake Elmo but he said there's too many memories in his house and it's too big anyway for just him. His wife is not doing well ... she doesn't even wake up much. Poor guy."

Angie checked out the refrigerator and came back with two muffins and a glass of milk. She sat down on the sofa next to Ruth. "I like George. He's really nice to me, but I don't know ... his wife's still alive, even if she's fading away and doesn't recognize him anymore. I don't know ... I guess we'll take it slow."

"Taking it slow is good," Ruth said." We should both take things slow, very slow."

Angie sighed, brushing crumbs off her ample bosom. "So, what's happening with Mr. Gorgeous?"

Ruth blushed and shook her head. She really didn't want to discuss it.

Angie went on. "I haven't had a 'date' for years, but George is easy to be with, and to talk to. I don't know what to do. I just feel ... so right with him."

"You're a good woman," Ruth responded, patting her shoulder. "And I think taking it slow is a very wise thing to do." Then, deciding to confide in Angie a little, Ruth added, "I'm starting to feel more comfortable with Del. And he liked my paintings."

"Yeah. You little artsy-fartsy theatre wannabee gal, you!" Angie chortled.

"And don't forget," Ruth laughed, "I'm also from the middle of nowhere!"

"I love the middle of nowhere," Angie retorted.

Both women laughed.

Angie changed the subject. "I think I know who Tracey is seeing."

"Who?"

"I have a hunch it's that Danny Ancino. I just have a feeling about him. I saw them talking together a lot while I was in the hospital. There seemed to be some chemistry there."

"Danny Ancino?" Ruth was alarmed. *Oh-oh,* she thought. *He could be trouble with a capital T.* But to Angie she merely said, "Well, if it *is* him, I hope she takes her time. Gets to really know him before she, well, you know ..." She was genuinely concerned, but didn't want to worry Angie unnecessarily.

"I hope so too," Angie sighed as she got up. "But she's a big girl and she can take care of herself—I think."

"We can't live their lives for them," Ruth said.

"And thank God for that," Angie said as she headed up the stairs. "It's hard enough living our own."

Vivian called and cancelled rehearsal that week because of "Rodney's trouble on the boat." She informed Ruth that most of the children had been removed from the show by their worried parents.

"Bad new travels fast," Vivian said sorrowfully. "Elena Cordova is still in the show, thank God, but her grandmother has insisted on being in the chorus so she can keep an eye on her."

After talking with Vivian, Ruth wondered if Rhonda had quit. Vivian didn't mention it, and Ruth didn't want to ask, which might have spurred Vivian to worry even more. Without rehearsals, the week went by slowly. Angie spent a lot of time at George's house, "helping him organize his stuff," she told Ruth. *Well, that's the blind leading the blind,* Ruth chuckled to herself, remembering Angie's disheveled apartment.

Del called on Wednesday to remind Ruth about their date on Friday.

As if I needed reminding, she thought. "Have you heard any new ideas about the theatre group, about who might want to hurt us?" she asked Del.

"No. That sergeant—Don Olson—called me, though. He left a message on my answering machine. He thinks for some reason that it was intended as a warning for the governor—because of the governor's proposed increase in the tax on liquor. That seems far-fetched to me."

Ruth agreed. "I hope they don't put us on the back burner and then someone else in our group gets hurt or killed. You know, until this gets solved, I think we'll all just have to keep our own eyes and ears open and watch out for each other."

"I would be glad to watch out for you," Del offered.

"You can watch for me on Friday," she told him primly. "I'll meet you at the restaurant. I'd rather drive in there than have you come all the way out here to pick me up. There would be no need for that."

Del argued that he didn't mind the drive, but Ruth held fast. She wanted to be under her own steam, as her grandmother would have put it. She felt more independent that way.

Chapter 18

The Date

FRIDAY FINALLY ROLLED AROUND. Ruth had her hair washed and styled in the morning at the little beauty shop on the main street in Lake Elmo. While getting ready, she frequently checked her appearance in her bedroom mirror.

"Well, babies," she told Morrie and Griselda, who were curled up on separate sides of her bed, "Mama has a date. What do you think of that?"

"We all think it's great!" Angie walked into her bedroom. "Oh, you look so nice! I love your hair wrapped up that way! And what are you wearing? Show me." She sat down in the chintz wing-backed chair by the window. "It's show-time!" she exclaimed as she rubbed her hands together.

Ruth started pulling things out of her closet and laying them out on her bed. "No, that's too tight" she murmured, holding it up to herself and looking in the mirror.

"No." said Angie. "I like it. It's sexy!"

"You *would* like it!" Ruth laughed, putting the offending dress back in the closet, then pulling out two more.

"This one's too 'churchy' and that one's too dressy. We're only going to the Muffuletta. Oh god, I'm acting like a teenager." Ruth was embarrassed that Angie was watching her, but her friend was enjoying it immensely.

By the time Ruth settled on the perfect little black dress and matching jacket with red, blue and yellow Mexican-like trim, she was already behind schedule.

"I'd better call Del and tell him I'm running late. I don't want him waiting there wondering. He might think I'm not going to show up."

Angie handed the bedroom phone to Ruth and moved out of the chair. "I've got a hot date with a good book. Have fun." As she left the room she looked back at her friend. "You look *very* nice," she said with a broad smile.

Del laughed when she called.

"I've been busy cleaning my house. I don't want you to feel sorry for a poor old widower when you come back here for an after-dinner drink." He told Ruth not to worry about the time and not to drive too fast. "Just tell me how long you think it will take you to get to the restaurant and I'll be there waiting for you."

Ruth told him she'd be about twenty minutes late and Del assured her that that was well within the bounds of good manners.

"I can't wait to see you," he said before hanging up.

"Me too," Ruth said. And she meant it.

I hope we have enough to talk about, she thought as she drove past the U of M's St. Paul campus and onto the meandering tree-lined streets of the comfortable St. Anthony Park neighborhood.

As she entered the Muffuletta, she saw Del rise from his table near the back. He gave her a small nosegay of flowers and bowed slightly. "Miss Ruth, may I present a little tribute from my neighbor's garden. He told me I could take some." He smiled and pulled out her chair.

Ruth thanked him for the flowers, adding, "And please thank your dear neighbor."

They were wrapped in a wet paper towel and tin-foil. She laid them next to her plate.

Ruth looked around. The restaurant wasn't crowded, but those who were there were obviously enjoying the wine and exceptional cuisine. The Muffuletta was intimate and quasi- upscale, nestled in the corner of a group of Tudor-style buildings called Milton Square. Its menu touted the savory New Orleans sandwich from which the place took its name, as well as salads, assorted sandwiches, a few main dishes and especially good desserts. The décor was understated, with subtle paintings on the walls, white table cloths, and a candle at each table. The lights were dimmed and gentle music played above the murmur of conversation.

"This is nice," she said.

"I think so too. I've always liked this place."

We probably look to everyone else as though we may be old friends, Ruth thought as the waitress took their orders. *And no one cares anymore who goes out with whom ... and he* is *a delightful dinner companion.*

She actually forgot, during their very pleasant meal together, all the trouble that befell the rehearsals of *Show Boat*. She forgot about Fritz. She forgot the sense of impending disaster she felt when she thought about opening night. She forgot Lionel and Angie and the Rosenberg's car and Rodney. Ruth concentrated instead on her chicken Caesar salad, the wonderful crusty rolls and, of course, Delancy Mays.

Del talked about his wife and daughter, Elizabeth, and some highlights of his career on the stages of musical theatres in the Twin Cities, New York, San Francisco, and others. He told Ruth that he'd been lucky to have some very good mentors and some fortunate breaks. He'd had a full personal and professional life.

"But you know," he added sadly, "when you have a good marriage, it's lonely when your partner is no longer there."

Ruth nodded in agreement and told Del about her family. She talked about Tom, about her daughter, Hannah and her husband, Rolf, and her granddaughter, Annika, and about her son, Robbie, and how proud she was of them all. She talked about her days as an art teacher in the public schools, about her painting and finally, about how she missed Tom and how she tried to fill her days with activities so she wouldn't feel lonely.

"And," Del put his hand over hers, "does it work?"

Ruth looked down at her empty plate. "Not always."

"Well, I think ..." Del began, but he was cut off before he could say another word.

Ruth had not noticed the clacking, but she felt a chill.

"Well, Delancy Mays, as I live and breathe!" It was Blanche, coming from out of nowhere, swooping down upon them, smiling with all her teeth. "And, Ruthie? Isn't it? How *wonderful* to run into you both!" She tossed her lime green shawl over the shoulder of her tight-fitting turquoise satin dress. "I was just telling Maxie here," she said as she flung a be-jeweled hand toward her escort—a stout, red-faced, elderly man who was a head shorter than her— "I was just telling him about your little community theatre group. How *absolutely wonderful* it is, and how he should invest some of his money in theatre groups that let *absolutely anyone* sing and act in them. Didn't I, Maxie?"

"Yeah, sure, you did that," Maxie managed to stammer.

Ruth was dumbstruck, but Del took the interruption in stride. He rose gracefully, introduced himself and Ruth to Maxie and, ignoring Blanche, said, "I hope we can meet some other time when we can sit and talk. It was so nice of you to stop by our table. We were just leaving. It was good to meet you." He reached out to shake Maxie's stubby fingers. "Excuse us, please." He touched Ruth on the shoulder and hastily guided her to the front of the restaurant, paid the check, and hurried outside, leaving Blanche and Maxie to themselves.

"What was that all about?" Ruth whispered.

"I have no idea," Del whispered back.

"Could she be stalking you?" Ruth asked.

"Lord, I hope not." Del sounded grim.

He led her to his car and opened the passenger side door for Ruth. "We'll come back later for your car."

Del slid into the driver's side. "I think we need that after-dinner drink," he sighed. "Maybe two."

Ruth started to laugh, putting her head in her hands.

Del started laughing, too. "And some Bavarian chocolate."

"Oh, yes, and two of those, too."

Now they were both laughing. Del flung his tie over his shoulder and said in a falsetto voice, "Oh Maxie! I want you to meet two *wonderful* people!"

Ruth giggled back. "And they're in a *wonderful* theatre group!"

"That takes absolutely *anyone!*" Del said in falsetto.

They collapsed into sidesplitting laughter and it took a minute or two before Del regained enough composure to drive. What they didn't see, however, was the furious countenance of the ditched diva, watching them from the window of the restaurant.

Del drove straight to his townhouse, which took less than fifteen minutes. It was tucked into a hillside surrounded by large oaks and maples. "This is lovely," Ruth exclaimed as he helped her out of the car. "All these trees. Right in the middle of the city."

"I was lucky to get this place. The units are almost never listed. One of my friends told me about this one. He's a pianist and said he wanted me for a neighbor so we could practice together without driving anywhere. And, by the way, he's the one with the garden."

Ruth walked with him up to the front door, which had a shiny brass door-knocker inscribed "D. R. Mays" in gothic letters. Before turning the key in the lock, Del reached down to pick up a scrap of paper that lay near his door jam. Crumpling it, he said, "Don't you hate litter? I pick it up all the time."

"Is there something written on it? Maybe someone left you a note." Ruth said.

"Well, let's see." Del unfolded the paper. "Hmm, it says, 'It's not over yet.'" He looked at a wide-eyed Ruth. "What the ...?"

"Del!" Ruth gasped. "Quick! Get inside!"

Del did not question Ruth until they were in and locked the door.

"Ruth, what's the matter?" He guided her to a brown leather couch where they could sit down together. "What does this mean? What's going on here?"

Ruth's hands were shaking.

"Del, you are in danger. We've got to let the police know. He knows where you live! He *knows* where you live!"

"You think this was left by the murderer?" He put the wrinkled note on the coffee table and walked across the room to a carved chest. "I think you need some of my good brandy. I think we both do." He poured two snifters of brandy from a crystal decanter.

"Here," he said, giving Ruth the one with a little less liquor. "So what's this about?"

She took the glass, sipped, and winced as the liquid burned its way down her throat. Del looked at her with searching eyes.

"There was a message on my phone after Angie was assaulted," she told him. "It said the same thing: 'It's not over yet.'"

Del shook his head. "And you suppose it's from the same person and I'm a target?"

"That's exactly what I think."

"Well, if I'm next on their list," Del continued, "it has to be someone with a motive. Someone with a grudge against Fritz. Or against the whole company." He took a deep breath and another sip of brandy. "We'd better call Sergeant Sullivan and let him know."

"Maybe we'd be safer if we went straight down to the police station," Ruth said.

"I am not letting some mad man chase me out of my own home." Del rose and went immediately to the phone, which hung on the kitchen wall.

Ruth listened. She could tell he was put on hold. After a brief time, Del said, "Well, yes. Thank you ... yes, I would ... yes. Delancy Mays. D-E-L-A-N-C-Y-- M-A-Y-S. That's correct. Yes, that's my home number. Yes ... that's right. Yes, please have Sergeant Sullivan call me as soon as he gets in ... Tomorrow? Okay, tomorrow then ... yes ... thank you."

Del returned to the sofa. "He wasn't there but I'm sure he'll get back to me as soon as possible. They're probably thinking the man from Angie's apartment isn't the right one because of what happened on the boat. This ought to clinch it."

Ruth and Del spent the next hour trying to relax by drinking more brandy, eating Del's Bavarian chocolate, and listening to an album he had made when his wife was still alive. It was full of Gershwin songs and Ruth loved it. When she told him so, he handed her the album cover.

"It's yours."

Ruth demurred, saying that she couldn't take his only album, but Del just laughed.

"My only album? My dear, it's just like publishing a novel. The artist always gets extra copies." He went to a large built-in bookcase on the wall of a short hall separating the living room from the kitchen. It held books, music, record albums, family photos, and some prestigious-looking awards. Ruth watched as he picked up half-a-dozen of the albums and showed her. Then he sat next to her again.

During the song "How Long Has This Been Going On," Del gently kissed her. Ruth kissed him back.

"To be honest, I feel a little as though I'm being unfaithful to Tom," she murmured, leaning back.

"I know what you mean," Del said quietly. "Elaine and I were married for so long I don't even know how to ..." He let out a breath and raised his free hand to his eyes, rubbing them as he took a deep breath. "Let's take this very slow," he told her again.

"Slow is good." Ruth tried to relax with Del's arm around her shoulder, listening to the music.

"Del, I hate to break the mood, but you know he could be watching the apartment." She looked around the refined, understated room with its ebony grand piano, leather furniture, soft sofa pillows, and small tribal sculptures on the coffee table. "I'm sorry, I just can't think straight about you, or about anything, as long as he's out there lurking, focused on his next victim. I think I need to go home. And you need to lock up and be very careful when you go out."

Del sighed and got up. "I know, and I understand your concern. I just didn't want him to ruin our first real date."

"I'm sorry." Ruth rubbed her eyes. "Maybe when this is all over." Ruth looked down in her lap. "I'd better be going now," she said as she got up. "And please, you really need to take this seriously."

They drove in silence back to Milton Square to retrieve her car. As they stood there, he held Ruth and kissed her briefly again.

"I'm not going to let anyone ruin this," he whispered. "This is good. I feel it. I know it." He pulled her close. "I'm not letting anyone or anything take this away from us."

"Thank you for a great evening," she said softly, and then giggled. "I don't think I'll ever use the adjective 'wonderful' again, but it really was, you know. I'm just sorry I'm such a worry-wart."

"My mom used to say that," he said with a smile. "Oh Ruth, I haven't enjoyed myself this much in … well … a long, long time."

He waited while she got into her car, then motioned for her to roll down the window. "Please drive carefully," he said. "Call me when you get home?"

Ruth said she would and watched him get safely into his car before she started her engine. He turned and waved as he drove away.

Oh Del, Ruth thought, waving back. *Be careful. I don't want to lose you.*

When she arrived home, Ruth carried the album and the flowers inside and set them on her kitchen counter. While she was looking in the cupboard for a vase, Angie came into the kitchen, her eyes red and watery.

"George's wife died this afternoon," she sniffed. "He called and told me. I told him we should cool it for a while."

"Oh Angie. I'm so sorry."

Angie shrugged. "He feels terrible and he doesn't have any kids. He's so alone!" Ruth didn't know what else to say, so just hugged and held her friend for a moment.

"Mickey Sullivan also called," Angie finally said, regaining her composure. "He wants to see you. Maybe you should call him back in the morning and … oh." Angie noticed the album with Del's picture on the front. She picked it up.

"Did he give you this?" Ruth nodded. "So, how was your date?" she wondered, wiping her eyes.

"Well, my date was fine, but Del got the same kind of note at his apartment as my message."

"What?!" Angie's eyes widened. "Did you call the police?"

"Del called right away, but he wanted to talk with Sergeant Sullivan, who wasn't there. Dell left word for them to call back, but I'm going to call the sergeant myself in the morning. Maybe I won't have to drive in. Did Sullivan say anything else when he called?" She looked at her friend. "I just don't want anything to happen to Del."

"No, nothing else, but you'd better call bright and early." Angie opened the refrigerator, looking for leftovers. "That Sullivan sounded kind of grim, like maybe he knows something."

"I hope he knows who's doing this," Ruth replied. "I want this over!"

Then, as if to remind Ruth and Angie that they had other responsibilities, the animals came into the kitchen.

Ruth reached down to scratch Griselda, who was rubbing against her leg, wanting attention. Then Morrie came over for affection, too.

"Well, hello, you big baby," she told him as she scratched the back of his neck. "Have the dogs been out tonight?"

"Yeah, I let them both out about twenty minutes ago. George thinks they're cute." She looked at Ruth. "D'ya think I'm awful for seeing George before his wife died?" She looked troubled.

"Angie," Ruth consoled, "don't even think that! You talked with him, had breakfast with him … big deal." She shook her head. "You said he was lonely. For three years she hasn't even recognized him. Three long years!" She put her arm around her friend. "George is lucky to have you for a friend. And so am I."

Angie gripped Ruth's hand and said, "Thanks, I needed that." She turned to go up the stairs. "I'm just about done-in. Goodnight." She stopped and gave each dog a pat.

Ruth looked at the two little dogs. *They're like matching bookends,* she thought. "Well, I had a very nice evening but I'm exhausted too." Ruth drew the curtains on the windows in the living room, something she seldom did, and then checked the back door to make sure it was locked.

Angie said good night again as she headed up the stairs.

"Good night, Angie," Ruth told her as she followed.

Ruth lay in bed remembering Del's embrace, his kiss, his laughter, and his rich baritone voice singing that old love song, "How Long Has This Been Going On."

What a fine man ... with such kind eyes.

Then, for no apparent reason, she thought about Charlie and Toby.

What is going on? What am I missing in all of this? Something ... there's something I'm missing ... and then she fell asleep.

She woke with a start in the middle of the night. The dogs were growling down in the living room. One began barking and then the other chimed in. She turned on her bedside lamp and hurried to Angie's bedroom. Angie had been awakened, too, and was sitting up, wiping her eyes and yawning.

"What time is it?" she asked. "Whatsa matter with the dogs?"

"I don't know." Ruth was wide awake now and the dogs continued to bark and growl.

"The dogs are going crazy down there," Angie said. "I'm afraid to go down. Maybe we should call 911 from up here." She reached for the phone on her bedside table.

Ruth grabbed her arm. "No, not yet. It might not be anything. I don't want the police coming out here for a squirrel or a bat or something like that."

"But it might be some guy down there." Angie whispered. "Do you have a gun?"

"Not anymore," Ruth whispered back. "Tom had a hunting rifle but after he died, I gave it to a young guy at church who didn't have much money and liked to hunt."

"Well," Angie said uneasily, "we've got to have something we can use to protect us before going down there."

They rummaged madly around both bedrooms for something with which to hit an intruder. Finally, Ruth, armed with a heavy candlestick and Angie with a high heeled shoe, began descending the stairs. Half way down they were met by the dogs.

"What's wrong, babies?" Ruth asked them quietly. "Is there a squirrel in the house?"

"A squirrel would be good," whispered Angie nervously. "I can scare a squirrel."

The dogs led them to the kitchen, where Ruth looked around and couldn't see anything amiss.

As the two friends turned back into the living room, a shadowy figure was slowly driving a dark car, its headlights out, along Ruth's street, out of Lake Elmo and toward St. Paul.

Chapter 19

Undercover Reinforcement

Ruth and Angie spent the next fifteen minutes checking every inch of the downstairs in Ruth's house. They even checked out the basement, Angie right behind Ruth, going through it together. They walked gingerly around the assorted old furniture, tools, cross-country skis, sleds and boxes of family junk of the sort usually found in basements. They turned on all the basement lights.

"I have got to get down here one of these days and get rid of some of this stuff," Ruth said, more to herself than to Angie.

They found nothing amiss in the house except the front door, which hadn't been locked. "I always keep it locked because we never use it," Ruth said.

"I might have used it. I just don't remember, but maybe I forgot to lock it," Angie admitted to Ruth. "I'm really sorry."

"It's okay," Ruth assured her. "I don't see anything out of place. I'm sure it was an animal—a squirrel or chipmunk in the chimney or something—and the dogs heard it or smelled it and got upset."

After a cup of Sleepy-Time tea, the two women made certain the dogs had settled down for the rest of the night. Charlie was especially nervous, and continued to shake behind the big blue chair. Angie went to him and knelt on the floor near him, talking to him in low, soothing tones while she scratched his ears.

"What's the matter, baby? Do you have the heebie-jeebies? There's a good boy, nothing's wrong."

Ruth did the same for Toby, who, while not as anxious as Charlie, was still upset. Morrie and Griselda had been upstairs on Ruth's bed when the ruckus started. They were not used to people up at this hour and both cats wandered into the kitchen to see what was happening. They looked into their empty dishes.

Ruth put a bit of food in the animal's bowls and gave them fresh water. "Okay, you guys. You might as well have a little snack."

The two women headed back up to their bedrooms but Angie was far from sleepy.

"I hope it was an animal. I just can't help thinking someone was in here, though. I don't know why, I just do. If the front door was unlocked, they could have gotten in while I walked the dogs. Geez, d'ya suppose someone coulda been in the basement while we were asleep upstairs?"

Ruth put her arm around Angie's shoulders and tried to sound calm for her sake. "I'm sure no one was down there. But I'll call Sergeant Sullivan in the morning. And Angie, let's both of us make sure to always lock all the doors from now on, even when we are home here in the house." Angie nodded.

Ruth lay awake for almost an hour before finally drifting into a fitful sleep. The next morning, groggy and out of sorts, she managed to put on a cheerful face while making breakfast, but forgot that Sergeant Sullivan had wanted her to call. Ruth decided she would make Tom's favorite breakfast: Swedish pancakes and crisp bacon.

"Things look a lot better in the daylight, don't they?" she said reassuringly to Angie as they ate.

"Yeah," Angie said. "Late at night it's like everything's worse." She broke off two pieces of pancake and gave them to the two canine beggars sitting expectedly at her feet.

Just then, Ruth glanced out the kitchen window and saw a St. Paul police car pull into her driveway.

"Oh no! I forgot to call Mickey Sullivan. And I didn't expect anyone to come over. I'm still in my robe!" She hurriedly rose from the table. "Angie, at least you're in sweats. Please give him a cup of tea or something. Offer him breakfast. Tell him I'll be right down."

A few minutes later, clad in black slacks and a navy tunic sweater, with her hair combed but no make-up, Ruth returned to the kitchen to find Mickey Sullivan and Angie, eating and talking quietly. He rose as she entered.

"Ma'am," he said, extending his hand. "I'm sorry to bother you, but I wanted to talk to you personally and decided to just come over." He looked outside. "I know it's a long drive for you to come into St. Paul." He smiled, wiping his mouth on a napkin. "I'll have to admit I don't often have such a good breakfast. Usually only a doughnut or two ... forgive the cliché."

"It was good of you to come all the way out here," Ruth said. "Is it about last night and Mr. May's threatening note?"

"Well, yes, and something else." The sergeant looked at Angie hesitantly. "Okay, I guess you know what's going on so you might as well hear this, too."

This could take a while, Ruth thought as she refreshed his cup of coffee.

Mickey Sullivan cleared his throat, took a big sip of his coffee, and put both hands on the table.

"I thought I'd get somewhere with you. God knows, your director is difficult." He hesitated. "Or should I say impossible?" He smiled and shook his head.

"Fritz?" Ruth laughed. "I suppose you asked him to close the show."

The sergeant nodded affirmatively.

Ruth went on. "We open the weekend after next. This is the Gerhardt's summer money-maker. It would be a real mess to close it now."

"That's what Mr. Gerhardt told me, in so many choice words." He looked at the two women and held out his hands in a helpless gesture. "My advice to him was to cancel the show and try to keep all of you good people safe."

"And that's not an option with Fritz," Ruth said as she looked him in the eye. "I know him. He won't back down. Against all odds he'll somehow go ahead with this show."

Sullivan continued. "Oh, he wants all his people safe, that's for sure, and we had to let the man we arrested go for lack of evidence. Frankly, I don't think he was guilty of anything except being in the wrong place at the wrong time. But now Mr. Gerhardt wants half the police force to stand guard at the pavilion while the show is on, under cover of course. Obviously, we don't have the manpower for that sort of thing." He looked out the window at a pair of squirrels chasing around a big oak tree. "Anyway," he sighed, "I think we've come up with an alternative that's well ... it's something. Better than nothing, I guess. But your director wanted me to discuss it with you. He respects your judgement. He wanted your input."

Just then the phone rang and Angie jumped up to get it. Ruth hoped it was Del.

"Yes," Angie said, "he's here right now, talking to her. Yes. I'll have her call you as soon as he leaves ... Okay, thank you. Goodbye." Angie turned to Ruth. "Call Fritz as soon as you can," she said.

As soon as she stepped away from the phone it rang a second time. Ruth's heart leaped. *Let it be Del!* she prayed.

Angie shrugged her shoulders and rose again to get the phone. "I might as well be your secretary," she said before picking it up.

"Oh hi!" (She mouthed "George" to Ruth.) "Yeah, I know," she smiled. "I know ... you're right." She drew a heart on the tablecloth. "Yeah ... you're right about that too." She shook her head and smiled. "Well ... I think that would be okay." She sat down. "No, we really haven't, have we?" She cleared her throat. "George, I'm sorry, but can I call you later? Ruthie's waiting for an important call, and I really want to talk to you ... yes ... we could ... definitely ... Okay then, okay ... me too. Bye."

Angie's cheeks were pink as she put the receiver back. Actually, Ruth thought she looked radiant.

"How is he doing?"

"He sounds pretty well, considering." Angie blushed. "He wants to see me." She shrugged her shoulders. "This coming week for sure, and I said okay."

Then the phone rang yet again, and once again Angie went to pick it up, shaking her head and murmuring "grand central station."

"Hello ... yes, yes, it is. She's here, Mr. Mays." She smiled broadly at Ruth. "Well, yes, he is, too. Sergeant Sullivan is here. He's talking to Ruth right now ... Well, that would be nice. I'm sure she'd love to see you." She held the phone out to the police sergeant. "He wants to talk to you first."

Ruth watched the sergeant's face as he talked with Del.

He looks pretty grim. I wonder if Del had any more trouble.

After another few minutes he passed the phone to Ruth.

"Hello, Ruth," Del said. "Well, I told Sergeant Sullivan about that note we found last night and he wants to have it as evidence. Ruth, is it all right if I drive out to see you today ... around noon? I want to show you some river property I'm looking at. We could go to lunch somewhere along the way. I wanted to get your opinion of the site and," he laughed, "of course it's an excuse to get to see you."

"No excuse needed," Ruth smiled. "Do you remember how to get here?"

"Oh yes," Del replied, "I remember. I'll see you at noon, then. I suppose you should get back to the sergeant. We'll talk about it all while we're driving. Well ... goodbye." He seemed unsure about how to end the conversation.

"Yes, thank you. See you soon." Ruth hung up the receiver and turned to Mickey Sullivan and Angie. "I'm sorry. Maybe I should take the phone off the hook." She sat down and took a sip of her tea. "Now, what is your alternative plan?"

"It's not as much as I would like," the policeman said, looking into his empty cup, "but we *can* provide a little more police reinforcement for you." Angie tried to pour him another cup of coffee, but he held his hand over it. "No thanks, it was good, but I've had enough for now. Anyway, this is what we've decided to do. One of our men, Don Olson, used to sing in a men's chorus. He sounds pretty good when he sings at our Christmas parties. So, he's going to join your group and be in the chorus. Undercover of course, to keep an eye on everybody, and to watch for anything suspicious. You already have Danny Ancino, so that's two policemen who are now actually in the cast. And during performances I plan be there too, out front and sometimes back stage, at every performance. I'll send a good man to take my place if for some reason I can't be there myself. How many performances do you have? Nine, I think Mr. Gerhardt said."

"Yes, nine. Thursday, Friday and Saturday nights for the last two weekends in July and the first weekend in August."

Then Ruth told him about last night's mysterious "visitor."

"I don't think anyone was here, but it was strange and I want to be careful." She looked at Angie.

Mickey Sullivan stood up and walked over to the sink, depositing his cup and saucer. "I can only tell you to lock up tight and keep an eye out for things." He peered out the window over the sink.

Ruth agreed with him and then remembered Rodney. "How about Rhonda Olson and her little boy?" she asked. "How are they doing?"

"I guess she took both herself and her son out of the cast, which is a smart move, if you ask me." He headed for the door. "I think all of you would be better off if you weren't in this show."

"I know you do." Ruth smiled at him as she held out her hand and shook his. "Thank you for everything you're doing." She watched him through the porch window as he walked to his car, picking up acorns on her sidewalk and throwing them off to the side. She was amused when she saw him look at one and put it in his pocket. *Just like Tom used to do,* she thought. *I hope his plan works. God knows we need help.*

The Cabin

DEL ARRIVED A BIT before noon, looking very "Land's End" in khaki trousers and a maroon and navy plaid shirt. Ruth was glad she had chosen her jeans skirt with its matching vest and a blue plaid blouse to wear on their trip to the St. Croix River.

"We match," he laughed as he hugged her.

As they got into Del's Lexus and pulled out of Ruth's driveway, Angie came to the back door to wave good-bye. Ruth called out to her, "Don't forget to lock all the doors if you go out."

Angie gave a thumbs-up sign and responded: "Don't worry. No more squirrels!"

"Did you get a squirrel in the house?" Del asked Ruth. "How did you handle that? With those dogs and cats of yours I'll bet that was fun!" he joked.

"Well, a squirrel or chipmunk or some kind of small animal. Something apparently got in and set off the dogs in the middle of the night. They were really excited. Angie and I got up and looked everywhere, but found nothing. I don't know ... maybe it was a just a squirrel—or maybe something else," Ruth said quietly.

"What do you mean? A prowler?" Del was immediately on alert.

"I can't say for sure. But whatever or whoever it was, it left before we got downstairs."

"Did you tell the police?"

"Sergeant Sullivan came over this morning to discuss his plans for 'protecting' our group. I thought maybe I should at least mention it as long as he was here, but with nothing to show him, nothing except my gut feelings, I downplayed it. There would have been nothing he could do about it, and I don't want him to think we are just a couple of dithering old ladies who are not to be taken seriously. He did tell me to be careful and to always keep the house locked."

"And what's the sergeant's plan?"

"He's going to put another policeman in the chorus. He'll be under-cover, to help keep an eye out. It's the policeman who I first talked with after Angie got attacked, the one who had Charlie. I guess he's a good singer."

"I think I met him on the boat." Del told her. "He seemed like a nice enough fellow. And of course our group takes *anybody*!"

They both laughed, and then drove in comfortable silence, enjoying the rolling hills, forests and fields north of Stillwater.

Finally, Del spoke. "I'm glad Angie is living with you. I feel better knowing you're not alone out there."

They headed north up Highway 95 on the Minnesota side of the St. Croix River. Del told her that they were going to look at a cabin for sale on the Wisconsin side. It sat on a bluff overlooking the river and belonged to a percussionist with the Minnesota Orchestra. He hadn't been using it much and decided to sell it. Then Del changed the subject.

"So ... someone is trying to kill off the cast," Del said, "and apparently, I'm going to be next? Good thing I'm getting out of town."

"You're getting out of town?" Ruth was surprised. She looked toward Del and then out of the window at the passing fields and woods, trying to act more nonchalant than she felt. "Where are you going and what about the show?"

"Oh, that's no problem. We'll be home before the dress rehearsal. I've already cleared it with the Maestro. Besides, you have a son in the Chicago area and I'd like to meet at least one of your kids."

This was all going too fast for Ruth. "*We'll* be home? Would you mind telling me what exactly is going on here?"

Del slowed the car and glanced at Ruth just as they were driving through the historic village of Marine on St. Croix. "I'm sorry. I shouldn't tease you. I got a call last night from my Chicago friend, Ed Millard, who is directing Verdi's *Otello* at the Lyric. They've got a crisis. The baritone playing Otello caught some kind of bug that's affecting his voice. They need someone to stand in for him for their final two performances, which start in three days. Ed knew that I could do the role without a lot of prep because I did Otello in San Francisco only a few months ago." He kept his eyes on the road but seemed to hold his breath.

All Ruth could say was, "You said we. *We'll* make it back by dress rehearsal." She turned to look at him. "You've already made the arrangements?"

"Ah ... well ... no, not really." Del glanced at her pleadingly. "Of course I needed to talk with you first." He cleared his throat. "I mean I have to go, and, well, I was hoping that, ah ... you would go with me?"

Ruth said nothing, but she looked out the window and shook her head "no."

"Please, Ruth." Del turned onto the road leading to the bridge between Minnesota and Osceola, Wisconsin. "The Lyric will pay for everything. First-class airline tickets, limos, accommodations at the Drake, everything first-class." He paused. "You'll have your own suite, of course."

"Of course," Ruth sighed as she finally started to wrap her head around it. "Well, I suppose it would be an adventure. And they say *Fritz* is impossible!" She shook her head. "All right. I'll go. But only if you tell me how you got Fritz to agree to it." All of a sudden Ruth remembered something. "Oh dear! I was supposed to call Fritz and I forgot! You see what a tizzy you've got me in?"

"A tizzy?" Del chortled. "I've got you in a *tizzy,* have I?" He began to sing a sort of aria, "A tizzy ... a tizzy ... a-a-a-a-tiz-z-z-y!"

"Oh, is that in *Otello?* I don't seem to remember the tizzy aria." She laughed.

They drove across the bridge and through the town of Osceola. After Del stopped to look at his directions, they found themselves driving down a narrow county road toward the river. After passing a couple of farms, Del said, "I think this is it," and turned sharply into a long, uneven gravel driveway bordered on both sides by stands of pine. The Lexus bounced and swayed with each rut. "I hope I don't break an axle!" Del muttered.

The realtor was already there, waving at them as they got out of the car.

"Isn't this just beautiful!?" she exclaimed cheerfully, moving her arm in an arc toward the bluffs.

The building in front of them was rustic, to say the least. Del set his jaw and cleared his throat. Ruth sighed.

"It needs a bit of work," the realtor said in a reassuring tone, "but the view is astounding!"

They went inside.

"Oh dear," Ruth whispered to Del.

It was dark and surprisingly uninviting—nothing but a large single room with cheap sheet paneling covering the walls. Brown. Everything seemed to be brown. The small windows (not clean) did little to brighten the space, which contained an assortment of mismatched furniture, including a vintage chrome and Formica kitchen table and a decrepit upright piano. For "bedrooms," there were two swayback double beds surrounded by faded drapes that could be pulled for privacy. A 1970s-era Franklin wood stove appeared to be the only source for heat. Near the entrance stood a large trash can overflowing with empty beer cans. A musty smell tinged with old burnt wood hung in the air.

"I'm sorry it's such a mess," said the smiling realtor. "It hasn't been listed yet and we haven't had a chance to clean it up."

"Um ... We'll need to really think about this," Del told the realtor as he scanned the dreary room. "Is there a bathroom?" He didn't see one.

"Oh that's out back," she told him. "You'll probably want to put in plumbing, but that shouldn't be too hard to do—easy peasy," she smiled broadly.

They took a walk around the property. The setting was beautiful, but Del had seen enough. "Do you have a card?" he asked the woman. She handed Del her card. "We'll be in touch," he told her, betraying his true feelings. "Thank you."

"I have a couple of other wonderful properties you might like to see," she said hopefully, "Maybe we could ..."

"I'm sorry," Del said as kindly as he could. "We don't have time today. I have your phone number. I'll let you know."

They followed the realtor back to the main road. Ruth put her head in her hands and started to giggle. "Easy peasy?" They locked eyes and burst out laughing. "Oh my! Did your drummer-friend have something against you?"

"Ha! Maybe so," Del answered with a grin. "Looks like his college-age son used this as a party house."

They drove back to Osceola and stopped for a lunch of hamburgers and fries at a little bar with booths covered in fake Holstein cow-hide.

"Well, it was a fixer-upper alright," Del told Ruth, chuckling as they waited for their food. "The drummer as much as told me it would surely sell quickly. We can believe that or not. The land is nice, but the cabin has about as much charm as a worn-out welcome mat!" He shook his head. "I admit this trip today was really more of an excuse to be alone with you and to talk about Chicago. We'll be there for three nights. I'll come out and get you tomorrow morning. Can you be ready by nine? We should try to get to the airport by ten."

"Tomorrow?" Ruth gasped, "I can't possibly ..."

"I know," Del said as he reached across the table and put his hand on Ruth's arm, "it's last minute ... and I'm sorry, but they just called me last night."

Ruth nodded and said, "Okay, why don't I just drive in to your place and leave my car there?"

"Can you be there at nine?"

"Of course." *But no time to get my hair done*, she thought.

"Thank you, Ruth. It will be much more enjoyable if you can be there with me."

The ride back to Lake Elmo was serene. The hills and forests and the farms and cornfields always made Ruth feel peaceful.

They rode along in the comfortable silence of people at home with each other. Del kept reaching over to hold Ruth's hand. "Thank you for coming with me to Chicago," he repeated. "I really appreciate it." Ruth wished it was the "old days" so she could cuddle next to him on the seat instead of having to wear a seat-belt with a console between them.

"Penny for your thoughts," he finally said.

"Oh nothing," she blushed. "Just longing for the old days, when a girl could sit right next to a guy in a car." She looked at him and smiled.

"Modern things aren't always an improvement," he replied, grinning.

"Well, they sure would improve that cabin!" she laughed.

Del hugged Ruth long and hard when they got back to her house. He kissed her hair, her cheek, her lips.

"You are very dear to me," he said.

"And you, to me," she whispered back.

They said goodbye and Del kissed her again at her door. "See you tomorrow at nine. As he walked to his car he said, "Pack something dressy too. There's a reception."

Ruth rolled her eyes. "Okay, I'll do it, for you." *Please tell me we won't run into our old friend, Blanche!*

After he left, Ruth went inside and told Angie about her upcoming trip. They sat in her cozy living room, talking quietly. Charlie and Toby were on their rugs in front of the fireplace. Griselda lolled on Ruth's lap and Morrie was next to Angie on the sofa.

"I don't have to go to Chicago, you know. I hate to leave you here alone."

"Don't be silly," Angie answered. "Anyway, I won't be alone. George called again, and doesn't want to wait to talk. We have a sort of a date at his house, tomorrow night. He's making supper. I hope you don't mind my leaving the critters for a couple of hours."

"Of course not. Why would I? I'll be gone. You can have him over here if you'd like."

"He's barbecuing us some steaks on his deck, and he has some old records he wants me to hear." Angie hugged herself. "He's so nice to me, and, well, I never had a man be this good to me. Maybe we could come over here afterwards for some ice cream. You sure it's okay for him to come over here?" she added, looking at Ruth for her approval.

"Of course it's okay. I want you to feel at home here. Me casa es su casa." She smiled at Angie. "And of course he's good to you—why wouldn't he be? You're a good person!"

Angie smiled. "Who would'a thought we'd both have new beaus at the same time?"

Chapter 21

The Show Must Go On

RUTH REMEMBERED, FINALLY, TO call Fritz at nine in the evening, her mental cut-off time for polite phone calls. She hoped he and Vivian weren't in bed, but she needn't have worried.

"Hello," rasped the familiar voice. Fritz almost always answered after the first ring. "Gerhardt residence."

"Maestro, this is Ruth. I'm so sorry. I forgot to call you earlier. What can I do for you?"

Fritz, as usual, came right to the point. "I want you to talk to Rhonda." Aside, he called out to Vivian: "It's Ruth. Get me the cast list with those phone numbers." Then returning to Ruth he continued: "I need Rhonda as Julie. It's a big part. She can't just quit! My god! How can I get anyone else at this late date? The show might as well be cancelled! I don't know what I'm going to do. Please call her. She'll listen to you." He gave Ruth Rhonda's number and asserted that old theatre adage: "The show must go on!"

Ruth agreed to talk with Rhonda because it was pointless to argue with Fritz. She reassured him that she would try, and promised to call him about Rhonda's decision as soon as possible. "I'm going to Chicago tomorrow, though. I'll be gone for three days."

"He! He! He! Oh, I know all about that," Fritz laughed. "Del's already cleared it with me." He went on. "You know, I was the first chair bassoon, oh ... thirty or forty years ago, when Mama had the Lyric up here for a benefit performance at Northrop Auditorium. We did *Otello* as no one has ever done it!" He laughed, remembering.

"Mama got so mad at their Desdemona. Their baritone Otello was pretty fat and he threw himself across Desdemona's body in the last scene. You could see her hands pushing at him, trying to get him off her so she could breathe—and she was supposed to be dead!" Fritz laughed gleefully.

"Mama saw it, and most of the audience saw it, too. You could hear them snickering." He stopped, and Ruth could hear Vivian laughing and saying something to him in the background. "Well, when 'Desdemona' came off-stage after her bows, Mama went right up to her and shook her finger at her, 'Dahlink, vhen you're dett, you're *dett*,' she yelled at her, 'und you're dett in diss town!' And then she went over and yelled at the baritone. 'Und you, you big pig, you should lose some veight!'"

Ruth couldn't help but laugh, "That's one of the better opera stories I've heard."

"I've got a million of 'em! Mama was a real doozie!" Fritz was suddenly in a better mood. He always was when he reminisced about his Mama Gerhardt and the good old days. "I should write a book. You know, all the things I've ..." Vivian could be heard speaking again, apparently trying to get him to cut it short. "Yes ... okay dear ... well, my bride says it's time for bed. She wants me in bed ... hee hee hee! Bye, Ruth!"

Ruth hung up the phone, exhausted by the late hour and by Fritz's mood swings. From despair to manic exuberance in so short a time. "Oof!" she said, shaking her head and smiling as Angie walked toward the kitchen for a bed time snack. "I wonder what it would be like to be married to someone that temperamental? Vivian is a saint."

"Maybe someday soon you'll find ah—out," her friend intoned in a sing-song voice as she went through the kitchen door.

"Angie! Honestly!" Ruth chided. "We're just going to Chicago. And we have separate rooms," she added, more for herself than for her house-guest. She could hear Angie's singing "shuurre you do!" out in the kitchen.

Ruth went to her room and packed. She filled her suitcase with what she thought were suitable outfits, including a black sleeveless silky dress with matching black jacket and a black scarf with sequins. *When in Rome* ... she thought, as she threw in some black patent leather high-heeled shoes that she knew she could only wear for a couple of hours, along with an evening purse that matched them. Finally she packed her black lace nightgown, one she'd worn during her marriage on trips and "special occasions" with Tom. She paused for a moment and then took it out of the suitcase and put it back in the drawer.

Not yet. I don't even want to think about that, she thought as she rummaged in the drawer for something less sexy.

She finished packing and closed her suitcase.

I hope I'm doing the right thing. I wonder what opera folks are like? I hope they're not all like Blanche!

She sat down in her blue and white chintz easy chair and put her feet up on the matching ottoman. She loved this bedroom. It was where she went when she wanted to think things over. Ruth called it her "blue room" with its restful blue wallpaper, white lace curtains, and the blue and white chair and ottoman with upholstery that matched the spread on her queen-sized bed. The colors and furnishings gave it a serene dignity.

I wonder what Del would think of it? she mused, and then she thought again. *Oh, this might be too much too soon.*

She tried calling her son. The line was busy. *We probably don't have enough time in Chicago anyway.* She frowned. *This is getting way too complicated.*

The next morning, Ruth couldn't reach Rhonda Olson but left a message on her answering machine, asking her to please reconsider. She told her that her leaving at this late date would mean they probably would have to close the show. Ruth appealed to Rhonda's sense of fairness. Angie said she'd help watch Rodney while Rhonda was on stage, and Ruth relayed that message.

As Ruth left the house with her suitcase, Angie hugged her good-bye and said "Have fun! Don't do anything I wouldn't do!"

"You take care too. Bye now!" Ruth put her suitcase in the back seat of her car and drove out of Lake Elmo. *What a glorious day!* she thought. *It's early summer, the weather is gorgeous, and I'm flying first class to Chicago with a handsome opera star!* As she drove to St Paul, the traffic was light and moving along rapidly.

She started singing, "Fish gotta swim and birds gotta fly ... I've gotta love one man 'til I die ... Can't help lovin' that man of mine!"

On her way to Del's, Ruth had a conversation with Tom. She used to 'talk' to him all the time right after he died. Now it only happened occasionally.

I know you'd like him, she said to her dead mate. *He's a good man. An honest man. I'm taking it slow. Not jumping into anything. After all, the kids haven't met him, and I haven't met his daughter, so we're just friends. That's all. Good friends. And I'm not so lonely anymore …*

Fire

When Ruth arrived at Del's condo complex, she couldn't get near it. Two fire-trucks and three police cars were parked in front. Red and blue lights flashed. Yellow plastic "crime scene" tape wound around the trees circling what would have been Del's unit and the one next door.

As she stopped her car, Ruth felt panic rising sharply in her chest. She could see that the unit next to Del's had minimal damage, but Del's was now a smoking ruin. "Del!" she screamed as she bounded from her car. "Del! Oh my God! Del!"

In the next instant, Ruth's heart began to settle down when she saw him sitting in the front seat of a police car. Ruth ran up to the door and tapped on the window. Del turned and rolled it down. He was wearing striped silk pajamas and held a bunch of brown notebooks in his lap.

"Scores," he said weakly. "I saved my scores." He looked dazed, then started to sob. "But my photo albums—all gone." His shoulders heaved. "Couldn't get to them in time. All the pictures of my family, Elaine,

Elizabeth. All gone." He rambled on. "Your paintings weren't in there. I just didn't think I could do them justice so I took them to a frame shop."

"Oh Del." Ruth patted his shoulder through the window. "Your daughter will have photos—of you, and Elaine, and your family. I'll even paint a portrait of Elaine for you if you'd like." Then she laughed and cried at the same time. "Besides, even if my paintings had been in there, I can always paint more landscapes. What's important is that you're safe. That you're alive. That's all that counts. You're alive!"

Del just sat there, staring blankly at firefighters hauling hoses back and forth in front of him.

"What happened? How did this start?"

"I don't know. I was asleep and there was some kind of explosion in the house that woke me up and then heavy smoke started pouring into my bedroom."

Ruth leaned her head on the top of the police car and took a deep sobbing breath. When she straightened up, Sergeant Sullivan was behind her.

"Mr. Mays says he doesn't want to go to the hospital. I personally think it would be best if he would get checked out, but he ... ah, has a mind of his own." Mickey Sullivan looked pleadingly at Ruth. "Maybe you could ...?"

"Let me talk to him," Ruth said as she looked back at Del. His fine-boned profile looked fragile, as if it might crumble, and her heart ached for him.

"Del? Del?" she repeated, trying to get him to look at her. He finally turned his head to her, tears in his eyes. "Del," she said patiently, "you can ride with me. I'll take you to urgent care over on Lexington Avenue just to make sure you're all right. Okay?" She felt as if she was talking to a child. "You might be in shock. We need to take you to a doctor. Okay? Can you get out of the car?"

She took a blanket from the sergeant and wrapped it around his shoulders as he got out and stood up.

"Ruth, Ruth, can you get more photos for me?" He sounded like a frightened child or a very old man, still clutching his musical scores.

"Of course I will!" She walked him over to her car. Mickey Sullivan held the passenger-side door open for him. After Ruth made sure Del was belted in and she had closed the door, she spoke quietly to the sergeant. "How on earth did this happen?"

The sergeant shrugged. "We don't know yet. A 9-1-1 call from a neighbor came in about seven this morning. He saw smoke pouring out of the place after hearing a boom. A team from the Fire Marshall's office will be checking it out. Your friend is one lucky man."

"He told you about the note he received?" Ruth asked. He nodded yes.

Sergeant Sullivan closed his eyes and rubbed his forehead. "Damn! I wish Gerhardt would close this show."

Ruth shook her head. "I know Fritz. He won't do that. I'm going to take Del to urgent care now," she said, "and then, if he's all right, I'll take him to my house. We'll call his daughter from there." She looked at the sergeant. "Thank you for everything."

"Looks like arson to me," said Mickey grimly as he surveyed the scene. "Seems likely under the circumstances." He spoke quietly, gesturing with his hand toward the ruined condo.

"It seems pretty likely to me too," Ruth said, as she opened the driver's door of her car and slipped behind the wheel.

Ruth left Sergeant Sullivan walking slowly back toward Del's destroyed condo.

Patting Del's knee she said cheerfully as she could, "We'll get you to a doctor. Get you checked out. You must have breathed in a lot of smoke. And then you're going to the Carson Clinic. No, not clinic … the Carson Spa!" She smiled at him. "The Carson Spa for Indigent Musicians—on the beautiful shores of Lake Elmo." She saw a faint smile come over his face.

While a doctor at the Lexington Avenue Urgent Care clinic was examining Del, Ruth tried to reach Del's daughter Elizabeth on the lobby pay phone. She used the phone number he had given her but there was no answer, so Ruth left a message on Elizabeth's answering machine. Without going into all the detail, she said there had been a fire at Del's house, that he seemed to be okay, was being seen by a doctor for smoke inhalation, and that she could reach her father by calling Ruth's home phone.

The doctor gave Del a clean bill of health, but told Ruth to watch for signs of disorientation or clamminess or shivering. Ruth promised she'd take Del home, get him in a warm bed, and give him chicken soup and lots of attention.

"All my patients should have such a great nurse," the doctor told them.

Del nodded in agreement.

By the time they reached Ruth's house, Danny Ancino's police car was in the driveway. She could see Del's whole body stiffen up as they came upon the black and white vehicle.

"It's okay, Del, he and Tracey are probably visiting Angie. He's a friend of Angie's daughter."

They walked by Morrie and Griselda on the back porch, who looked up and then returned to grooming themselves as if a strange man in his pajamas walking into their house was an everyday occurrence.

As she led Del into her sunny kitchen, Ruth could hear loud rock music coming from the living room. They were met by both Charlie and Toby, who had taken up residence under the kitchen table, as if to get away from the noise. Del was still clutching his precious scores. Ruth took them from him and set them on the table; she could see they were from various operas. *Otello* was on top. "We'll call the Lyric in Chicago and cancel," she said, looking at Del.

"No!" he said emphatically. "I have to get there. They're counting on me." The old Del had suddenly snapped back. He looked down at his pajamas and gasped, "Wha ...? I've got to get some clothes. Ruth, I need clothes!" He looked around her kitchen in panic. "I've got to be on a plane to Chicago!"

"Sit," Ruth ordered as she pushed him gently into the only chair with arms at her kitchen table. Both little dogs sat down too. She smiled at this, thinking how authoritarian she must sound. She poured him a cup of hot coffee from Angie's breakfast brew. "Drink this. Please." She softened somewhat as she held the white Corelle mug up to his mouth. "And then we'll decide what to do."

He complied with an audible sigh and a drop of his shoulders.

The white wall phone rang and a very disheveled Tracey ran into the kitchen to answer it. She let out a surprised "Oh! Hi! I ... we ... just came over to see mom," she said upon seeing Ruth and Del. "But then George called and she went over to his place for a bit."

She answered the phone and then gave it to Ruth.

"It's for you."

Ruth could see Danny Ancino hurriedly tucking his shirt into his pants as Tracey, smoothing down her clothes and hair, dashed back through the living room door.

It was Del's daughter on the phone. The conversation was brief. In very terse tones, Elizabeth Mays informed Ruth that she wanted to speak with her father, who rose wearily from his chair to take the call. Ruth could hear his pleas to her.

"No, darling ... no ... I'm fine. No, you don't have to do that. Please don't bother ... I'm ... yes ... well, yes, if you have them handy ... I could use some ... no, I don't ... oh ... oh ... I wish you wouldn't ... well, okay ... if you think it's best." He told her the name of the director at the Lyric, as well as Ruth's address.

After hanging up he told Ruth, "I'm sorry. She's coming out here. I couldn't stop her. But she has some of my clothes from our last vacation trip we took, so that's good. She's cancelling Chicago, though." He shook his head. "I sure hope they can find another replacement at the drop of a hat."

By now, both Tracey and Danny were in the kitchen, looking a trifle sheepish. Ruth didn't comment, except to explain Del's predicament.

"Would you sit with him awhile, please? I'm going upstairs to put clean sheets on my bed. And Tracey, honey," she added, "why don't you heat up some chicken soup. You'll find cans in the pantry."

After he'd had a bowl of soup and a shower, Ruth tucked Del—somewhat against his wishes but wearing clean pajamas that had once belonged to Tom—into her bed. She plumped a soft blue comforter up around his shoulders. He leaned back into the soft pillows with resignation.

"I'll just rest until Elizabeth gets here," he said quietly.

Ruth closed the blinds on the big windows that looked over the lake, darkening the room.

"I'll wake you as soon as she gets here," she whispered and leaned down to kiss his forehead.

"Thank you. You're such a good ... friend. I want to ... I love you," he said quietly as his eyelids closed. He fell asleep in seconds. Ruth tip-toed out of the room.

By the time Ruth got back downstairs, Tracey and Danny had cleaned up her kitchen and were preparing to leave. Tracey told her that she and Danny were going to go to an afternoon movie before he had to be on duty.

"Mom said she'd be back late from George's. Would you please tell her that, um, I'll see her in a few days?"

As the two young people hurried out the back door, Ruth thought Danny seemed almost hen-pecked around Tracey.

Maybe he's met his match!

Alone, at last, she thought with relief. She made herself a cup of hot tea and sat down at her kitchen table to wait for Del's daughter. The view out her kitchen windows into her spacious back yard always gave Ruth quiet pleasure. A half-dozen large oak trees provided ample shade. A sparrow flew from the lilac bushes and perched on the edge of her birth bath.

I love this place, she thought. *I would hate to lose it.*

She lost all track of time as she sat mulling over the morning's events while sipping her tea.

Who is doing this? Why would anyone want to hurt Del? Or Rodney? Or Mimi and Al? Angie? Lionel ... or me? What did I ever do to anybody?

She shivered. She felt cold but did not have the energy to get up and put on a sweater. She just sat there for about half-an-hour, pondering what awful thing was happening to her theatre group, thinking, on the other hand, how nice it was to have Del safe and asleep up in her bedroom.

Maybe I should go up to check on him, but I want him to sleep. Sleep is restorative.

Finally, a dark blue sedan pulled up and a young woman who looked like a model got out. Ruth watched as she purposefully strode toward Ruth's back door carrying a duffle bag. Her face had Del's fine features, but lighter skin. Her hair was pulled back and fastened into what Ruth called a "French roll." She wore a white blouse and a straight dark skirt, with dark pumps. She had the no-nonsense look of someone who was used to taking charge.

Ruth felt flustered as she jumped up to open the door.

"I'm Ruth Carson, your dad's friend," she said, extending her hand.

The handshake she received in return was stiff and formal.

"Elizabeth Mays," said the woman on Ruth's doorstep. "I've come for my father."

A Formidable Daughter

*S*HE IS ABSOLUTELY STUNNING! Ruth thought to herself.

"He's sleeping right now," she told her. "Why don't you come in and have a cup of tea and I'll fill you in on what happened."

Elizabeth Mays walked silently into the kitchen where Ruth guided her to a chair with the best view of the back yard. The young woman sat down gracefully and folded her long fingers in her lap. Griselda approached her and rubbed against her legs. She glanced down but did not pet the cat.

"I really don't need any tea, thank you," she said. "I appreciate your kindness, though, for bringing my father to your home. When he wakes up, I'll take him to my apartment." Her tone was polite, finishing-school perfect, business-like. "How long has he been asleep?"

Ruth looked at her watch. "Oh, about forty minutes. I ... I'd like to let him wake up naturally." She looked imploringly at Del's daughter. "He's had a pretty rough morning."

Ruth was nervous. The girl did not seem happy that Ruth was her father's friend, and Ruth didn't know if it was because she was white or because she was not the girl's mother.

Maybe both? she mused. Ruth busied herself with pouring water into her tea-kettle. "Are you sure you won't have a cup of tea with me?"

"Ah …" Elizabeth answered, with a hint of hesitancy, "all right, just one, nothing in it." Ruth set the cup in front of her guest. "So, what happened to dad's condo?"

Ruth told her as much as she knew, explaining that the fire department would be trying to determine the cause. "Del's unit looks like a burned-out shell, I'm afraid. I'm not sure anything is salvageable."

Elizabeth took a sip of her tea and stared out the window toward the trees in the yard. Finally she spoke, changing the subject, as though the enormity of what had happened to her father was just too much to take in. "My mother loved oak trees," she said. "We had so many of them in our yard out at the farm. She called them 'The Druids'."

"It must have been a beautiful place to grow up in." Elizabeth said nothing, so Ruth continued. "And speaking of your mother …" The girl looked up with raised her eyebrows. "Your father lost all his photos in the fire. I promised him I would try to get as many replacements as possible. I told him I was sure you would have some." She didn't think it politic to tell her that Del managed to save his musical scores.

"Of course I do." Elizabeth spoke more softly now. "I have the originals. Dad had mostly duplicates. I'll get more made for him." She continued to sip her tea. "He and my mother were very much in love." Without looking at Ruth she reached over to Morrie, who settled in on the chair next to her, and scratched his ears. Griselda noticed, and began rubbing against Elizabeth's legs once more. Elizabeth smiled. "Your cats take to strangers better than mine. Mine hides under my bed if anyone comes over."

Thank God she's warming up a little.

"They don't take to everyone," said Ruth. "I think they like you." She looked around, but didn't see Charlie and Toby. "I have two little terriers, too, around here somewhere. I think they might be guarding your father."

She went to the refrigerator where she kept a bag of dainty little tea-cookies with chocolate centers. She put some on a blue and white Swedish plate and set it on the table in front of Elizabeth. The girl gestured "no" with her hand but Ruth just sat down and looked at her guest.

"I wish I could explain what's happening with our little theatre group this summer. It's all so strange and hard to believe."

"What do you mean? Is my father in danger?" The young woman's expression was cautious.

"I think he might be. I think we all are." Ruth reached for a cookie. For the next twenty minutes, as carefully as she could, Ruth told Elizabeth Mays about the "it's not over yet" note on Del's doorstep, and more about the fire in his condo, and about the other cast members who had been killed or attacked. "I don't think it has to do with your father, specifically. I think it may be anyone who is in the theatre group."

Seconds went by and finally Elizabeth spoke.

"I wasn't aware of any of this. I haven't talked with him in a while. We've both been very busy. As for the theatre group, he obviously needs to extricate himself from it." She set her cup down forcefully and said, "That's final."

"I won't do that, darling," Del said softly from the door to the living room. He stood there, a dog on either side of him like sentinels. Even in rumpled pajamas he looked dignified. "I won't let these good people down."

Elizabeth jumped up and ran to her father, flinging her arms around him. "Dad!" She began to sob. "Oh dad!" She was no longer a stand-offish, self-sufficient young woman. Suddenly she was a little girl who had almost lost her father and was thankful he was alive.

Ruth busied herself with the tea kettle and cups, feeling, somehow, that she shouldn't intrude on this private moment between father and daughter.

"It's bad enough I let the Lyric down," he said ruefully. "I am not about to give Fritz Gerhardt a stroke." He sat down at the table and accepted the cup Ruth put before him, winking at her as he did so.

"Fritz Gerhardt!" The girl's eyes widened. "He's still doing shows?"

"He is," Del told her.

"And this is *his* troupe that is being attacked?"

"One and the same."

Ruth watched from across the kitchen. *He's himself again. Thank God! And she takes after him. Same face. Same eyes ... I wonder if she sings?*

Just then the phone rang. Ruth answered it.

"Is this Ruth Carson?" It was Rhonda Olson.

"Yes, yes it is. Is this Rhonda?" Ruth covered the phone and mouthed to Del, "Rhonda Olson." Del nodded yes.

Ruth told Rhonda how much she was needed in the production, how important the part of Julie was in *Show Boat*, but to no avail.

Rhonda Olson informed Ruth, politely but firmly, that there was no way she or her son would be returning to the musical.

"It's too dangerous. It looks like someone is trying to hurt, or kill, people in the cast. Besides, Fritz knows better than to try and push me. He knows me from the old days. Once I make up my mind, nobody can change it. Nobody. You remind him of that, will you?"

Ruth didn't know what "old days" Rhonda was talking about, but she promised to relay the message to Fritz. She hung up the phone and looked at Del and Elizabeth, who had been taking it all in. She held up her hands in a gesture of resignation.

"Well, it seems we don't have a Julie. I don't know how we'll proceed. Maybe it's for the best." She looked crestfallen.

"Oh, you'll have a show, all right," said Elizabeth, who stood up from the table. "You just call Mr. Fritz Gerhardt and tell him little Lizzie Mays is back. I can do Julie."

"Oh no, you're not!" Del stood up and faced his daughter.

Ruth turned to her. "You were in Fritz's shows?" she asked, flabbergasted.

"Yes, I was," Elizabeth answered, "and, oh yes indeed, I am going to be in one again." She looked her father in the eye.

"Liz! You can't!" Del cried.

Father and daughter stood nose to nose.

"Do you think for one minute I'd let you get up on that stage without me being there to watch over you?" the young woman told him.

"I don't need you to watch over me!" Del's hands were in the air. His voice was more exasperated than angry, but a little vein stood out in his neck.

"Well obviously you do, Mr. 'it's not over yet,'" the girl said with both hands on her hips.

Del's shoulders sagged and then he started to laugh. "My God! You sound just like your grandmother!" He looked at her and then at Ruth. "You traitor! Did you have to tell her everything?"

"I thought she had a right to know."

Elizabeth smiled.

"Women!" Del exclaimed. "How can I win against two of you?"

Elizabeth walked over to Ruth and put her arm around her shoulders. "You can't. So don't even try."

Scream in the Night

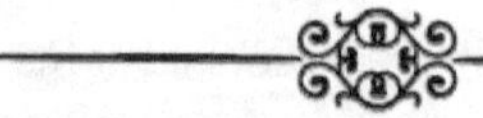

RUTH ASKED DEL AND Elizabeth to stay for supper, but the young woman insisted on taking her father back to her apartment in Minneapolis. Del gave Ruth an imploring look, but didn't argue with his daughter.

Elizabeth winked at Ruth and told her, "We'll stop at Ted Cook's Barbecue on the way home. Dad needs his soul food."

While Del was getting dressed, Ruth gave his daughter a tour of the house. Elizabeth stopped in front of a wall of family photos, gazing intently at a picture of Ruth's daughter, dressed in a theatre costume.

"Hannah is *your* daughter? No way! We were in several shows together. Fritz called us the Katzenjammer Kids. What one of us didn't think of, the other one did. I'm not sure I even knew her last name. I called her 'Hannah-Banana.' And she called me 'Lizzard!'" Elizabeth laughed at the memory. "What's she up to these days?"

Ruth brought Del's daughter up to date on what her daughter had been up to since her days in Fritz's shows.

Overhearing them as he came downstairs, Del was astonished. "What's this? You actually knew her daughter?"

"I didn't just know her," Elizabeth laughed. "Hannah-Banana and The Lizzard were co-conspirators! I just can't believe it! We were together in *Oliver, Sound of Music, Fiddler ... Oklahoma ...* Dad, do you remember the rubber chicken that was tied to the bridal canopy during the wedding scene in *Fiddler*, opening night?" There was a mischievous glint in her eyes.

Del tried to look stern, but he couldn't manage it. "The rubber chicken that caused your esteemed musical director to pop a gasket?"

"I remember that rubber chicken," Ruth exclaimed suddenly. "Hannah swore she never touched it."

"She didn't. We wore gloves!" Elizabeth doubled over with laughter at the prank.

They spent the next ten minutes rehashing the "good old days" in Fritz's productions. Ruth remembered Elizabeth now, although she had changed drastically from the gangly, silly child she once was, to the poised and beautiful young woman in Ruth's living room. She couldn't remember the girl's mother, but after Elizabeth told her that her grandmother usually brought her to rehearsals, Ruth recalled an older woman who sat and knitted while her granddaughter rehearsed.

After Del and his daughter left, Ruth felt exhausted.

"I don't even want supper," she said to Toby and Charlie. She let the two little dogs run around the back yard while she sat on the back steps watching. "Come on, you two. Hurry up. Mama's tired."

As she went back into the kitchen, the phone rang again. This time it was Angie.

"What're you doing home?" Angie asked. "We saw lights when we drove by and I thought it was Tracey and Danny."

"She and Danny left for his place," Ruth informed her. "They really are a cute couple." Then she soberly told Angie all that had transpired with Del.

"I'll be right home!" Angie told her.

"It's okay. Stay there as long as you want. I'm fine."

"I'll be there in a few minutes," Angie insisted.

Angie let herself in the back door and locked it.

"You look like hell," she said.

"Gee thanks," said Ruth yawning. "All I need is a good night's sleep."

After making sure all the doors were locked and the animals were fed and had water, the two women went to their respective bedrooms. Ruth dropped her clothes on the floor, put on her nightgown and flopped down on top of the bedspread, pulling her chenille "throw" over her as her head hit the pillow. *I'll change the bed and pick up my clothes tomorrow. I'm too tired now.*

She smelled the trace of smoke from where Del had slept on her pillow, but she didn't care. The last thing she saw before falling into a deep, dreamless sleep was the oak tree keeping watch over her bedroom window.

Keep Del safe, she thought, then slept through the night without waking.

She didn't see Del all weekend. He called every day, and even wanted to drive out to get her, but she told him he should rest.

"The insurance adjuster called my condo a total loss and it looks like I will get a good settlement, but Elizabeth won't even consider helping me look for a new place until after the show closes," Del complained.

"She's right," said Ruth. "You do what she tells you. She's a smart girl."

They talked a while longer and Ruth finally told him she had to go and let the dogs out. "I miss you, Miss Ruth," Del said. "I really do."

"I'll see you at rehearsal on Monday," she assured him.

"You know what I mean. Alone."

"Opening night is a week from this Thursday. We don't have time for alone."

"I know, I know. But promise me, when this is all over, you and I have a date. Just the two of us."

"Okay, I promise. Just us two." Ruth closed her eyes and said goodbye.

The following day, Ruth wrote to Hannah. She said nothing about the cast troubles because she didn't want her daughter to worry, but told her about Del and the fire and meeting 'Lizzard'."

Next she picked up the phone to call Robbie in Illinois. To her surprise, he was home. She told him about the *Show Boat* production but, as with Hannah, said nothing about the attacks. Then she said she was seeing a guy in the cast who was playing Joe, an opera singer whose big solo was "Ol' Man River."

"Good for you, mom."

"His name is Delancy Mays."

"Delancy Mays? I've heard of him!" Robbie whistled. "I think I've even seen him at the Lyric. He's famous. Good job, mom!"

"You sure it's okay with you?" she asked. "He's Black, you know."

"Yeah, mom," he chuckled. "Times are changing. Most people don't care about that race stuff so much anymore. It's no big thing. As long as he's good to you, I'm good with him." They talked a while longer and he told her about a new program he was inaugurating in his school, one that would put an Apple Macintosh computer in every classroom. He sounded excited about it. Then he told her about a lady professor he had been seeing, and that he had to get off the line and get ready for a dinner date with her. Ruth was happy for him and happy for herself.

Monday's rehearsal was wild. With opening night a week and a half away, Fritz was in high gear. He was furious at Rhonda for leaving.

"She'll never be in another show of mine!" he proclaimed. But a minute later he was positively gleeful that his little "Lizzy" was back. "She's her father's daughter. A real trouper!"

Fortunately, Elizabeth had quickly memorized most of her lines and music.

"Dad saved the score," she told Ruth. "Good thing, too." She moved across the stage with all of Del's grace and then some. Her lusty rendition of "Can't Help Lovin' That Man" got rousing applause from the rest of the cast.

Ruth noticed that officer Olson was lingering with the chorus. Billy Hammer had introduced him as an "extra baritone to fill out the men's parts." Since this sort of thing sometimes happened in the final days before a show's opening, no one in the cast seemed curious about his presence—and no one remembered that he had been a uniformed police officer on the paddleboat that day when they performed for the governor.

Ruth also noticed Sergeant Sullivan. He sometimes sat on the benches and sometimes walked the perimeter of the pavilion. He was not wearing his uniform and looked like just another father waiting for his child to finish rehearsing.

"I'm so glad he's here," thought Ruth.

Del glanced at Ruth often throughout the rehearsal. Once, during a crowd scene, he managed to squeeze her arm and whisper, "Coffee? Afterwards?"

She nodded yes, adding, "But Angie and I came together."

"As did Elizabeth and I ... so, we have chaperones."

After Fritz and Billy reviewed their cast notes, Fritz once again welcomed Elizabeth as the new Julie, telling everyone what a prodigy she had been years earlier as "one of my kids."

As Ruth, Del, Elizabeth, and Angie were leaving to go for coffee, Ruth noticed a black Lincoln Town Car parked near the pavilion. She watched a burly man get out and beckon impatiently toward someone.

Then she saw Susie, their accompanist, being pulled into the car. She thought she heard her scream, but it was silenced by the slamming car door.

Chapter 25

Who Killed the Piano Player?

R UTH GRABBED DEL'S ARM. "Did you see that?!"

Del turned to her. "See what? I'm sorry, I wasn't paying attention."

Elizabeth and Angie were walking ahead of them and hadn't noticed anything either. They stopped when they heard Ruth cry out.

"That was Susie, our piano player! Over there! Someone just grabbed her and forced her into that car!" She looked at everyone frantically, then scanned for Danny, but he had disappeared.

Elizabeth was of no help. "I'm sorry Ruth, I didn't see or hear anything. My mind was on my score, but if you think there's some kind of trouble, let's get Billy." The others agreed.

A small group of people were on stage discussing their notes with Billy Hammer. His wife Lorene, always his help-mate, was gathering up props and putting them into a large cardboard box. Gloria-June Kimmel was gesturing and arguing over some minute point in the script while her husband, Howard, stood quietly by her side. Don Olson was there, too. He turned to Ruth as she ran up to the group.

"Billy! Excuse me, please, but I think there's trouble!"

"What now?" said Billy, smiling at her. As a theatre director he was unflappable. He'd seen and heard it all and was good at calming excitable actors, especially right before opening night.

"It's Susie!" Ruth tried to catch her breath. "I think she's ... she's ..."

Del came up and put his arm around her shoulders. "Ruth saw her getting into a car and thought maybe she'd been forced in."

"A big black Lincoln?" Billy smiled a rakish smile. "A town car? Ritzy-looking?"

"Yes. And I thought I heard her scream."

The group began chuckling, albeit uncomfortably. Ruth looked puzzled.

The implacable Billy went on. "Screaming? Probably in delight. She's been Tony Ancino's ... uh ... 'honey' for, let's see, how many years now? Since *Brigadoon?*" He looked to the group. Like Billy, most of them measured time in theatre seasons and productions.

"Before *Brigadoon*," Gloria-June chimed in. "She started going with that guy way before *Brigadoon*. During *The King and I,* wasn't it? Don't you remember he was always in the front row, night after night, right next to the orchestra as the kids marched in?" Howard nodded in agreement.

"Okay, so it's been about four years," Billy said to Ruth. "You've got to keep up with the company romances, Ruth." He patted her shoulder. "I'm sure she's okay. Ancino ... yeah, that's Danny's uncle—Tony ... right, it's Tony." He chuckled. "They've had their little spats over the years." He looked at Gloria-June. "Remember after *Brigadoon* and that clarinet player who asked her out?"

"Oh God," laughed Gloria-June. "Did anybody ever see him again?" She gestured a slash across her throat with her hand. The group broke out in nervous laughter, except Don Olson, who didn't know what they were talking about.

Billy looked at Ruth and held his hands up in a gesture of helplessness. "She can't help lovin' that man of hers," he sang in a mock falsetto voice.

"Well, okay." Ruth felt relieved and a little embarrassed, wishing she had not reacted so frantically. If you think she's all right."

"Well, that depends on your definition of 'all right.' I suppose it's all right for a moll or for women who like it rough."

"Billy! For God's sake," Lorene muttered. Billy shrugged his shoulders but shut his mouth. Lorene shook her head and continued to throw props in the box, only now with force. The small group of actors, looking uncomfortable, began to disperse. Howard just sighed.

Del finally spoke up. "Let's go have some coffee, Ruth. I'm sure Susie can take care of herself."

Angie took Elizabeth's arm. "That Danny seems like a nice kid, though, don't you think?"

"He sings well," Elizabeth told her. "Not that that's an indication of his character," she added, more to herself than to Angie.

Billy went over to Lorene to help her. Del had noticed Don Olson's reserved countenance during the discussion of Susie's affair. He turned to the undercover policeman. "We're newcomers here, too. I don't know about the company romances, either. Would you like to join us for coffee? We're going to Keys."

The man looked surprised. "Oh, uh, thanks, but not tonight. I've got to get home to my new puppy. She's, well, she's a bit un-trained and you know how it is. I need to let her out." He waved as he walked off. "Maybe another time."

Back in the parking lot, Del opened the car door for Ruth and tried to give her a peck on the cheek as she slid into the front seat, but she ignored it. She still thought Susie was in trouble and was still smarting from the laughter of the group.

Maybe he's abusive to her. Or maybe I've seen too many gangster movies.

"I don't know about you people," Elizabeth piped-up from the back seat, "but I'm down-right starving. If we're going to Keys, I want one of their old-fashioned turkey dinners, with all the fixings."

"Oh, you lucky thing!" Angie chimed in. "So nice and skinny! I bet you can eat all you want and not gain weight."

"Ah, the young." Del looked over at Ruth. "My doctor says I can't eat for at least three hours before bedtime. Acid reflux. One of the delights of old age."

"You're not that old," Ruth told him, softening a bit.

Angie chimed in, "I'm not either. And I might just have that turkey dinner too."

"I wish Don Olson had seen Susie getting into that car," Ruth murmured. "Maybe he would have done something about it. He *is* a policeman, after all."

Del reached over and touched her hand. "I think we all feel safer having someone in the police force in the cast—we've got two, actually—but you know, they can't be everywhere at once."

"Do you think we really need the protection?" Elizabeth asked her father.

"Damn straight we do!" Angie piped up.

"Well, I'm just going to chalk this up to nerves," Ruth told them all. "And I don't know about you folks, but I plan on sleeping well tonight," she said, steering the conversation away from her fears, "so I don't want a heavy meal or anything with caffeine." She squeezed Del's hand.

Ruth had herbal tea and Del had decaf coffee and they both had some toast and jam. Elizabeth enjoyed her turkey dinner while Angie finally decided on a plate of onion rings, slathered in ketchup. They talked "shop" and tried to be positive about opening night. After they finished, Del insisted it was his treat and picked up the check.

Del drove Ruth, Angie, and Elizabeth back to the pavilion parking lot. Del told Elizabeth to "Sit here and digest your food for a minute. I'm going to walk the ladies to their car."

"Lock the doors," Ruth couldn't help saying, and then she glanced at Elizabeth in the back seat and blew her a kiss. To Ruth's delight, it was blown back.

"She's a wonderful girl," Ruth told Del as they walked across the darkened lot toward her car. Ruth could smell the flowers from the Bridal-Gate Garden and hear the nearby man-made waterfall as it cascaded over a wall of rocks into a pool of koi. She breathed in the warm summer air, letting the night surround her senses.

"She likes you, ya know," Angie told Ruth as they walked along.

Del's grip on Ruth's hand tightened. "I agree. She likes you ... a lot."

When they got to the car, Angie got in first and closed the door to give the two some privacy.

"*I* like you too," Del said tenderly to Ruth.

"It's mutual," Ruth whispered back.

They stood there for a moment, not wanting to leave each other.

It was Ruth who broke the spell. "You can't leave Elizabeth in the car and I can't leave Angie. We all have to get home."

"I'll call you in the morning." Del hugged her as if he didn't want to let her go.

As both cars drove out of the lot, the waterfall continued its night music, falling softly into the pool. Unfortunately, in a few short hours it would also fall onto the strangled body of Susie, the accompanist.

Chapter 26

The Police Can't Be Everywhere

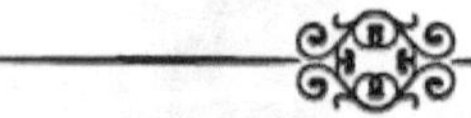

EARLY FRIDAY MORNING, GROUNDSKEEPERS at Como Park discovered the body. Angie was still in bed and Ruth was alone in her kitchen having her morning tea when her little countertop TV began broadcasting the news.

"The body of a young woman found dead this morning in the waterfall pool across from the pavilion in St. Paul's Como Park has been identified as 35-year-old Susan Ormstad of St. Paul. Joggers discovered the body just after seven this morning. Cause of death is under investigation. More on this breaking news at noon."

Ruth nearly dropped her tea cup.

"Oh my god!" Ruth cried. "Susie! It's Susie! He killed her! I knew she was in danger! It had to have been him!"

With shaking hands she stood up and reached for the kitchen phone, which rang just as she touched it. She jumped. After the second ring she picked it up.

"Hello?" Her voice trembled.

It was Del. "Have you seen the news?"

"Oh God," Ruth blurted out, sobbing. "We could have saved her. We could have stopped it!"

"We don't know that," Del said quietly, more to comfort Ruth than by any conviction he had. "It could have been totally unrelated." He took a deep breath. "We should talk to the police, though, and tell them exactly what you saw and heard. And when. I'll call Sullivan first, but I'm sure he'll want to talk with us in person at the station. I'll pick you up in about an hour."

"No," Ruth countered. "I'll meet you there. You don't need to drive all the way out to Lake Elmo."

"Nonsense." Del sounded firm. "I don't want you on the highway while you're so upset."

Ruth felt too ill to argue. "Well, okay. I'll be ready." She put her hand in front of her eyes, feeling dizzy. "Bye, see you soon."

She slumped down at her kitchen table and put her head in her hands. The phone rang again. She tried to get up to answer it, but she just couldn't. She sat there and let it ring, stunned by the evil consuming her theatre company.

It went to her answering machine. "Hi, Ruth. Hi, mom. It's Tracey. Just calling to tell you I got to Milwaukee okay. Mom, do you remember my company was sending me? The weather here is nice. Today we're going to see a new computer setup and tonight we're seeing some kind of a musical production at a comedy club. I don't know much about it, but I hope it's good. Anyway, I'll be here for four more days. Kiss the critters for me. I'll try calling again later. Bye now!" The phone clicked off just as Ruth finally reached for the receiver.

Ruth sat there, holding the phone, and stared at the oak tree outside her kitchen window. She could see two squirrels chasing each other 'round and 'round the huge trunk. She noticed the sunlight on the leaves.

The world is beautiful, she thought. *Or rather, nature is beautiful. It's people that ruin everything.* Tears rolled down her cheeks. She didn't even try to wipe her eyes. One of the dogs licked her right hand, which had fallen to her side.

"Oh, little baby," she gulped, as she patted Charlie's furry head. Or was it Toby's? She couldn't tell with her tear clouded eyes.

Just then Angie padded into the kitchen. "Didn't you hear the phone? I was in the bathroom and I couldn't get it." Then she saw Ruth's tears. "What?! Is it Tracey?" Her hand went over her heart.

"Yes … I mean *no*! Tracey's fine. She's in Milwaukee." Ruth put the phone back on the hook. "It's Susie, the accompanist. She was found dead this morning. In the waterfall pool across from the pavilion at Como Park. It's all over the news."

Angie paled and plopped down into the nearest chair. "Oh lord!" Her eyes grew wide. "I bet it's that mobster guy. The one in the car you saw." She stood up and started pacing the floor. "You gotta tell the police!" Her eyes got even wider. "Do you think Danny Ancino's mixed up in this? I gotta warn Tracey!"

"Hold on, hold on now." Ruth was upset but beginning to get her emotions under control. "We don't know that. Besides, that call was from Tracey. She's in Milwaukee on business with some others from her company. She's fine."

Neither woman had much appetite, so after a piece of toast and coffee for Angie and tea for Ruth, Angie took the dogs out in the back yard and Ruth went upstairs to get dressed. As soon as she reached her bedroom, the phone rang again. This time it was Fritz. He'd seen the news too. Ruth could tell he was trying to be calm, but he wasn't managing very well. He filled her in on what he'd heard about Susie's apparent murder and that, according to Channel 11, the police were looking for Susie's boyfriend, Tony Ancino.

Ruth asked what he was going to do about the accompaniment for the show?

"I've already called a guy I know from the musician's union," he told Ruth. He said he'd try to find me another pianist," and then he broke down. "I've worked with her for fifteen years!" he sobbed. "Oh my god! She was dating that gangster. I *told* her he was no good. She should have listened to me! Oh. My. God!"

Ruth let Fritz ramble on, holding the phone up to her ear while she pulled on a light gray blouse and a pair of dark gray slacks. Finally she said, "Maestro, I'm so sorry, but I need to get off the phone. Del is coming over and I have to get ready." She didn't want to go into the details of her impending visit to the police or what she thought about Susie's murder.

Ruth hung up and went downstairs. Angie was back inside with the dogs.

"Did Tracey say what hotel she was staying at?" she asked Ruth.

"No, I don't think she did. Here, listen to her message." Ruth played it back for Angie.

"Well, she sounds okay. But I wish I could have talked to her."

"I'm sorry I didn't get the phone in time. I was in shock."

"That's okay. Anyway, she calls a lot when she's out of town. I know she'll try again later." Angie poured herself a second cup of coffee and made two more slices of toast. "I think I'll just stay around the house so I'm here when she calls back." She put it all on a small tray and headed for the living room where they had a larger TV. "I'm going to see if they have anything more to say about it," she told Ruth as she left the kitchen. "Say 'hi' to Del for me. I'll give you two a little privacy."

"Oh Angie, you don't need to do that. It's not like we're teen-agers or anything."

"Mores the pity," Angie quipped back.

By the time Del pulled into her driveway, Ruth was having her second cup at the kitchen table. She'd been watching for him and let him in the back door.

He immediately took her in his arms. "Oh, my dear, my dear." He stroked her hair, her back. "Nothing will happen to you, my sweet lady. Nothing. I won't let it."

They stood there for some minutes, Ruth not wanting to leave the warm protection of his embrace, and Del not wanting to let her go. Finally, she said, "We have to go. We have to tell Sergeant Sullivan what we know."

"Bye, Angie!" Ruth called through the living room door. "I'll see you later."

"Bye!" Angie called through a mouthful of toast.

The ride to the station seemed surreal. Everything was so green and lovely. They passed grassy country meadows where she could see birds perched on phone wires and Queen Anne's Lace waving in the wind. They passed well-kept suburban developments where kids rode their bikes. Even as they entered the city, it seemed bustling and busy and happily unaware that a killer was loose within.

They walked into the downtown police station and Del spoke for her.

"We have an appointment with Sergeant Sullivan," he said with authority. "I called earlier this morning. I believe he is expecting us."

As they were being taken to Mickey Sullivan's office, they passed Don Olson's open door. He was on the phone, but waved to them as they walked by.

"It's our undercover man," Del said quietly to Ruth."

"Yes, the one who's supposed to keep us safe. Too bad he didn't follow Susie home."

"The police can't be everywhere at once." Del patted her shoulder. "They do the best they can."

Sergeant Sullivan was also on the phone when they were ushered into his office. The sergeant finished his conversation with a terse, "Well, I guess that's that then. Good bye." He sat back in his chair, looking grim.

"I know what you're going to tell me," he said to Ruth. "But Tony Ancino's lawyer beat you to it. It seems the old boy dropped Susie off next to her car in the pavilion parking lot about an hour after he picked her up there, and it sounds like his whereabouts can be documented for the entire evening. He looks clean."

"Can you tell us how she died?" Del asked.

"An autopsy hasn't been completed yet, but she had bruises on her neck. It looks like she was strangled."

"Strangled? Oh, poor Susie!" Ruth countered. "I don't understand. I saw her being dragged into that man's car! I'm sure I heard her scream!"

Danny Ancino stood in the office doorway. "You may have thought that my Uncle Tony pulled her into his car, Mrs. Carson, but she was probably laughing. They were always joking and foolin' around. The two of 'em acted like a couple of kids." Danny looked squarely at Ruth. "Uncle Tony loved that woman. He told me this morning he won't rest until he has her killer by the throat." He looked at Mickey Sullivan. "Uh, sorry, sir. I didn't mean to interrupt."

Ruth started to say something, but stopped.

Del tried to smooth things over. "I think everyone's upset by *all* the things that have happened. And now this. It's monstrous. Somehow we need to get to the bottom of it, and fast."

"I know, I know," Danny said, "but I want you to know that my family—while technically they might not always be on the right side of the—you know, but when push comes to shove, they're good people." He looked at Ruth imploringly. "They really *are* good people."

"I believe you, Danny," she told him. "And I don't want to hurt your feelings, but what I witnessed didn't look like they were just kidding around."

Sergeant Sullivan took down Ruth's statement and told her the police might need to talk with her again. Then he repeated the concern he had voiced earlier. "I think whoever did this was the same person who killed Mr. Worthing and assaulted Mrs. Corbello ... and also tried to kill the Rosenbergs, the Olson boy, and *you*." He looked at Del. "Please, try to convince Mr. Gerhardt to cancel this show."

As they left Sullivan's office and walked down the hall, Del said under his breath, "Fat chance!"

Chapter 27

Enough is Enough

DEL INSISTED ON TAKING Ruth to lunch.

"I've finally got you to myself," he said, squeezing her hand. "You're not going to get away from me this time!" He drove through the Cathedral district toward Grand Avenue. "How about Le Grande Café?"

"I'm not very hungry," Ruth replied. "I still feel as if we should have done something to save Susie." She sighed and looked out the window at the graceful old houses lining Summit Avenue.

"You are not responsible for the whole world," he gently told her, "even though you think you are."

"Do *you* think Tony Ancino did it?" she asked as Del maneuvered his Lexus through the noon-time traffic on Grand.

"It's difficult to say." He was looking in vain for a parking space. "Usually the first suspect is a spouse or a lover ... except for present company, of course. Hey, I think I see a spot! Say a prayer, it's a block away." Prayer answered, Del pulled into a space not far from Grand and Victoria.

Ruth thought a moment. "If what Danny says is true ... that his Uncle Tony loved Susie and wouldn't hurt her for the world, then what about the 'rough stuff' Billie mentioned? And I could swear I heard her *scream*, not laugh." She shook her head as if to clear it of the sound.

"I know you heard something." He reached for her hand as they walked. "But you could have been reading things into it. It's easy to do. We've all been upset at the murders, and the attempts." He stopped short on the sidewalk and looked deeply into Ruth's eyes. "I'm upset too. Maybe it's a guy thing, but I am trying to be brave, and use logic"

"Somehow, I just don't think this killer is logical," Ruth responded.

Although she initially picked at her food, Ruth eventually managed to down most of Le Grande Café's famous salad sampler and a piece of crusty parmesan bread. Del had the turkey, bacon and guacamole sandwich with corn chips. They both had raspberry iced tea. In the upscale, cosmopolitan atmosphere of this popular establishment, they both felt at home.

Ruth decided to change the subject while they ate.

"How's living at your daughter's place?" she asked him, more to make pleasant conversation than anything else.

"Well," Del hedged, "let's just say we are getting to know each other better and leave it at that."

"It's not a good arrangement? Why don't you look for someplace else?" She already knew the correct answer and smiled down at her plate.

"Don't you tease me, woman," he whispered. "I'm hoping for a better offer. Maybe a place on a lake so I can fish." He took her chin and raised her face so she had to look at him.

"Del, you know I'd ... I'd love to, but Angie's my house guest." Ruth could feel her face getting warm. "What would she think?"

"That you're a cool modern woman who does what she wants." He leaned his elbows on the table. Ruth just smiled and shook her head.

He offered her his pickle, which she took, but after one bite, she grimaced and handed it back. He popped the rest of it into his mouth.

They continued eating in relative silence. Not an uncomfortable silence, but the quiet of two people who know and like each well enough not to worry about keeping up a conversation. At one point, Ruth took her napkin and absentmindedly brushed a crumb off Del's collar. He sighed contentedly. They looked, for all the world, like an old married couple.

"Oh no!" Del whispered as he looked over Ruth's shoulder. "I don't believe it. Here we go again."

"What?" Ruth tuned to look, just in time to see Blanche Voorhees and a young man get into the line to order food at Le Grande Café.

In spite of herself and what had transpired that morning, and perhaps because of the stress of it, Ruth began to laugh. It started out as a giggle and within a few seconds she was looking down at her lap, holding her hands over her mouth, her shoulders quaking.

Embarrassed by her own uncontrolled mirth, Ruth rocked back and forth and shook her head. "I'm sorry, Del. It's just so, so ridiculous and so funny. I can't help it."

Then Del started laughing also, a low chuckle that grew into a muffled guffaw as he tried to keep quiet. "I know. God, it's so ... awful. I mean ... she's everywhere!"

"Maybe she won't see us," Ruth whispered, lowering her head, but to no avail. The woman spotted Del and Ruth and immediately left the line of people, dragging her bewildered friend with her.

Again, the clacking of her stiletto heels announced the arrival of Blanche Voorhees. Dressed in a hot pink suit, she had two matching pink spots on her cheeks, more perhaps from rage than overdone rouge.

"Well, we meet again," she declared, but not pleasantly. "I swear you people are following me around." Her escort stared intently at the wall, then the floor.

"But we were here first," Del countered.

Ruth nodded, trying not to smile, and not quite making it. She shrugged her shoulders and gave a palm up gesture with her hands.

"You think you're pretty smart, don't you, Mrs. Carson?" Blanche said icily to Ruth. "Playing the innocent. Laughing at people. You make fun of everything and everybody, don't you? I see your little game. I'm wise to you!"

Ruth opened her mouth to object and Del stood up as if to protect Ruth, but Blanche kept right on, her voice low and menacing.

"And *you*, Del. How can you be so, so completely taken in by this conniving, this ... plotting, no-talent wannabe?"

"All right, that's *enough*, Blanche!" Del was no longer laughing. He spoke in low tones so as not to be heard by other diners. "Mrs. Carson and I are good friends. With time, I hope we'll be even better friends." He put his hand on Ruth's shoulder. "And *you* need to understand that.

And respect it. Enough is enough! My companions are absolutely none of your business!" He emphasized these last words while peering into Blanche's eyes without flinching.

"Come on, Blanche," said her escort. "Let's go. Please."

Blanche glared imperiously at Ruth, swung around with a flourish and headed for the exit, escort in tow.

Ruth and Del tried to finish the remains of their lunch, pretending nothing much had just happened. Del even remarked about the large paintings hanging on the walls.

"Look at that landscape. What do you think about those birch trees? Did the artist know what birch trees really look like? Those leaves are more like oak leaves, don't you think?"

"Oh Del." Ruth was solemn now, her eyes beginning to well with tears. "Maybe this is wrong. Maybe we shouldn't see so much of each—"

Del cut her off. "Stop! We are not going to let that woman ruin this for us."

"I know. I don't want her to, either," Ruth stammered, "but maybe we shouldn't see so much of each other in public." She looked furtively at the tables around them, but the other diners had already lost interest in the little melodrama and were deep into their own conversations.

"Enough of such talk. Just listen to yourself." Del reached over and put his hand upon hers. "You're going to let someone like, like that awful woman dictate your life? I don't believe what you're saying."

Ruth lowered her voice. "Just how close were you two?" Even as the words came out of her mouth, Ruth wished she could take them back. "I'm sorry. I have no right to ask you that." She looked down in her lap.

"No ... no ... you have every right to ask me about her. She acts as if we were lovers, and believe me, we were *not!*"

"I want to believe you, but why would she ...?"

"Because she's not only delusional, she's an arrogant, malicious, self-absorbed *bitch!*" "Sorry, for my language, Ruth," Del said with disgust, "but there's no other way to say it. She thinks she's superior to everyone else, and she thinks she can push everyone around, make them fall at her feet and do whatever she wants."

Ruth started to say something, then hesitated, allowing Del to continue.

"All I did was take her to a cast party—one cast party. That's it, and I was even finagled into that!" He shook his head. "Her publicist set up the whole thing. Then she started sending me notes and calling me on the phone. She got it into her head that I belonged to her. My God! The woman is like a leech!"

Ruth pushed the salt shaker toward him. Del laughed and set it in front of his plate. "That's exactly what I need! Salt was my grandmother's cure for leeches."

"My grandma's, too."

"Don't let her get between us. What we have is very special."

"I just hope she doesn't know where I live," Ruth told him.

"Maybe I should move in with you to protect you," Del teased.

"You don't think *she's* the one who's doing all this, do you?" Ruth said, ignoring his comment about moving in. I heard she and Fritz hate each other. You don't think she would ... ?"

Del shook his head. "I don't think she'd risk breaking her nails to strangle someone." He held his stomach. "Ooh. This drama isn't good for my digestion."

Ruth immediately dug in her purse for a Tums and gave it to him. "We need a no-stress meal," she said.

"We need a no-stress *life!*"

⁂

When Ruth and Del finally arrived back in Lake Elmo, they could hear Charlie and Toby frantically barking as they approached the house. "What's eating them?" Ruth said, more to herself than to Del as they headed for her back porch door.

She opened it and found the reason for all the fuss. A chipmunk had broken through a tear in one of her window screens. The poor critter was sitting on the highest shelf of the old bookcase she kept on the porch, the one she used at Christmastime to store Tupperware containers full of cookies.

"Well, my goodness, look at you!" she laughed at the little creature who sat stock still, frozen in fear at yet another creature larger than itself. She let both dogs out the back door as Del slipped past them and entered.

He saw the chipmunk and quietly said, "Shh. Let me see if I can catch him." He held his hand out. "I used to be pretty good at this."

"Del, be careful," Ruth chided. "He's wild, you know. What if he bites and has rabies?"

Del ignored her, holding his hand perfectly still and making a soft clicking noise with his tongue. The chipmunk seemed mesmerized.

Ruth held her breath, watching the man she loved try to lure the little critter onto his hand.

He looks like someone out of a nature film, she thought to herself. "*Wild Kingdom.*" She stood still and didn't make a sound.

After a few seconds, Del moved nearer to the shelf, his long fingers edging toward the frightened creature, and then, as if by magic, the chipmunk sniffed Del's hand and crawled onto it. Del did not move, just stood there, looking into the creature's eyes while continuing to make soft clicking sounds with his tongue. Then, he edged toward the door, and as Ruth opened it for him, he gently moved his hand toward the window ledge of Ruth's back porch. The chipmunk saw his chance and without a backward glance scampered across the ledge and down the wall, disappearing into the bushes bordering Ruth's house.

"Where did you learn to do that?" Ruth laughed, amazed and delighted at this surprising feat.

"My grandmother," Del said with a grin. "She called it 'calmin the critters.'" He repeated the sound to demonstrate.

"I think you have a bit of St. Francis in you." She turned and looked at her torn screen. "And if I'm lucky, maybe some Bob Vila, too?"

"You will find me a very handy man to have around," Del told her, as he encircled her waist with his arms. "I can fix a lot of things."

Ruth let herself be held, there on her back porch, feeling the cool breeze as it came up from the lake. "I don't know how my screen got torn," she wondered. "It was okay the last time I remember looking at it."

"What's this?" Del let go of Ruth to stoop and pick up a well-worn music booklet on the floor. "This is the score for *Show Boat*. Ruth, you shouldn't leave it out here. It could get rained on."

"I wouldn't do that," she scowled, taking it from Del to examine it. "This isn't mine. It has someone else's handwriting on it." She looked at it more closely. "Oh my God, it's the piano score." She felt a cold shiver of fear, more than any cool wind off the lake could bring. "Del, look. Look at the front page. It's Susie's!"

Del winced. "S.A. Ormstad" was written in Susie's neat handwriting at the top of the title page, and immediately after it someone had scrawled in black marker pen, "It's not over yet."

"It's our killer. He's been here," Del said quietly. Then he bent down and took a closer look at Ruth's torn screen. "This screen wasn't torn. It's been cut."

The Storm

RUTH STOOD STILL, HER breathing coming in short gasps. She felt as though nowhere was safe, except in Del's arms.

What am I going to do? If he knows where I live, he must know Angie and I are alone out here! ... Ohmygod! ... Angie! Where's Angie?! She yanked the back door open and called into the kitchen. "Angie? Angie!"

Del was right behind her. "Ruth," he said firmly, grabbing her shoulders. "Let me go in first." As he strode into the kitchen, he noticed a large, hand-written note taped to the refrigerator. It read: "George and I are out looking at condos. We're going out for supper. Don't wait up. I'll probably stay over. Will call you later. Love, Angie"

He showed Ruth the note and, instantly relieved, she laughed. "She's in love! She's in love with my neighbor, George. She's staying over at his house? Oh, Angie!" She laughed and cried at the same time, trembling as she put her arms around Del.

Finally her mind shifted back, perplexed by the cut screen and the piano score still clutched in one hand. "I'm sorry, Del. It's just that, well, *why*? Why does this killer, this person, whoever he is, leave that kind of thing ... that kind of 'message' at *my* house?"

"I don't know," Del sighed, "but Sullivan needs to see this right away. Can they get finger prints off of paper? We need to make another trip in to the police station."

"Oh, I just can't." Ruth looked at the musical score. "I'm too tired to drive into town again now. Let's just call him. You can drop Susie's score off there tomorrow." She blushed as she realized what she'd said. "I mean tonight. Tonight, when you, ah, go back in town."

Del raised his eyebrows. "Oh ho," he said with amusement. "Was that an invitation?" He ran his fingers down the side of her cheek. "Was it?" He smiled down at her.

"Del, behave!" she chided, moving away slightly. She looked around the room. "It's just that, with Angie gone, I don't know if it's safe for me to be here alone."

Del brightened at the thought. "I'll call Elizabeth. I'll tell her what happened and that I'm going to bunk out here for a while—in your guest room, of course." He looked pointedly at Ruth. "That's really what you want, isn't it? For now?"

"Oh Del." She breathed easier. "Thanks for being so patient with me. I guess I'm not one to rush into things." She went into the kitchen and checked the cat's dishes, which were empty. "Poor babies!" she muttered to herself. As she proceeded to fill them, Morrie and Griselda moved in to eat and drink.

They carefully checked out the whole house, with Del insisting on going ahead of her. Ruth was glad to have him with her, especially when they searched the gloomy basement. Other than the cut screen and the music score on the porch floor, they found nothing else amiss.

When they finished scouring every room and every closet, Del insisted that he look around the yard too.

"And your garage, starting with your car, and see if everything's okay out there." Ruth went with him, not wanting to be alone in the house any more than necessary.

After making certain the outside was as safe as the inside, they walked down to the lake with Charlie and Toby at their heels.

"I could get used to this," Del kidded as he stepped out on the dock. "Any walleyes in this lake?"

"I see fishermen out here all summer, but I don't know what they catch."

"This is beautiful," Del stated, drinking in the scenery.

"It's quite a deep lake. About a hundred fifty feet, I've heard. And the water is nice and clear."

"Then it probably has good fishing. I used to fish as a boy. I was proud to bring my catch home to my mother. She was always appreciative."

"Did you also clean them?"

"Oh yes. In our family, the men-folk caught and cleaned the fish, and the women-folk fried 'em up."

"Tom fished, but not as much as he wanted to. He passed away two years before he was supposed to retire." She looked down. "I'm sorry. That was ..." Her voice trailed off.

"It's okay." Del put his arm around her and gave her a squeeze. "We're going to have to tell each other our memories from time to time, but I hope we can make some memories of our own."

"I think we already have," Ruth said as she looked up at him. "I only wish they were better ones."

"You just let me take care of that," he told her. "I promise you we'll make some great memories."

"We'd better go inside and call the police."

They held hands as they walked up to the house.

Del called Sergeant Sullivan and left a message to call Ruth's number. Ruth made some tea. They settled down on the sofa to drink it and watch the news.

The television droned—*protesters are still being rounded up by the Chinese government after a deadly crackdown in Tiananmen Square … cleanup continues in Alaska's Prince William Sound after a massive oil spill … St. Paul's mayor, George Latimer, announces a new housing initiative … need a brake job? Midas will do it for only $79 an axel …*

Charlie and Toby lay contentedly at their feet, giving Ruth a feeling of normalcy. *The animals would be more upset if someone had been in the house,* she thought to herself. *Maybe whoever it was went no farther than the back porch.* As she sat on the sofa with Del, Ruth felt the house take on an air of comfort, something she hadn't truly felt for a long time.

"This is nice," sighed Del as he leaned over to Ruth to click her cup with his. "To us," he said simply.

"To a quiet evening," Ruth answered, "and no more visitors." She leaned back against the soft blue and tan plaid pillows.

"Oops!" Del set his cup down on the coffee table and got up quickly. "I forgot to call Elizabeth." He winked at Ruth as he hurried to the phone on the kitchen wall. He kept the door open so Ruth could hear the conversation.

"I don't think she's home yet," he whispered as he held his hand over the receiver. "I'll leave her a message to call here ... Hi, honey. This is Dad. Something has come up and I need to stay out at Ruth's tonight. It's not terribly urgent, but please call us when you can." He left Ruth's number. "'Bye now. Love you, baby girl."

"I'm not sure when to expect her call," he told Ruth. "She has grueling hours. It may be late when she calls back, or she may just wait until tomorrow."

"I don't care," Ruth told him, feeling secure in his presence. "Whenever she calls will be fine." Then she thought for a moment and looked at him. "Do you think she'll be upset that you're staying here?"

He sat down next to her and covered one of her hands with his. "She already thinks we're an item. I heard her tell her grandmother all about you the other day. She was on the phone when she thought I was napping. She was actually defending you to her."

"You're lucky your mother is still alive."

"Not mine, Elaine's. Her name is Wilda. She's a tough cookie, but I have a feeling she'll like you. Besides, she's always telling me to get married again."

"But maybe not to a white woman?"

"Oh, I don't think that will be an issue," said Del. "Her father was white—the son of a plantation owner. He left a fortune to run away north with her mother so they could marry."

"How romantic!" Ruth exclaimed. "I hope they had a long and happy life together."

"They did. I never saw two people more devoted to each other. You know, every morning of their married life, he brought her first cup of coffee to her in bed." Then he sat back and sighed. "I did the same thing for Elaine—when I wasn't on the road."

"She was a lucky woman. They both were." Ruth snuggled closer.

They turned off the television and sat quietly on the sofa for some time, watching the sun go lower in the sky over the lake. They could hear the birds chirping outside and the quiet breathing of the dogs at their feet. Morrie and Griselda flanked them on the sofa, purring.

Ruth felt like purring, too.

Finally she looked at her watch. "It's almost seven o'clock. Are you hungry? How about I fix you something to eat?"

"'You know what I'd really like?" he grinned boyishly.

"What?"

"Popcorn. I'm hungry for some popcorn." He leaned back into the pillows and put his arms behind his head. "Popcorn, woman!" He clapped his hands. "That's what I want—if you have it."

Ruth laughed as she got up and went into the kitchen. "Popcorn it is!" she called back. "Buttered or non-buttered?"

"Oh, I guess 'none.' Got to watch my cholesterol."

About ten minutes later, she returned with a big stainless-steel bowl of hot popcorn, lightly salted. She set it on the coffee-table and went back to the kitchen. This time she returned with two small wooden bowls, two napkins and a salt-shaker, in case Del wanted more seasoning. "Here you are, m'lord," she said, teasingly.

"Ah, woman, you are a jewel, a rare jewel." He dug his small bowl into the large one, filling it to overflowing. "This smells so good."

The storm came up suddenly, as summer storms in Minnesota some-times do. The early evening sky turned from reddish-gold to a dark greenish-gray. The branches of the oaks nearest the house began whip-ping at the roof and rain began coming down in sheets amid plenty of thunder and lightning. Ruth jumped up to close the windows and Del got up to help.

"Is it always this noisy out here?" he yelled, over the racket outside.

"Sometimes!" Ruth yelled back. "I'm going upstairs to see if there are any windows open up there." By this time, Morrie and Griselda had run off to hide, frightened by the thunder. Charlie and Toby were obviously frightened too, but they followed Ruth upstairs and stayed with her as she went from her bedroom, to Angie's, and finally to the bathroom, which had an open window. Rain was blowing in.

"This might be a bad one," she said to herself as she hastily shut the window and mopped up some of the floor with a big bath towel. "I'm glad Del's here."

Back downstairs, she heard the television in the living room, which Del had turned on. The usually perky weather lady on Channel 4 looked serious as she described the storm.

"... with straight-line winds up to seventy miles per hour. We have eye-witness reports of tornadoes sighted in the Hugo/Lino Lakes area but no word on whether anything touched down. The storm is traveling in a southeasterly direction. Residents of Grant Township, Stillwater, Bayport, and Lake Elmo should take cover immediately."

Ruth switched it off. "We should go down to the basement. You grab the dogs," she told Del. "I'll try to find the cats. Hurry!" When he didn't react right away, she raised her voice a few decibels. "Del, get the dogs!" She spotted Morrie and Griselda crouching under a low cabinet and managed to get hold of both squirming cats, putting one under each arm before heading toward the basement door. "Come on, Del, we've got to get downstairs."

"Okay, okay," he answered. He scooped up Toby, but Charlie eluded him by racing into the kitchen. Del chased after him. "Come here, you!" he called, running after the frightened little terrier.

"Leave him!" Ruth yelled up the stairs. "Get down here quick!" The storm had been surging in intensity and then suddenly the wind stopped blowing. "It's too quiet," she called up to him. "That's bad." There was fear in her tone. "Del! Please get down here—*now!*"

"Maybe it's done?" he said, out of breath as he finally reached the basement.

"That's not the way it works." She motioned him toward her. "When it gets suddenly quiet, then we're in real trouble. Let's get under the stairs. Please!"

While they hunkered down beneath the basement stairs, she called to Charlie.

"Here Charlie, here, boy. Here Charlie!"

The wind began to howl again, sounding like a freight train, which brought the dog scampering down the steps. As soon as his paws hit the floor, the lights went out, plunging the room into blackness. Seconds later, Ruth and Del heard a deafening crash on the floor above.

"Oh no!" screamed Ruth. "The house!" Without thinking, she started to get up.

"No!" Del snapped as he held her back. "Stay here." He pulled her close. "We're safer here." The two dogs quivered next to them. The two cats found another hiding place somewhere in the basement. Outside, the storm raged.

Chapter 29

A Good Cop Dies

THEY SHELTERED UNDER THE basement stairs for what seemed like an eternity. Ruth felt safe in Del's arms, even though she knew they were in danger. *It's just a house, just a building,* she kept telling herself as her eyes became accustomed to the dark. *I should be thankful we're all alive.* She knew the animals were down in the basement with them.

After about ten minutes the storm quieted down.

"I think it's probably okay to go up now," Del said softly. "Let's see what happened upstairs." He shifted to get on his feet and Ruth let go of his arms. Distant sirens could be heard outside.

"Be careful," he cautioned. "There might be broken glass on the floor, or electric wires." He helped her up. "Let's keep the animals down here for now. They'll be safer."

As they ascended into Ruth's kitchen and closed the basement door behind them, they heard someone in the back yard.

"Is anybody in there? Everybody all right?" Raindrops could also be heard, and beams from several flashlights could be seen dancing around outside.

"Looks like the police," Ruth said to Del. "Lake Elmo police I think. They got here fast."

Del led her toward the kitchen. "We're in here," he shouted. "We're okay!"

Someone was rattling the back door knob. Ruth hurried to open it for him, wiping her eyes on her sleeve.

A heavy-set police officer stood before her. It was Lake Elmo's popular police chief, Captain Henry Stoltzman, whose "don't-mess-with-me" demeanor belied a big heart. Ruth recognized him right away.

"We just came up from the basement. We haven't had a look, yet," Ruth told him. Del was rummaging through kitchen drawers.

"Do you have a flashlight somewhere?" he asked Ruth.

"It should be in the drawer by the stove."

The chief pointed his flashlight in that direction and Del found what he was looking for. "I think the batteries are dead."

The stream of light landed on Del's face, then quickly moved to the floor and then to the opposite wall.

Oh boy, thought Ruth with an inward laugh, *I'm in for it now. This is a small town.*

As if he'd read her thoughts, Del spoke up. "I'm Delancy Mays. I was a dinner guest of Mrs. Carson's and I was just leaving when the storm hit." He held out his hand to the policeman.

"Pleased to meet you," the burly chief said as he shook Del's hand with a good-natured smile. "A little more of an evening than you bargained for, eh?"

"That's for sure. I'll be glad to get back into town."

"I'm afraid nobody's goin' anywhere for a while," the man told him. "Power lines and big trees are down on all the roads around here. Let's check out the rest of your house," the officer continued. "Most of the damage is along the lakefront." He stepped cautiously into the living room. "Whoo boy!" he said, under his breath.

"What?" Ruth hurried to the door and peered in, eyes following the beams of light. She gasped when she saw the branch of a huge oak tree in the room. It had crashed through the front window, destroying the frame, crushing one of her antique ladderback chairs and grazing a table before stopping inches short of her piano. "Oh dear!" she blurted out. "What a mess!" Broken glass, fragments of wood, and wet leaves lay everywhere. Then, looking at her piano, she sighed with relief. "I just had it tuned and some of the pads re-done." She ran her hand over the smooth surface of the instrument. "It seems to be okay," she said, wiping water off the top with her hands.

"Maybe we should find something to cover it," Del told her. "Moisture and pianos don't mix."

"Yeah, well you'd best do that, Mrs. ... uh ..." mumbled the policeman.

"Carson," Ruth told him. "Ruth Carson. I co-chaired the fall pig-roast last year. Remember? I worked with your wife." Ruth was trying to recall the woman's first name. She could see her in her mind: short, plump, dark-brown hair, full of energy, a bit disorganized.

"Pat knows you? Oh, sure," he smiled broadly, "I remember you now." He rubbed his stomach with one hand and pointed at Ruth with the other. "I remember your apple pie." He looked around and returned to the emergency at hand. "You people will need to find a dry place to sleep tonight. Let's see if the upstairs is livable." Just as he started up the stairs an urgent-sounding male voice yelled from outside.

"Captain Stoltzman! There's a guy out here under a tree. Hurt pretty bad. We need to get the tree off him. He'll need paramedics!"

"Who is it?" the chief yelled back. Then, "Get on the radio and ask if we can we get EMS over to ... what's the house number here?" he asked Ruth. "Over to 216 Lakeside Avenue ... stat!" One officer ran to the police car, the other was trying to remove the branches off the man on the ground.

"Do you know who it is?" Stoltzman shouted through the yawning hole in the wall.

"I don't know, but he's in a uniform ... he's a cop!" came the voice from outside. "I'm tryin' to clear the branches off him ... Oh geez!" he cried once more. "You better get someone out here fast!"

Captain Stoltzman pushed his considerable bulk against Ruth's front door, which was jammed. She heard it creak and groan and then finally open, admitting more oak branches into her living room but allowing the policeman to exit. Ruth and Del followed.

"Move outa the way. Let me see 'im." You could tell he was used to giving orders. "Does he have any I.D.?" He gently pushed branches away from the upper portion of the man's body and directed his flashlight upon the form lying before him. "Lord have mercy!," he whispered, turning his head away from the gaping wound in the man's chest.

Ruth was looking over his shoulder and could read the name inscribed on the man's bloody shirt: "Sullivan." Tears welled up in her eyes.

"He's still alive," said the younger officer, astonished. "He's trying to say something."

The Chief had seen dying men in his career. They sometimes rallied, backing away from death's door in order to say one last thing. Usually it wasn't very important or was unintelligible. Sometimes they didn't know who they were talking to. This man seemed to be no exception. "I ... I ... was going ... " the injured man whispered, bloody saliva forming bubbles at the corners of his mouth.

"Shhh, fella. Save your strength. The storm's over and everybody's okay. Hold on. The ambulance is on its way," he gently told the man, brushing wet twigs away from his face.

"I was ... was ..."

They were Sergeant Mickey Sullivan's last words.

Chapter 30

House Bound

R UTH AND DEL WATCHED, horrified, as the paramedics put the body of Mickey Sullivan on a gurney and covered him with a sheet.

"How did you know him?" asked Captain Stoltzman. "Why was he in your yard?"

Del started to say something and then looked at Ruth.

"It probably had something to do with the murders surrounding our show at the Como Pavilion," she said, shaking her head. "We're in the cast. We've been working with Sergeant Sullivan. Maybe he came out here to tell us something and just got caught in the storm. It came up so suddenly."

"Maybe," said the chief hesitantly. "Well, whatever he knew, or was trying to do, may have died with him. The St. Paul police have a bad situation on their hands with that Como Park music thing." He went back to his squad car but when he reached it, he turned around. "If anything comes up in regard to those murders, if anyone threatens you out here, or there's something you want to tell me, don't hesitate to call us immediately. What's been going on is nasty business and we don't want you or anybody else to get hurt. You hear?"

Ruth and Del assured him that they would, and thanked him. Then they walked over to check on her neighbor, George, to see if he and Angie were okay. They were fine—happily and safely holed up in George's little house. There were some downed branches in his yard, but the place appeared otherwise untouched.

"I love this house!" Angie told Ruth. "It's so cozy. I'm trying to talk him out of moving to a condo."

Ruth told Angie the bad news about Sergeant Sullivan.

"Oh no!" Angie cried. "He was such a nice man." She guessed he had come out to tell Ruth something about the murders and got caught at the wrong place at the wrong time. "I wonder what he found out?" she said.

"I wish we knew," Ruth answered softly.

Ruth's house had sustained less damage than initially thought. Her front window and part of the sill and frame had been torn out. She had a big downed tree, a very messy yard, and some missing shingles, but other than that, things could have been much worse. The storm, later reported to be an EF2 tornado, caused real havoc not far away. Some houses farther down the street lost their roofs.

Fortunately, Ruth was able to get through to her insurance agent the next morning and within a day an adjuster came to survey the damage and provide an estimate for repairs. Del in the meantime found a buck-saw in the garage that he used to cut up the living room tree branch. After removing the pieces, he headed for the Lake Elmo lumberyard where he bought what he needed to temporarily board up the gaping hole in Ruth's living room wall.

"My goodness! You really are handy!" Ruth called to him as he pounded in the last plywood panel. "But be careful!"

"I am making myself indispensable to you, madam. I will ... be ... yo ... handyman ..." he sang out.

Later, he also took a look at Ruth's broken ladderback chair, but they decided it was a lost cause.

Roadblocks cordoning off the storm-damaged area lasted three days. Gawkers were kept out by National Guardsmen who only allowed residents to come and go. Checkpoints were located at key intersections and passes were issued for each household. It was well organized and, as a result, the people of Lake Elmo felt certain their property was as safe as could be under the circumstances.

A week after the storm, the Immaculate Heart of Mary Church in St. Paul held a funeral mass for Sergeant Sullivan. Ruth and Del decided not to attend. "I wish we could go, but I feel like such a mess!" They had both been taking sponge baths using water brought up from the lake, or just going swimming to wash up, because there was no running water for bathing. The electricity was still out, disabling the pump, and every household in Ruth's neighborhood had its own well. On the day of the funeral, Del brought the morning *Pioneer Press* back from Gustafson's.

"It says Sergeant Sullivan died accidentally when he was struck by a falling tree in Lake Elmo during the storm, but nothing more about why he was out here." He shook his head. "I still can't figure this out. Why would he be out here, alone, at night, in your yard? Was he going to tell us something, or was he looking for something? Was he doing some kind of stake out, watching for something?" He paused to let that idea float. "Maybe we shouldn't even talk to the police in St. Paul. Maybe we should just look out for ourselves and not depend on anybody for anything," he sighed. "If you were Black, you'd know what I mean about being wary … and on your own …" His voice trailed off as he looked vacantly out the window. "We've learned to take care of ourselves."

"Oh, I don't know," mused Ruth. "In that respect, maybe our worlds haven't been so different. My Swedish grandparents came here with nothing but the clothes on their backs. At first, they were looked down on because they were poor and barely spoke English. They depended heavily on their own family and friends. They *had* to in order to get by. You and I, we'll do the same. We'll just take care of each other." Ruth put her arms around him.

"I would never let anyone or anything hurt you, if I could help it," Del told her as he kissed her.

Ruth hugged him extra hard and then started emptying the bag from Gustafson's Grocery, smiling as she took out three plastic jars of Orville Redenbacher's Gourmet Popcorn.

"Was this on my list?" she asked teasingly.

"It's for when we get electricity again, which will be very soon, I'm sure. Anyway, I thought I'd splurge a bit."

Because they were the only grocery store in Lake Elmo, Gustafson's Grocery was doing a booming business. Nobody had electricity except those with generators, such as Gustafson's. Mr. Gustafson was from one of the oldest families in town. While the electricity was out, he gave away bottled water and bags of ice, free of charge, to the locals who needed them. He said he considered it "payback" to the town.

"You wouldn't see anything given out for free in the city," Del remarked.

Ruth agreed. "Lake Elmo is his town and he cares about it. And it's probably good for business in the long run. Builds loyalty."

"When I was walking up to that little store this morning," Del said, "it reminded me of my home town in Illinois where I grew up. People were good there, just like they seem to be here." He smiled at Ruth, who smiled back at him from the open door of her dark refrigerator while putting two large bags of ice on the middle shelf.

"This ice reminds me of when I was little," she told him. "Remember ice boxes? When I was a kid, my grandparents didn't have a refrigerator. They had an old-fashioned ice box with a big block of ice in it."

"Those bags of ice were free too, from Mr. Gustafson," Del told her. "He's a good one."

"There are lots of good people in this town," she said. "Big cities are okay to visit, but I wouldn't want to live in one. Too anonymous. I'm a country mouse."

Del thought for a moment. "My grandmother always said 'It takes a whole town to raise a child.' Oh boy! If we did anything wrong in our town, the mothers, grandmothers, aunties, and even the neighbors would be on the phone in a flash. We never got away with much."

"Were you a naughty boy?" Ruth asked playfully, putting the lunch meat near the ice.

"Sometimes," Del chuckled, reaching for her.

"How naughty *were* you?"

"Oh, not really very bad. Stealing apples from Mr. Odey Jackson's orchard was about as bad as I got." His voice softened as he closed his eyes and wrapped his arms around Ruth from behind. "Oh," he breathed into her ear, whispering, "how I loved those apples."

Ruth felt the slow, sweet pressure of his hands on her breasts. She felt the inherent gentleness of the man himself. She felt other things she hadn't felt in years. After a few moments, she took a deep breath and said to herself, *Now or never*. She turned around and kissed him. Then she took him by the hand and led him up the stairs to her bedroom. There, in the quiet of the morning, with birds chirping outside the window and sunlight falling across Ruth's bed, they made sweet, un-hurried love.

Afterwards, as they lay peacefully in each other's arms, Del whispered, "Now you'll have to marry me. Make an honest man out of me."

Ruth kissed his shoulder, "I love you, Del. You must know that."

"And I love you," Del said quietly. He sighed. "We would have had beautiful children."

"We did." Ruth told him. "Three, to be exact, and we will have to tell all those beautiful children of our intentions."

"I suppose you're right. And the sooner the better. I'm kind of old-school. I don't go for all the casual stuff that seems so common today." He stroked her cheek with his long fingers. "I liked being married. I've had to travel a lot, but at heart I am basically a homebody who likes to have a wife beside him in front of the fireplace—and a dog at his feet."

"Two dogs," Ruth corrected, "and two cats. And Angie my house guest." Ruth poked him gently in the ribs.

"Do you think she'll stay with George—I hope?" Del asked.

Ruth looked at him. "Who knows? Angie's in love. Anything can happen."

"So am I." He leaned back into the pillows.

They napped for a time in each other's arms. Ruth woke up first.

"The house is humming!" she cried joyfully.

"What?" Del was groggy.

"Don't you hear it?" Ruth got up and grabbed her robe from the chair beside the bed. "The house is humming. We've got electricity."

"Well finally! Does that mean I get popcorn tonight?" Del asked her, looking hopeful.

"Anything your little heart desires tonight," she said as she headed for the bathroom.

Suddenly the phone rang. Ruth jumped.

"Wow, everything's working!"

She went to her bedside table and picked up the receiver. It was Fritz.

"Ruth, can you get out of there and come to dress rehearsal tomorrow night?"

"Some of the roads are still blocked off, but I think I can get through."

"Do you know where Del is staying? I need to reach him and we can't do the show without him." Fritz's voice cracked with exasperation.

Ruth briefly explained that Del had been staying with her since the storm hit. She handed the phone to Del. "It's Fritz," she whispered. "Just tell him everything will be all right."

"I'm not sure about that," Del whispered back. "This show is jinxed."

Chapter 31

It's Not Over Yet

A FTER ASSURING FRITZ THAT they would both be at dress rehearsal the following evening, Del and Ruth walked over to Captain Stoltzman's office in the Lake Elmo City Hall. They had decided to tell him about the unnerving "it's not over yet" notes and the musical score that mysteriously showed up on their porch just before the storm hit. When they got to the station, the chief invited them into his office and sat down at his desk. Ruth and Del took seats across from him.

"We ought to just quit the show," Ruth began, "but Del is a leading soloist. Without him we have no 'Ol' Man River'." Del demurred at her comment, but she looked him squarely in the eye and said, firmly, "You know we can't do the show without you."

"So tell me more about what is going on with your theatre group," said the chief, "and more about how Sergeant Sullivan was involved. I've heard good things about him. Too bad about his death. Odd of him to drive out to warn you about something in person, though. Unless he was out there on a watch, I can't help wondering why he didn't just call you.

He used an unmarked squad car, by the way. We found it parked about a block from your house."

"Maybe it had something to do with Susie's music, although I don't know how he would have known about that. He hadn't had the time to call us back yet. That's why we decided to talk to you. Del, tell him about the music and all the notes."

Del cleared his throat. "Whoever it is, has left messages—notes—sort of a calling card, letting us know that he or she had done the killings. They said 'It's not over yet.' They also left a musical score at Ruth's house that had belonging to Susan Ormstad, the woman who had been strangled in the park."

Chief Stoltzman perked up. "So tell me about these notes. Have the St. Paul police seen these notes you're talking about?"

Ruth had to think a moment. "Well, it started with a message left on my phone after my friend Angie was assaulted, saying 'It's not over yet.' I gave my answering machine to the St. Paul police. They still have it." She looked at Del. "And what about the note outside your condo?"

"Slow down now," the chief told her, holding his hand up. "One at a time. Let me get this in order. So, who was the first person from your group to be killed?"

Ruth sat up in her chair, her hands clasped together in her lap. "Lionel Worthing was the first one killed. He was stabbed outside in the alley behind Fritz Gerhardt's home in St. Paul—it's also his studio—and we were there for auditions. We're doing *Show Boat*. Lionel was there to audition for the show. And then my friend Angie Corbello, one of the actors, was assaulted in her home. While she was in the hospital, I got the message I told you about. It was on my phone's answering machine and it said, 'It's not over yet.'"

Chief Stoltzman took a tablet and pen from the top drawer of his desk and began writing out notes to himself.

Ruth went on, relieved to be able to talk to the police about her fears. "Then someone blew up the Rosenberg's car. Fortunately, they weren't in it. And Rodney Olson, one of the children in our cast, was deliberately pushed overboard into the Mississippi from the deck of a paddleboat where we were doing a benefit performance. Del dove in and saved him." She reached out for Del's hand and held on tight. "And then we found a written note saying 'It's not over yet' on the doorstep of Del's condo."

"Don't forget you were attacked in the costume room," Del interjected while Stoltzman scribbled furiously.

"Oh, that's right! That was after rehearsal one night when I went down to the costume room alone to look for my keys. It was dark and someone pulled an old costume over my head, pushed me down, and then ran off."

"Wait." Captain Stoltzman stopped writing and looked up at Ruth. "And you didn't see who it was?"

"Oh no. It was too dark. Everyone else had already left. The building was deserted—or so I thought. That happened after someone blew up the Rosenberg's car." Captain Stoltzman shook his head, squeezed his eyes shut for a brief moment, and resumed writing.

Ruth continued: "Anyway, right after we found that note on Del's doorstep, someone exploded something in Del's condo in the middle of the night and it burned down. Thank God he's okay!" Ruth rubbed her face with both hands and moaned slightly. "And the last thing, before

Mickey Sullivan died, Susie Ormstad our piano-player was strangled in Como Park, only a few hours after our rehearsal. And the next night, which was the night of the storm, a note saying, 'it's not over yet' was left on my porch—written on Susie's piano score."

"Hold on a minute." Captain Stoltzman looked at Del. "The note outside the condo, the one you said you found on your doorstep. Do you have that one?"

"Didn't we give that one to the St. Paul police?" Ruth asked Del. "So much has happened, I don't remember for sure."

"I think we did ... didn't we?"

Captain Stoltzman looked back and forth at the two of them as if to say "Actors!" and then returned to his writing.

Finally he said, "What about the note written on the music—the one you found on your porch. Is it still at your house?"

"Well, the storm came, and then the electricity went off, and we were down in the basement with our pets, and then ... and then you came and you found Sergeant Sullivan ..."

"Sergeant Sullivan was our contact person on the St. Paul Police Force," Del clarified. "When he died, and everything at Mrs. Carson's house was in turmoil because of the storm ... we didn't tell anyone about that note. We've had other things to think about."

The chief looked puzzled. "Why do you think that note on the music was left at *your* house?"

"I wish I knew," said Ruth. "As I said, we found it on my back porch the day of the storm. Someone had cut my screen and pushed it through into my porch."

"It has to still be in your kitchen," Del said. "I think it's on the counter by the phone." He looked at the policeman. "Would you like us to bring it up here?"

Chief Stoltzman rubbed his eyes and looked exasperated. "Yes, we'd like it, but I'll send an officer home with you to get it. Right now." He picked up his phone and punched a number. "Sammie, would you have Lubach bring a squad car around?" He turned to the couple. "What happens in St. Paul is normally the business of the St. Paul police department. But when a resident of Lake Elmo is threatened, in her home, as you were, particularly in light of what's going on, then it becomes *our* business too. Now this music score you mentioned, I suppose you've both touched it."

"Well, yes, of course. We both did. At first we didn't even know what it was."

A young woman stepped through the door.

"Lubach, get an evidence bag and take these two people back to Mrs. Carson's house. And bring me back a music book and a note they have."

"Yes sir," said the young woman with a clipped, military bearing.

"And Lubach," the captain added as they headed out, "remember to take gloves."

After stopping by a storeroom to get a plastic bag and some vinyl gloves that looked like the ones worn in doctors' offices, the young officer led Ruth and Del to a black squad car parked by the side of the building. She opened the back door for them and they slid in while the youthful officer adjusted her uniform jacket over her slender hips. After pulling the car key from her pants pocket, she stiffly got behind the wheel. Sitting with her shoulders back as if she were passing muster, she buckled herself in, turned slightly to her passengers and said "Buckle up, please."

Ruth stifled a smile while she and Del complied with her request. They sat there for a moment, waiting, as though the young officer was trying to remember what to do next.

"Your address, ma'am?" she finally asked Ruth.

Ruth told her and they drove in silence the half mile to Ruth's house. When the three entered the house by way of the back porch, Toby, playing guard dog, barked at the stranger while Charlie ran into the living room, tail between his legs.

Officer Lubach carefully bagged and labeled the music with the note she retrieved from the kitchen counter top. She brushed some long fur fibers off the top of the music, giving Ruth a knowing, tight-lipped smile.

"Cats," she declared, looking at Morrie and Griselda, who sat innocently next to their empty bowls. "You can never trust 'em. They go by their instincts."

Then with a business-like nod, she left.

Ruth and Del sat down at the kitchen table and stared at each other wordlessly. Del finally spoke. "It's my fault we forgot about the note and the music score. I was so happy just being here alone with you."

"It's nobody's fault. I forgot about it too."

"I guess there's not much more we can do right now," Del said. "We've told your Lake Elmo police chief everything we know."

"He seemed genuinely interested," Ruth replied. "Maybe we aren't so alone in this?"

"Maybe not." Del rose and went to the now-running refrigerator. "I'm hungry. Want me to fix us one of my famous sandwiches?"

"Yes." She paused and then returned to the earlier topic. "Do you think he'll work with the St. Paul police?" Ruth wasn't ready to stop thinking about the danger they might be in when they go to the upcoming rehearsal. "I wish we didn't have to go back into town ... to the pavilion." She shivered. "I feel as if that place, I don't know, that we're just not safe there. *Any* of us."

Del, rummaging in the refrigerator, poked his head out. "We won't be safe if we *don't* go back for the dress rehearsal. Fritz'll kill us!" he laughed as he removed the bags of ice and dropped them in the sink.

"I know. I know." Ruth shook her head. "But this 'show must go on,' stuff—this time I think we're all just nuts to be involved in this. We should cancel the show. Just call a halt to all of it. Going on with it is just crazy."

"Trouble is," Del told her, "rental for the pavilion has already been paid. Musicians are counting on being paid. Royalties were paid. A lot of people depend on this show." Then he added, "by the way, I'm donating my time." Del put the turkey-mustard-cheese-green pepper-black olive sandwich he had concocted on the table. Then he kissed her on the forehead. "And Fritz ... I think the summer ticket sales at Como are a large portion of his yearly income."

"I know that. Poor Fritz and Vivian." Ruth looked askance at the sandwich. "Really? Green peppers and olives? With turkey?" She shook her head, sighed, and ate it all. Actually, it wasn't half bad.

The night of dress rehearsal, Del and Ruth picked Angie up from George's house. Angie was positively glowing.

"I guess we're an item," she told the two of them as she threw a kiss to George and scooted into the back seat of Del's Lexus. Ruth smiled and reached back to squeeze her friend's hand, but said nothing.

"Can you take me back to George's afterwards?" she asked. "I hope you don't mind, Ruth. You know, with his wife gone, and all ..." Her voice tapered off. "He's a lonely guy."

"I think he's a lucky guy!" Del assured her.

"How 'bout you two?" Angie asked. "Any news?"

They told her about the mysterious note in Ruth's porch and their meeting with Captain Stoltzman.

"Has anyone from the St. Paul police been in touch with you?"

"No," Ruth told her, "but I think we all need to look out for ourselves and be careful."

"Keep our eyes open," Del added.

The dress rehearsal did not go smoothly. For starters, the actors were told to meet in the pavilion's basement rehearsal room, without sets, although the set was already in place on the stage.

Angie was disappointed. "For this we should be on the real stage," she whispered to Ruth.

"I wonder what's going on?" Ruth asked Del, who shrugged his shoulders.

Just then, Lorene Hammer walked in and motioned to Billy to stop talking to the stage-hands and come to her side. She looked fire-in-her-eyes angry.

"They *promised* we could have our dress rehearsal on stage tonight!" she said loudly. "We set everything up. What happened?"

Billy tried to shush her, which was a mistake.

"Don't you 'shush' me!" she retorted. "What the hell happened?"

"It was just a misunderstanding," Billy told her. "The pavilion restaurant supervisor booked some community band from Fridley for tonight, by mistake. We'll just have to rehearse down here in the basement again."

"They better not move our sets!" Lorene said vehemently.

As if on cue, the restaurant manager of the pavilion restaurant came in and quietly said something to Billy, whose face turned crimson.

"I'm afraid we'll have to take our sets down," Billy reluctantly told his wife.

"We are *not* taking our sets down," she snapped back.

"But you'll have to," the manager interjected. "The band director says he can't work with that river boat taking up half the stage."

"To hell with the band director!" snapped Lorene.

Billy sighed, "I'll make you a deal," he said to the manager. "We'll move the boat off to the side, and give comp tickets to all the members of the Fridley band."

Tim the Stagehand, standing nearby, adjusted his Twins baseball cap and looked back and forth between the speakers as if watching a tennis match.

Fritz, who had also been listening, immediately chimed in. "No, you won't! We don't give away tickets! I know the Fridley director. *I'll* talk to him."

Once again, Fritz's network of Twin Cities music contacts paid off. He knew the man in question, who Fritz suddenly treated like his oldest, dearest friend. The sets, including the showboat, remained on stage although the rehearsal still had to take place downstairs.

Once the overture began, Ruth breathed more easily. She gave Del a wave, which he returned.

The young accompanist taking Susie's place tonight looked to be in her teens and didn't know the music very well. Although Fritz tried hard to be patient with her, one could hear him mutter expletives under his breath as he conducted. Because Fritz had to pay union scale to his orchestra members, he only used them during actual performances.

The chorus forgot some of the words to the 'Captain Andy' song, prompting Fritz to yell, "Come on now, chorus! Pay attention!"

Some of the actors still didn't know their lines. Gloria-June flubbed her scenes, as did Al Rosenberg. Mimi didn't look as angry with Al, but she was upset when he improvised some of his lines. "Say it like it's written," she chided loudly.

Danny Ancino and Sandy Westerling did their parts passably well, but Ruth noticed that Danny seemed distracted. He kept glancing at the stage exits when he should've been gazing longingly at Sandy.

"Frank and Ellie" forgot their dance moves and had to start over. Fritz motioned to Vivian, who quickly retrieved her purse and gave him some pills, which he downed with a swig of his Pepsi.

Elizabeth Mays was, as was her father, professional and stunning. Ruth was proud of them both.

Billy Hammer's notes were lengthy that night. Ruth tried to concentrate on the play, taking out her knitting in order to keep awake, but she looked up frequently so Billy would know she was paying attention. She also kept sneaking little glances at Del, who nodded and smiled at her each time.

We'll get through this together, she mind-signaled him.

After the rehearsal, just as they were leaving, Vivian motioned to Ruth. She still had four costumes that needed to be altered before the next evening and she asked Ruth to take them home with her. It was not what Ruth wanted to hear, thinking, *if Del is staying at my house, I don't want to spend all my time on the sewing machine.*

"We're still in such an uproar after the big storm, I don't even know if we'll have electricity. It goes on and off," Ruth said to Vivian. This was not exactly a lie, because after storms that sometimes happened.

"Well, maybe I can get Mimi to help me," Vivian said. She sounded tired. "God knows, Gloria-June won't cooperate."

"Maybe I could take one," Ruth told her, feeling guilty for not being more obliging. "Is there one that just needs some hand-sewing?"

Vivian found one that needed hemming, which could be done by hand, and gave the costume to Ruth. "Thank you," she told her, "I can always count on you."

Which only made Ruth feel more guilty.

Don Olson and Del were at the back of the hall, talking together. As Ruth came toward the two men, Don waved good-bye and walked off.

"I told him what we thought about Sullivan," Del told her, "... that he may have come out to tell us or warn us of something. Or maybe to stake out the house, watching for whoever was coming or going. Don said he thought that either could be the case and that he'd look into it."

Elizabeth came up to kiss her father good-bye.

"I think you should stay out at Ruth's house for a while longer and help her clean up after that storm." She winked at Ruth, who blushed.

"Good idea!" Del said, smiling. "What's this?" he asked, as she gave him a large grocery bag full of clothes.

"I threw some of your things in here, right before I left tonight. Extra clothes ... they're all clean, but not ironed. I'm sorry, but I've been pretty busy at work."

"I can iron them," Ruth told her quietly. She didn't want Vivian to hear that their power was on.

As they left the pavilion, Ruth spoke quietly to Del. "They always say that a bad dress rehearsal means you'll have a good opening night."

"Then our opening night ought to be a smash hit," he answered.

Chapter 32

Break a Leg

"THERE IS NOTHING QUITE so terrifying, or exhilarating, as an opening night," Ruth observed the following night as she and Del pulled into a shady section of the pavilion parking lot.

"Oh that's good!" Del shot back. "Did you make that up?"

"I probably wasn't the first person to say it," she laughed, "but it's true. I've got butterflies and I'm only in the chorus." She carried the finished costume, as promised to Vivian, on a hanger.

"Never say 'only the chorus,'" said Del as he took the hanger from her. "Where would we be without the chorus?"

"At least I don't have to memorize any lines, or even know exactly when I go on stage." Ruth fumbled with her parasol and basket. "I just follow the pack. I go out when they go out, I sing when they sing, and I leave when they leave."

Just then, George and Angie drove into the parking lot. Angie yelled out the window, "Hey, you guys! Wait for us!"

Ruth and Del waited while George found a parking spot.

"I'm sure glad I'm not playing Ravenal in this production," he said.

"Why is that? I think you'd be a great romantic lead."

"Woman, don't you tease me!" he said playfully. "I need my concentration."

"But why wouldn't you want the lead?" Ruth asked again. "It's a meaty role, with those wonderful songs: 'I Drift Along with My Fancy' ... 'Make Believe' ... 'You Are Love' ..."

"Because I think the lead in this play is too vulnerable, too much, oh ... out there." He paused and took a deep breath. "There's a killer still on the loose in St. Paul, able to, well ... what would hurt this troupe the most?" The thought of it gave him the creeps.

Ruth answered his question in barely audible tones. "Killing off the leading man, or lady. Or the director," she added as she realized that Fritz could be a target, too.

By now Angie was out of the car, arm in arm with a smiling George who was carrying her costume. "Who's killing who?" she wanted to know.

"Nobody's killing anyone if we can help it," Ruth told her friend. "We were just worrying about the leads in the show—and Fritz."

"Hah!" Angie retorted. "The cops are really watching now. We'll be okay. And that Danny Ancino is a good guy. Tracey told me how nice he is to her. I'm not worried."

Then Angie remembered her manners. "You all remember George?" she said to Ruth and Del.

Del shook hands with George. "Sure I do. We ran into each other at Gustafson's"

As George and Del walked in front of the women, Angie whispered to Ruth, "He's good in bed."

"Shh!" Ruth whispered back. "He'll hear you."

Del pretended not to hear this exchange, but Ruth detected a little smirk. George kept walking, looking straight ahead. Ruth hoped he was hard of hearing.

The moon, nearly full, hovered over Lake Como like something in a fairy-tale. The July air was warm. The smell of nearby picnic barbeques coalesced with a pungent fishy odor off the lake. Small groups of actors and their families walked excitedly toward the side of the pavilion that spread out along the shore. Carrying costumes in their arms, they entered the basement door, manned tonight by Officer Don Olson—in uniform. He checked their names on a list as each one entered.

"That's a first," said Ruth.

"Good security tonight," Del commented.

"They just want to keep us all safe."

"I wonder if anyone can really keep us safe?" Del said quietly as they reached the basement door of the pavilion and were checked off Don's list. Dodging around a couple of burley young men carrying in canoes, they hurried down into the dimly lit hallway to their respective dressing rooms.

Ruth ignored Del's question. She didn't want to think about it.

"Bye," she said to him before entering the women's dressing room. "Break a leg." It was the time-honored way actors wished one another good luck before the curtain went up.

"Break a leg," he said back, and threw her a kiss.

The scene in the women's dressing room was noisy and chaotic. Women of all ages and girths, in various stages of dress and undress, jockeyed for a look in the long mirror that stretched across one wall. The ledge in front of the mirror was laden with makeup, hair brushes, combs, hair pins, and tissues. Used tissues, some smudged with red lipstick, lay upon the floor along with brown grocery bags, plastic bags, bundled up clothing and shoes of all sorts. Above the clamor Ruth could hear the penetrating voice of Gloria-June.

"Excuse me. Ex*cuse* me! I've been waiting for *ever!*" The self-proclaimed diva elbowed one of the younger chorus members away from the crowded mirror.

Ruth had put on her costume and applied her makeup at home, as had Del.

As she handed the finished costume to a grateful Vivian, she felt a tug at her sleeve.

"Mrs. Carson?" It was little Elena Cordova. "Could you please try to zip me up? My dress is stuck."

"Let's see." Ruth put down her things and looked at the back of Elena's dress. The zipper on the peach lace frock was more than stuck; it was broken. "Oh dear," Ruth told the girl. "Hurry, get out of this. I'm going to have to do a quick repair-job on it."

"But I have to go on in half-an-hour!" She looked panic stricken. "I have to be in costume!"

"You will be, sweetie. Don't worry, I can fix this quickly." She helped pull the dress over the child's head, trying not to mess up the curls that someone had laboriously styled into her shiny black hair. "I carry all my sewing stuff with me in my basket," she reassured the girl. "I can fix this in ten minutes."

Elena Cordova managed to smile and ran off in her slip and pantaloons, leaving the frothy lace dress in Ruth's hands.

I should have come earlier, Ruth thought, as she got out the needle and thread she kept in her basket. *I wonder if there are any more last-minute repairs? I hope not.*

Ruth found an empty folding chair in the corner of the dressing room and began repositioning the zipper so that it would start zipping above the broken part. She sewed the broken part completely closed while thinking about what Del had said.

Nothing will happen here. There are too many people.

Suddenly Gloria-June swished her bright purplish pink skirt over Ruth's more subdued blue one, making it impossible for Ruth to continue sewing for a moment.

"Don't stand too close to me on stage, Ruthie!" she said gaily. "Your costume clashes. I don't want you making me look bad!" Gloria wasn't really looking at Ruth, but simpering at her own reflection in the long wall mirror.

"What? Oh, I could never do that," Ruth said quietly, shifting her body so she could continue working on Elena's costume.

You do that all by yourself.

"Ruth, Ruth ... someone wants you outside." This time it was Elizabeth, speaking softly in Ruth's ear. She looked elegant in a pale-yellow satin dress.

"Oh, hi." Ruth looked up and gave her a broad smile. "I didn't even see you in here, there's so many people. What does he want? Tell your dad that I'm busy repairing Elena's costume."

"It's not dad," Elizabeth told her. "It's our esteemed director."

"Oh Lord, what does he want now?" She got up and hurried to the door.

Fritz looked frazzled. His eyes were unnaturally wide and his normally pallid countenance seemed even more pale. Perspiration beaded on his forehead. Under his red blazer Ruth could see his thin shoulder blades and chest heaving. This wasn't just opening night jitters; this was real fear. Her heart went out to him.

"What can I do for you, maestro?"

"You can get Del to lead the cast prayer. He said he'd rather not, but I know he'll do it for you. We've got fifteen minutes!" Fritz looked at his watch and then turned on his heels and left. He knew Ruth and he knew her loyalty to him. He knew from years of working with her that if he wanted it, and it was reasonable, Ruth would make it happen.

"But, but, I don't think he'll ..." Ruth watched in exasperation as Fritz disappeared into the crowded hallway. Then she saw Del coming out of the men's dressing room. "Del, please?" She looked at him with pleading eyes.

"All right. For you. I haven't really wanted to pray much since Elaine ... well, I just haven't had a mind for it." He looked at Ruth and then up at the ceiling. "Okay, maybe I have a lot to be thankful for. Maybe a short one."

"We gather in five minutes to warm up in the rehearsal room. We always have the prayer in there, just before we go upstairs."

"Mrs. Carson!" Elena's dark head poked out of the door. "Are you done with my dress? I'm going to be late!"

"Just one more minute, sweetie," Ruth said as she ducked back into the dressing room and finished the repair job. "Here, let me help you get it on."

Lorene Hammer stuck her blonde head through the dressing room door and called out, "Five minutes! Everyone meet in the rehearsal room for warm-ups."

Last-minute touches were hastily added to makeup and costumes. Soon the menagerie of harried-looking amateurs stood transformed in a circle of respectable-looking actors.

The woman in charge of warm-ups was in the chorus. Ruth couldn't remember her name. Jane ... something. She had been, or still was, the director of an elementary school chorus somewhere in the city. She started them out with *"I lo-ove to sing,"* in rising changes of key. Then came *"Many mumbling mice are making merry music in the moonlight. Mighty nice!"* which was fun and Ruth's personal favorite. They ended with *"Aaaaaaah"* and *"Eeeeeee"* and *"Ooohhhhh,"* a concluding full-body exercise that involved stretching out the arms and then bending over. It was supposed to not only warm up your voice but make your body more supple. Ruth wondered about that, but did it anyway.

After that last exercise, the room became quiet and Jane looked at Del. "Let's have our prayer," she said.

The older members of the cast knew the drill and reached out to hold the hands of cast members next to them, forming a circle. When all were holding hands, Del began:

"Heavenly Father, we come to you tonight, all of us actors, knowing that you are the true author of all good plays, the true composer of all beautiful music, the inspiration behind the sets, the costumes, the direction. Everything we do comes from you. You are the creator of all of us. Of love. Of laughter. Of music. Be with us now, Father, and help us to do our best. Help our voices sing to your glory, and Lord, please keep us all safe. We ask this in Jesus' name, Amen."

Ruth heard a few sniffles during the prayer, and she joined in with the group's solemn "Amen" at the end. She looked across the room at Del, her eyes misty, and mouthed "thank you." Then everyone trooped upstairs where they could hear the orchestra tuning up. It was Showtime!

Chapter 33

Opening Night

RUTH SMOOTHED DOWN HER skirt as she stood in the wings with the other chorus members waiting to go out for their opening number. A slight breeze blew off the lake and the evening air had begun to cool.

Thank goodness, she thought. *We'd die in these costumes, otherwise!* She peeked through a tiny slit in the set to see how full the house was. It looked packed. *It's a good house. High ticket sales. Fritz will be happy.*

While the orchestra played the overture, many in the audience continued munching on snacks, but most were just listening and waiting for the action to begin on stage. Ruth noticed one little boy who intently watched Fritz and moved his arms to the music, as if he was the conductor.

Then she caught her breath. Blanche Voorhees was sitting in the third row center, resplendent in a white designer suit. She held a bouquet of blood-red roses.

Oh god, not her again ... *not tonight!*

"Do you see who I see?" Angie whispered, singing the beloved Christmas carol in jest, as she came up behind Ruth. "She's heee-ere!"

"Shhh!" another chorus member whispered. Ruth nodded silently to Angie, then stretched to her full height and clenched and unclenched her hands. She took deep breaths, trying to relax her body and her vocal cords.

I don't care, she thought. *I love Del and tonight I will make him proud.*

Ruth could see Del and Elizabeth on the other side of the stage. Both of them smiled at her at the same time.

"Break a leg," she mouthed. They both nodded and mouthed, "You, too."

Suddenly Ruth heard a peeping noise. She looked up and saw a mother sparrow that had built her nest on top of an unused backstage light fixture. The mother bird fluttered around her nest and then flew out through the set and over the audience. Ruth lost track of her over the lake.

Poor thing. The music must frighten her. Well, sometimes I'm frightened, too. And then I wish I could fly away over the lake.

Finally, the overture was over and it was time to go on.

"Here the folks work on the Mississippi," the riverboat men sang. Ruth could hear Del's clear, strong baritone, floating above the voices of the other men.

He is wonderful, she thought, and smiled at him, although he was concentrating on singing and didn't see her.

"Cotton Blossom, Cotton Blossom, love to see you, growin' wild!" the women's voices sang out as they swished their long, heavy skirts to and fro. Ruth watched Elizabeth's entrance as Julie Laverne. The pale yellow

of her dress and huge picture hat set off her features. Her luxurious black hair was pulled to the back of her neck, with tendrils of curls hanging over her ears. Her smile was radiant, her bearing, queenly.

Oh Del, how proud you must be! Ruth looked over at him as Elizabeth made her regal way to center stage while the chorus danced and sang around her.

"See the sho-o-w boat! That's old Capt'n Andy's Cotton Blossom. Will you go-o-o. Let me take you to the sho-o-w" sang the men as they pointed to the paddle boat painted on a shaped set. The white railings of the boat were painted with dark gray shadows, to look three-dimensional. Even the windows looked real. It was one of the best sets ever, Ruth thought. The man who made it (another volunteer) had worked as a designer for Dayton's Department Store before he retired. You could tell he had been a designer. Even the water at the base of the boat had reflections. For an amateur production, it was perfection.

Danny Ancino's first solo, "Make Believe," received rousing applause. Shouts of "Bravo!" came from Danny's Uncle Tony, who sat in the front row, clapping diamond-covered hands. The dark-haired woman sitting two rows behind him also called out "Bravo! Bravo!" and Uncle Tony turned to see who it was. It was Blanche, who mouthed him a flirtatious "kiss."

Just as Danny and Sandy's duet was wrapping up, Howard Kimmel ran down the steps and breathlessly whispered, "Have you seen Gloria-June? She's due on stage any minute!" He looked wild-eyed, and Ruth instinctively put a hand on his sleeve to comfort him, which he shook off.

"Have you looked in the women's dressing room?" Ruth asked.

"Of course I have." He was wringing his hands now. "I've looked all over. Upstairs and down. She's nowhere!" He looked anxiously at Don and Del. "Help me find her."

"We'll find her. Don't worry," Del told him.

"Don't worry?" Howard looked at him with disbelief, his hands clenched and his thin shoulders shaking. "With all that's been happening in this group?"

"Shh, "said Del. "The audience will hear you. Come on, Howard. I'll help you look. We'll find her."

Ruth watched the two men go quickly up the darkened steps towards backstage. She followed and there found Billy's wife, Lorene Hammer, who had filled in once before when Gloria had to miss a rehearsal. Lorene was already in costume and sitting on the long bench that ran the length of the backstage area, resting her head against the wall, eyes closed, an open script in her lap.

"Lorene," Ruth said softly, touching her on the arm.

"I know," she said in a resigned voice. "Billy already told me. I may have to go on."

"Do you know her part?"

"Yes," Lorene sighed. "I know all the parts, even the men's." She closed the script and smiled at Ruth. "I'm sure they'll find her. She's probably in front of a mirror somewhere, putting another layer of make-up on that face of hers—and she needs all she can get!" she added derisively. Lorene turned her attention to what was happening on stage. Her slender form, clad in pink and black silk, strained forward to hear.

Ruth was surprised at the venom in Lorene's voice but chalked it up to some gossip she recalled from many years ago, after Billy's divorce, about him and Gloria-June. Ruth never put much stock in backstage gossip. Theatre-folk were sometimes unfairly maligned and their personal indiscretions magnified. Ruth knew that even when there wasn't anything going on, some people still relished the assumption that there was. Romance, especially when illicit, was a favorite topic.

And if there isn't any romance, how about murder and mayhem? Ruth thought with a shutter.

When the cue came, Lorene Hammer went resolutely onstage, taking Gloria-June's role.

"She's good," Ruth told herself as she watched from the wings. Lorene moved with cat-like grace and delivered her lines flawlessly. Billy stood behind Ruth, also watching.

"Why is she always a stage hand?" Ruth whispered. "She's missed her calling."

"She was in a theatre group out in California, before I met her," Billy quietly answered. "Always said she preferred backstage work over the backbiting and one-upmanship that sometimes goes on among actors. She's a great stage hand, though. Knows more about wiring than any woman I've ever met."

"Where did she learn that?" Ruth asked him, awestruck.

"Oh, here and there," Billy answered, evasively.

If Ruth thought Billy Hammer was sounding odd, she didn't have time to mull it over. Shirley Hammond, who played Ellie, was getting ready to go on. Ruth stepped aside from where she was watching to let her through. She looked particularly cute tonight, thought Ruth.

That red and white polka-dot costume is perfect for her. Ruth tapped her foot as Ellie's big solo number, "Life Upon the Wicked Stage," began.

It was a good thing Shirley Hammond went onstage when she did because she hadn't seen Del and Don Olson, struggling up the basement stairs, carrying Gloria-June Kimmel. If she'd seen that, she wouldn't have been able to perform her song.

Chapter 34

Frightened but Alive

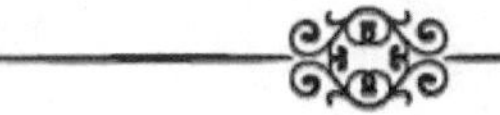

GLORIA-JUNE HAD BEEN ASSAULTED, that much was certain. Del found her in a darkened inset hallway to the restaurant's basement storage room, hit on the head, hair matted with blood. Del and Don carried Gloria-June up the stairs and laid her gently on the cement just inside the door to the backstage area.

While Don went to call the park police, Del spoke softly to her, "Poor lady, poor little lady." Tears ran down his face. Gloria-June Kimmel moaned and opened her eyes.

Ruth heard the commotion and joined Howard, Del, and Gloria-June at the top of the stairs. "Oh, good, you've found her!" she said at first. "Where was she?" Then she saw the blood and gulped. "Oh no! What happened!?"

"She was in the back hallway downstairs," Del said very quietly, wiping his eyes. "She's been hit on the back of the head." He looked horrified. "Don helped me carry her up here. At first I thought she might be dead. I don't know why, but I just started talking to her, and, well ..." Del looked at Ruth. "She woke up."

Howard bent over Gloria-June and asked, "Who did this to you?" His thin face was contorted with a mixture of shock, fear and rage. "Who did this to you? Tell me!"

"Shh! the audience will hear you," said the same woman chorus-member who had earlier shushed Angie. Howard shot her a murderous glance.

Before Gloria-June could answer, however, Don Olson opened the door, accompanied by a uniformed officer. "We've called the ambulance. Wha …?!" His eyes grew wide when he saw Gloria-June partially sitting up, embraced by Howard.

Gloria-June looked at Don and then at Del. "Thank you," she said faintly. "You saved my life." Then she laid her head back on Howard's chest and sighed deeply. "Howie, take me home. I want to go home."

"Who did this … thing?" Howard Kimmel was now in tears, his arms wrapped tightly around his wife, his cheeks next to hers.

"I didn't see anyone," Gloria-June answered weakly. "It was so dark. I was down there to practice my lines a little. I was looking for the light switch when someone hit me from behind … and then everything went black."

Don and the other officer went outside to talk and wait for the ambulance. Gloria-June wanted to go straight home, but Howard insisted on going to the hospital.

"Don't expect us back here," Howard told Billy in terse tones. "We're done." Soon Gloria-June, elaborate costume and all, was lifted onto a gurney and into the waiting ambulance.

Act One ended just as the ambulance pulled away. Most of the cast had been onstage, unaware of what had taken place. During intermission, the pavilion audience always packed into the restaurant for snacks—mostly ice cream, soda, and popcorn. A few of them questioned Billy about the departing ambulance, but most were so intent on getting something to eat and drink they didn't even notice it.

"Nothing to worry about," Billy said, coolly. "Just an actor who wasn't feeling well. She'll be alright."

Angie ran up to Ruth. "Who was sick?" She looked around. "Not Danny, I hope."

"No, it was Gloria-June." Ruth thought it best not to go into the details just now.

"Good," Angie told her. "I think Danny and Tracey are in love. I don't want Tracey catching anything." Just then, Angie spotted George, who was standing near the steps leading up to the stage area. She ran to hug him.

In the same instant Del spotted Blanche.

"Oh no," he said to Ruth, stepping behind the curtain so no one from the milling intermission crowd could see him.

"The flowers are probably for you," Ruth told him.

"What flowers?" Del looked through the curtain at the diva. "I don't see any flowers."

"Red roses. She might have left them on the bench."

"I hope they're not for me," Del told her. "I don't want them."

"You can always be gracious and take them during our bows, and then toss them later. Or give them to one of the youngsters in the cast."

Del groaned and took Ruth's hand. "Let's just get through this night. Then we'll see what happens. I can't think about Blanche or her damn flowers right now."

"I know. We won't worry about it." Ruth squeezed his hand. Del put his arm around her and hugged her, kissing the top of her head, lingering as if he didn't want to let her go.

Before the beginning of Act Two, Billy assembled the entire cast downstairs, including Fritz and the orchestra. Fritz was fuming. He had been holding court upstairs with some little blue-haired ladies—long-time fans of his park concerts—and wasn't happy to be interrupted when people were telling him how wonderful his show was.

"This had better be important!" he rasped. Vivian glanced over at Ruth and rolled her eyes.

"It's important," said Billie. Then he turned to the assembled cast. "Listen, people, we had an awful incident here tonight. Gloria-June Kimmel was attacked. Someone hit her hard on the head with something and knocked her out. That's why Lorene took her part. It happened downstairs."

The assembled troupe gasped.

"She appears to be okay. She's at the hospital now. She's frightened but alive." He looked to Lorene as if to ask what to say next, then proceeded. "We don't know who did it, and, well, the thing is ... I don't want any of you ... *any* of you ... and this means everyone ... to go anywhere backstage or downstairs alone!" He began pacing. "We have eight more shows and that means eight more nights. We're going to have to be very, very careful. That means you go with a buddy to the dressing rooms, to the prop room, even to the bathroom ... *you go with a buddy!*"

Some of the cast members giggled nervously.

The older woman who had shushed both Angie and Howie piped up. "Why don't you just close the show after tonight?" She looked around at the group. "I don't know about you people, but I, for one, don't intend to be the next victim."

Fritz jumped in. "Billy, you can't close the show. We owe too much!" Visibly shaking, he held his hand out to Vivian, who rummaged through her purse and finally put two pills in her husband's hand. He swallowed them with a large swig from the can of root beer he had been carrying around.

"Don't worry, Fritz," Billy said, trying to calm him down. "We'll get more policemen because of this. I'll ask for one on-stage, one back-stage, and one in the audience." He looked at Don, who nodded affirmatively.

During Act Two, the actors were noticeably subdued, although in *Show Boat*, the second act is subdued anyway. Six years have passed and Ravenal has gambled away his money. Nola, now pregnant, is living in a cheap boardinghouse. She gets a letter from Ravenal, who doesn't know Nola is pregnant. He tells her that he is leaving her because he is no good and that she should return home to her parents. Nola, who wants to support herself, instead tries to get a singing job in a dance hall. Julie has been singing at the same place and spots Nola, but doesn't want Nola to see her. Julie pretends to be drunk so they will fire her, which gives Nola the job. Then the act shifts to New Year's Eve and Captain Andy finds his daughter singing in the dance hall. In a poignant scene, the captain finds out that his daughter Nola is pregnant and begs her to come back home to have her baby.

In the final scene, it is some years later. Nola had a daughter named Kim. Ravenal learns this from Julie and returns to the show boat to see for himself. There, in a beautiful scene, the errant father meets his little girl for the first time and sings "Make Believe" to her. Captain Andy and

Parthy welcome Ravenal back to the show boat and Nola and Ravenal reconcile and Joe reprises "Ol' Man River" and by the time the curtain comes down there isn't a dry eye in the house.

Tonight was no exception.

As the cast moved on-stage for their bows, people from the audience came to the edge of the stage offering bouquets to the actors of their choice. To Ruth's surprise, Del took a very quick bow and pretended not to see the red roses being thrust in his direction.

Oh dear, thought Ruth. *Now what is she going to do?*

But Blanche Voorhees had always been a quick study. Without missing a beat, she handed her roses to a surprised Sandy Westerling, who looked at the woman with an amazed smile on her face.

Good one, Blanche!

The diva caught Ruth looking at her and glared.

"No notes tonight," Billy announced wearily, after everyone had taken their bows, "but please, please remember what I told you. The buddy system! No one walks around here alone!" He looked around. "Now I want you all out of here at once, before the crowd leaves."

The cast, hardly needing to be told, nervously exited the pavilion accompanied by friends, family, or fellow cast members.

"Bye you guys!" Angie called to Ruth and Del. "George and I are going to Old Mexico for margaritas and nachos. Want to join us?"

"Oh Angie, thanks," Ruth answered, "but maybe some other time."

Then Elizabeth ran up to Ruth and Del and informed them that her "office mate" was at the performance tonight and was taking her out for a drink. She waved toward a handsome-looking Black gentleman standing by the stage and called out, "Wait. I'll be right there." She turned to Del. "Dad, can you stay at Ruth's again tonight out in Lake Elmo?"

"I was planning on it," Del said as he looked at Ruth. "I don't want her alone in that big house."

"Okay, that's great!" Elizabeth seemed relieved. "You guys have fun. I'll see you tomorrow night? Six-ish?" She ran toward the man waiting by the front of the stage.

"She was glad to get rid of us!" Del said with a chuckle as he took a large wicker basket from Ruth. "What on earth have you got in here? It weighs a ton."

"Everything I need for on stage and back stage: my water bottle. my knitting, my props, my purse, a few snacks. I always carry that basket when I'm in these productions. It holds everything. It's my 'lucky basket.'"

"Snacks?" Del opened the flap on the top of the basket and began rooting around inside. "What snacks?"

Ruth laughed, "Oh, wonderful snacks! Raisins, fat-free crackers, fat-free pretzels ..."

"Ah, no thanks." Del closed the lid. "Want to go to Snuffy's for a burger and fries?"

"Oh, I don't know. I'm tired." She began to lean on him as they walked through the darkened parking lot toward his car.

"That's because you haven't eaten tonight. Come on," Del told her. "You'll perk up if you eat something. They're open 'til ten and it's only nine-twenty. We can still get in if we hurry." He walked a little faster toward his car.

"We shouldn't eat late at night," Ruth said without much conviction. "But okay. I don't want you passing out on the way home."

He helped Ruth into the car and put the basket on the back seat. As they drove to Snuffy's, Ruth told Del about Billy's conversation with her.

"He said Lorene gave up acting to get away from all the backbiting, and prefers being a stage hand."

"Frankly, I'm beginning to think that Lorene's being from California is just a weird coincidence," Del told her.

"I'm not so sure."

After feasting on Snuffy-burgers, fries, and Diet Coke, Ruth and Del drove back to Lake Elmo. Ruth fell asleep on the way home and didn't wake up when Del pulled into her driveway.

He turned off the ignition and lights and sat there, listening. Ruth began to stir.

"Shh." Del put out his hand to quiet her. "I think we've been followed. Look." He pointed to a pair of headlights a half-a-block away. "Those lights have been behind us for the past ten miles at least."

"Are you sure? Lots of cars use this road."

"I'm not a hundred per cent certain but ... Quick! Duck down! They're turning into your driveway."

"Let's run into the house right now and lock the doors," whispered Ruth.

"It's too late." Del scrunched lower in the seat.

Ruth could almost hear her heart pounding as she ducked down even further. "Can you see who it is?" She wanted to look, but was afraid to stick her head up.

"I can't see. It's too dark," Del said. "Boy, they're brazen. They're going right up to your back door."

"Okay, that's enough!" Ruth sat up and grabbed the door handle. "No one goes into my house without my permission." She jumped from the car before Del could stop her and yelled, "Stop! Right where you are!"

It was loud enough to wake the neighbors.

Chapter 35

Rising Domesticity

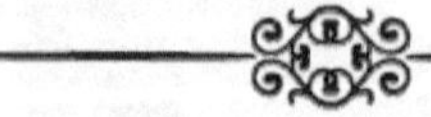

"**R**UTH!" CRIED TRACEY. "YOU scared the shit out of me!"

"Tracey? What are *you* doing here?" They both collapsed, laughing and crying in each other's arms.

Del, somewhat sheepishly, got out of the car and walked up to the back door.

"Hi, Tracey, remember me? I'm Del ... Ruth's friend?"

"Sure, I remember." Tracey held her hand out to Del. "Hi, I just came over to see my mom. Sorry it's so late."

"Everything okay, Trace?" Danny Ancino said as he emerged from the darkness.

"Danny and I, well, he got a new place—a house, that is. I'm going to rent it with him and, I thought I'd, ah, talk with mom about it," Tracey stammered.

"She's at George's house. I'll call her and see if they're back yet. Everyone, come on in." Ruth by now had regained both her composure and her sense of duty as a hostess. "Danny," she said as she looked at the young man, "you did a wonderful job tonight."

"Thanks, Mrs ... uh, Ruth. I'll do better when I know my way around the stage more."

Wow, thought Ruth. *Will the real Danny Ancino please speak up?*

When they entered the kitchen, Charlie and Toby excitedly jumped up and down.

"Hey, guys," Tracey said to them as she scratched their heads. "Did you miss me?" Morrie and Griselda appeared at the living room door, interested, but not ready to join in.

"Here." Ruth pointed to the kitchen chairs. "Danny, you and Del sit down and I'll get some tea—herbal tea for this time of night." She looked at Tracey. "George's number is on that list by my phone. Do you want to give them a call?"

"Sure." Tracey dialed the number but there was no answer. "Ruth," she said, "I was wondering if mom's okay with this. Danny's place is big enough for pets. It has a fenced-in yard with big trees, and everything ... and ..." Tracey looked across the kitchen at Charlie, who lay contentedly with his now inseparable pal, Toby, next to the refrigerator.

"And you want to take Charlie?" Ruth's heart sank. She had become unexpectedly attached to the little animal. "Of course," she said with a forced smile. "But it's up to your mom." She looked down at the two terriers. "She'll probably be alright with it. I hope you'll bring him back here for a visit from time to time."

Charlie and Toby both cocked their heads at Ruth.

"Come here, babies." She bent down and held her hands out to the dogs, who both came over to her at once. Ruth knew that the terriers were only temporary guests, but it would be difficult to see them move away. She looked up at Tracey, fighting back her emotions. "We can't separate them, you know. Can you also take Toby?"

"Thank you, Ruth," the girl said with a hug. "I was hoping you'd say that."

"How 'bout that tea?" Del ran some water into the tea kettle and turned on the burner.

"You bet," said Ruth, dabbing one eye. "And we've got some cookies."

"Come on, you two," Tracey called to the dogs, who came to her at once. "You are going to a nice place!"

"So you and Tracey are renting a house?" Ruth asked Danny.

"Yeah, it's kind of on the edge of the east side. Not too bad a neighborhood. We're renting with an option to buy. My uncle owns it. I wanna live there a while before I ... before we make up our minds." Danny looked uncomfortable.

"Your uncle owns it?" Del said. "You'll probably get a good deal."

"Well, yeah, only my mom doesn't know about it yet." Danny looked down at his feet. "Tracey and I, we're goin' to need to get engaged or my mom will throw a fit. Ya know what I mean?"

Ruth smiled at him. "Yes, I know what you mean. I'm a mom, don't forget."

The kettle started to whistle. Ruth took it off the burner and poured the contents into four cups, adding a tea bag to each.

Danny seemed to want to talk. He looked at Del and Ruth intently, as if trying to judge whether or not he could trust them. Finally, he spoke up.

"There's something goin' on down at the station house that I think I should tell you about. I can't put my finger on it, but there's somethin' weird goin' on." He looked at Del. "Don't tell anyone I told you, but somebody'd rifled through Mickey Sullivan's office just before he died. Then this memo came out that we all hafta keep our desks locked when we're not at 'em." He hesitated a moment as though he was thinking it through and then went on. "I heard that Mickey was helping on a case in California. Don Olson told me. He said that there is this on-going investigation, and a woman who might've been killin' off the actors in her theatre group. I don't know if it has anything to do with what's been goin' on here, but I thought you should know." His eyes scanned the faces at the table. "I just don't want anythin' else to happen. I really like this show, and these people. I want everyone to be safe and I don't want the show to close."

Ruth looked down at her tea cup and, for some reason at that moment, decided not to say that Sergeant Sullivan had told her about the community theatre in Sausalito, or that Billy had told her Lorene was from California, and that he'd met her in a theatre group. She'd tell Del later.

"More cookies?" she said instead.

They drank their tea and ate their chocolate-filled cookies in silence.

Finally Del spoke up. "I really don't know if we can have enough policemen on hand to keep us all safe." He turned the delicate tea cup round and around in his slim hands.

"Yeah, I know what ya mean," Danny said with a shrug. He put down his cup. "If it's someone in the group, they'll still be around. And even if we have buddies, what if it's *your* buddy? Maybe we should go in groups of three. That way, at least you'll have one other person to help ya."

"Good idea," Ruth added. "Let's tell Billy during vocal warm-ups tomorrow night." "Danny," Tracey asked him, "can you help me with these dog dishes? Let's bring them out to the car."

"Right!" Danny was out of his seat and through the door. "At your service," adding a salute.

"Hmm," Ruth said after the two left the kitchen. "He seems to be good husband material."

Del looked into Ruth's eyes and placed his hands over hers. "Am I good husband material?"

"Would you jump up and run every time I called?" Ruth arched her brows at him.

"Oh, would I ever! I'd jump up and run, Miss Ruth. *Every time you called,*" he said quietly in her ear.

Ruth blushed.

"Well, we're ready," said Tracey as she reappeared at the kitchen door. Charlie and Toby were at her feet and Danny behind her. "Thanks so much for everything, Ruth. Just ... everything. Tell my mom for me, will you? I know she'll be okay with this arrangement. After all, Charlie is really my dog—my birthday present when I was fifteen." She smiled up at Danny who seemed to melt.

"Take the dogs' food," Ruth said. "There's some left."

"No, no, I don't want to do that. What'll they eat when they come for a visit?"

Ruth stood up to hug both Tracey and Danny goodbye. "Alright, but you'd better come back here soon. I'm going to miss these little guys."

Charlie and Toby ran excitedly around Danny and Tracey as they headed for Tracey's car. When they got to it, however, the little terriers stopped and then ran back to Ruth.

"It's okay, babies," Ruth said as she walked over and petted each one. "It's time to go to your new house. Here, take these too." She handed Tracey the basket of dog toys and the blankets they had used. "They'll want these. It will help them feel more at home in the new place."

Tracey hugged Ruth again with her free arm. "I know why my mom loves you so much," she said, and put it all in their car.

That night, Ruth and Del fell into bed, exhausted, too tired to even talk.

We'll talk tomorrow about Lorene ... about everything, she thought as she fell asleep with her back snuggled up to Del, listening to the sound of his quiet snoring.

The next day, Ruth woke up late. Past ten! She felt ill, not seriously, but as if she had a summer cold coming on. And Del was gone. A note on his pillow read "I didn't want to wake you. I have to go to Schmitt's Music. I'll be back around two or so – with lunch. Love, Del." The bottom of the note read "P.S. – I fed the cats."

Ruth smiled. She knew Del needed to go to Schmitt's in downtown Minneapolis to pick up the music he'd ordered for a fall engagement with the St. Paul Chamber Orchestra. She was disappointed that he went without her, but also glad to have a few hours to herself.

I still need to convince Del about Lorene. I think she's dangerous.

She went downstairs and was greeted in the living room by Griselda, who rubbed against her leg.

"Where's Morrie?" she asked the cat, who just continued purring and rubbing against her.

She found Morrie sitting on one of her kitchen chairs, staring out the window at something.

"So what do you see?" Ruth came up and scratched the back of Morrie's ears. He simply arched into her hand and continued looking straight ahead.

She made her usual morning cup of tea and some toast with peanut butter. Then took it into the living room, snuggled down on the couch, opened her book, and pulled the purple and navy-blue afghan over herself. Morrie and Griselda jumped up to join her.

"Now, babies," she said to the cats as she opened a new Margaret Atwood novel, "Mama is going to be lazy today."

But Ruth didn't get much reading done. She kept thinking about Lorene, playing out the mystery in her head.

Why? What would be the purpose? Why kill Lionel? Susie? And try to kill or harm the others? And why me? Could she have pulled that costume over my head down in the basement? Ruth couldn't fathom someone doing that. *And how could she?* She felt dog-tired, emotionally as well as physically, and kept dozing off.

When Del came home later that afternoon, he found Ruth sound asleep on the sofa with the book on her stomach, glasses half way down her nose, and the cats nestled at her feet. He brought chicken wild rice soup and a crusty loaf of French bread from Byerly's. He put his grocery bag on the coffee table and was coming back from the kitchen with bowls, silverware, and napkins when Ruth woke up. The cats had smelled the soup and were already nosing in the bag.

"Get out of there, you little beggars!" He gently pushed Griselda and Morrie off the coffee table and looked at Ruth. "Your body must have needed that extra sleep. That's what my mother always said when we stayed in bed for a day. How do you feel?" He opened the bag and took out the loaf. He broke off a piece of bread and handed it to her, still warm.

"Oh," Ruth moaned as she bit into the savory crust. "I feel like I'm in heaven. I think I'll have to keep you around."

Del grinned as he took out the containers of soup. "Good! That's what I like to hear."

Ruth was still in her housecoat. "I am actually feeling much better, and what is that I smell, wild rice soup? Oh! This *is* heaven!" She watched as Del carefully ladled some into a bowl for her. "I should get up and get dressed and we can eat this out in the kitchen," she told him.

"You stay right there," he told her. "We have to get dressed for the play in about two hours anyway so you just relax. We'll have ourselves a picnic." He began eating his soup. "I'm glad you're feeling better. Tonight we'll have to look out for each other, you know. I'm going to be your buddy."

"You're my buddy anyway," she teased. She took the second piece of bread he handed her. "Del, do you remember last night when Danny was talking about the police station?"

Del was rubbing her shoulders. "Sure. He said something about the desks being locked and someone out in California." He kissed the back of her neck. "Is your costume ready?"

"Yes ... oh, that tickles! I wanted to tell you about California, Del." He had nibbled her ear.

"Well, I know Lorene's from California." He continued rubbing her back.

"That's what I wanted to talk about. Lorene's from California." Ruth tried to continue but Del's hands and mouth were distracting her.

"Good, she's a California girl. Good for her. We have an hour and forty-five minutes before we have to leave," he reminded her, rubbing her shoulders.

"I have to do my hair, and my makeup," Ruth told him. "And I wanted to tell you about Lorene and California ... oh ... that feels good!"

"Now, Miss Ruth," he said quietly as he kissed her cheek, "you are already beautiful. It won't take much time to put on your makeup, and we really don't have to talk about Lorene or anyone else right now." His hands moved from her shoulders to her neck and then down the front of her housecoat.

We'll talk about California later, Ruth thought, as some of her soup spilled on her mauve and white flowered housecoat. "Oh, now look what you made me do!" she mock-scolded him. "Now I'll have to take it off and wash it."

"Let me help you," Del said, as he followed her up the stairs, opening his shirt as he went.

Ruth's housecoat didn't get washed immediately. And neither did she have time to discuss what she thought about Lorene.

Chapter 36

Stay Together!

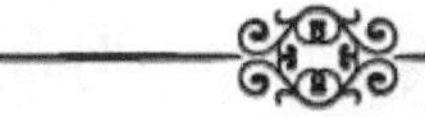

Two hours later, Ruth and Del were on their way to Como Park.

Now, Ruth thought, *he's a captive audience.* She felt she had to tell him what she knew.

"Del, I should have just come out with this before, but I had to think it all over and get it straight in my mind. I think that Lorene Hammer is our murderer. I really think she is."

"Well, Ms. Sherlock, I don't see it, but right now I'd agree with about anything you say to me," basking in the after-glow of their lovemaking.

"Please, Del, be serious for a moment." Ruth sounded insistent.

"You really think she is?" Del decided to pay attention this time.

"Yes, I do."

"But why? She would have to have some kind of a motive, wouldn't she?" His hands tightened on the wheel.

"Not if she was just plain crazy," Ruth told him. "And remember, they never caught that killer out in California—the one who killed the members of that theatre group."

"Yes, I know." Del looked straight ahead, concentrating on the road. "I remember. This is something you've thought a lot about?"

"I've been going over it in my mind for quite a while. I've really struggled with this. The murderer has to be someone in our troupe, someone who knows the people. So who?" She clasped her hands in her lap. "The other night, Billy came up behind me when Lorene was on stage. He told me he had met her in California, and I did tell you that Mickey Sullivan told me about a similar problem with a cast in California. Members of a community theatre group were getting killed and they never found out who did it."

She took a deep breath. Billy told me he met her in a theatre group in California, and he said she was good at wiring. Your house fire started with an explosion. And the Rosenberg's car blew up. Wiring. Lorene!"

"Whoa! That's quite a leap." Del shook his head. "Lorene's not a big woman. She doesn't look that strong."

"You don't have to be strong to wire things so they blow up," Ruth said vehemently, "and neither Lionel nor Angie would have been able to put up much of a fight. Nor would Gloria-June and Susie. It would have been easy to sneak up behind and push little Rodney Olson in the water. And I didn't fight back when that dusty old costume was pulled over my head because I was so completely surprised by it. I've seen Lorene lug around stage props that the men had a hard time with." Ruth gazed out of the car window, took a deep breath and looked back at Del. "She's the only logical one. So ... do we go to the police with this? Do we tell them? What? What should we do?"

Del shook his head. "I don't know. You have no proof. It's just conjecture. It would be terrible to make that kind of accusation and then find out it wasn't her. I think we should just watch her—try to make sure she doesn't get alone with anyone." Del glanced over at Ruth just as she looked at him.

"Her buddy. Who's her buddy?" they said in unison.

Ruth remembered. "It's Billy. I heard him tell her that they'd be buddies." Ruth thought for a moment. "They live together, so he's probably safe, but you know, Billy seemed so strange when he told her that they would be buddies. I watched him. He looked resigned, almost. Do you think he knows, or suspects ... something?"

"I don't know, but ... a murderer? His wife a murderer?" Del shook his head as if to make sense of it. "How could he keep that to himself?"

"Love can make people do strange things."

"Not *that* strange."

"Well, I think *we* have to do something. We can't let more people get killed." Ruth was wringing her hands now. "Maybe I should talk to Don Olson. Danny said he knows about the California case." Ruth looked blankly out the car window. They would soon arrive at the pavilion. "I wonder if Don knows Lorene is from California?"

Del shrugged. "We'll have to ask him."

Ruth had nothing further to add until they reached the north parking lot and found one of the few remaining spaces. "I know that just because someone's from a California theatre group, it doesn't mean they're a murderer." She shivered as she reached in the back seat for her shawl. "I know that."

"Okay," Del told her, smiling. "Keep that in mind." He patted her hand. "And remember, we don't personally have to figure this all out—that's what the police are for and they will know what to do." He pulled her shawl around her shoulders.

"What happened to 'we're on our own?'" Ruth asked him.

Del put his arm around her shoulders. "I just want things to go smoothly. I just want us to be okay."

Ruth smiled up at him, putting her arm around his waist. "Whatever happens, we're going to be okay."

They walked into the pavilion restaurant and headed for the double doors leading to the stage. They could see people lined up half-way around the building, waiting to purchase tickets for the show.

Fritz and Vivian sat at their usual table by one of the restaurant windows. Fritz, wearing his signature red sport coat, was eating a hamburger and drinking a cola. Vivian nibbled on a few of his French fries while writing in a ledger book.

"Looks like a great night. Weather's holding. There's already a good crowd," Fritz declared as Ruth and Del stopped by his table. He seemed to be in a good mood, as he usually was when the weather was not too hot and there were plenty of people in the audience. "I talked with Billy about everyone using the buddy system. I think we should all watch each other's backs. Of course, everyone watches *my* back—hee hee hee!" he cackled.

Vivian rolled her eyes but said nothing.

Ruth laughed in spite of herself while thinking, *Fritz always takes credit for the good ideas.* "We'll do that, maestro. There's sure lots of people tonight." She looked out at the crowd gathering along the outside walls of the restaurant, waiting to buy tickets.

"They love this show!" Fritz said. He looked at Vivian, who nodded in agreement. "Say, Del," he went on, "the other night I meant to tell you. You can sing an encore if you want. You don't have to stop at the end of 'Ol' Man River' in the first act if the audience gives you rousing applause. Just like on the boat. You can go ahead and sing it again, or repeat the last part of it. The people love it!" Then Fritz grinned at Del. "You sing almost as well as I do!"

Del grinned back. "Am I that good? Why, thank you, maestro!"

Fritz's singing voice, or lack thereof, was frequently the subject of his own mirth. He joked about it frequently, telling casts and audiences alike that his mother used to say to him, "If you ever sing for an audience, please don't tell them you're related to me." Fritz told this joke over and over, but people always enjoyed it—Fritz most of all.

"You two need to get downstairs for vocalization," Vivian reminded them. "Billy was up here a minute ago, trying to round up his cast."

"Do you know if Gloria-June is coming back?" Ruth asked.

"Howard said they were both out of the show. Howard was just in the chorus and didn't have any lines. Lorene agreed to do Queenie again tonight but the understudy will have to take over starting tomorrow," said Vivian. "Can't say I blame them much." She looked at Fritz. "I think I'm going to start selling tickets early tonight. The line is already pretty long." She noticed a bit of mustard on Fritz's lapel and dipped a napkin in her water glass so she could sponge it off. "You'd better get your orchestra rounded up," she reminded him.

"Break a leg tonight," Fritz said with a grin as he got up from the table.

Ruth and Del proceeded down the steep stairway to the basement rehearsal room. As they descended, Ruth noticed that all of the lights were on—in the hallways, the dressing rooms, the storage and costume rooms, everywhere—and all the doors were propped open with chairs. Billy, it seems, was taking no chances.

When the cast was finally assembled in a semi-circle around Billy, he again gave explicit instructions to stay together.

"I don't care if you have to pee together. You stay together! No wandering off, anywhere, without a buddy." There were a few chuckles again at the "pee" bit, but the normally upbeat cast didn't say much.

As they did their warm ups, Ruth tried to watch Lorene out of the corner of her eye. The woman looked the same as she always did, no better, no worse.

It's hard to believe she's capable of murder, Ruth thought, scrutinizing Lorene's placid face while she sang.

Elena Cordova's grandmother, now wearing a costume, stood next to the little girl.

She must have joined the chorus and is sticking like glue to her granddaughter. I don't blame her. I'd do the same.

It was time to go upstairs. As they walked past the women's dressing room, Ruth touched Del's arm. "I need to run in here for a second," she told him. "Wait at the door."

Del leaned against the wall. "I'll be right here waiting."

Ruth went into the empty ladies' dressing room and was busy in the bathroom stall when she heard the door slam shut. She called out, "Del? Is that you? Who's there?"

"It's me, Lorene."

Chapter 37

An Engagement

RUTH FELT THE HACKLES on her neck rise, but she tried to keep her voice even. "I'll be out in a minute, Lorene. I'm almost finished." She hurried, trying to arrange her slip under her dress so it wouldn't show. Her hands shook badly, making the task more difficult.

"Don't hurry," Lorene said quietly, "there's plenty of time. But I need to talk to you."

Ruth thought for a moment that she should stay inside the stall and be safe, but she knew Del was right outside the door, so she came out and quickly washed her hands. Lorene stood in front of the closed door to the hallway, blocking it.

Panic rose in Ruth's chest. "Del is waiting for me out there. I'm sorry, I can't talk right now. I really have to go," Ruth told her.

"Not just yet, Ruth," Lorene said, calmly. "I'd like to have a few minutes alone with you."

"I ... you ... maybe later." There was urgency in her voice. "Del is right outside the door waiting for me to go upstairs with him."

"Let him wait," Lorene said coolly. "I need to talk with you."

"Del!" Ruth called. "Del, are you out there?" She was so frightened she could hardly breathe.

Del opened the door immediately from the other side. "Ruth!" he yelled. "Are you okay?" Lorene was still standing in front of the door, and Del had to push her aside in order to open it. "What's going on in there?" There was fear in his voice too.

"Chill out," Lorene told him. "It's just two ladies in the ladies' room. Nothing to get excited about."

"Hurry up, Ruth." Del thrust his arm past Lorene and took Ruth's outstretched hand. "We've got to get ready to go on. The overture is playing."

"Excuse us, please!" Ruth said to Lorene, as she hurried past her into the hallway.

"Sure. I guess it can wait 'til later," Lorene replied.

Not if I can help it! Ruth thought to herself. She clutched Del's arm.

"Thank you!" she gasped. "I thought ... I ... well I don't know what would have happened in there."

"She went in there and closed the door before I knew what was happening," Del said. "I thought ... damn! I didn't know if I should go in there or not. It *is* a ladies' restroom, after all. And we don't really know if she's the one." He put his arm around Ruth's shoulders. "I was listening at the door."

"I know, and thank you for being so quick opening it." Ruth leaned into his body. "Oh Del, she's the one, alright. The way she spoke to me? So cool. Calm." Ruth shuddered. "It's her. I'm sure it's her!"

"We're okay as long as we stay together," Del whispered. "Stand as close as you can to me tonight while we're on stage."

Ruth started to laugh. "We can do 'Ol' Man River' as a duet!"

"Shh! Here she comes!" Del whispered back. They could hear Lorene coming up the stairs behind them.

"We've got to talk to Don Olson," Ruth whispered. "He'll know what to do."

"Shh. Okay, you win. Talk to Don ... later," Del whispered back.

The second night of a show nearly always goes smoother than opening night and tonight's performance seemed to be no exception. The actors were less nervous and more accustomed to moving around the stage. They knew their lines and sung with greater certainty. The orchestra was more together. The sound and lighting people were better coordinated. All was going smoothly, so far. Billy kept pacing the back stage area, giving everyone the "thumbs up" sign, yet Ruth worried it was only a calm before the storm.

When Ruth heard the strains of "Can't Help Lovin' that Man of Mine," she knew Lorene was on stage doing the part of Queenie. Quietly she edged over to Don Olson, who was standing in the corner watching the stage through a narrow slit in the set. She touched his arm, startling him.

"Sorry," she whispered. "Don, I need to talk to you about the murders."

"What about them?" he whispered back. He took her arm and led her over to the steps leading to the room where the orchestra kept music stands and chairs. "If you know anything, anything that might help us catch this person, you need to tell me." He held on to her arm while they walked down the steps.

Ruth scanned her surroundings. "I think I know who is responsible. It's a long story." Ruth looked up at him trustingly. "Oh, I'm so glad you're here."

"That's my job, to keep everyone safe." A group of actors stood nearby, waiting to go on stage. "We really need to solve this case," he told Ruth.

"I know, I know, and I think I can help. But I need to tell you everything. From the beginning."

Just then, Lorene came off stage and down the steps. She saw Ruth and Don talking together and walked quickly over to them, catching them off guard. "Watch out, you two," she said with a smirk. "People will think you're a back stage romance."

Ruth immediately stepped away from Don, who looked embarrassed. "I'll check back with you later," she whispered.

"Promise?" He looked at her. "I want to hear what you have to say."

"I know," Ruth told him. "For sure, we'll get together. Maybe at the cast party tonight?"

Don gave her a thumbs up and walked away.

That night during curtain calls, Ruth again saw Blanche in the audience. Tonight she was resplendent in a pale lavender silk pants suit. No flowers this time—only a small beaded bag that looked expensive. "I see that awful woman is here again tonight," Angie commented to Ruth as soon as they had finished their bows.

Ruth scowled. "I wonder if she's going to come to every performance?"

"Maybe she's writin' somethin' for the paper," quipped Angie. "A ... what do you call it?"

"A review," Ruth answered. "I bet she won't give me a very good one. Say, are you going to the party tonight?"

"Not tonight," Angie told her. "George is nervous about me bein' around this crowd. He wants me to come right home with him. He has some shrimp cocktail and a bottle of wine and we're goin' to have our own little party," she said with a comic little shrug.

"Oh Angie! That sounds so romantic."

"Yup!" Angie grinned from ear to ear. "Oh, hi, sweetie! I'm ready to go!" she called to George, who had just come in from the restaurant area. He held out a cold looking bottle of water for her.

"Oh ... hi Ruth," he stammered. "Would you like me to get you one?"

"Thanks, but no, I'm okay," Ruth assured him.

"How ya doin', Del?" George asked as Del came up behind Ruth.

"Very well, and you?" Del put his arm around Ruth's shoulders.

"Better than ever, due to this little lady!" George followed suit and put his arm around Angie's shoulders. "Mighty good singing tonight, Del. Mighty good."

"Well, thank you, George," Del said with a bow. "I thought the whole cast did well."

"We'd better get going," Angie giggled. "Don't want that shrimp to go bad." She looked impishly at George.

"Yes, well, bye now, folks." George shouldered Angie's heavy bag of clothing and makeup with one arm, and encircled Angie's waist with the other.

"They are so cute together," Ruth commented quietly to Del, as the couple walked away.

"Are we cute together?" Del asked.

Ruth leaned into his shoulder. "I think we're just dandy togeth ..." she started to say.

"Well! Isn't this just too, too sweet!" said Blanche, her voice dripping with sarcasm. The opera star had come up quietly and stood just behind them. "A backstage romance. My, my, my. But then, you know how long *they* last, don't you, Del?"

I didn't hear her high heels clacking! thought Ruth as she looked down at the woman's feet. They were clad in soft leather ballet slippers.

"Please excuse us, Blanche," Del answered tersely. "We have a cast party to go to." He quickly ushered Ruth out of the pavilion.

"She'll probably show up at our wedding!" Del said angrily, as they hurried across the dark parking lot.

"Maybe I should ask her to sing for it?" Ruth laughed.

"Maybe she could be a bridesmaid?" Del added as he opened the passenger door for Ruth.

As they drove out of Como Park, Ruth's ire began to rise. "I wonder how long this is going to go on—her acting like this? She's like a snotty junior high mean girl."

Del held the steering wheel with one hand and patted Ruth's leg with the other. "Maybe I should get a restraining order."

"That's giving her way too much importance," Ruth murmured. "If we keep giving her the brush off, maybe she'll finally get tired of this foolishness and just go away."

"Not to change the subject, but I wonder what Lorene wanted?" Del asked.

"I don't know. I was too freaked to find out."

"Maybe she'll be at the cast party," said Del. "We can talk to her together."

"And to Don Olson too," Ruth added. "I promised I'd talk with him and tell him about who I suspected."

As often happened after a Friday or Saturday night performance, members of the cast had a cast party, sometimes impromptu at a nearby restaurant and sometimes more organized and held at a cast member's house. This evening's party was being hosted by Sandy Westerling's mom. Sandy acted a little embarrassed as she passed out Xeroxed invitation flyers to the cast and orchestra before their performance. It came with a map. "My mom, you know, she's so excited to see me in this show. She's been cooking all day. You don't need to bring anything."

Everyone was on edge and a party offering fun, relaxation, and free refreshments was too good to pass up. Most of them assured Sandy that they'd be there. "Feel free to bring your friends, too." Sandy had told them. "My mom's made enough food for an army!"

As they drove along, Ruth helped Del navigate by reading a map to the Westerling's place.

"I think it's near the lake, yes, Lake Owasso. Stay on this road for about two more miles and then we'll need to turn left."

He said "our wedding," she thought to herself, smiling.

Del cast a glance in her direction. "What are you smiling about, woman?" he teased.

Ruth teased back. "Oh, it's just something you said when we were talking about Blanche. You sure take a lot for granted."

"About our wedding? I thought ... I *did* ask you, didn't I?"

"Oh, I guess you did, sort of."

"Then would you do me the honor of wearing this for me?" Del was serious now. Keeping his eyes on the road and one hand on the steering wheel, he dug into his right pocket and took out a miniature box covered in blue velvet.

"What?" Ruth took the box and opened it. "Ooh!"

"If you don't like it, I can get a different one. Anything you'd like."

Ruth looked closely at an elegant emerald cut diamond ring. She was breathless. "It's just beautiful! I love it!"

"Lizzie helped me pick it out. She approves of us, you know."

Tears welled in Ruth's eyes.

"I love you," Del said. "And please marry me."

"Yes, you know I will. I guess I'd better tell both Hannah and Robbie," she added. "They know I'm going with you, and they both approve. I know they'll love you ... but ... I *do* need to fill them in on this. I'll write to Hannah again tonight, and call Robbie in the morning."

"Does the ring fit?"

Ruth took it out of the box and put it on. "Oh, Del. It's just so beautiful. I've never had such a lovely ring. It feels a little big, though. I'm afraid I might lose it."

"We can get it resized. The jeweler told me to bring it in if it didn't fit right. We'll do that on Monday. *Then* will you wear it?"

"Proudly!"

Del took the ring, returned it to the blue case, and slid it back into his pocket.

Chapter 38

Cast Party

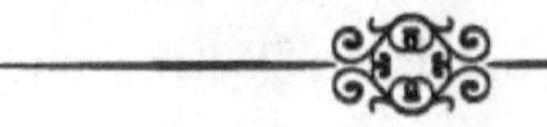

THE WESTERLING'S HOUSE, A spacious 1960s rambler, was on the south side of Lake Owasso in Roseville. Mrs. Westerling greeted them warmly at the door.

"Glad to have you here," she beamed. "Wonderful show, just wonderful! Please come in." Ruth thought the mother was the very image of her daughter Sandy, if you added twenty years and twenty pounds.

The party was well underway and Ruth was happy to be among familiar people. Don Olson was already there, standing with Elizabeth in the dining room next to a makeshift bar. "Hi, Don," Ruth said as she sided up to him. "I'm so glad to see you here."

"How about me?" Elizabeth interjected with a smile.

Ruth hugged her. "Of course! I'm happy to see you, too. You should have come with us."

"I thought I'd leave you two love birds alone." Then she looked at Ruth's left hand. "I was hoping ... I assume he showed it to you."

"It's beautiful, just lovely! But it was a little big. We need to get it resized."

"Oh, sure." Elizabeth sounded disappointed.

"I was beginning to worry you wouldn't be here," Don said to Ruth. "Do you want to discuss the, well, what you wanted to discuss with me?"

"Yes, I definitely do," Ruth said quietly. "Is there someplace ...?" She looked around the room.

"Good, now we can leave all this to the police," Del said.

Elizabeth stopped sipping her drink. "What about the police?" she said quietly, staring into her father's eyes. She looked back at Ruth, then back to Del. "What's happening?"

"Let's all go outside," he told her, spotting a set of French doors that appeared to open onto a patio. They headed toward it, went out, and closed the doors behind them.

Elizabeth, as usual, was the first to speak. "Dad, what's going on?"

"You sound just like your grandmother!" Del couldn't help laughing

"Oh, by the way," said Elizabeth. "I forgot to tell you. She's coming to our next performance. But please, what's going on?"

"Are you going to bring her?" Del asked. Ruth could feel her stomach begin to tighten.

"Yes, and don't worry, Ruth. She'll love you! She'll be coming with a friend of mine—that man you saw the other evening." Elizabeth peered once more into her father's eyes. "Now, *what* in sam hill is going on?"

"Ruth thinks she knows who the murderer is," Del answered.

Elizabeth looked at Ruth and then at Don.

Don turned to Ruth. "So, how about telling me what you know."

"Well, I'm not really sure," Ruth began hesitantly, "but I think it may be Lorene ... Billy's wife." She paused. Her fears were beginning to color everything and she stared warily out toward the lake that lay beyond the dark, indiscernible back yard. She hoped Lorene wasn't out there somewhere, listening.

"Go on ..." Don said quietly.

Ruth continued. "Well, Mickey Sullivan told me once about this theatre group in California ... how the members were being killed, one by one ... and when I found out that Lorene was from California, and that she knows all about wiring ... you know things have been blown up ... and seeing how physically strong she is, well, that, and that she acts kind of strange, kind of angry about some of the actors, like Gloria-June. Well, I think perhaps you ought to look into it."

Don said nothing.

"This has to be an inside job," Ruth added. "Someone who is in the show or connected to the theatre company in some way. There's no other explanation, and it could be Lorene."

"I really appreciate your giving me this information," he said quietly. "If everyone was as thoughtful as you and remembered things as well as you, and were willing to share their gut feelings, our jobs would be easier."

"Are you going to question her?" Del asked.

Don looked out into the yard as if lost in thought. "I'll do a little checking to see if there is any kind of police record on her. In the meantime, we need to be watchful. Keep an eagle eye on her comings and goings."

"Do you think we're safe?" Elizabeth asked him.

"Oh, I think as long as you stay together and are watchful. So how long have you people been in this theatre group?" He looked at Del.

"This is my first show," Del told him. "I sing in other venues. This is the first time I've been in one of Fritz's shows, although I've known him for years. Everybody seems to know him."

"I was in a few of his shows as a child," Elizabeth said. "Only a couple of the people in it now were in it when I was doing it as a kid."

"I've been in a lot of his shows over the years," Ruth chimed in, "but I was out for about five years when my husband was sick. For instance, I didn't know Rhonda. She must have started after I left ..." Her voice trailed off.

"Okay, then," Don said in a heartier voice. "I think we should get back to this party. You let me take care of things." He smiled reassuringly as he clapped Del on the back and started toward the doors. Ruth, Del, and Elizabeth followed him back into the dining room.

A little later, while standing in line to get a plate of salad and lasagna, Ruth noticed Don saying something to the hostess. He shook her hand and then departed via the front door.

"Maybe he's going back to the station," Ruth said to Del. "Maybe to see if Lorene's got a record."

"Who knows?" Del replied. "I sure hope we did the right thing."

"All I did is tell him what I suspected," Ruth said with more conviction than she really felt.

"See you two later," Elizabeth told them as she took her plate and joined a group of younger cast members.

Ruth looked around. She could see that Lorene and Billy weren't at the party, which seemed strange because Billy loved parties.

This party should be more fun, but it's not.

Mrs. Westerling was a gracious, attentive hostess, but in Ruth's eyes the party had a somber undertone. She and Del ate their food in relative silence.

Soon—perhaps in an attempt to liven things up—some members of the cast gathered around a piano in the living room to sing old Broadway favorites, accompanied by an animated Mimi Rosenberg. Ruth was about to join in when Del motioned for her to come with him.

He led her back out to the empty patio, drinks and cheesecake in hand. They sat down on a porch swing. "I'm surprised Lorene isn't here tonight," Del said. "And I just can't imagine Billy missing a cast party."

Ruth looked around. "I'm glad she's not here ... and what do you know, neither is Blanche!" she added with a laugh.

Del smiled and nodded and then thought for a moment. "So, what do you think about setting a wedding date?"

"Let's wait until the show is over. As I said in the car, I need to let my kids in on what's been going on with us. Good grief," she laughed. "I barely told them that I'm dating you, and now I'm engaged to you?" She chuckled to herself. "And I always told them not to rush into things." She shook her head.

"Am I rushing you, Ruth? I mean, with the ring and all?" Del looked concerned.

"No, of course not." She snuggled up to him. "I think, considering our age, and that we are in a loving relationship, it was the gentlemanly thing to do." She smiled at him and kissed his cheek. "I promise I will write to Hannah tonight when I get home and call Robbie tomorrow morning." She patted his arm. "And I will gladly wear your beautiful engagement ring—when it fits."

He kissed her back. "Ah Miss Ruth, I made a good choice."

They sat for a while, finishing off their dessert and drinks.

"So, let's leave all this for the police to figure out," Del finally added as they swung slowly back and forth. "We'll concentrate on us."

"I like that," Ruth said, snuggling closer.

Just then, Danny rushed out to the patio through one of the French doors.

"Good. I thought I saw you two come out here. Tracey just called. One of the dogs got out. It was Charlie, and she's goin' crazy lookin' for him. I gotta get home and I thought I should say goodbye and tell you why I'm headin' out."

He turned to go back and then stopped in his tracks. "Oh, geez! How could I be so stupid? I don't have a car!" He hit the side of his head with his hand. "My uncle dropped me off here."

Del was up in an instant. "We'll take you," he told Danny. "Just a minute, I'll tell Elizabeth we're going and thank our hostess." He hurried inside, carrying the empty dishes and glasses with him.

"Do you know what happened?" Ruth asked Danny as he impatiently shifted from one foot to the other.

"I don't know what happened. He's just gone. The backyard is fenced in, but there must'uv been a hole in it or somethin'. There's a lot of traffic around there. Geez, I hope the little guy is all right!"

It took them about half-an-hour to drive from the Westerlings to the east side of St. Paul where Danny and Tracey had rented a small, sturdy-looking two-story house. When they arrived, the place was lit up top to bottom. They hurried in by way of a side door. "Trace!" Danny called out. "Trace!"

A shaken Tracey came running into the kitchen with Toby at her heels. She threw her arms around Danny. "Charlie's gone! I went out there to bring them both into the house after I got all the boxes in from the garage and Charlie was gone!"

Chapter 39

Lost and Found

THE FOUR OF THEM looked all over the yard and down nearby alleys and streets. Tracey and Danny had just moved in, so didn't yet know any neighbors to call. It was late, well past dark.

"It's almost midnight," Danny said. "Someone might have taken him in. He's such a cute little guy. Let's start again in the morning. We'll go house to house and ask."

"We'll come back in the morning and help you," Del said. He glanced at Ruth. "Won't we?"

"Of course," she quickly replied. "And I'll bring breakfast. Tracey, I'll bring one of Gustafson's famous coffee cakes, the one you said you liked so much when you were at my house a few weeks ago." She put her arm around the girl's shoulders. "Don't worry, honey, we'll find him. We did it before. We can do it again." Ruth was thinking back to the first time they had lost Charlie.

"Oh, my poor mom loves him so!" Tracey wailed, "what are we going to tell my mom?"

"We don't need to tell her anything right now," Ruth said. "Anyway, it's too late tonight. I'm sure we'll find him tomorrow. We can also call the city pound after it opens and let them know, just in case someone brings him in there. Maybe they already did."

"You two go in now and get some sleep," Del told Tracey and Danny as they stood out in the street. "Ruth and I will take one more swing around the neighborhood before we head back to Lake Elmo." The four said their good-byes and Ruth and Del got into the Lexus. "Let's go back to that little park we saw. Just to make sure," Del told Ruth.

They drove slowly around the small park. Ruth had the window down to listen for barking and both peered into the dark, shadowy landscape for any sign of a white animal.

"Del! Stop the car!" Ruth suddenly cried. "I think I see him! I think that's Charlie!"

Del pulled the car to the curb and Ruth jumped out.

"It is!" she screamed. "Oh! Charlie! Here, Charlie! Come here, boy!" When the little dog saw Ruth, he ran excitedly to her, jumping up and down and licking her face when she knelt to pick him up. Ruth's worry over Charlie instantly dissolved as soon as they got the dog into the back seat of their car.

"I hope I can find their house," Del told Ruth as they began to drive back to Tracey and Danny's. "I was so caught up in finding the dog I didn't pay attention to the address."

"I didn't either," Ruth admitted. "Wait, I think it's on this block." She pointed to a large Victorian style house with gingerbread trim. "I remember that house. It was on the end of the street they were on." They drove slowly down the street. "There it is. I recognize it. Oh dear, the only light is upstairs. I suppose they're in bed by now."

"Somehow, I don't think they'll mind us bothering them tonight," Del said confidently.

"You're right. Come here you little rascal." Ruth took Charlie into her arms and cuddled him.

Charlie's homecoming was indeed joyous. Tracey and Toby were ecstatic. Danny flashed a big grin and told Ruth and Del, "Thanks so much! I've got my family back."

"And speaking of family," Danny went on, "Next week, my uncle Tony wants to give the cast party on Saturday night. He has a place on White Bear Lake. I sure hope you guys can make it." He looked hopefully at Ruth and Del.

Tracey came up behind him and put her arms around Danny's waist. "You've got to come. We're announcing something special that night," she said, beaming.

Oh gosh, She's pregnant! thought Ruth.

"We're getting engaged," Danny told them. "My mom and my uncle Tony helped us pick out this humongous ring."

"I didn't want anything nearly that big ... but those Ancinos ... they're kinda flashy!" Tracey laughed.

"Someday, I hope I can pay Uncle Tony back for that bit of *flash*," Danny retorted.

"I think that's wonderful! We wouldn't miss it for the world," Ruth assured them.

As they headed back out to their car, Danny stayed inside with the dogs and Tracey walked out with them.

"Ruth, please don't tell my mom before we announce this at the cast party. I want to surprise her. And then please whisper in her ear that I'm not pregnant ... so she won't worry."

"Okay, mum's the word," Ruth said with a hug. "It'll be our secret until then. But your mom will be so happy about your engagement I don't think she'd care if you were pregnant."

"Still," the girl said, "I want to do this right. There'll be plenty of time for all that."

Saturday dawned sunny but cooler than usual. A breeze blew in from the lake, ruffling the curtains in the bedroom. Del stretched as he got out of bed and looked out the window.

"I'm goin' fishin'!" he told Ruth.

"You need a fishing license," she murmured sleepily. "You can't fish without one. Tom always had to have one, even if he just went out for one day." She buried her head back into her pillow.

"So where do you get those? Nothing is simple anymore," he muttered as he padded off to the bathroom.

Soon Ruth heard him singing lustily in the shower. She snuggled down in the bedclothes until he stopped singing and then went over to the bathroom door. "I think I know where you can get a fishing license," she called through the door. "In fact, if you take me out to Perkins for breakfast, we can stop at the license place in Stillwater. It's right nearby."

"You drive a hard bargain, woman," he called back. "Perkins it is."

This feels familiar, Ruth thought as they drove to the restaurant. "This is where we often went after church," she said as they exited the car. "It was kind of a tradition ... church ... then often as not, Perkins."

"With any luck, we'll run into our friend, Blanche."

"Couldn't you just see her at a Perkins?"

"Well, no, I guess not." Del put his arm around her.

The Stillwater Perkins was a family place. Even at nine o-clock on Saturday morning it was bustling. With lots of windows, and photos of long-ago Stillwater on the walls, the place was homey and inviting. A glass case full of delectable-looking baked goods greeted them upon entry. A dozen paintings of Minnesota wild flowers by two local artists were displayed in the entry area.

"You should show your work here," he told Ruth. "This stuff is good, but yours is too."

"I did, a long time ago," she answered. "I even sold a couple of watercolors. It's a lot of work, though, and I'd rather give my paintings to deserving friends."

A manager smiled genially as they came up to the matre d' stand. He held up five fingers and told them "About five minutes, folks."

When their name was called, they were taken to a window table overlooking shrubbery tinged with a hint of fall colors.

"I love it when the leaves start turning," Ruth said as she took her seat. "I think fall is my favorite time of year."

"You know what I'd like to do in the fall—*this* fall?" Del said as he looked over his menu. "I'd like an outdoor wedding ... under those big oak trees, next to your lake."

"We can't," Ruth said, patting his hand. "Hannah won't be back from Sweden yet and I want both my kids to be there."

"Oh, I'm sorry. I forgot." Del looked a little crestfallen.

"Don't worry. It'll happen," Ruth laughed. She shook her finger at him. "Smile! You're going fishing today, remember?"

After a big breakfast of cheese-omelets, crisp bacon, and cranberry muffins, Del and Ruth left for the license bureau, just down the street from the restaurant. The line moved rapidly and soon Del was walking out to the car, the obligatory license in his pocket.

Ruth squinted up at the late morning sky. "If you're going to be out in that boat this time of day, we'd better also get you some sunscreen." Then she stopped and looked at him, embarrassed, "Oh! You don't need it, do you?"

"I don't get any tanner than this," Del grinned with a wink, "but if you have an old hat of your husband's, I could use it. It'll keep the sun off my head."

"There's a couple of them in the basement," she told him. "I use them myself when I go out rowing in the boat, which isn't all that often."

"Want to come with me today?" he asked hesitantly.

"No. I don't horn in on fishermen," she told him tartly. "Besides, I have to write to Hannah and call Robbie. And after that I have a wedding quilt to start for Tracey and Danny."

"You are indeed a fine, fine woman," he explained, relieved, as he opened the passenger-side door for her.

Del spent the rest of the afternoon on the lake, content with a casting rod and other fishing gear that had once belonged to Tom. Ruth spent the rest of her day writing lengthy letters to her daughter Hannah and son Robbie. She had tried calling Robbie, but all she got was a message that his answering machine was full. Then she remembered that at this time of year he always went camping with his buddies in Colorado.

After finishing her letter to Robbie, Ruth went to her sewing room and began cutting out pieces of fabric for Tracey's quilt.

I hope this wedding doesn't take place too soon, she thought. *I need more blue fabric for this, and I need more time.*

The phone rang around four o'clock; it was Don Olson. "Mrs. Carson, I called Fritz and suggested once more that he close the show, but he told me in very colorful language that there's no way he would shut it down." He cleared his throat. "He was pretty upset."

"Well," said Ruth, "I think he really depends on the money he makes in the summers."

"I suppose so," Don sighed, "but if you carry any clout with him at all, would you talk with him?"

"I'll try," Ruth told him, "but I don't think I'll have any better luck than you did."

Del came in from the lake a half hour later, empty handed except for his rod and reel. Ruth told him about Don's call.

"As if you could get Fritz to cancel the show. Did you call your son?" he asked Ruth. "I'm not so worried about Hannah" he told her. She would love being the "Lizzard's" sister. It's Robbie I'm wondering about. What did he say about us getting married?"

"I couldn't get through and his answering machine is full. I think he might be on a camping trip in Colorado, so I wrote to both of them. But stop worrying. I know my kids and I know they'll both be fine with us getting married. Please don't worry."

"So, where are all your fish?" she asked him.

Del shrugged, "I think I'm out of practice. Soup and a sandwich will be fine with me."

Chapter 40

Mama Wilda

Thursday and Friday performances the following week went smoothly. Nothing out of the ordinary, on stage or off. No attacks on anyone. Good size audiences.

Then came Saturday and Ruth felt a change in the air.

Just as they were walking up to the pavilion, they saw Angie and George park and get out of their car. They waited so the couple could join them.

"So, whatcha think, Ruthie?" Angie ran up and paraded in front of them, turning around in a circle, showing off a new hair color and cut. "Do ya like it?"

"It's beautiful!" Ruth said, awestruck. "What ... what did you do?"

Angie was transformed. Her once bilious red hair had been toned down to a soft auburn and cut to frame her face, just touching her shoulders. She looked years younger; more than that, she looked classy.

"I went to George's hair-cut place. It's right downtown in Lake Elmo. The lady who did me, knows you, Ruthie. Didn't she do a good job? I told her I usually do my own hair and she told me, "Not any more, you don't!" George was grinning and shaking his head.

"Angie, you look just wonderful!" Del told her.

"I thought, with Tracey's hookin' up with the Ancino bunch, I'd better start lookin' like I belonged with all those ritzy types." She made a snooty face and pirouetted again. Ruth just hugged her.

"Come on, classy lady," Ruth told her, "we'd better get going. You know how the Maestro is about late-comers."

Vivian, already in costume, had set up her ticket table by the main entrance and there was a long line. It was pleasantly cool, the kind of weather that usually attracted a bigger audience. Once they bought their tickets, excited theatre-goers hurried in to find good seats. Because of the weather, many carried blankets.

"Look at that crowd!" Ruth exclaimed to Del. "I think this is the biggest night yet."

They descended the steps to the dressing rooms.

"Hi, folks." It was Don Olson. "Big crowd tonight. Fritz will make a bundle on this one," he mused. "But you know, he probably has a few enemies out there."

Now, that's a happy thought! Ruth thought to herself.

Del said nothing.

Billy Hammer was ushering everyone downstairs. "Come on, people, let's get downstairs for our meeting. We've got a show to do." He looked up at his wife, who was on a ladder repairing a tear in the backdrop. "Honey, would you do the prayer for us tonight?"

"Yeah, right!" she yelled back at him, laughing derisively.

Billy got the message and then spotted Ruth.

"Ruth, how 'bout you? Do the prayer for us tonight?"

Oh Lord! Ruth thought, looking at Billy. She hesitated.

"I'll do it for you tonight," Don said, putting a hand on Ruth's arm. "That is, if you don't mind."

Ruth turned and smiled at him. "Why thank you. I owe you, Don," she answered quietly. He smiled back.

Just then Del nudged Ruth. "Look out there, walking in toward the first row, the queen mum—my mother-in-law." He pointed at an older but ram-rod straight little woman, dressed in a navy-blue satin suit and carrying a matching evening purse.

Ruth looked where he was pointing.

"She's Elizabeth's grandmother? My! She's elegant! I can see where Elizabeth gets it."

The woman saw them, gave a little "queen" wave, and primly sat down next to her escort, who Ruth recognized as Elizabeth's boyfriend, Richard.

"She will adore you," Del whispered in Ruth's ear.

Don Olson said a reasonably good prayer. The cast, less subdued than the night before, seemed happy they had only one week of performances left. The first act started without incident. Toward the end of it, however, a sharp wind began to whip up waves on the lake, followed by a downpour that blew soaking rain on folks sitting in the last few rows. Most moved forward, finding new places to sit. "Minnesota nice" prevailed, as the other audience members squeezed together to make room on their benches. Soon everyone was settled in and enjoying the show once more.

During intermission, Danny Ancino hurried around backstage, inviting all to the cast party at his Uncle Tony's home on White Bear Lake.

"Uncle Tony's really gone all out for tonight," Danny told Ruth, as he handed her an envelope containing an engraved invitation along with a map. "It's kind of last minute, but I sure hope everybody can come. He's even hired a jazz combo to play for us."

"Oh my!" exclaimed Ruth. "This looks pretty fancy. We'd love to come."

Tracey suddenly came up and, putting her arms around Danny's waist, pulled him to her with a hug. "His Uncle Tony wants to 'announce us' tonight, and I decided to tell my mom," she told Ruth. "So it won't be a surprise."

Danny looked down at Tracey's ring finger. The huge diamond sparkled in the artificial light of the pavilion. "I think he wants to make sure she doesn't get away from me," he laughed, leaning into Tracey's arms.

"She'd better not!" Angie said as she walked by, wagging her finger. "I bought a dress already, and ... well ... although your Uncle Tony's kind of ... well, you know how he is. I kinda *like* you!" She kissed an embarrassed Danny on the cheek.

"Mom," chided Tracey, "behave yourself!"

"Like *that's* gonna happen any time soon." Angie gave Ruth a wink. Danny just grinned, basking in Angie's approval.

Ruth went in search of Del.

Apparently the 'buddy system' has gone by the wayside tonight, she thought, as she saw actors, musicians, and stage hands milling around, some walking singly, seeming not to care that they were alone.

"Really? Another party?" Del responded when Ruth reminded him about it. "Do we have to?"

"I'm afraid we have to," she told him. "It's Tracey's engagement party. We can't get out of this. We can't disappoint her, or Angie, or Danny ... or Uncle Tony!" she laughed.

"No, I suppose we can't then. Oh, look who's here! Ruth, I would like you to meet the matriarch of our family, Mrs. Wilda Hartford-Smith." Elizabeth's grandmother had just walked up to them.

"Mama Wilda, I would like you to meet Ruth Carson, the woman I want to spend the rest of my life with."

"It's about time! I'm glad this boy's finally found someone," she said to Ruth with a broad smile. "It's no good for a man his age bein' alone."

"Thank you." Ruth told her. "I'll try to make him happy."

"Of course you will," she said as she patted Ruth's arm. "I can tell—just by lookin' at you."

Just then a deafening clap of thunder and flash of lightning shook the pavilion, knocking out the power. Lights everywhere went out, even in the parking lot. Ruth reached out for Mama Wilda, who said, "What in the sam hill is happenin' here?!"

There were gasps, both from the audience and the cast. Above the din, you could hear Fritz scream, "Oh my god! Vivian! Help me! Oh my god!"

Ruth, who believed in the old Girl Scout motto "Be Prepared," said to Mama Wilda, "Just a minute. I think I can help." She reached down and grabbed for the basket at her feet. Fishing around in the bottom of it she retrieved a small flashlight and turned it on. She aimed the beam in Fritz's direction.

"You marry this one," Mama Wilda told Del. "She's prepared!"

Fritz's music had fallen in disarray off of his music stand.

"Whoever you are, keep that damn light on!" he yelled toward Ruth. She continued to aim her flashlight at him, although she felt like turning it off, just to annoy him.

Uf! I could just throw this thing at him!

"You," he pointed at the new pianist, "Help me get all this music back up here! Pick up those clips for me! I need to get this in order!" The young piano-player jumped up quickly to comply.

Mama Wilda snorted. "That man sounds like an absolute nightmare."

A few minutes later, the lights on the stage came on, illuminating the faces of the audience near Fritz. Ruth saw a predatory-looking Blanche Voorhees clutching the arm of Danny's Uncle Tony.

Del noticed her too.

"Look who's latched onto poor Uncle Tony," he said grimly. "That woman is like a rampant plague!"

"Well, we can't stop her. She's a paying customer," Ruth told him.

"My goodness!" Mama Wilda laughed, looking at Blanche and Tony. "Will you look at those two. You'd think they were doin' *Guys and Dolls*!"

Blanche simpered and smiled and raked Tony Ancino's arm with her long, red nails. Tonight, she looked the part of a gangster's moll, complete with tight black satin cocktail dress adorned with a bright red rose in the bodice. Red stiletto heels and a matching clutch bag completed her ensemble. She smiled at Tony and leaned her breasts into his forearm. He obviously enjoyed the attention.

"I won't see you two after the play tonight," Mama Wilda told them. "Lizzie and Richard are driving me back to my place and then I think they have a party to go to." She patted Ruth. "Oh look, I see them." She waved at Elizabeth and the young man with her. They waved back.

"It was so wonderful to meet you, Mrs. Hartford-Smith." Ruth was still chuckling at the *Guys and Dolls* comment. "You are an absolute delight! I can see why Del and Elizabeth love you."

"Mama Wilda, to you, my dear. I'm happy for you, Del. She looks like a good one." With that benediction, Mama Wilda turned and headed back to her seat. Ruth could see Elizabeth hug and kiss her before returning backstage.

Apparently, the restaurant had a backup generator that also provided enough power to illuminate the stage and orchestra area.

Lorene came up to Ruth and asked, "Have you seen Tim the Stagehand? Billy's looking for him." Ruth shook her head. Tim the Stagehand had been with their group as long as anyone could remember. Ruth glanced around backstage, hoping to spot his white hair and the old Twins baseball cap he always wore, indoors and out.

He's probably helping with the generator, she thought, *or he just left and went to a bar.* Tim didn't always stay around for second acts or clean-up, and his erratic behavior and drinking habits were well-known to the group.

Billy Hammer walked to the middle of the stage. Like a man used to dealing with disasters, he was calm and collected and prone to shop-worn humor.

At the top of his voice, he announced, "Okay now, folks ... just a bit of Minnesota weather. You know, if you don't like the weather here in Minnesota, just wait a few minutes and it'll change. So, nothing to get upset about. Take your seats now. We're gettin' ready for the second act. You don't want to miss this. You want to find out what happens, don't ya? Sure, ya do!"

The second act of *Show Boat* went off without another hitch. After the final curtain call, Billy assured the group that the generator was also providing light for the dressing rooms downstairs. "Thanks everyone!" he beamed. "You did an awesome job tonight!"

Valuables you didn't want to lose were never left unattended downstairs. Most of the women carried small purses with them on stage, either in baskets, like Ruth, or in pockets sewn into their costumes. The men simply used their pant pockets. No one, however, wanted to wear their costume to a cast party, so everyone trekked down to the dressing rooms to change.

In all the commotion, no one noticed that Tim the Stagehand was still missing in action. And luckily for him, he'd gone to a bar on Dale Street—he was a regular—to enjoy the evening with his buddies. He didn't realize it, but that decision saved his life that night.

Chapter 41

Uncle Tony's "Lake Cottage"

WHEN DEL AND RUTH drove up the long tree-lined driveway to Tony Ancino's "lake cottage" (as the invitation called it), Del whistled. "Whew! Look at this place!"

"Da deee da dummm," Ruth hummed the theme from "Tara," the fictional plantation in *Gone with the Wind*.

"Some lake cottage he has here," she observed as a stately, white columned structure came into view. Even at night in the rain, the place looked palatial. Every window was lit up.

"I'd love to know the history of this place," Del said as they parked the car in a paved area near the entrance. They sat for a moment, taking it all in.

"I think it might have been a sanitarium at one time," Ruth told him. "I remember my mother, who was a nurse, telling me something about a place here in White Bear Lake—it might have been this one—where people used to come for their tuberculosis cures."

"I wonder how Uncle Tony came to have it?"

"From what I understand, Uncle Tony can buy pretty much anything he wants."

"How's the fishing on White Bear Lake?"

"You have a one-track mind."

"Actually, Miss Ruth …" He reached over and squeezed her thigh. "Two tracks."

"Del!" Ruth chided, but she leaned into his body for more.

As they got out of the car and came to the front door, which was flanked by two small pine trees set into two stone containers, an elderly man in a black suit opened the door and said, very formally, "Welcome, please come in."

When the man turned his back, Del slipped a glance to Ruth and mouthed, "a butler?" Ruth just shrugged.

As Del and Ruth began to remove their wet shoes, the man said, "Oh, do please keep your shoes on if you'd like. Don't worry about the floors. The floors here are terrazzo and nothing can hurt them. Mr. Ancino is waiting for you in the party room. Just head down the hallway toward the back of the house. You'll hear the music. Just follow the sound."

As they reached the double doorway into the lakeside party room, Ruth gasped. It was huge, like something out of a 1930s Fred Astaire movie set, with cream-colored wood paneling and tall, floor to ceiling windows framed by sheer, white curtains. Various furniture groupings lined the walls.

Small clusters of early arrivals stood around chatting and laughing. Mimi and Al Rosenberg, looking a bit uncomfortable, stood next to a pink marble fireplace. Ruth waved to them and they hurried over to Ruth's side. Mimi was breathless. "Isn't this place something?"

"It sure is," Ruth answered as she scanned the room. "By the way, you were both wonderful tonight. Of course," she added with a wink, "you're both wonderful *every* night!"

Off to the left, a five-piece jazz combo, clustered around a grand piano, was doing a smooth rendition of "Ain't Misbehavin'." The piano player was a well-known jazz musician in the Twin Cities and Del, who knew him, gave him a wave. The pianist beamed at Del and nodded to Ruth, Mimi and Al.

The right side of the room held a long table set with a white cloth and at least a dozen pink candles of various heights. Wonderful-looking appetizers—shrimp cocktail, chicken on skewers, little quiches, and much, much more—were heaped on the elegant table. A bar was set up next to the table and a bartender in a white jacket stood ready to dispense whatever people wanted.

"Come on, Del," said Al, "let's wet our whistles." He started toward the bar.

"Sounds good. Can I get you anything?" Del asked Ruth.

"Not right now, thanks," she told him. "I think I'll look for the powder room."

"Oh! Me too," said Mimi.

As the two men went for drinks, the two women walked back into the hall, hoping to find a bathroom. There were several closed doors and Ruth and Mimi tried to guess which one might lead to a lavatory.

The first room they tried was a linen closet.

"Not this one!" Ruth laughed. The next one led to another closet.

"Not this one, either!" Mimi said and they both laughed nervously.

Ruth tried a third door and both women were shocked at what they saw. In a room that must have been an office or library, Uncle Tony Ancino sat in a leather lounge chair, his pants around his ankles. Straddling him with her skirt hiked up around her waist and her blouse open, revealing voluptuous swinging breasts, was none other than the inimitable Blanche Voorhees. The two were so engrossed in what they were doing, they didn't notice or hear the door opening. Ruth shut it silently.

"Oh dear!" she whispered to Mimi.

"Whoa! Isn't she that opera singer?" Mimi whispered back, her eyes like saucers.

"The one and only," Ruth told her quietly. "We better stop looking behind closed doors."

As they headed back toward the front entrance to seek directions, they encountered a maid who told them where to find the ladies room. It was in the same hallway, right next to the "office." When they entered, they could hear Blanche on the other side of the wall. *"Oh god! Oh baby! Oh! God! That's so good! Yes! Ohh! I like it that way, baby! That's so good! Ohh ... Yes!"* They could also hear Tony Ancino grunting in satisfaction.

Mimi started to giggle, then Ruth. They held their hands over their mouths so they couldn't be heard through the thin wall.

"They're having quite a party," Mimi whispered, "just for themselves."

"I wonder if they're going to make it over to ours?" Ruth whispered back.

When they returned to the party room, they gave each other conspiratorial glances and joined Del and Al who had drinks and plates of food waiting.

"You both look like cats who swallowed the canary," Al told them.

Both women burst out laughing. Ruth looked at Del, who had a quizzical look on his face. "Later," she said.

"Okay." Del offered her a shrimp. "I can wait."

Ruth took the shrimp. "Delicious! Thank you!" But she was smiling way too much.

Del gently guided her toward the food table. "Okay, what's up?"

"Uncle Tony, apparently ..." Ruth burst out laughing again. She covered her mouth and leaned into him, trying to control her laughter. "I'm sorry, Del, I just can't ..."

"What?" Del looked at her with an air of reproach, but before she could answer, Tony Ancino and Blanche Voorhees made their entrance. Both were flushed and Tony had an arm around Blanche's waist. He looked happy. She was smoothing her skirt down with one arm and checking the buttons of her blouse with the other.

"Welcome to my lake place!" Tony ebulliently bellowed as he sidled up to Del and Ruth. Part of his shirt was un-tucked.

"Thank you for having us here," Del replied.

"It's a beautiful house," Ruth told him, trying not to smile too much. "Just lovely!"

"You guys know Blanche?" he asked with a nod toward her. He looked at Del. "I understand you're an opera singer. Blanche here is in that business too. But not for long. Not if I can get her to be my gal, permanent-like."

"We've met," Blanche said, smiling at Del, and while she tried to smile at Ruth, she stiffened, and her smile didn't quite reach her eyes.

"Whoa!" laughed Tony, who immediately noticed the chill in Blanche's expression. "Ain't this lady a friend of yours, honey? Want I should take care of her for ya?" he laughed again. "Just kidding lady," he said to Ruth. "Blanche's temper-mental ya know."

Ruth didn't know what to say, so said nothing at all and smiled weakly at Uncle Tony. Del set his plate down and put both arms around Ruth, from behind, kissing the top of her head as he did so.

"Hey, Blanchie!" Tony whacked her on the bottom. "Take a lesson from these folks, babe. See how in love they are? We want to be that way, don't we, babe?" Tony licked his fore-finger and put it on Blanche's hip, making a "pssst" sound as he did so. "My Blanchie, she's a hottie, she is!"

Ruth could see Blanche stiffen even more, but Tony didn't notice and kept on. "Well, folks, enjoy yourselves. Eat, drink, get crazy. Come on, baby-cakes, let's see who else is at this shindig of ours." At this, he steered Blanche around Ruth and Del and took her to greet other guests.

"Baby-cakes?" Del said quietly, a huge grin on his face.

Ruth was laughing now. "Please don't ever call me that." She looked toward Uncle Tony and Blanche and whispered, "He sure got over Susie quickly."

"I think he's an opportunist, and as a matter of fact, so is Blanche."

"Made for each other."

Del saw Mimi talking in hushed tones to Al in the corner and noticed that Al was getting a big kick out of whatever he was hearing. "So, what were you and Mimi laughing about?" he asked.

"I promise to tell you later," Ruth smiled. "You can anticipate it." She looked toward the bar. "I would like a Diet Coke. I know it's late, but it sure would taste good right now."

"Woman, I know when you are distracting me. Come on, let me in on your secret." He walked her toward the bar.

"Okay, but we have to be quiet," she told him. "Let's get our drinks and sit over there by that book case." She nodded toward an alcove off to one side of the room where no one was sitting.

A minute later, drinks in hand, they sat down on a craftsman style bench facing a tall, oak bookcase. Ruth noticed that all the books looked new, probably unread

"He's got a lot of good books," she said to Del, "but look at them. They're all brand new."

Del looked into her eyes. "You don't want to tell me, do you?"

"Well ... it's pretty risqué." She looked down at her lap and started to smirk. "And pretty funny!"

"Okay, you and Mimi went out to the bathroom. What happened?"

"We opened the wrong door, and we caught two people in a compromising position. *Very* compromising! They didn't see us, though. They were too busy."

"Don't tell me—Uncle Tony and Blanche?"

"Yes."

"Good lord!" Del snorted. "She's known for that, you know."

"You never said anything ... before." Ruth looked up at him.

"Well, you know how opera people gossip. I didn't want to ... and I never had any experience with her. Anyway ... I wasn't interested in her. Never." Del seemed embarrassed.

Just then, Mimi and Al walked over to them. It was obvious that Al was now in on it.

"Did you tell Del what we saw?" Mimi asked Ruth.

"And what you heard?" Al snickered.

"You heard them?" Del said.

"Oh god! Oh baby! Give it to me! That's the way I like it, baby! Yes!" Al said in a falsetto voice, while he moved his hips suggestively.

"Al, shh! Not so loud!" Mimi chided. "They were in the room next door to the bathroom," she explained, "and it was hard *not* to hear them."

Ruth was blushing. "I think maybe we should just get some more to eat," she said.

As the four of them went back to the food table, Elizabeth came in, looking upset and disheveled.

"Elizabeth!" Del rushed over to her. "What on earth?"

"Someone tried to run me off the road!" Her hands shook as she reached for her father.

Chapter 42

Suspicions

"**A**RE YOU OKAY?" DEL hugged his only child.

"Yes," she told him. "Fortunately, I was able to get back on the pavement again. And my car's fine ... but my nerves are shot!" Her shoulders shook. "I'm glad Richard wasn't with me. He's got a brief to work on."

"We need to call the police," Del told her.

Just then Don came up from behind. "And tell us what?"

"Someone tried to run my daughter off the road."

"Are you alright?" Don looked concerned.

"Yes. And my car's okay, too," Elizabeth said quietly. Ruth was relieved to see the girl had stopped shaking. "But if Richard had been driving, I think he would have turned around and followed, and maybe picked a fight with whoever it was. I'm really glad he wasn't with me tonight."

"This is just unthinkable," Del muttered, clearly incensed.

"But it happens." Don said. "Usually it's teen-agers out on a spree." He shrugged. "Since you're okay and your car was not damaged, unless you remember a license plate number there's not much we can do about it."

"Here, take this," Ruth said as she handed Elizabeth a Coke.

"Thanks," she said and took a sip. "I think I need the sugar." She smiled wanly. "I'm okay, dad ... really." She looked at her father. "Just shaken."

"Maybe so, but I'll drive you home," Del told her. "And I'll stay the night with you." He looked at Ruth, who nodded *yes*. "Ruth can drive my car to her house." Del thought a moment, then looked at Don Olson. "Would you be willing to follow Ruth home? I know she'll be safe if she's with you."

Before Ruth could say anything, Don agreed. "I'd be glad to. I wanted to talk with her some more anyway ... about ... you know ..."

"Um, sure." Ruth wasn't keen about having Don Olson at her house that late at night, but she rallied. "You can come and have a cup of herbal tea with me, and we'll talk. For a little bit."

The gathering had become louder and more festive by the time Danny and Tracey arrived. Most of the cast and orchestra, including Fritz and Vivian, were there, as was Angie and George. When Danny and Tracey walked in, Angie whispered something to the piano-player, who started playing "Here Comes the Bride!"

This, apparently, was Uncle Tony's cue. He clapped his hands together and yelled, "Quiet down and pay attention now!" The crowd hushed immediately. "I know all you theatre folks are romantics at heart," he boomed and then winked at Blanche. "And I know you all love a happy ending." He grinned at Tracey and then at Danny, who blushed. "So,

I want you should put your hands together for the happy couple. My nephew, Danny Ancino and his new fee-awn-say ... ah ... Tracey!"

Cheers, laughter, and shouts of "speech! speech!" resounded from the crowd. Uncle Tony went over and put his arm around both of them. Then he pushed Danny forward to give his "speech." Danny grinned uncomfortably as he looked at his uncle.

"Tracey *Corbello*, "Danny said with an emphasis on Tracey's last name, "has made me the luckiest guy in the world by agreein' to become my wife. And I wanta thank my Uncle Tony for helpin' us out. And for givin' us this great party!" Danny looked around the room for his mom and spotted her. "And my mom ... thanks for everything! I love ya, mom." He looked at Tracey, who was standing with Uncle Tony's protective arm around her. "I can't believe how lucky I am ..." His voice started to break. "I ... I think my family ... that I grew up with ... and my family of the future ... are so fine. Well, I ... I just don't see how I deserve all this good luck."

Cries of "Yes you do, Danny!" and "Kiss her! Kiss her!" kept going until Danny took Tracey in his arms and kissed her on the lips, at which the crowd cheered once more.

Ruth went over to Mrs. Ancino, seeing that Danny had referred to her as his mom. "He's a nice boy," Ruth told her. "I think they'll be very happy."

"Huh!" said the woman, "*Boy* is right! That's what he is, *a boy*. I'm his mother and I ought to know!" She sniffed. "He's way too young to get married. They both are."

"No, they're really not," Ruth started to tell her.

Just then Angie came up.

"Tracey and Danny—both those kids have good heads on their shoulders," declared Angie while glaring at Mrs. Ancino. "So get used to it!" With this pronouncement Angie walked away, head held high. She went over to George and said something to him. Ruth was proud of Angie but she smiled at Mrs. Ancino, who merely sighed and turned to talk to someone else.

"Trouble with the in-laws so soon?" Del said, quietly.

"I think Angie will give the Ancinos a run for their money," Ruth said.

"It seems they have enough of it," Del mused, looking around the room. "I'm going to go and get some more shrimp. Want me to get you something?"

"No, thank you. I'm stuffed. I probably won't be able to sleep tonight."

As Del walked away, Ruth scanned the massive party room and noticed that Billy and Lorene Hammer had still not arrived. It was always easy to spot Billy at a party: you just looked for the loudest group with the most laughter.

I wonder why they're not here? Billy loves parties. Maybe Lorene has a headache. Maybe they were both tired ... maybe ...

Ruth's thoughts stopped abruptly as Blanche came up to her like a dark cloud.

"I see you're still with Del." She looked Ruth up and down, as if taking her measure.

It's now or never, Ruth thought.

"Blanche," she said calmly, "let's just call a truce, okay? I don't know what to say to you. I'm sorry you feel the way you do about Del. I'm sorry he didn't choose you, but for God's sake, give it up, will you?"

"I never give up," Blanche said quietly with an air of self-satisfaction. She turned sharply and headed into the next room, hips swaying.

Ruth sighed and went in search of Del, who was talking with his daughter. "We've been here a while and Elizabeth is tired and wants to get home," Del said. "I think we need to say goodnight."

"So I'll see you tomorrow?" she asked Del, not wanting to tell him just then about Blanche.

"Yes, I'll probably be there by the time you usually head for church. Why don't I take you out for lunch afterwards? Any place you like."

"Bring Elizabeth, too," Ruth said. She took the girl's hands in hers.

Elizabeth kissed Ruth on the cheek. "We'll leave it open.'"

They said their "thank you and good night" to Uncle Tony. Blanche, happily, had disappeared. Ruth looked around for Don Olson.

"Have you seen Don?" she asked Del. "He was supposed to follow me home." She really didn't want him to, but after hearing Blanche's venomous words, it seemed like good idea.

"I saw him go outside," Del told her. "Maybe he's sitting in his car waiting for you."

That was exactly what Don had done. As Del gave Ruth the keys to the Lexus and walked her over to it, Don Olson waved from his car, which was parked behind Del's. He rolled down the window and called out, "Ready to go?"

Ruth gave him a thumbs up and slid behind the wheel. "See you tomorrow," Del whispered as he kissed her before shutting the car door. Then he and Elizabeth got into her car and drove away. Ruth waved to Don as she started Del's car. It purred to life and she glided carefully down Uncle Tony's long, winding driveway.

The rain had stopped and traffic was light. Along the way she kept turning things around in her head, trying to think about what else she could tell Don. *There's got to be a missing piece that I haven't thought of, something that connects everything else. Lorene? Blanche? And what about Mickey Sullivan? He must have been on to something ... but what?*

It was almost midnight when Don and Ruth pulled into Ruth's driveway. She was exhausted, but felt duty-bound to ask him in and offer him something. As Ruth opened her back door, she was greeted by Morrie and Griselda, who, upon seeing Don, turned and scurried into the living room. "Cats are funny," Ruth told him apologetically. "It's not you; they don't like anyone they haven't met before."

"Yeah, but it's not only cats. My puppy is that way, too," Don assured her. "He only likes *me*. Won't even eat if someone else tries to feed him."

"A one-man dog," she laughed.

"For sure."

Ruth invited Don to sit down at her kitchen table. She felt a little funny having him sit on the sofa in her living room. *Too intimate a setting,* she thought. She offered cookies to go with it.

"No thanks," Don told her, holding up his hands in a "stop" gesture. "I've had way too much to eat tonight. Just the tea ... thanks."

For a few minutes they sipped their tea and made small talk. He asked Ruth again what years she had been in the group and who she knew. For a moment Ruth wondered if Don suspected anyone else in the group. "Do you think it could be someone other than Lorene?" she asked point blank.

"Most of my suspicions steer in her direction, but there is a lot about this case we don't know."

"But what motive would she, or anyone, have? None of this makes any sense."

"Intentional murders seldom make sense," he told her, "except to the murderer."

Ruth asked Don if he suspected any of Fritz's enemies. She thought of Blanche Voorhees, but decided not to mention her. *She might hate me, and Fritz, but I doubt if she gives any thought to the others in the cast,* she quickly concluded.

Don looked thoughtful. "There seems to be a lot of people Fritz has had run-ins with. I think the list would be pretty long." Then he changed the subject to something more cheerful. "Say, didn't you have a dog? Angie Corbello's dog?" He looked around the kitchen.

"I did," Ruth said. "We even went to the pound and bought a 'friend' for him to play with, but Tracey and Danny decided to take them both. They have a fenced-in yard. It's a lot quieter around here now."

"And Mrs. Corbello? Wasn't she staying with you?"

"Ah, well ..." Ruth didn't want to go into Angie's relationship. "Tonight she's staying with another friend."

"That guy she was with tonight?"

"A very nice man, a neighbor in fact." Ruth didn't want to go into it any further.

"Lots of 'lovey-dovey' goings on in this group, that's for sure."

"Cast members sometimes get emotionally close when they do a show together," Ruth answered with a sheepish smile. "All that time spent working on it, it's natural for people to ... become friendly ... to get to know each other."

"I guess." Don became quiet.

"You're a widower, aren't you?" Ruth asked. "Did you have any children?"

"Yes, my wife passed away several years ago, and I have a daughter, but we're estranged. She wanted to live a lifestyle that I could not agree with. We don't see much of one another anymore."

"I'm so sorry." Ruth put a hand on his arm.

"Well, it's getting late." Don cleared his throat and rose quickly from his chair. "Thanks for the tea. And don't worry. I'll keep an eagle eye on things."

After he left, Ruth sat for a while and poured herself a second cup of tea. Don seemed like a nice man. But obviously lonely. She hoped he would find someone again and be happy. *No one should be alone if they don't want to be,* she thought. *There's a lid for every pot.* Her grandmother used to say that.

She finished her tea and locked herself in, checking the doors and first floor windows twice.

"It's just you guys and mama," she informed her cats, who had finally returned to the kitchen. She added some food to their bowls and gave them fresh water. Then went upstairs and took a hot shower. When she finally crawled into bed, even though she was alone in the house she fell asleep as soon as her head touched the pillow.

Chapter 43

Amazing Grace

THE NEXT MORNING ELIZABETH drove up just as Ruth was walking out the door to go to church. "Need a lift, lady?" Del said, his head out the passenger side window. He looked dapper in a navy-blue summer sports coat with dark gray slacks and a light gray knit shirt. He jumped out and hurried to open the back door of the sedan for her.

Ruth got in, noticing how clean the car was. No costumes. No playbills.

Not messy, like mine.

As Del slid in and sat beside her, she smoothed down the skirt of her black knit dress and buttoned the top button of her white linen jacket.

"Why didn't you two come earlier?" she asked them. "I could have made you breakfast."

Elizabeth turned around. "The alarm didn't go off. We barely made it here on time." She wore a sleeveless dark-brown knit sheath with a large white belt. "He rushed me so much I forgot my earrings."

"You look beautiful," Ruth assured her. "You always look beautiful."

"I was the one who set the alarm," Del told her. "And I set it wrong. Anyway, now we can go to Perkins and have pancakes after church."

Ruth laughed, "Oh ho! So it's not just going to church with me that's the draw here. It's pancakes at Perkins!" She shook her finger in Del's face.

Del grabbed her hand and kissed the inside of it. Ruth felt the tingle all the way through to her toes.

"It's a bit of both," he said. Then he kissed her on the lips.

"Okay love-birds," Elizabeth called from the front seat. "Where is this church?"

Ruth recovered quickly. "Turn right when you get to the street. Then go all the way down to Highway 5 and turn right again. Then another block and another right turn. You'll see the church."

The congregation of Christ Lutheran in Lake Elmo—mostly of German and Scandinavian stock—had previously welcomed Del into their midst, so they were not overly surprised when he and Ruth showed up for services with Del's daughter in tow.

"Well, this one's sure got to be one of your kids," one of the elderly women joked with Del as he entered the narthex. "Does she sing, too?"

"She's my *only* kid," Del told her, "and she does sing—just like an angel." He glanced at Elizabeth, who rolled her eyes and shook her head.

"Good!" the woman said briskly, "because our soloist is sick today and left us in the lurch. We don't have any music during the offering." She looked at Elizabeth.

"I can't ..." Elizabeth stammered. "I've got to prac ..."

"My favorite is 'Amazing Grace,'" the woman interrupted. Then she smiled hopefully. "Bet you know that one."

Elizabeth looked up at her dad and made a silent *no* with her mouth.

"Oh come on, I'll sing it with you," Del coaxed. "Remember when we did that duet for your mom?"

The girl's eyes misted over. "Yes," she sighed. "Well ... okay. But I'll need the words ... just in case."

"They're right here," the woman said as she handed her a red hymnal, already turned to the correct page. "'Amazing Grace.' Thank you both!"

The young woman who preached that morning was an intern still attending Luther Seminary. She had taken over for a few weeks while the regular pastor, an elderly man, was on vacation. Ruth thought she attended to her notes too closely, but was probably nervous. Her sermon was oddly pertinent to their predicament, Ruth thought to herself—all about watching out for wolves dressed in sheep's clothing. It gave Ruth the willies.

I wonder who our 'wolf' is?

As the sermon proceeded, Ruth couldn't help parading the names of suspects around in her head. *Lorene? Danny's Uncle Tony? Blanche? All seem possible. And what was Sergeant Sullivan doing in our yard that night of the storm when the tree fell on him? What was his part in all this?*

Ruth's dark thoughts evaporated, however, during Del's and Elizabeth's beautiful rendition of the old favorite hymn. She noticed some members dab their eyes. When they finished, there was even appreciative applause, which seldom happened in that church. Later, as they left the building, the young woman who gave the sermon thanked Del and Elizabeth profusely. Several other parishioners did the same.

As they got to her car, Elizabeth put a hand on Del's arm. "Dad," she said, "I'm sorry. I really can't go to lunch with you and Ruth today.

Richard and I have a proposal to work on. I promised I would meet him at one o'clock. We really need to do this. It could lead to a raise for both of us."

Del looked disappointed. "I suppose ... okay ... just drive us over to Ruth's and we'll drive back to the restaurant in my car."

Ruth and Del said their good-byes to Elizabeth, who looked relieved after she dropped off them off.

"She's a good girl." Ruth told Del as they got into his car.

"She is that," he nodded.

After lunch, Del went upstairs for a nap. Ruth took off her shoes and snuggled into her living room sofa with the Sunday paper. She had fallen sound asleep with the paper, unread, on her lap when the phone rang.

It was Fritz, apoplectic! "Oh my god! Ruth! It's Mimi!" he rasped. "Someone broke into her house this morning and stabbed her!"

Ruth thought she was having a nightmare. "Is she ...? Is she dead?"

Del came downstairs just then and immediately went to Ruth, putting his arm around her shoulders. "Mimi Rosenberg," Ruth whispered.

"No, not dead." Fritz seemed to have calmed down some. "At least she wasn't when Al called me." He started a fit of coughing and Vivian took the phone from him.

"Ruth?" she said. "We don't know much, but when Al found her, she was unconscious. He told us she was rushed into emergency surgery at Regions Hospital. He hasn't called us back."

"I can't believe it!" Ruth exclaimed and then turned to Del. "Mimi Rosenberg was stabbed in her home earlier today. She's in surgery." Del's mouth dropped open.

"Vivian," Ruth continued, "where was Al when this happened?"

"I guess he had gone to the store to get a Sunday paper."

Fritz took the line again. "Can you believe it? He said he was only gone about twenty minutes. My god! It could have been any of us. None of us are safe!"

"Well, the show has got to close," Ruth declared. "It will be harder to hurt anyone if we're not together anymore."

"We can't," Vivian said, taking the phone back. "We need to do one more week to break even."

Ruth could hear Fritz bellowing in the background. "We've got to keep going! We've got to have enough to pay my musicians, and the rental fee for the pavilion! I need three more performances!" He started coughing again. "Oh god, who's going to do Parthy? We don't have a Parthy!"

"I can do Parthy," Vivian said to Fritz. "She doesn't have all that many lines and she doesn't sing solos. I can take over for Mimi."

Ruth could hear Fritz talking excitedly to no one in particular. She looked over toward Del, who had been listening in on the kitchen phone. He stood in the kitchen doorway with his hand over the phone's mouthpiece.

"Ask Fritz if he wants us to bring him over to Regions," he said to Ruth.

Ruth nodded. "Del wants to know if you want us to pick you up and take you to Regions Hospital."

Fritz came back on the line. "No ... no, I don't think so. I think we'll just wait here to hear more from Al ... and hope and pray she'll be okay."

After Fritz finished ranting about how "people aren't safe in their own homes—even in good neighborhoods" he said that he had to hang up and call other members of the cast so they would know the show was still on for one more week.

"I'll see you on Thursday," he told Ruth. "Would you please tell Angie?" and hung up.

Ruth was stunned. "How could this happen?!"

"I don't know." Del shook his head. "And in broad daylight."

"Stabbed!" Ruth put her hands to her face. "But still alive." She sat back down on the sofa and Del sat down next to her.

"Fritz was right. This could have been any of us. There but for the grace of God go I ... or you." They sat like that for a long time, neither saying anything.

Ruth finally broke the silence.

"If Mimi lives through the surgery and wakes up," she took a deep breath, "she'll know who did it."

Del gasped. "She'll know who the murderer is. She'll need 'round the clock police protection."

"We've got to call Don." Ruth reached for the phone.

"No, hold on. I'm sure he knows already."

"I suppose you're right." Ruth closed her eyes for a moment. "When Angie was in the hospital, I remember Danny Ancino was stationed outside her door. He told me in cases like this the police always stayed to protect the patient—just in case the would-be murderer might want to come back and finish the job. And also in case the patient woke up and could give them information." Ruth began to breathe easier.

That night, before falling asleep, Ruth and Del each said their own private prayers for Mimi Rosenberg's recovery and safety.

By Thursday's performance, everyone in the cast knew about the stabbing. According to a very haggard Al, Mimi had come through the surgery but was now in an induced coma. "They're watching her all the time," he told the other actors. "But she'd want me to continue playing Captain Andy. I just know she would." He had a determined look on his face.

The show went on as planned. A good crowd. No storm or power outage. No one attacked. Ruth could sense the underlying tension in the cast, though. When on-stage, the actors continually pitched furtive glances toward the shadowy sides of the stage. When off-stage, they kept an eye on one another and the audience. They adhered to the buddy system but no one seemed to trust anyone.

Ruth thought Vivian was just "okay" as Parthy. Unsure of her lines, Vivian kept peeking surreptitiously at little slips of paper that she slipped in and out of her apron pockets. As Captain Andy, Al simply played it by the numbers, without his usual exuberance. He looked terrible and left immediately after his curtain call. Mimi was no longer in a coma.

The Friday night performance also went without incident. As they waited in the wings to go on, Del whispered to Ruth, "I heard Fritz tell Billy he was glad tomorrow will be the last night."

"Break a leg," Ruth whispered to him as she moved onto the stage for the chorus's opening number.

Chapter 44

Closing Night

JUST BEFORE THE CURTAIN went up on Saturday night—closing night—Vivian announced to all the cast that they, including friends and family, were invited to the Gerhardt residence for a "last night party."

"Everyone, you've been a wonderful cast!" she said with a brave smile. "I know this show has been extremely difficult, for reasons you are aware of, but Fritz and I hope all of you can come to our house tonight for a small gathering." She looked around the room. "You have to come over—or Fritz and I will be eating leftover deli food for the next two weeks!" People laughed quietly. "You know where we live," she added, glancing toward Fritz, who had already invited the orchestra. Most cast members assured her that they would indeed attend the party.

The show itself that night went better than the previous two nights, but the spirited *joie de vivre* that usually accompanies closing night performances was missing.

After the final bows were taken and they had changed out of their costumes, Del and Ruth were emotionally exhausted. "I don't think I could have taken another night of this," Del said as they walked toward his car.

"I still think Lorene looks as if she knows something," Ruth said. "I don't know … she has that look in her eyes."

"Why don't you just talk to her?"

"Because I'm afraid of her."

"Speaking of being 'afraid' of people," Del said, "did you see Uncle Tony and Blanche in the audience again tonight?" He looked grim.

"She's been here every night," Ruth said quietly.

"I'm so sorry." Del put his arm around her. "I can't believe she's doing this. She's got to know I don't care about her."

Ruth looked up at him. "I don't know what her problem is. Or, rather, I *do* know what her problem is—unfortunately," she said ruefully.

Del pulled her more tightly toward him. "Well, she has a real problem if she thinks she's going to get me interested in her. I'm already taken."

"I wonder if her obsession is not just with you," Ruth mused. "Maybe it's with the whole cast."

"Well maybe," Del thought out loud. "She hates Fritz. I know that for a fact."

"Lionel … and Susie … Sergeant Sullivan … all dead." Ruth, too, was thinking out loud. "And Angie … the Rosenberg's car … little Rodney … you … me … Gloria-June—all of us targets in some way. We could very well have been killed. And now Mimi again. There has to be something we've forgotten."

"Or someone we don't even know exists."

"I wish we could just go straight home tonight."

"It's the last night of the show. We have to at least put in an appearance at Fritz's."

"I suppose." Ruth leaned into him. "They want the tradition of their last night cast party to go on. It means a lot to them."

As they continued walking through the parking lot, Lorene caught up with them. "I'll bet Vivian's glad about Mimi," she said to Ruth.

"What?" Ruth stopped in her tracks and turned to look at the woman. "What on earth are you talking about? Who's glad?"

"Vivian. That's what I wanted to tell you about the other night." Lorene was out of breath. "I know you probably think I'm up to no good, especially after what happened to Gloria-June. God, I could not stand that woman!" Lorene pursed her lips. "But I swear to you, it's not me who's doing all this … stuff. It's Vivian! I *know* it's her. She's crazy." Lorene's voice lowered to a whisper. "But crazy like a fox."

"You can't be serious," Del said. He turned to Lorene while putting his hand on Ruth's arm to move her behind him, as if to protect her.

Ruth, her mouth open, stared dumbfounded at Lorene.

"Why do you think that? Vivian? What is she? In her sixties? Do you think she's physically strong enough to take on Lionel or do all those other things?" Ruth sounded incredulous. "Besides, Lionel was in the alley, wasn't he? Wasn't Vivian in the studio when he was killed?"

"I don't know about Lionel. I can't explain that. Maybe his death had nothing to do with the others." Lorene shook her head. "I *do* know that there was some talk about Mimi and Fritz. It was years ago, before Vivian and Fritz were married, but Mimi and Fritz apparently had something going on. And I know Vivian. I know she has never liked Mimi."

"Oh, there's always 'talk' in the theatre," Del told her, "and most of the time it doesn't amount to a hill of beans. Theatre people love drama."

"And how could Vivian have blown up the Rosenberg's car?" Ruth continued. "She couldn't have done that, and besides, she was in the house at the time. It just doesn't make sense."

"Maybe ... maybe she paid someone." Lorene began to look embarrassed. "She ... she runs all the money for the shows, you know. As for Fritz, he's no money man. He doesn't even look at the books."

"How do you know that?" Del confronted her.

"Billy told me." Lorene looked around the parking lot, as if she hoped Billy would appear.

"Why don't you tell Don Olson all of this," Ruth said gently. "He's looking out for us. He'd probably be interested in your theories."

"Sure ... okay." Lorene started to walk backwards away from them. "I'll do that. I'll talk to Don." She turned and walked quickly toward the pavilion. "Thanks anyway."

Just then, as Del opened the car door for Ruth, they heard a woman calling from a distant side of the parking lot.

"Dad! Dad! Please! Wait a minute. I want to talk to you!"

"That sounds like Rhonda!" Ruth turned to look in the direction of the voice, but in the darkness could see nothing.

"I don't see anyone." Del said, looking around. Hearing nothing more, he got into the car.

"I doubt it was Rhonda," he told Ruth.

"It sure sounded like her." Ruth fastened her seat belt. "What do you think of Lorene? Can you believe she would bad-mouth Vivian that way?"

"No. And why would Vivian, of all people, want to kill off the cast? That's silly. This is their livelihood! But I suppose we do have to go to their party," Del groaned, aiming to change the subject.

Ruth leaned back and groaned too. She patted his leg, "I promise we'll leave early," she said as she nestled into the comfortable seat. Within minutes she fell asleep.

The night was chillier than usual and there was no moon. Del maneuvered his car silently down Lexington Avenue, crossed University and turned left onto Summit. Driving slowly, not really wanting to go to the Gerhardt's party, he wondered about what Lorene had said as he drove past the avenue's stately mansions. He finally dismissed it as complete nonsense. He turned left onto Dale Street and turned left again onto Portland.

Chapter 45

Final Act

"WAKE UP, SLEEPY-HEAD," DEL whispered to Ruth. Cars lined the street, but he found a parking place about a block down from Fritz's and Vivian's house.

"I'm cold," Ruth breathed, as she stretched and tried to wake up. "Do I have a shawl in the back seat?"

"I think you do." Del reached behind him. "What's this?" He pulled Ruth's blue shawl into the front seat, noticing that there was a note pinned to it. He gave it to her.

"A note? It says it's for both of us." Ruth immediately felt queasy. "How did someone get into your car? Don't you always lock the doors?"

"I thought I did," Del answered, "but there was so much going on. Maybe I forgot."

"Oh my god!" Ruth gasped when she opened the note. "It's from Blanche!"

"Read it. Go ahead. Let's just get this over with," Del sighed. He switched on the dome light and leaned back in the seat.

"Dear Del and Ruth -- This is just a note to say how very sorry I am for everything. I don't want any trouble. I realize now that I was acting like a spoiled brat. Could you two please come over to my apartment tonight? I have a gift for you—something I should have given you a long time ago. Please come. I really need to see you both. Regards, Blanche" The address of her apartment was written on the bottom of the note.

"Go over to her house tonight? I don't think so," Del said angrily. "She's probably got a gun."

"There sure are a lot of 'I's' in that note," Ruth said as she examined it closely.

"Well, that would be Blanche."

"Anyway," Ruth reminded him, "we've got a party to go to."

"You can call her tomorrow."

"No, *you* can call her tomorrow. Blanche is *your* friend."

"No, you can call her tomorrow. She's *your* enemy," Del mimicked.

Ruth tried to give Del a hit on the arm, but he grabbed her hand and held it against his chest, bringing her close to him.

He kissed her. "You are so dear to me. You sure you want to go in there?" he said as he motioned toward the Gerhardt's with his head.

"You're dear to me, too," was all Ruth said.

After a few minutes they finally headed inside to the party. Not everyone in the troupe was there. Don Olson was absent, as well as Billy and Lorene Hammer. Vivian was in fine form, however, holding forth in the Gerhardt's large, formal dining room. Several Chippendale chairs were arranged along the white wainscoting that lined the room. Pale blue flowered wall paper covered the upper wall, matching the pale blue carpeting on the floor. Vivian stood at the head of the table, dishing out potato salad, warm rolls, and thin slices of ham. Everyone got a full plate.

Fritz was pouring white wine into plastic wine glasses.

"I know you are all upset," he told the group, "but you've worked hard tonight, and you've got to eat!"

Danny Ancino was there, but not with Tracey.

"Where's Tracey tonight?" Ruth asked.

"I hafta work tonight," Danny answered. "I told Tracey that I would just stop for a minute to put in an appearance and then come home to get ready for my shift."

Del and Ruth didn't want to stay much longer than Danny, but they lost track of time. People were congratulating Del on his performance, admiring Ruth's engagement ring, which had now been resized, and wishing them both the very best. It was half-past eleven when she looked at her watch.

"My gosh," she yawned, "no wonder I'm so tired."

Del looked at his watch, too, but it was missing from his arm. "Ruth, did I have my watch when we left Lake Elmo?"

"Yes, don't you remember? I told you when we were in the car. Be sure to take it off for the play ... to stay in character."

"Oh boy!" He hit his head with his hand. "Do you mind if we go back home by way of the pavilion? I left my watch backstage. I remember now. I put it on top of the sound box just before I went on. It's my good one, the one with the diamonds. Elizabeth gave it to me."

"Of course we'll go back for it," Ruth reassured him. "Don't worry, I'm sure it will still be there."

They said hurried thank-yous and good-byes to Vivian and Fritz, and shook hands with many others. When they finally left the Gerhardt's, Del drove quickly through the night toward Como Park.

The pavilion building was dark when they arrived but the parking lot was lit and held one car, a police car. Del pulled up next to it and turned off the ignition, feeling safer there.

"I wonder why an empty squad car would be here?" he said to Ruth as they got out of his car.

"It's not empty!" exclaimed Ruth. "Look! That's Charlie in the back seat!" The little dog barked and franticly scratched at the window.

Ruth immediately tried to open the doors to get the dog out, but they were locked.

"Isn't Como Park Danny's beat?" Del asked.

"Yes," Ruth told him, "but why would Danny take Charlie along?" Ruth was getting an uneasy feeling. She looked toward the pavilion.

"I don't know, but right now I need to go and find my watch."

"Ok, you go and get your watch. I'll wait here in case Danny comes back." She shivered. "Maybe it's okay. Maybe he just found Charlie running around and was going to bring him home after his shift."

"No, you come in with me," Del stated. "I don't want you to be alone out here. It'll only take a minute."

The street lights gave the pale structure an eerie, shadowy cast. At any other time, the graceful columns might look romantic, but tonight, to Ruth, the building looked menacing. She and Del walked past the table where Vivian sold tickets, around the iron gate leading into the pavilion, past an overflowing trash can, and up the side stairs to the back stage.

"It's so dark, I can hardly see," Del said to Ruth in a low voice. "Do you still have your flashlight?"

"No. It's in my bag in the car."

They turned to go back for the flashlight.

"Stop. Right. There." It was Don Olson's voice.

"Oh Don!" Ruth spun around. "Are we glad to see you! So that's your car parked out there? What is Charlie doing in your ..."

"Just turn around and walk downstairs ... easy now," Don said quietly as he pressed a gun against Del's back

"Don, why are you ...? Del forgot his watch backstage. We came back, hoping it was still there." Then Ruth saw the gun and stared, dumfounded, uncomprehending. "What's going on?!"

"Both of you, downstairs!" he growled, nodding toward the stairway. "As a matter of fact, I left something backstage, too, that I came to get—my wallet." He waved the gun at them. "Hurry up! Both of you, downstairs, *now*!"

Stunned, Ruth and Del made their way down the dark steps and into the hall. A dim light from one of the rooms cast ghostly shadows against the walls.

"What?" Ruth looked back at Don. "What's going on ... why are you ...?"

"Just. Shut. Up!" Don growled. "I hadn't planned for this, but you've given me an opportunity. Now I can add two more to my score card—and a dog for good measure. Ha! Three birds with one stone."

"Don, this is crazy! I don't know what this is about, but you don't need to do it," Del told him.

"Shut up," snarled Don, "Or I'll finish the job right now."

"Finish the job?!" Ruth was crying now. She took a deep breath. "Why? I don't understand! I can't hurt you ... and Del ... Del isn't going to hurt you. He's a good man. And Charlie can't hurt you. Why are you doing this?!"

"I have to get rid of that damn dog." His voice now sounded calm.

Ruth paused, not sure what to say next as fear battled confusion. "What did Charlie ever do to you?"

"He knows I'm the one."

"The one?" She paused, letting the idea soak in. "You mean ... it was *you*? It was *you* who hurt Angie? *You* killed Lionel and Susie? And tried to kill or frighten me and Del and the others?" Ruth felt horrified but resolved to keep talking, to keep buying some time. "Tell us what this is about—why you're doing this. And why Charley?"

"Might as well tell you. You're not going to be around long enough to spill the beans to anyone."

The policeman smiled at his own cleverness. "That Corbello dame, she was a fighter, alright! But she got away and her dog knew it was me. I had to get rid of it."

Ruth shook her head. "What are you saying? Angie's dog loved you. I saw you feeding him a bagel that day when I picked him up from the police station."

"Well, I was feeding a dog a bagel ... but not the dog that's in my car." He smiled slyly at Ruth. "I was lucky. There was another dog in the pound that looked a lot like Corbello's dog. I just told them that my dog had a behavior problem and I needed a replacement ... for my grandson. Yeah, my grandson." Don suddenly sounded angry. "Rhonda's little bastard."

Ruth gasped, "Rhonda? Your grandson? Are you talking about Rodney? Were you the one who ... on the boat ...?" She couldn't bring herself to say it.

"Pushed him off?" He was smirking now. "Yeah, I nudged him. It was easy. There was a crowd of people. No one was looking. So the kid just lost his balance. Too bad your boyfriend here jumped in and pulled him up," he said as he looked at Ruth and then at Del. "I ... my daughter ... having this kid ruined her life. This whole damn theatre group ruined her life. Not only that, it *killed* my wife. She was so upset it put her in a tailspin that she never got over. Her health issues all started when Rhonda got pregnant with that kid—thanks to Fritz's theatre group. So, I decided to get rid of it, once and for all."

Incredulous, Ruth looked at Del. *We've got to keep Don talking for as long as we can,* she thought, leaning into Del.

Del, his voice calm and controlled, said, "I understand, as a father of a daughter myself, how hurt you must have been by your daughter's, ah ... trouble." He cleared his throat. "But why ...?"

"Why did I kill all those people?" He stared at Del. "Well, I didn't kill Worthing." Don paused and shook his head as if to clear his thoughts. "It could have been some mugger out in the alley ... or maybe his fag-lover ... I don't know ... but it wasn't me. It gave me a good start, though. When Sullivan told me about that group in California, I got an idea. If it hadn't been for that god damned theatre group Rhonda was in, everything would have been different."

"I suppose you could call it revenge. Doesn't matter. Did you know that idiot Corbello woman actually gave my daughter a baby shower? And that bitch Mimi, she kept giving Rhonda money to live on. And that little slut who played the piano, she babysat! And don't think I don't know who the father is. He's *next!*" He spit the words out with venom.

"But all those good people *helped* your daughter!" Ruth sobbed, "Why would you want to kill them?"

"Helped, my ass! You mean the 'good people' who helped drive a wedge between Rhonda and her mother and me? And the 'good' theatre creep who 'helped' her get pregnant? And every one of those other 'good' theatre people who 'helped' my wife die and 'helped' ruin my daughter's life?"

Don glared intensely at Ruth, then at Del, as if trying to decide who he'd shoot first.

"Don, you need help," Del said as calmly as he could. "We can help you. You're not yourself, Don. You're a better man than this. We can ..."

"Shut up! You're the one who needs help." Don began to ramble. "And the best part of all was I could blame it all on Lorene! I was sprinkling clues. Ha! *You* even thought it was her!" Don laughed. "You heard she'd been in a community theatre. She was a sound technician. I checked on her. She'd lived for a while in southern California near LA, nowhere near Sausalito. Still, that made it easy for me to put her on our suspect list." He chuckled at his own brilliance. "You know, they'll probably blame all of this on her."

Del spoke up again. "We didn't even *know* your daughter until this show."

Don looked at Ruth. "I thought your *boyfriend* here was a part of the group." He sarcastically emphasized the word. "And you, lady, you've been in this company a long time. You're kind of an insider. You should have stayed away from it after your husband got sick. Too bad, 'cause now you know too much ... way too much."

Ruth was desperate to keep talking. "What about Charlie? He's a dog. He can't say anything. How about letting the dog go?"

"I hate dogs! It'll be a pleasure sending that one to hell along with the two of you."

"But what about your new puppy?" Ruth pleaded. "You told me you had a new puppy."

"Oh, you are *so* gullible, lady. You believe anything anybody tells you."

"Okay! Stop right there! Drop the gun, Don!"

The loud, authoritative voice came from the end of the hall. Don instinctively swung toward the voice and as he did so Del lunged at the would-be killer, throwing Don off balance. Ruth screamed as she heard three shots.

When Ruth realized she wasn't hit, she opened her eyes. Del stood unscathed next to her and Don Olson lay on the floor, clutching his chest. Danny Ancino walked out from the shadows and wrenched the gun away from the wounded man.

"Sorry I waited so long," Danny said, "but I needed to hear what he had to say."

Del wrapped his arms around Ruth.

"How did you know how to find us?" Ruth asked him.

"Just luck. I went home tonight to change and Tracey was all upset because Charlie was gone again." He grabbed a costume from a nearby chair and used it to staunch the bleeding. "I hafta admit, I was a little suspicious of Don because of things he'd said, things about this case that none of the other guys on the force had heard anything about." He put pressure on the wound. "It was weird that he seemed to know stuff about what happened to the victims that none of us knew."

"But how did you know to come here to the pavilion tonight?" asked Del.

"I couldn't help Tracey hunt for Charlie 'cause I had to be on duty. This area around Como is part of my patrol area. I was drivin' through the park and I saw Don's squad car in the parking lot next to your Lexus. That seemed pretty odd, so I pulled up next to Don's car." He took a breath. "And then I saw Charlie in his back seat. I thought I better come into the pavilion and find out what was goin' on. Damn good thing I did!" Danny looked down at Don, who by now was unconscious.

"I didn't wanna shoot him, but when he fired toward me after Del bodychecked him, I fired back."

"Damn!" Danny said as he tried harder to staunch the flow of blood from the wound in Don Olson's chest. "I think we're losin' him. Del, I gotta call for back-up. Here, you hold this and press down hard!"

Danny ran back to his squad car to call for aid while Del continued to put pressure on Don's wound. Sirens could already be heard by the time Danny returned to the pavilion basement, but it didn't matter. Don Olson never woke up.

Chapter 46

Curtain

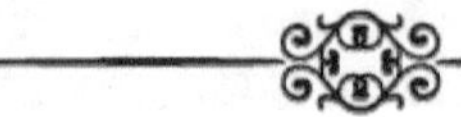

D*URING THE NEXT FEW* days, Ruth and Del met with police, retelling all they experienced. It was sensational front-page news in both the Minneapolis and St. Paul newspapers. Don Olson's motives were treated as a mystery, although it was suggested that he simply snapped, that he was mentally ill, that he couldn't deal with the stresses of being a cop after his wife died. Not much was said about his daughter except that they had been estranged. Ruth was grateful for the omission.

Al Rosenberg was still by Mimi's bedside. She was improving slowly while her husband barely knew, or cared, what else was happening. Ruth and Del understood that he'd been told about Don Olson. When they called the Rosenberg's house to ask about Mimi, Al's son answered. "Mom's going to have a long recovery," he said. "As soon as she gets out of the hospital, we're all going up north to the cabin. Dad just wants to get away from it all."

They never did get to talk with Blanche or find out what her "gift" was.

I can do without it, whatever "it" is! thought Ruth.

Angie called and said she and George were taking a vacation to Door County in Wisconsin. "George says he wants t take me somewhere where I'm not gonna be reminded of all this."

Ruth and Del attended Don Olson's funeral service a week after his death, basically for Rhonda's and Rodney's sake. It was held in a neighborhood funeral home on the east side of St. Paul. As they walked in, recorded organ music played tranquil hymn melodies in the background. Six or seven pews faced a closed casket at the front of a small, chapel-like parlor. Colored light spilled across the floor from two stained glass windows, giving the room a soft glow. They took a seat in the back. Only a handful of people were there, some of them policemen, and Ruth didn't recognize any of them.

A few minutes later, Danny slid quietly into the same pew and sat next to Del. "Tracey didn't wanna come," he whispered. "He tried to kill her mom. And her dog. She's pretty upset." He shook his head. "Ya know, Don was my patrol partner for a while. I guess I should be forgiving … but it's hard after what he did. He'd been acting kinda strange ever since his wife died, but still …" His voice trailed off and then resumed. "Ya know, when his daughter got pregnant it embarrassed him a lot. One guy made a joke about it and we had to hold Don back so he wouldn't slug the guy! Then his wife died and I guess he must have blamed Fritz's theatre group. I think that was the kicker, the last straw. He was angry and depressed and it spiraled completely outa control."

"Was he getting help from anyone? Counseling? A program or somebody to help him deal with his feelings?" Del asked.

"Nah, I'm pretty sure about that," Danny answered. "Don wasn't the type to ask for help—and he probably didn't think he needed it. He just hadda get back at *somebody,* though, and it all started with this theatre group his daughter was in, so they became the target. It was all in his head of course, but he decided to get even—punish everybody in the group, even the ones who helped Rhonda and even the boy himself. Just think of it, his own grandson!" He shook his head, staring down at the floor. "It don't make no sense. No sense at all. I guess those things, and maybe other things in his life that we don't know about, made him go completely off the rails. Who knows? He turned crazy ... just plum crazy."

Just then, Rhonda and Rodney Olson came through the door and walked slowly to the front of the nearly empty room, stopping at the casket to bow their heads. Rodney was supporting his slender mother, who held on to his arm, braced by his sturdy little body.

Ruth choked up at the sight. "That sweet wonderful girl ... that beautiful talented boy ..." She wiped her eyes. "Don missed out on so much."

Danny reached into his pocket. "Del, is this yours? I found it on top of the sound box. It has the initials 'DM from EM,' and I thought maybe it was yours." He handed a watch to Del.

"Oh, thank you! In all the excitement I forgot about it that night. We went back the next day but it was gone," Del whispered as he took the watch.

Danny sat uneasily for a few more minutes and then said, "Well, I gotta go." He reached over and shook Del's hand. "I really wasn't going to stay for the service ... I mainly wanted to return your watch."

He gave Ruth a quick hug and started to exit the pew, then stopped and added, "By the way, Stoltzman says he might need another guy on the Lake Elmo police force and Tracey really would rather live farther away from the city. Ya never know," he grinned before slipping out of the room, "we might end up being neighbors."

"Well, well," Ruth whispered as she snuggled closer to Del. "Who would have thought he'd turn out to be such a nice young man?"

"Why do you say that?" Del whispered back. He put his arm behind Ruth, resting it on the pew as he gently rubbed his fingers along the collar of her navy-blue suit. "Didn't you like him?"

"Not at first. At first I thought he was just a self-centered macho guy looking for some poor girl to fool around with. But I was wrong about him."

Del just pulled her closer.

"I forgot to tell you," he whispered. "Danny told me why his Uncle Tony wanted him to join the theatre group."

"Why was that?" Ruth looked straight ahead.

"He said he'd meet nice girls there."

Ruth leaned into Del's shoulder. "Smart man," she whispered back.

About the Author

Judith Johnson, who lives with her husband and cat in rural Stillwater, Minnesota, has been performing in summer musicals at St. Paul's Como Lakeside Pavilion for many years. It all started in 1981 when her eldest daughter was in *The Sound of Music* and the director needed more nuns. Judith was hooked!

She has sung her heart out on that stage many times since, always as a member of the chorus and often joined by her children and grandchildren. This mystery (because she loves a good mystery) was written out of love for the directors, actors, musicians, and helpers who, every summer at the pavilion, say with gusto, "Break a leg!"